If you play with dynamite, it could blow up in your face.

BACKFIRE

If you live on the wrong side of the law, you may find out you can't trust anybody.

BACKFIRE

If you live on the right side of the law, ditto. . . .

BACKFIRE

BACKFIRE

Christopher Newman

FAWCETT GOLD MEDAL • NEW YORK

A Fawcett Gold Medal Book
Published by Ballantine Books
Copyright © 1990 by Christopher Newman

Library of Congress Catalog Card Number: 89-91906

ISBN 0-449-13295-1

Manufactured in the United States of America

First Edition: March 1990

for Don and Abby Westlake

back•fire *(-fīr)*, n. 1. a fire started counter to an advancing forest or prairie fire, to check the latter by clearing an area; hence, figuratively, any counter activity against all attack.

—*Webster's Second*
International Dictionary

Prologue

Phillip DeWitt was anxious. The silly girl had either changed her mind or was having trouble finding the motel. At half past eight she was already thirty minutes overdue. He didn't want to believe she'd chickened out. Her tuition at the state university was paid up for the next semester, and the new car had been delivered three days ago, so perhaps she *had* missed the place. It was a mist-heavy, moonless night, and because it was deep in the off-season, the management hadn't bothered to switch on their garish roadside sign. Connie knew the area, but up on the road only the occupancy indicator lit her way; VACANCY, in pale, forlorn pink.

DeWitt sat behind the wheel of his 1962 Chevrolet Impala coupé; a car as black as his mood and the Ozark night surrounding him. Ricky Nelson was playing at low volume on the station out of Harrison, Arkansas. A news announcer had just finished highlighting the events of that day, foremost being the latest stall in the nuclear-test-ban talks. Two and a half months after Jack Kennedy had won the showdown over Cuba, Khrushchev was still posturing with menacing determination. As the minutes ticked by, DeWitt's anxiety saw fear creep in around its edges. There was something about

1

the role he was playing, and the fact that he played it in this part of the world, that irritated him. Since managing Senator Franklin Coulter's besieged campaign to a landslide victory, he'd been stuck out here, tying up a thousand loose ends while his boss returned to Washington. It made him feel like a man in a fast car trapped in the slow lane. Down here in these mountains, moving at half speed was a way of life. It didn't matter that the hunting in the region was good and the fishing excellent; these hillbillies were as backwards as they were backwoods.

Bundled against the biting cold, Phillip envied his pal from their old St. Louis neighborhood, who was waiting for Connie inside the warm motel cottage. Once Erv Orton had agreed to do the job, he admitted that as a first-year intern at the U.S. Medical Center for Federal Prisoners he'd never actually performed an abortion. But the other guy Erv brought along tonight, the Polish intern from Chicago, claimed to have done several while still a medical student. Right now those two novices were in there smoking cigarettes and playing cribbage, all warm and comfortable. The radio report had predicted a fifty percent chance of snow, and in these hills even the slightest dusting could be treacherous. When this night was over, Phil didn't want to find himself in a ditch, his name in some tow operator's log.

Headlights bit through the misty gloom up on the road. Seconds later the brand-new TR-3 ragtop could be seen swinging down into the motel lot, advancing toward De-Witt's position. The black Chevy wouldn't be hard for her to find. It was the only car parked in front of the crescent-shaped cluster of motel cabins. He could finally move, and climbed out into the bitter damp to stand shifting from foot to foot as the girl parked.

"Hello, Connie," he greeted her. "I thought we agreed on eight o'clock."

The girl hopped out of her car in such haste that she dropped her purse and keys. She was still fifteen feet away and hadn't yet met his eyes as he addressed her. A tall wisp of a thing, beautiful in that long-limbed, bloom-of-youth way, she got his heart racing, just looking at her.

"I couldn't come all the way down here from Springfield without seein' my mama, Phil. Supper just sorta dragged on. I'm sorry I'm late." The effort of retrieving her spilled things left her breathless as she rose to face him. The words were gasped.

"I've got a nice room for you, hon." Just ten years older than she, DeWitt felt silly, trying to carry off the comforting confessor bit. As she came closer into the soft, ambient light leaking through the curtains of the cabin, he was struck again by her beauty. It stunned him the same way it did that first day she showed up to do volunteer work for his boss in the 1962 senatorial campaign, all eager and dewy-eyed with the Kennedy era's political fervor.

"And the doctor?" she asked, guarded suspicion in her tone.

"Inside, hon. Not just one, but two. Both from the federal hospital in Springfield. I've known one of them since grammar school. Come on, let's go inside. It's freezing out here."

DeWitt led the way into a pin-neat cabin, the walls paneled in knotty pine. Twin beds, one with the coverlet pulled back, straddled a nightstand which matched a simple oak lowboy dressing table and chest. Underfoot, a hooked rug worked to pull it all together in a feeling of down-home coziness. Two men loitered against the dresser, clad in surgical gowns. One smoked a cigarette, while the other had his forearm draped over a black leather grip.

"This is Connie Dahlrymple, gentlemen. Connie, Doctors Orton and Solokowski." As he spoke, DeWitt turned to beam reassurance at the girl. "We wouldn't want to take any chances, right?" He wished to hell Orton didn't look so fidgety, the way he rolled that butt back and forth between thumb and forefinger.

Solokowski, the bigger of the two and the more self-assured, wasted no time. He handed the apprehensive girl a hospital gown.

"Why don't you take a nice hot shower and change into this? It's important that you try to relax, Connie."

As soon as she disappeared behind the closed door to the bath, Solokowski set about spreading the shiny instruments of his profession atop a towel.

"I'm going to wait in the car," DeWitt announced.

Orton, still smoking nervously, raised his eyes to regard him. Fresh hatred could be read in that look; the sort grown from seeds of envy. Erv was all too aware of the fact that Phil was currently on a roll. While Erv worked as a low-paid intern for the government, Phil had just managed a highly visible United States senator's embattled campaign to victory by an impressive margin. Phil sauntered with a winner's confidence. Phil drove a late-model car and ate at fancy restaurants, while Erv faced even more impoverished years as a cardiological resident before he would realize a decent level of income. Erv was deeply in debt. The fifteen hundred dollars he and Tim Solokowski were being paid to perform tonight's little favor was money neither of them could afford to refuse.

Phil had just finished tamping his pipe and relighting it for a third time when a knock came at his fogged-over window. He'd been sitting out here in the cold, the radio playing low, for a little more than half an hour. As he rolled the window down, he discovered Tim Solokowski, his topcoat pulled on over the medical gown, hands on knees, confronting him. There was a look of panic in the doctor's eyes.

"It's going sour. We've got to get her to a hospital. Fast."

DeWitt scowled, reaching to knock his pipe against the side mirror. Solokowski had to step quickly aside to avoid the shower of embers.

"Slow down. What do you mean, sour? What's wrong?"

"She's *bleeding*. I must have nicked an artery with the curette. She's losing a lot of blood in a hurry."

With a yank of the release lever, DeWitt heaved the door open and climbed out. As he moved toward the cabin he absorbed the fact that no late arrivals had shown, looking to rent lodging for the night. The absence of all but the faintest light in the manager's window told him that the proprietor and his wife had called it an early night.

"A hospital's out of the question," he muttered, following Solokowski toward the cabin door. As he moved, he tried to work the kinking effect of the cold from his muscles.

The frightened intern whirled to confront him. "Maybe you're not getting what I'm trying to tell you! That girl is bleeding to *death*!"

DeWitt pushed past to grip the knob with an impatient roll of his eyes and swung the door wide. The scene confronting him on the bed caused him to pull up and stand rooted in his tracks. Enormous quantities of blood soaked the sheets beneath the girl. She was deathly pale and seemed to be barely drawing breath.

"For Christ's sake, when did this happen?" he demanded.

Across the room Orton was hurriedly stuffing the last of the instruments back into the black bag.

"We knew something was wrong about fifteen minutes ago," he told him. "We thought we could handle it." There was real panic in both the way he spoke and moved. "If we don't get her over to Skaggs Memorial in the next ten minutes, there's no way she'll pull through." He snapped the clasp closed on the case and nodded to Solokowski. "Let's get her into the car."

That shocked DeWitt out of his inability to move. He dug into his pocket for the keys and tried to push them into Solokowski's hand. "Wrap her in a blanket or something, for God's sake. I don't need blood all over my backseat."

Solokowski wouldn't take the keys. "Why do I need those? You didn't lock it, way out here, and you're going to drive."

DeWitt's eyes narrowed as he pointed at himself, shaking his head. "Not me, friend. You fucked this up, you take her to the hospital."

Across the room Erv was stripping out of his gown. When he spoke, his voice dripped disdain. "Forget it, Phil. You drop us off at Tim's car, back in town. This isn't our dirty laundry. We get caught performing an abortion—on a minor, no less—they'll cancel our tickets.''

Solokowski was hovering over the girl now, his hand on her wrist, monitoring her pulse. ''C'mon, DeWitt. You continue to argue instead of act, it'll soon be academic.''

Phil's mind raced over his options. He had no intention of destroying his own life in an effort to save the girl's. Even were she to live, he would surely be arrested. And at the same time, weren't the risks the same for these two? Slowly, he turned toward the door.

''Where the hell are you going?'' Orton snarled.

DeWitt gave it a slight tilt of the head. ''Same place you are, Ervin. Away from here. I mean, isn't it *already* academic? I've got just as much to lose here as you do, and I'm not the one who swore any Hippocratic Oath, *Doctor*. You're right about her not being your dirty laundry, so when you're ready, I'll be waiting for you in the car. I assume you'll be wanting to wash your hands.''

''No rush,'' Solokowski murmured. He dropped her hand and reached to unknot the ties of his gown. ''There's nothing a hospital could do for her now, anyway.''

Connie Dahlrymple was left where she died, the two doctors riding with DeWitt to where they'd left Orton's car parked in the middle of town. Parting company, none of them spoke. Once Erv got his ten-year-old Buick started, he wasted no time warming it up. He and Solokowski got out of there. For nearly fifteen minutes Phil sat alone in his car on Fifth Street in Branson's little business district. Surrounding him, the plate-glass windows of every storefront lining both sidewalks were darkened. Once Orton's clunker departed the scene, there were no other cars. By nine-thirty even the diners down near the highway had closed for the night.

Phil thought that he'd never felt more alone. Everything that he'd worked for, coming up off the streets of St. Louis, was now in jeopardy; the scholarships to Duke and Georgetown Law, the state-level work on the 1960 Kennedy campaign, and all the fast-track hustling that followed. An hour ago he'd been on a roll. Men wise to the intricacies of the political game spoke of his magic touch—his intuitive sense. God, he prayed that they were right. Phil had a hunch he knew he had to play, and the ante was going to cost him a dime.

The phone booth beckoned in his rearview mirror, standing out there on the far corner like a fluorescent-painted prostitute. He crossed to wedge himself into it, paid the ante, and dialed the number. The blaring of a television reached his ears from down the line as a woman's voice said hello.

"Is this the Scranton residence?"

"Sure is. Who's this?"

"My name is DeWitt, ma'am. Is the sheriff in?"

"DeWitt? Hold on a minute."

Phil could hear the receiver being set on some hard surface and then the woman's voice call out, obviously trying to be heard in some distant room. "Boz? Telephone, baby. Some fella, name of DeWitt."

Bosley "Boz" Scranton was the second-term Taney County sheriff who had run on the local Democratic ticket that past November. He'd been challenged by an energetic young Republican with a criminology degree from the big university up in Columbia. Even as the incumbent, Scranton's reelection was seen to be anything but a sure thing, and the local party bigs had gone to the state machine looking for help. DeWitt's boss, Franklin Coulter, all but owned the state apparatus. Because Coulter's own candidacy was being threatened by an upstart rustic off a mid-state hog farm, DeWitt had focused much of the campaign's efforts toward winning over rural pockets of Republican strength. Bosley Scranton's plight was tailor-made. The Ozarks were a Republican stronghold. Coulter troops had campaigned like hell down here, with Scranton reaping the benefits and triumphing with a vote margin of mandate proportion.

"*Phil* DeWitt?" The hearty, hail-fellow voice of this

backwoods, good-ol'-boy sheriff fairly exploded down the line. "How the hell are ya?"

"I've been better, Boz. I've got a problem."

Scranton's whole tone changed, his voice dropping to a level of conspiratorial confidentiality. "Somethin' I can help with?"

Outside the booth, DeWitt noticed that a light, freezing rain had begun to fall. "You may be the only one who *can* help me, Boz. I hate to drag you out on a night like this, but it's time to repay a favor."

One

Senator Richard Coulter could feel the crowd now, and it was with him. He could feel the net worth out there, the eagerness to embrace his message, the righteous indignation. And he'd thought Phil DeWitt was crazy. San Francisco was teeming with faggots and lily-livered liberals, while the Richard Coulter candidacy was being forged as a Democrat's call to arms. Old values in bright new armor. A championing of the ethics of hard work and fair play. Yet, precisely as Phil had predicted, here he was, a carefully assembled dream audience turning to warm putty in the palm of his hand.

"*You* are the generals of this crusade, ladies and gentlemen! I stand up here, gazing out across a sea of faces, and catch a glimmer of hope in eyes weary of watching an entire great nation sold down the river. *Weary* . . . of corruption and self-interest in high places. *Weary* . . . of seeing the products of our sweat and inspiration turned away at ports across the globe, while the bloodsucking foreign bedmates of the Republican Administration steal the wealth of this great nation.''

Coulter paused, drawing himself up to square his shoulders and scowl down at them. He let the powerful, aristocratic jaw, the six-foot, five-inch frame, and the fierce glint in those deep blue eyes work them for a beat. Then, from the shoulder, like a fighter's jab, a fist shot out across the rostrum, index finger extended.

"*You* are the heirs to that wealth! *Not* Mitsubishi Heavy Industries! *Not* the European Economic Community! It was built by your fathers, *grand*fathers, and *great*-grandfathers; by the sweat of honest toil. Stacking bricks, stoking ore furnaces, hauling timber out of wildernesses, standing day in and out on assembly lines."

His voice dropped now, going husky with reasoning confidence.

"Just north and south of this beautiful city, we have a treasure that all the sweat and toil of seven generations could never buy. It is the most remarkable stretch of coastline along the entire rim of the greatest ocean in the world. It, too, is our heritage. And before we let this current administration or any future administration sell our birthright to that breathtaking beauty, to litter it with oil scum, kill its habitats, and create yet another of the countless monuments to pure greed which stretch like a shameful blight across this land, I suggest we look long and hard at the *facts*, ladies and gentlemen. That oil would not be used to heat our homes, generate our electricity, and fuel our cars. Ninety percent of all the oil pumped from Alaska's north-slope fields is shipped directly to Japan, to fuel *their* industry. *Japan*, ladies and gentlemen. The same country that will not take our farmer's grain, our cattlemen's beef, our auto industry's cars."

Again, a pause. Let it sink in. Let them chew on it. He was tempted to glance over to the side of the stage, to see if he could catch the expression on Phil's face. That expression would be his barometer. It would confirm something Richard already knew; that he had them eating out of his hand. But Richard didn't want to break contact. Not when he had them mesmerized like this.

"You all know who my father is; that he gave forty-two years of his life to seeing that *your* fathers got a fair shake

10

from their government. You know that my *grand*father helped
see this nation through the greatest economic depression of
modern times. You know their records and you know mine.
Standing in their shadows, I would be ashamed to also stand
by . . . and watch the greed of the self-interested few destroy
the dreams of the embattled men who founded this country.
Tonight, I take my heritage of public service one step further.
Tonight, a Coulter declares himself as candidate for the presidency of this great country our collected ancestors built.
And I serve warning here tonight that I will not spend this
campaign in *flag factories*.''

Coulter paused to beam his first smirking smile as the
audience broke into enthusiastic applause.

''No!'' All seriousness now, the senator gripped the edges
of the lectern and leaned forward across it. ''*This* campaign
will be fought in the trenches of education, commerce, and
winning back our streets. My battle cry will demand a return
to the ethic of fair play. Tonight, the time has come, ladies
and gentlemen. The time for the doors of justice and opportunity to start swinging both ways!'' A pause, as he quickly
gathered his notes.

''Thank you.''

The ovation was thunderous, many of the entertainers,
educators, business people, and environmental activists
leaping spontaneously to their feet as Richard Coulter turned
to leave the stage. They'd all come to San Francisco for a
symposium on pollution and the rapidly developing global
environmental crisis. This crowd, attending a five-hundred-
dollar-a-plate dinner in the elegant setting of Nob Hill's Mark
Hopkins Hotel, represented the cream of the crop. To get the
proper mix of ardent enthusiasm as well as outright financial
clout, the Coulter campaign had dropped fifty thousand dollars to ensure that one hundred of the guests would be aca-
demics and storefront activists. More of Phil DeWitt's
strategy; to establish an equal footing and sense of importance for all the players.

The senator moved from the stage, his eyes searching out

Phil's self-satisfied smile. Where the hell was he? They'd just finished firing a devastating first salvo, and Phil was generally the first to report the body count. It had been that way through Richard's father Franklin's last two senatorial campaigns, his own five elections to Congress, and the subsequent filling of his father's seat.

"Where the hell is Phil?" he asked Lester Dworkin, the speechwriter.

"He said he wasn't feeling well, Senator. Left for his room about ten minutes ago."

Coulter was visibly surprised. "He didn't stay for the end?"

"No sir. He'd gone sort of gray, and was sweating. I think it was something he ate."

"Jesus," Coulter moaned. "I can see the headlines. 'Three hundred poisoned at Dem's debut.' So what did *you* think?"

Dworkin, a short, intensely high-strung man who wore wire-rimmed glasses and carried a Zenith lap-top computer with him almost everywhere he went, grinned. "The way you punched all the catch phrases made my skin tingle. Those people out there ate it up like they hadn't been fed in *weeks*."

"More like years," Coulter growled. "I like that last line. About it being time for the doors to swing both ways. Try working with that. Maybe we can make it some sort of theme."

"Already on it. Mr. DeWitt had a sense that it was going to play well. I've got half a dozen things sketched out."

Coulter nodded, glancing around him at the milling crowd of well-wishers who now pressed toward the stage. In addition to the press photographers on hand, Phil had hired one of their own to make sure they got him with as many of the famous faces in the crowd as stepped up to offer their support. For the next half an hour Richard was caught up in the campaign whirlwind of pressed flesh, kissed cheeks, and slapped backs. As he came out the other end, he realized that Phil hadn't returned and thought he'd better look in on him.

The senator was grateful for the silence that enveloped him as the doors closed on the elevator and he rode up from the lobby. It had been a crazy summer, spent trying to assemble the best talent they could buy for the upcoming ordeal, and at the same time trying to keep it all under wraps. Everyone involved knew that the time was ripe for the sort of candidacy he could offer a Democratic Party that had long been in disarray on the national level. The excitement that grew as the date of declaration neared was almost palpable. From the family ranch in Aurora, Missouri, his father had been a great help, sounding out the feelings of old-line Democrats and enlisting their support. Now the die was cast and the pressure was on to produce.

As the doors opened on the hallway of the sixth floor, a pair of hotel guests, dressed for a night on the town, stared at him in open recognition as he stepped from the car.

"Evening, folks," he greeted, beaming his best, confidence-inspiring smile. With his stature, thick mane of swept-back gray hair, and chiseled features, he had communications tools crafted for the electronic age. Phil and other political managers liked to refer to such a package as being "television compatible."

He received no reply when he knocked on DeWitt's door, and tried again.

"Phil?" He called it out, and again getting no reply, he stepped down the hall to his own room and dialed the desk.

"I'm sorry, sir," the switchboard operator reported. "That line is engaged."

"This is Senator Richard Coulter, in 610. I just knocked on Mr. DeWitt's door and got no reply. Can you check to see if anyone is on that line?"

After a brief silence the operator came back on. "That phone is off the hook, but there is no conversation on the line, Senator. Would you like me to call security?"

Richard felt a queasy, panicked clutching high in his gut.

Two years ago DeWitt had checked into Johns Hopkins for a week of tests after experiencing severe chest pains. In the time since, he'd shrugged off any concern when he appeared to be experiencing a degree of discomfort. Richard thought he'd read something else there, a sort of false bravado.

"Yes. I think that might be a good idea."

The dog-day heat of a late August day in St. Louis was only serving to make matters worse for Phil DeWitt's son, Carter. Friday nights were generally an event for the young attorney, but this afternoon he'd canceled all plans of revelry. Instead of going out, as was his custom, to prowl the fashionable downtown nightspots where beautiful women always seemed to be in plentiful supply, he sat home in his fifteenth-floor condominium apartment and stared out at the lights along the Mississippi River, contemplating his predicament. A month ago, while legitimately representing the syndication efforts of a thoroughbred horse-breeding enterprise, Carter had taken half a million investor dollars and gambled them on a sure-thing over-the-counter issue going for five dollars a share and promising to go to ten in the very short run. The stock was sold on a company that proposed to manufacture a revolutionary new fire extinguishant, freon-free and non-damaging to the earth's ozone layer. A quick doubling, to ten dollars a share, was a conservative estimate of how far this stock would go once the EPA issued its environmental-impact report in late August.

The report had come out just that morning, and a curious report it proved to be. While refusing to take the new product out behind the shed and simply shoot it in the head, the EPA scientists whose task it was to evaluate it were also refusing to give it a clean bill of health. The report suggested that while the new compound seemed, in the short-term, to perform admirably and present less health risk than chemicals currently in use, it also stated very clearly that the jury was still out on the long-term effects it might have on the environment. Further study was called for, and at least another year would be needed to see such a study completed to the government's satisfaction. A permit to manufacture was at least temporarily being denied.

In one day's trading the worth of a single share had plummeted from a previous-day high of $8.16 to $2.37. Carter had lost more than half of the five hundred thousand he'd invested. Money that wasn't his. And to further compound his dilemma, the report left open the possibility that a production permit might be in the offing somewhere down the road. The very real possibility existed that the stock could rebound. Sure-Fire, the company attempting to market the extinguishant, was known to be conducting a lot of tests of its own. Even if the EPA study wouldn't be concluded for at least a year, news of any breakthrough on the long-term effects of the stuff would no doubt boost the price of the stock to some more acceptable level.

Ever the optimist, Carter was working on his fourth double scotch of the evening, listening to old country tapes and trying to fine-tune his perspective, when the phone rang. Sure-Fire may have backfired, but it was going to come back. All he had to do was be patient. Be patient, and figure out how to get his hands on the half million he'd appropriated from the horse-syndication investors.

"Yes, I'm really home on a Friday night," he announced cheerily into the receiver.

"Carter?"

"Yeah?" Said more slowly. It wasn't a girlfriend or the voice of one of his buddies.

"It's Franklin Coulter, son. Richard just called me from San Francisco and asked me to call you."

Carter's father served two generations of Coulters in Washington, but the son had never received a personal call from either of those nationally prominent figures. The last time he'd seen or heard from the old man, now a few years into his eighties, was at last year's annual Coulter Thanksgiving gathering.

"Yes sir. How are you?" What the hell else was he *supposed* to say?

"I'm afraid I've got bad news, son. Your daddy passed on tonight. In his room at the Mark Hopkins. They think it was a heart attack."

Stunned, Carter opened his mouth to speak and found himself unable.

"Carter?"

"Y-Yes . . . ?"

"You'll never know how much we depended on your daddy. He was a good man. The best. We considered him family. Richard had his staff book you a room and a flight out tonight on TWA. Flight 403 at eleven-fifteen. You just pick up your ticket at the counter and Richard will have someone meet you at the other end."

As Carter moved to hang up, his head swam. All of his underpinnings had just been cut from beneath him. One thing neither Franklin nor Richard knew was the fact that his father had been dying for nearly ten years. That's what the doctors at Johns Hopkins had told him; that he suffered from an inoperable deteriorating disease of the heart muscle. His only treatment option was transplant, and Phil had vetoed it. Still, it had progressed very slowly, and Carter always assumed that the eventuality was something lurking somewhere down life's road, always further away than today.

Two

For Marilyn Hunt it had been a long, hot New York summer in more than the usual sense. Every Tuesday and Thursday since early May she'd appeared before the bar in U.S. District Court, anointed to do battle as chief prosecuting attorney in the United States v. Anando, Phraya, and Jenkins. The case had involved more slow, ponderous, and carefully calculated moves than a chess match. Because it involved an IRS attempt to confiscate $430 million worth of prime commercial real estate in mid-Manhattan, it had also grabbed its share of headlines. The defendants were the suspected kingpins of a Vietnam-era heroin cartel, and because all the early press about them had been of an extremely negative nature, presiding judge Harold Hirschbaum had granted them a lot of leeway in mounting their defense. Finally, just yesterday, after four and a half months in the trenches, defense had rested its case. Closing arguments were to be heard Tuesday, and Marilyn had all weekend to prepare.

She'd chosen the steakhouse on John Street because it was convenient, and damn the exorbitant prices. She was going to win this one. Win big. All morning she'd pored over the ledgers presented by the firm handling the defendant's so-

17

called legitimate assets in the United States. She was a criminal prosecutor, not an accountant, and felt the need to assure herself without a doubt that the inconsistencies uncovered by the IRS investigators were unassailable. She had done just that, and marched to the restaurant in triumph to eat the heartiest meal she had had in many months.

The place was crowded with the special breed of suits and ties that infests Manhattan's financial district. In spite of the calming influence of polished oak, tarnished brass, and great expanses of forest green, the air was heavy with the feel of hunger, aggression, and greed. The voices of the well-manicured patrons were loud and forceful as they all strove for the ever-elusive upper hand. Still, Marilyn could not have felt more at home. She matched wits every day with people just like these, trying to beat them at their own games. Today she was Daniel, lunching right alongside the lions in their den.

Her entrée finished, she ordered a cappuccino, stood, and started across the restaurant toward the phone alcove. There were a few items from her morning's notes that she wanted to dictate for inclusion in the closing argument being word-processed by her secretary. As she moved between tables and then along the back wall, she was not unaware of the attention her passing drew. Though diminutive in stature at barely five feet, she cut an impressive figure, with masses of honey-blond hair, huge brown eyes, and a body that was statuesque in miniature. Today she was dressed in a gray flannel suit fashioned to flatter but not accentuate. An emerald-green silk blouse was open only one button at the throat, and both the Coach bag and briefcase she carried were no-frills elegant. Marilyn was justifiably proud of her looks, but at the same time frustrated by the sorts of reactions they encouraged. Judges and opposing attorneys were not so much different than the red-blooded young Turks in that dining room. To the legal power structure, beautiful, thirty-four-year-old blondes were objects, not worthy adversaries.

As she dropped a quarter and proceeded to punch her

office number into the key pad, she caught an explosion of jocular mirth from one of the nearby tables. Seconds later one of its occupants stood to move in her direction, apparently headed for the rest rooms down that same shallow hall. Her secretary, Georgiana, came on the line.

"Georgie? Hi. I want to play you a few notes I made this morning. Get them down and we'll figure out where I want to work them in later. You set?" As she asked it, she lifted a handheld dictaphone to the mouthpiece and stood poised to depress the play button.

"Got you, boss. Go."

Simultaneous with hitting the button, Marilyn caught the approaching patron out of the corner of her eye. He pulled up behind her and turned to signal his pals with a jaunty thumbs-up gesture. In the next instant she felt his hand close on the left cheek of her buttocks, giving it a purposeful little squeeze.

As much out of reflex as anger, she whirled, the phone receiver becoming a weapon as she swung it in a quick, slashing arc. Pure outrage and a lot of rigorous physical conditioning put vicious force behind the blow. It caught her assailant hard across the right temple.

The guy was medium height, with silver-gray hair cut full, a blue pinstripe suit, and a serious sun-worshiper's tan. He let out a pained yowl and reached to protect his head as blood gushed quickly from a nasty scalp wound. For his trouble he caught an instep in the groin. It doubled him up and sent him crumpling to the floor. Just as he was hitting the deck, his cronies leaped to their feet and rushed to his aid. Marilyn watched in astonishment as a big, healthy-looking specimen in his late thirties arrived first and came directly at her. A forearm hit her before she had time to set herself. With its impact, she stumbled backward, fighting for balance, tripped over her briefcase and landed hard on her backside.

"You son of a *bitch*!"

"Fuck you, lady." It was tossed back at her over the big man's shoulder as he pressed his handkerchief to the gash in his tanned friend's forehead. "He was just having a little fun, and you half-fucking killed him."

She was on her knees now, struggling to rise. "Somebody call the police!"

All around her the restaurant was suddenly in an uproar. Many of the remaining patrons, having already paid their checks, now moved to hurry out of there. A few feigned obliviousness, while others rose from their chairs to gawk. When the downed man took that foot in the testicles, every male in the place winced and went a little white. Few had witnessed the actual precipitating incident with any clarity. From where she knelt, tears of rage streaming down her cheeks, Marilyn could see no one, not even from the restaurant staff, make any move toward a telephone.

When he emerged from the crowd of rubberneckers to cross and offer her a hand up, Marilyn remembered having seen the tall, casually dressed man enter in her wake to sit and dine alone.

"You all right, miss?"

Without waiting for her answer, he reached to reel in the dangling receiver and dug into a pocket for change. As he moved to lift a quarter to the slot, another friend of the guy who grabbed Marilyn moved to place a restraining hand on his bicep.

"What're you doing, pal?" It was muttered close to the rugged man's ear.

Marilyn watched in fascination as the man who'd helped her to her feet swung around to face the voice squarely. His pale, blue-gray eyes went cruel now, traveling slowly to the hand on his arm and back up. The hand left its purchase, becoming a fist as it fell to this shorter, stockier banker's side.

"The lady asked somebody to call the police."

"C'mon." It was punctuated with a nervous chuckle. "Nicky was having a little fun and the lady overreacted. He thought he knew her and was trying to play a little joke."

The curiously dressed stranger reached around to drop his

quarter into the phone. "She didn't appear to be amused. Not by him and not by your other friend there. The one who shoved her on her ass. Was that a little joke too?"

The words were spoken with a measured coolness, but plenty loud enough for the party ministering to his fallen friend to hear. Marilyn was alarmed to see him leap to his feet, hot fury twisting his face in a mask of rage.

"Hang that up!" He was nearly as tall as the man he addressed, with perhaps fifteen or twenty pounds on him. The command was delivered as though his size, health-club build, and station in life had accustomed him to being heeded.

"Pardon me?" Again, it was cool and controlled.

Marilyn's assailant took a quick, aggressive step forward.

"I'm telling you to wander off and mind your own business, cowboy. I tried to back her off and she tripped over her own fucking feet."

"He grabbed my ass and you pushed me, you bastard!" With the tears still streaming down her face and a quaver of disbelief in her voice, Marilyn was obviously struggling to pull herself together. "Is that what you call fun? It's what I call assault!" This last utterance came through clenched teeth, and as she spoke, she pointed at the phone, her eyes making direct contact with her benefactor's. "It's 911. *Please.*"

The fourth member of the offender's party got into the act now. He was several years senior and a bit more subtly dressed than his friends. His double-breasted suit in a pale gray with muted blue pinstripe was English in cut and probably hand-tailored. As he opened his mouth to speak he was already extracting a billfold from his inside jacket pocket.

"Can't we settle this thing reasonably, miss?" It was asked in his best amiable tone. "Our friend Nicky had a few drinks over lunch and thought he'd play a practical joke on a friend. It's an obvious case of mistaken identity. Let us buy your lunch and we'll call it all even, with Nicky's apologies."

The look the rugged stranger saw in Marilyn's eyes must have reflected what she was thinking with fair accuracy. For an instant she considered foregoing a knee to this one's balls and simply tearing them off instead. Three quick jabs at the telephone key pad turned the insulting offer into a dead issue.

The stranger listened a moment, reported the nature of the incident and location, listened another few beats and stated his name.

"Robert McElliot." A pause. "The man who precipitated the assault is bleeding a lot from a head wound. He may need medical attention."

In the next brief silence Marilyn realized that everyone in the immediate area was listening to every word said.

"That's correct. The offended party fought back."

When McElliot eventually hung up the phone, he turned to Marilyn, his look conveying nothing but sympathy for the awkwardness of her position.

"Unless the First Precinct just happens to have a unit in the area, there isn't much chance anyone is going to respond with emergency speed. I guess we're all going to have to just sit here and wait awhile." He turned to face the man with the recently opened wallet. His musclebound friend, still doing a slow burn, stood with his jaw clenched, just behind him.

"The lady and I are going to sit at one of those tables over there by the door. I advise you to keep your hotheaded friend there in line. If any of you try to leave, I'll be forced to stop you." There was no edge of challenge or even bravado in it. The man was stating facts. "I watched your buddy there give the lady a thorough going-over before he made his move. He winked at the three of you back at your table, so feed your case of mistaken identity to someone who *likes* horseshit."

Marilyn watched the older man size up this nail-hard customer with the scary edge to his speech. His scrutiny moved up from scuffed boots to intent, slate-colored eyes and short-cropped dark hair. It took in hands that were big and competent, the cuffs of his work shirt and bush jacket turned back to reveal sinewy forearms and wrists crisscrossed with prominent veins. The shoulders were wide and the hips slim, like an athlete's. The glint in those slightly narrowed eyes seemed to be almost begging him to press his side of the issue.

"I was just trying to be fair, and I've got to say that I find your attitude offensive, son."

There was no change in this Robert McElliot's expression. Just the continued, cool regard. "You've never seen me when my attitude gets offensive, *dad*. So don't push. Neither you nor your friend look like you'd have the stomach for it."

McElliot took Marilyn gently by the elbow, stooped to retrieve her bag and briefcase, and led her to an empty table adjacent to the front door. He stationed his own chair with his back to the wall, where he had a view of the entire dining room. When they were settled, he asked her if she'd like anything. She declined and he ordered himself a beer.

Perhaps it was his mention of blood, or maybe the name of the restaurant, but a pair of uniformed patrolmen appeared within ten minutes to begin sorting things out. When Marilyn gave them her name, in the process also identifying herself as an Assistant United States Attorney, her side of the story started carrying weight. McElliot backed her statement up with an account of what he'd witnessed, and eventually the bleeding Nicky and his pushy associate were cuffed and shown to a squad car. The officers provided her with a number she could call to get their report, and then she found herself following her rescuer as he drifted out into the sunshine of the late summer afternoon. While giving his statement, he'd described himself as a documentary filmmaker. That would explain his casual dress, but not his willingness to get involved. In that respect, he was an anomaly. New Yorkers never got involved.

"I don't think I've ever met anyone who does what you do," she said. "It must be fascinating." They'd stopped at the edge of the sidewalk and stood facing each other. "Is there anything that I might have seen?"

He chuckled good-naturedly. "I wish I had a nickel for every time someone's asked me that. My partner and I have done dozens of little segments you may have caught if you're a regular Public Television viewer. Shorts on troubles in urban neighborhoods, plant closings, labor unrest, how crime effects specific local economies . . . stuff like that. Usually between five and fifteen minutes. We've done two feature-length projects that drifted off into obscurity an hour or two after they were released.''

"I'm sure you're being modest."

He shrugged. "It's a lot of sitting around, mostly in out-of-the-way or uninspired places. It takes a certain temperament.''

"I want to thank you for what you did in there. If you hadn't, I don't think anyone else would have helped me.''

"No thanks necessary. That was a cheap, low-life stunt.'' He paused, seeming to consider what it was he'd just said. "But typical, I suppose, of the mentality down here.''

The man was gorgeous. It made her uneasy to realize that just being in his company was making her blood pump a little faster. She was a woman who prided herself on her control, and she was feeling anything but in control right now. She nodded toward the steakhouse door.

"So what's a documentary filmmaker doing eating by himself on John Street? Meeting with his broker?''

"A producer . . . and her money people.''

Was she crazy, or was the attraction she was feeling mutual? She thought she detected an amused twinkle in those unusual gray eyes.

"You suffer any damage from that spill?'' he asked.

"Mostly to my pride. It's nothing that epsom salts and a couple of drinks won't fix. In spite of it, I'm feeling decidedly up today, Mr. McElliot.''

"Call me Bobby. I'm afraid most everyone else does. I suppose you've got every reason to be feeling pretty positive, huh? What with all the press is saying about your chances of winning that trial.''

She knew she shouldn't be surprised that he'd made the connection, but she was. Surprised and flattered.

"It isn't over yet, but yeah, I do feel positive. You wouldn't happen to be free to have those drinks with me this evening, would you, Mr. McElliot?"

God, had she actually said that?

He laughed outright. "You look surprised that you just asked me out. Are you?"

Try as she might to fight it, color crept up across her face in a wave of flushed heat. "Surprised? I guess maybe I am. A little."

"How about dinner?" he suggested. "Without something in your stomach, all that alcohol might go to your head."

"I didn't mean to put you on the spot like this. Really."

"It's not a spot I much mind being on, actually. There's something about you that reminds me of the girls I used to know on the Junior Rodeo Circuit. They could take a shot as hard as any man might, get up, dust off their hats, and climb right back on. I haven't met a woman like that in a long time. Surely not in New York."

"Do you want to pick me up or meet somewhere?"

Three weeks after the fact, the shock of his father's death was something with which Carter DeWitt still hadn't come to grips. One day, a man of great presence and political prowess had confidently strutted the avenues of power, and the next day he was the stuff of dust and memory. As his only son and heir, Carter had been forced by circumstance to put all his own troubles aside to oversee transport of the body, funeral arrangements, and the burial. Franklin Coulter talked a good line about being as close as family, but when he and his son Richard learned that Phillip DeWitt had kept the fact of his illness from them, their reaction was less sympathy than anger. Neither had lingered once the burial was over, with Franklin slipping quietly back to his ranch and Richard off to the campaign trail.

In the three weeks since, Carter had moved from his apartment downtown to his father's big brick house in the affluent St. Louis suburb of Creve Coeur. He'd been forced to put his life on hold to deal with the estate, taking an indefinite leave of absence from the work he did as the youngest partner in his father's law firm. He held out hope that there might be enough liquid cash from the estate that, combined with the proceeds from the sale of his own apartment, he could cover the funds he'd appropriated from the breeding syndicate. But no sooner had news of his father's death gotten out than nearly a dozen creditors emerged from the woodwork, each petitioning the courts to freeze all assets. It seemed that part of Phillip DeWitt's up-by-the-bootstraps philosophy was to never pay immediately what he could put off for a few months or even a year. To make matters worse, the real estate market was soft all over the Midwest. In such a climate a man in need of quick cash had to be willing to take much less than he might think his property was worth.

Yesterday he'd finally made the dreaded trip down here to the lake house in Shell Knob. When Franklin Coulter had retired from public life, he'd made a sort of reverse retirement gift of thirty acres on Table Rock Lake to his faithful strategist, for services rendered. On it, Carter's father had built a four-thousand-square-foot home of fieldstone, rough-hewn oak, and glass. The place sat perched above the giant water-project lake, fronted by two hundred yards of private beach, a fieldstone boat house, and a dock. Phil had always regarded this place as his pride and joy; more, even, than his prestigious St. Louis address, and name on the letterhead of a venerable old law firm. The house had been completed late in Carter's sixteenth year, and was haunted with memories which he was not yet eager to relive. Memories of strong father-son bonding. Hunting and fishing. Being treated as an equal by men he admired and aspired to emulate. Before he turned eighteen, Carter bedded his first woman here.

He'd arrived late yesterday afternoon and spent the night in that same old room. He'd been too spooked by the experience of just being here to do much more than shop for a few necessary provisions, fry himself a burger, and sit out back on the terrace. A note discovered in his father's night-

26

stand drawer in St. Louis was his actual reason for making the journey, but being unable to shake that haunted feeling, he'd left the business of it until today. It suggested that some items had been put away for safekeeping in the game-room vault, saying that the combination was the same sequence of numbers stamped into the barrel of Carter's favorite rifle. Only a father and son would know which it was of the twelve guns in the game-room rack.

This morning he'd awakened late, driving into the ersatz town for breakfast at the diner, and returned to restlessly prowl the place before finally entering the game room in the early afternoon. His favorite rifle was an old Winchester Model 94 lever-action carbine. As a boy he'd chosen it because it reminded him of the gun wielded most often by heroes in John Ford and Howard Hawks Westerns. He'd cared for it lovingly, and had killed his first wild pig with it on the Coulter's Aurora ranch. The serial numbers stamped into its barrel were still readable, but worn smooth by years of polishing. He jotted them down on a scrap of paper, carried it to the wall safe—concealed behind a painting of two mallard ducks in flight—and worked the combination dial.

The contents of the safe were sealed in various-size manila envelopes. Carter stacked them on the edge of the pool table and left them there until he could pull a leather upholstered club chair over to one of the open terrace doors. A warm, late-summer breeze turned his skin clammy beneath a sheen of nervous perspiration as he opened the envelopes, one at a time. In the first he discovered a quantity of cash money, rubber-banded in packets. It took him better than half an hour to count it all; a little more than $110,000, mostly in tens and twenties. Under-the-table money. Hush money. Carter knew that a man in his father's position often had need for such funds, well-laundered and untraceable, to smooth over the rough waters generated by minor political storms. The hundred and ten thousand, combined with the two hundred and thirty his Sure-Fire stock was now worth, still left him a hundred and sixty short of replacing the syndicate-investors' money. The horse the syndicate's managing partner had her eye on was coming to auction in just three weeks. Instead of feeling buoyed by his discovery, Carter was embittered by the irony in it.

There were a number of stock certificates in the next envelope. From the names of corporations emblazoned in fanciful script across their tops, it was obvious that they were all long shots, most of them dying out of the gate. Still, he spent a little time checking the few more promising-looking issues against the market listings, on the chance that there was a pearl in there somewhere among the swine. When he eventually gave up, he turned to the last envelope in the lot. It was smaller than the others by quite a bit, and unlike them, it wasn't stuffed, but lay flat. Within it Carter discovered three typewritten pages, paper-clipped together and folded once. A letter, dated the first of July, just this year, and addressed to him.

This called for a drink. Carrying the letter with him, he poured a tumbler full of Maker's Mark from the game-room bar and pushed back the screen door leading onto the terrace. A week past Labor Day, the summer heat was still holding. There were a number of early weekend arrivals already out frolicking on the water, and as he pulled up a lounge chair to sit, a speedboat swept past below, skier in tow.

What he read in the letter was an account of an event that had taken place twenty-eight years ago. It told of how his father had arranged for a young, college-age campaign volunteer to have an abortion in an out-of-the-way Branson motel. Something had gone wrong. The two young doctors involved had nicked an artery, and the girl had bled to death. The local sheriff had helped his father tie up the loose ends, the two of them rigging her car to roll out of control over a cliff above Lake Taney Como. Since then, the sheriff had made it known that he had saved some specific piece or pieces of evidence as insurance, to make sure his contribution wasn't forgotten. In addition to being assured of reelection every four years until his retirement in 1986, Bosley Scranton had been paid a sum of money annually at Thanksgiving.

There was a second part of the letter. In it Phillip described the specific circumstances leading up to that girl's tragic death. He named names and made allegations associated with them which, if they could be proven, would surely destroy lives. He took pains to emphasize the weight of responsibility this knowledge carried, cautioning his son to use it prudently. His suggestion was, by doing so himself, he had seen his own nest well-feathered. It was his hope that his son might do the same.

Trembling slightly as he refolded and stuffed the letter back into the envelope, Carter saw the deliverance from his current situation suddenly revealed to him. His father advised caution, but in later life Phillip DeWitt had turned more the long-term strategist and less the gambler. Phil also hadn't recently lost control of someone else's half a million dollars. If Carter didn't recover that money and recover it soon, there would be only one sort of long term—the sort done behind bars.

As Carter returned his treasures to the game-room safe, a first oyster of untasted opportunity was already opening in his mind's eye. Within fifteen minutes he'd reached the St. Louis private investigator he used for particularly thorny litigational inquiries. He found Anthony Flood just preparing to call it a day and get an early start on Friday night. When Carter mentioned a particularly lucrative sum as compensation for his services, Flood agreed to pack a bag and drive down to meet with him.

Three

Asking men out wasn't exactly Marilyn Hunt's style. All the same, the prospect of seeing her filmmaker pass forever into the pages of a less than lustrous romantic history had been enough to see her throw caution to the wind. Since then she'd gotten stuck sorting out a host of last-minute final argument details at the office, and arrived home just an hour before Robert McElliot was due downstairs. As she raced through a shower and a feeble attempt at setting the blunt-cut ends of her business bob, her thoughts backtracked once again over the incident that afternoon. It seemed perhaps extreme, but at the same time so typical of her life lately.

As an Assistant United States Attorney, Marilyn had been assigned more than a year ago to prosecute a then barely developed case against the Asian dope cartel. The analysis and strategy had lacked complexity. She realized that any successful prosecution would involve months of fifteen-hour days if she wanted to completely document a sophisticated cash-laundering network and the purchase of Manhattan real estate. The stakes ran well into the hundreds of millions, and Marilyn had worked herself ragged to ensure that the case she brought into the Southern New York District of Federal

Court would stand airtight against an army of the slickest defense attorneys money could buy. Once she was in court, the prosecution actually under way, she found the twice-a-week schedule to be more advantageous to the defense than it was to her own effort. Each time she opened a wound, the other team had at least a day and often a long weekend to ferret out some way to close it. While proud of the job she'd done this summer, she was exhausted.

The rollers helped turn under the edges of the no frills hairstyle, softening it. In court she wore three-inch heels and a variety of suits selected because they lengthened her lines. Tonight she was throwing such contrivance aside in favor of comfort and a little femininity. Low heels and a floral-print silk dress. She surveyed herself in the mirror, the survivor in her screaming that the image was too soft.

McElliot's arrival was punctual. When the doorman called to inform her that her date was in the lobby, she hurried to the elevator and rode down.

"Hi," she greeted. The suit he wore was something of a surprise; European in cut, it hung from those wide shoulders and hugged his hips with the telltale cut of a garment made for him. "A reverse dresser. I'm impressed."

"You care to expand on that?"

Thank God there was amusement in his tone. So many men she met in this town took themselves with a frightening seriousness. She smiled her best disarming smile in return. "Casual by day. Killer-elegant by night."

As he moved to hold the door for her, his head-to-toe appraisal said he also appreciated what *he* saw.

"You hungry?" he asked. 'We've got a reservation in half an hour at Primavera."

Tailored Milanese suits. Dinner at a *very* expensive Italian restaurant in a city where the simplest day-to-day life was hard on most budgets. Marilyn felt distinctly lightheaded.

"Famished," she admitted, and laughed nervously. "Considering where you're taking me and that I invited myself, I'm not sure you wanted to hear that."

His response was warm and not the least forced. "It's a beautiful evening. You want to grab a cab or do you feel like walking?"

The restaurant was located on First Avenue and Eighty-first Street. Marilyn's apartment building stood at Sixty-third and Third. That made the distance a bit more than a mile, and they had time to kill. As she stepped out into the warm evening air, she slid her right hand under and up into the crook of his arm.

"I think I'd like to walk, if you don't mind."

They started off uptown, moving along at a slow, casual pace.

"I like your hair like that," he told her. "The dress too."

She smiled, enjoying the flattery. "I was in a mood for a change. You caught me with my game face on this afternoon. That case has become something like the final phases of a major chess match. I've been running around like a madwoman, trying to anticipate surprises and shore up against any potential collapse. That joker in the restaurant had his timing all off."

"I suspect he would have gotten his, no matter what day it was. I can't believe, prosecutor *or* beautiful woman in a pretty silk dress, that you take much abuse from anyone. We don't change that like we change our clothes."

She suddenly felt completely at ease with this man, and just as safe as she had in his company that afternoon.

"I have, by the way, filed assault charges against both those guys. I'm hoping you might be willing to testify."

"Sure. You do realize that a man in my line of work is in and out of town a lot."

"How about if I work it around your schedule? We could get a pre-arraignment deposition as early as next week, and go from there."

His eyes narrowed, smugness in them. "I suppose I'd better, huh?"

"Why's that?"

"I saw the way you clocked that clown. If I say no, I'll have to sleep with one eye open, well into middle age."

When he smiled, a pair of laugh lines manifested themselves on both sides of his mouth. Another something they had in common.

"I got him pretty good, didn't I?"

"Good enough to make *me* wince."

Throughout their stroll up along Third to Seventy-ninth and then east toward First, they talked more about the prosecution she was preparing to nail down. When asked, he described the film he'd made over the past few months at a steel mill in Pittsburg, California, explaining that the ailing American industry was collaborating with the Koreans to produce cheaper steel for the Orient than what was currently being offered by the Japanese. When they eventually reached the restaurant, it proved to be doing the sort of business that might be expected for a Friday night.

The maître d' eased his way through a small knot of people waiting near the door to greet McElliot, shaking his hand. The filmmaker slipped his arm lightly across Marilyn's shoulders as he introduced her. They were escorted to an intimate corner table, perhaps the nicest for two in the house. Without consulting the wine list, McElliot asked to have a bottle of Lungarotti Rubesco 1975 Riserva opened for the meal and asked Marilyn if she'd like white wine to start, or perhaps a drink.

"Wine, thank you. I'll defer to your choice."

He seemed pleased. "I think I'll join you." As he started to reach for the list, he suddenly stopped. "You seem to feel you're going to win this chess match of yours, am I right?"

"Chess match?"

"When I first picked you up. That's how you described your case."

Her confusion quickly vanished. "Oh. Yes, I do."

"I'm feeling sort of festive tonight, and I'm wondering if you've got reason to feel the same."

It sank in, and she quickly shook her head.

"I learned a long time ago not to count my chickens."

He grinned, mischief in it. "Then just indulge me."

The steward arrived with the Rubesco, and while he opened it, her date ordered a bottle of Roederer Cristal Rosé. Marilyn stared at him in open astonishment.

"*That* festive? Save your money, Robert, I'm already impressed." As she said it, she was hoping that he could handle a woman who didn't mince words.

"Bobby. I know it's not terribly dignified, but I'm too set in my ways to try and change it now."

He was ignoring her request to back away from his lavish wine selection.

"That's a three-hundred-dollar bottle of champagne you just ordered."

McElliot leaned back in his chair, absorbing the irritation in her tone. "I appreciate your concern, Marilyn. It's rare in a city like New York. But please. As an up and comer with the Justice Department, you would no doubt recognize the name Michael Harrington? He's my grandfather, I'm his only heir, and I can afford this."

The tailored Italian suits were suddenly explained. Michael Harrington was one of those names that needed no specific point of reference in American culture. His was one of the oldest and most enduring fortunes in the history of the country. It was so old, indeed, that a huge portion of the man's actual worth was buried in entire multinational corporations which his huge blocks of voting stock controlled. While his personal net worth was estimated in the financial press to be in the $500 million neighborhood, the worth his stewardship controlled was easily ten times that amount. Marilyn figured that if what Bobby McElliot had just revealed was true, he could probably have his suits tailored on the moon if he had a mind. Deep skepticism suddenly declared itself in her posture shift. The intimacy had disappeared.

"The Harrington Foundation? Harrington Institute for

Criminal Justice? The Harrington Chair at Princeton Law School?''

McElliot nodded. "And Eisenhower's United Nations ambassador."

Her mind was racing, something niggling back there, trying to click into place. "McElliot. McElliot . . ." she murmured. Then her eyes brightened, only to quickly narrow again. "*Terrence* McElliot. The guy who used to be Treasury's Director of the Secret Service. I remember reading somewhere that he was Michael Harrington's son-in-law. He must be either your father or uncle."

"Father."

"Jesus." Again, under her breath. "And that line about the Junior Rodeo Circuit? If you are who you say you are, what was that? Your idea of a disarming rich-kid come-on?"

McElliot seemed to take no offense, his tone unsettling in the way it remained calm and friendly.

"I am who I say I am, Marilyn. It's a fact of my birth, and I don't have much control over those basics. My mother died when I was five. I was raised by my paternal grandparents on a cattle ranch in Nevada, Missouri. I went to public school there because my dad's mother hated the idea of a little boy boarding somewhere. I'm the first Harrington since 1756 who didn't attend Princeton. I went to UCLA to play baseball. Nobody I knew in California had any idea I was a Harrington, and that was just fine by me."

Properly rebuked, Marilyn colored with embarrassment. "I'm sorry. Damn, I really put my foot in it, didn't I?"

He shrugged. "You're not the first. People hear my mother's maiden name, and in the same instant I'm generally prejudged."

"So if you hate that so much, why did you take me *here*? If we'd gone somewhere else, it probably wouldn't have come up. I'd never have known."

Only his mouth smiled while his eyes kept that wan, faraway look in them. "What was it that the man said? You can run but you can't hide? I run from drinking Dom Ruinart and partying with the glitterati; from living my life in a fish-bowl. But I refuse to hide, Marilyn. You remember what I said to you this afternoon? About not meeting women like you in New York? I'm afraid that's true. I don't generally like the women I meet in this town any more than I like the men. It probably sounds pretentious, coming from a man in my position, but New York's baby-boom generation seems infected with an ugly kind of avarice. You care about something a bit more inspired than simple greed."

She grinned. "It *does* sound a little funny, coming from a guy who's already got it all. You really rode on the Junior Rodeo Circuit?"

"Yep." He said it with pride. "National Teen Champion, Bull Riding, 1972. I was seventeen years old and had been riding, summers, for four years."

"And what did your grandfather Harrington think about that? It was dangerous, wasn't it?"

"Believe it or not, he flew out to Muskogee to watch me in the National Finals in '72. I think he was proud as hell."

The steward arrived with the Cristal and opened it. Marilyn sat digesting all she'd just learned as she watched the ritual process. When the blush-colored sparkling wine was poured, her date raised his glass to her.

"To shattered preconceptions, counselor?"

The feisty lady prosecutor's face softened. "You've been a surprise a minute, Mr. McElliot."

Several hours later they were back out in the evening air and again opting to walk. Now, with the warmth of the wine further relaxing her, Marilyn's hand gripped the crook of McElliot's arm a little tighter. Their pace was unhurried. As they approached within a block of her building, she turned her head to peer up into his face. He was a full foot taller, and for the first time in her experience she found that she didn't mind. There was no challenge in the difference. No threat. It felt right.

"When you spoke of people being infected with avarice,

I got the impression you don't much like this city. So why not base your operation in some place like Aspen or Jackson Hole?''

He sighed. "New York is where all the network assignments come from, not to mention grant funding and foundation money. Home here isn't much more than a big warehouse loft with a couple of bedrooms and a lot of equipment. Like I told you, I'm away three hundred days out of the year. Then I'm immersed in some other, completely separate reality. *Other* people's triumphs or problems.''

"You sound like a man who loves his work.''

He grinned, the evening seeming to have put him totally at ease. "You bet. I've enjoyed peering through windows into other people's lives from the day I first started doing it.''

"Sounds kinky.'' She delivered it with a wiggle of the brows.

"Maybe it is.''

When they reached the door to her building, he turned to face her, taking both of her hands. His own were huge, engulfing hers completely.

"Home safe and sound.''

"Nightcap?'' she offered.

He shook his head. "How about I take a rain check?''

"I had a wonderful time tonight.''

"Me too. You know that film I was telling you about? The one Stan and I shot out east of San Francisco? It's being premiered at the Whitney Museum, Sunday afternoon. It's black tie, and I know you're busy and this is pretty late notice, but I'd like you to come as my date.''

She hoped her delight was obvious as she stood on tiptoe, pulled his head down with both hands, and kissed him full on the mouth.

It was after eleven o'clock before private investigator Anthony "Tony'' Flood could complete the five-hour drive from St. Louis to the DeWitt Table Rock Lake house outside Shell Knob. When he finally pulled his late-model Jeep Cherokee into the drive in front of the garage, Carter emerged from the house to greet him. The contrast between the man who emerged from the Jeep and the man standing with a pair of Busch beers before him was marked. At a couple of inches under six feet, Flood appeared larger than the taller DeWitt. He moved as though he owned the space he currently occupied, while Carter seemed to be borrowing his. Tony had the thick bull neck, heavy shoulders, and stovepipe forearms of a hod carrier. His graying, bristle-cut hair further worked to define an edge of tungsten toughness. DeWitt, on the other hand, while trim, had an air of softness about him. His expensive casual clothes hung on him like a window dummy's. His jocularity seemed practiced; an act. He had the sort of face that photographed well but lacked any real presence. Flood, less classically handsome, was *all* presence.

"Carter boy. What y'all got that demanded draggin' my ass all the way down here on a Friday night? You seen the pair'a jugs on the bitch I had lined up tonight, you would'a known nothin's that important." Flood accepted the beer from the younger man, popped the tab and drank off close to half of it in a few deep swallows.

DeWitt forced a thin, locker-room laugh. "All the women you date look exactly the same, Tony. I don't suppose the twenty-five thou I mentioned had anything to do with you changing those plans?"

"Might'a." Flood opened the back driver-side door, grabbed his grip, and followed the attorney as he led the way up the footpath to the front door.

This was not Tony's first visit to the lake house, and he knew the layout well enough to head straight down a hall off the entry, drop his bag in a guest room, and use the plumbing. Some years back, at the successful conclusion of his first collaboration with DeWitt, he'd been invited down here for a week of barbecue, beer, and bass fishing. Privately, twenty-five grand for a couple weeks snooping around, and the prospect of getting his hook into the water hereabouts, was more than enough incentive to break a date. He wasn't getting any younger, sure; but lately he hadn't been getting any richer either.

He found Carter at ease in one of those huge steer-hide upholstered chairs in the living room, moved past into the game room to grab a second beer and joined him. The living room was the central shrine in old Phil DeWitt's monument to male bonding. A full fifty feet long and thirty wide, its exposed beams, vaulted ceiling rose to a peak some eighteen feet off the floor. The white plaster walls were hung with hunting and fishing trophies, Duck Stamp prints, and color-splashed Navajo rugs.

"So what the hell gives, good buddy? I thought you told me you was gonna be takin' a few weeks off. Sort out your daddy's affairs."

DeWitt nodded. "That's right; I did. This is personal. I came across something in my father's papers that seems to bear some looking into."

"To the tune of twenty-five thousand dollars? I bet it does. You care to let me in on it?"

The young attorney smiled, shaking his head. In his experience, Tony Flood didn't miss a trick . . . or an opening he could insinuate himself into. "Maybe, later on down this road. But right now I'm interested in finding out just how deep the well is." He reached into his shirt pocket, withdrew a folded piece of paper and handed it across. "Those are the names of three people I want you to run exhaustive checks on; develop profiles. Two of them are doctors, working in the Springfield area. The third is a former Taney County sheriff. Retired. For reasons I'd rather not go into, it would be nice if you could work the two doctors first. The sheriff is important, but you can take a little more time with him. I need the stuff on the medical men as soon as you can get it to me."

Flood took a moment to read the names before refolding the sheet and consigning it to his hip pocket. "Any of them gonna be expecting somebody like me t'come snoopin' around?"

"No reason to. This has something to do with a matter my father kept close to the vest for a number of years." Carter paused to purse his lips and consider just how much further he could go in explaining his motivations. "The sheriff may be in possession of something that, in conjunction with other information I have, could be worth a lot of money. If you manage to recover such, I think you can count on my doubling my already generous fee."

Flood came forward just slightly in his chair. "Care to give me a hint? Or is it somethin' real obvious, like an eighteen-foot Anaconda snake?"

His host chuckled, pushing himself to his feet to move off in search of a fresh brew. "Less obvious than that, but hopefully obvious enough to make you look twice. Something he's no doubt keeping in a very safe place."

"Bigger'n a breadbox?"

"Smaller, I'd think."

Four

One thing Robert McElliot failed to mention to Marilyn Hunt over dinner Friday night was the fact that as Director of the Secret Service, his father had recruited him into Treasury enforcement once he completed college. He also failed to mention that as a covert Treasury agent assigned to the Secret Service, he'd been pulled in off his regular beat to keep an eye on her. It seemed that there was a temporary manpower shortage at the New York Field Office, threats had been made against the prosecutor in connection with her current case, and both McElliot and his partner were between assignments. Whether the threats were real or not, the Secretary of the Treasury didn't want to see this highly visible prosecution interrupted, and the Attorney General didn't want to risk losing one of his fastest rising Criminal Division stars.

The van appeared ordinary enough, parked at the curb on Hamill Place, across from the U.S. Court House on Foley Square. From the outside it resembled any of the thousands of similar vehicles New York Telephone maintained in its considerable fleet. There were two ladders strapped to a rack on the roof, the usual painted logo and detailing, an empty driver's seat, and little else to draw any attention. A casual observer had no way of knowing that it had been parked in this same location every Tuesday and Thursday for a month. Today, a Monday in mid-September, Marilyn Hunt and the defense team were convening in the judge's chambers for some sort of special session. After a night of celebrating the premier of their new film, the partners had been rousted early to collect the van and begin this off-day protection surveillance.

"God, my aching back!" McElliot was seated at a tightly constructed video console, monitoring the street and foot traffic between his position and the courthouse steps.

"Your aching back, my aching *ass*." Wedged into the seat alongside, McElliot's partner, Stan Torbeck, was even less suited to the cramped conditions inside the van. If McElliot was big, Torbeck was huge; six-foot, four-inches tall and carrying 220 hard-muscled pounds. Both liked to think of themselves as men of action, and all this unaccustomed sitting around was killing them.

"You want some of this?" Torbeck lifted a thermos, unscrewed the cap, and poured himself a cup of coffee.

McElliot shook his head. "One more and I might crawl out of my skin."

"I think both of us are dangerously close to the end of our ropes, Bob."

"Can't imagine what might give you that impression, big guy. It's eighty-seven degrees outside. We're sitting here inside this hot box, being parboiled to near perfection. Meanwhile, the manpower that *should* be babysitting our beautiful blond prosecutor is off watching nearly a dozen early presidential hopefuls eat pan-fried chicken and apple pie. Whatever happened to that special status they conned us into ten years ago? There's no justice."

Torbeck snorted in disgust. "You're talking to me about justice? Who the fuck did she invite out to dinner?"

"And who asked me to take that shift alone so he could sleep in after a heavy night on the town?"

Torbeck slurped a swallow of his coffee, his eyes drifting

back along the row of monitor screens arrayed before them. When McElliot announced that he'd had dinner with the object of their current assignment, Stan thought his old pal had been pulling his leg. Later, when it became apparent that he wasn't, Torbeck chalked it up to his old friend's charmed existence. But then again, he'd long envied him his effortless touch. The way Stan figured it, all that easygoing cowboy simplicity aside, it was something a man like his partner was blessed with at birth. It was also something you didn't argue with, but just accepted.

If McElliot might seem, to those few who knew the facts, a strange candidate for this sort of work, so too was Torbeck. While the former was being raised in the shadow of immense wealth on a Midwest cattle ranch, the latter was growing up a towhead rowdy surfer in a California beach town. At eighteen they'd met at UCLA because they had baseball in common. In time both also wound up majoring in film, but there all similarity ended. McElliot generally preferred a quiet evening at home with a book, while Torbeck was an inveterate night crawler. McElliot was soft-spoken; Torbeck was loud. McElliot was slow to burn; Torbeck went off like lightning-lit tinder. Over the years, they'd inexplicably become the closest of friends.

Setting down his cup, Stan rubbed his eyes and stretched.

"So tell me. What gives with the lady lawyer?"

"What *gives*?"

"Yeah. It looked to me like you were actually getting on."

Stan had shown up at the premier party with a pretty, raven-haired date, dressed on the cutting edge of fashion. And as if McElliot's appearance with their current assignment on his arm wasn't already enough, the prosecutor proved to have brains to match her beauty. The four of them dined together after the party, and Stan's date, one of the trust-fund babies he was forever meeting in his night haunts, was soon left behind in a lively discussion of the government's recent attempts to break up wiseguy control of the Teamsters with RICO indictments.

"I think it's safe to say we seem to get along," McElliot allowed.

Stan rolled his eyes. "You know what I'm asking, buddy. Any potential there for a sustained run?"

McElliot had begun to roll his head and rotate his shoulders in an effort to relieve an aching tightness in his neck. One kink was refusing to be persuaded away.

"She didn't seem at all my type at first, but the more I see of her, the more I like it."

"How long you gonna play the wait-and-see game before you make your move?"

"My *move*? She's a protection assignment, for God's sake. I'm a professional."

"I *know* you, Bob. I saw the way you watched her when her attention was somewhere else . . . which wasn't all that often, I might add. She's hit you somewhere vulnerable."

This was not an exchange McElliot was sure he wanted to be having. With one hand spread, he ticked the negatives off on his fingers: "She's short. I've never trusted blondes. She works as a prosecutor for the Justice Department, and I'm a covert agent of the United States Secret Service. My father was *Director* of the Secret Service. I think there might be a conflict of interest buried in there somewhere. All that in mind, I haven't made my *move*, as you so gallantly term it, because I don't want to wake up the next morning, realize the whole thing's impossible, and have to cut out. This is a woman who seems to have a lot to invest emotionally, and as much to lose."

Torbeck turned from the monitors to face his old friend straight on. "Just for the record, Bob. I'd probably be trying to make a move on her myself right now if it wasn't my best friend who's fallen in love with her."

McElliot's eyes widened. "Fallen in *love* with her? I've had dinner with her *twice*."

"We're feeling a bit defensive, aren't we? It's okay, Bob. I keep wishing I'd meet someone who could storm my gates like that. Consider yourself lucky."

"How about I just consider myself confused?"

Stan's eyes had wandered back to the monitors, and suddenly he sat up a little straighter and leaned forward to peer closer.

"Give me a quick zoom on number seven."

McElliot sensed the urgency in his tone and wasted no time bringing the number-seven camera up, narrowing its focus on the center of its sector.

"Swing right a couple degrees."

The field of view moved, picking up the activity on the street around a stalled yellow cab. It hadn't been there long, stopping with the flow of traffic for a light up ahead and failing to move on. Torbeck jabbed his finger at the screen.

"That's the same fucking cab that stalled in that same fucking place an hour ago. Something's up, Bob."

"You're sure?" McElliot asked, leaning in for a closer look.

"Damn straight, I'm sure. I don't remember those two clowns in the backseat, but check it out . . . he's doing the same damn thing."

They watched as the driver got out, hurried around to the front, and raised his hood. As the light changed, several cars got stuck behind the stalled vehicle. Horns blared as other drivers tried to work loose of the snarl. As traffic thinned, the cabbie slowly worked his way back toward the trunk. As he got the lid open, his passengers opened their doors to climb out and join him.

"No good, Bob."

"But how could they know she's in there?" McElliot countered. "This isn't one of her scheduled appearance days."

"Maybe it ain't her they're interested in." Torbeck nodded toward the number-two monitor, above and to the right. It covered the side of the courthouse around on Pearl Street, including the ramp where vans parked to pick up prisoners for transport. There was a van in there now, flanked by two

U.S. Marshal sedans. A guard was just slamming the rear door of the van as the driver climbed up behind the wheel.

"With the way that cab's got traffic all tied up, those guys will be sitting ducks once they reach the corner."

As Torbeck spoke, McElliot was already up out of his seat and breaking out a pair of Uzi submachine guns from the weapons locker.

"Jesus God, Bob!" Torbeck, up out of his seat now, was staring hard at the number-seven monitor. One of the two cab passengers had lifted a four-foot-long, cloth-wrapped object from the trunk. For an instant some of the material fell away, revealing the forestock, barrel, and fully armed muzzle of a grenade launcher. By the time McElliot turned, the man carrying it had done a hasty rewrap job and was lifting it the rest of the way out of the trunk. Torbeck pointed at the shrouded object, panic in his voice. "That's a fucking RPG-7!"

By that time McElliot had their own firepower in hand and was now reaching for their radio mike. As he depressed the transmit button, he was hoping to God that the transport van was equipped to receive on restricted federal frequencies.

"Mayday, Mayday! United States Marshal parked at prisoner loading door on Pearl Street. Do you read?" As Bobby yelled it, Stan was already halfway through the access panel to the driver's seat. Once he was through, McElliot passed his Uzi in after him.

"Who the hell is this?" a voice demanded over the static crackling airwaves.

"Special Treasury surveillance unit. No time to explain. I don't know who you're transporting, but you've got trouble coming at you from the front of the courthouse."

Up front the Ford Econoline power plant caught and roared to life.

"What kinda trouble?" The voice was less demanding and more cautious now.

"Some maniac with a rifle-propelled grenade launcher, wrapped in a sheet. You picking up or delivering?"

"Pick up . . . that camel jockey they caught planting the bomb out at Kennedy. You in any position to render assistance?"

"Just keep your weapons handy and your heads down," McElliot growled. "And try not to shoot us, for Christ's sake."

"What are we looking to avoid?"

"Innocent bystanders and the only phone-company van you'll see driving up the courthouse steps."

On the number-two monitor a rush of activity could be seen around the transport van and the marshal's sedans, fore and aft. The number-seven monitor now showed the man with the grenade launcher start through traffic toward the sidewalk, his weapon carried casually, like a load of curtain rods. His fellow passenger moved to back him up, one hand wedged beneath a dark-colored sport jacket. Simultaneous with this action, the cabbie rushed back around to the front of the car and dropped the hood.

"You set?" Torbeck called back.

McElliot was busy wedging himself crosswise, just inside the rear doors. With his feet jammed up against the far bulkhead, he reached out to pop the door latch, his gun cradled in his other hand. All the while, his eyes flicked from screen to screen, overhead. The activity around the prisoner transport had ceased and no movement was evident.

"Right up on the sidewalk, Stanley! I want to be so close behind those two that I could stick the barrel of this thing up their asses."

Torbeck jammed his foot to the fire wall, the van's tires screaming and smoking as they left the curb. His path took them rocketing diagonally across Hamill, and behind them a horn honked before the screech of rending metal cut the air. Out in the middle of the street the cabbie, realizing that something was wrong, rushed to get back behind the wheel. Stan caught him and his door with the right front fender, crushing his legs.

"One down!" he hollered. "Brace for impact!"

The front tires of the van hit the opposite curb nearly perpendicular, the jolt all but tearing McElliot's hand free from the rear door handle. From his vantage, with the doors held open a few inches, he could see people scattering in all directions, and then he saw the guy with the grenade launcher. He was down on one knee and drawing bead on the lead marshal's unit when McElliot threw the door wide, tumbled out to sprawl prone on the concrete, and fired a short burst into the middle of his back. The sidekick, with a machine pistol, wheeled. Absolute bafflement was written in his dying expression as Torbeck dropped him with a single shot from the driver's window.

All around them hysteria seized the scene, even though not a single bystander had been hurt. Pedestrians, first rooted by the spectacle of a cab driver being hit by a telephone van, ran for their lives once that van hit the curb. No sooner did McElliot see the second man cut down than he was up and diving back between those rear doors.

"Get us the hell out of here!"

Torbeck needed no further urging. Fortunately, the fender bender they'd caused going in, along with the culprit cab, had stalled traffic behind them for blocks. The stench of rubber smoke seeped up through the floorboards as they jounced back into the street at high speed. There was no pursuit as they crossed lower Manhattan to a spot at the curb alongside the Javits Federal Building on Worth Street. By then McElliot had worked his way forward to join his partner in the front seat.

"You hit anybody outside your kill zone?" Stan asked.

"Nope. I got lucky," McElliot reported. "It's a miracle I wouldn't want to try duplicating." As he spoke his voice quavered almost imperceptibly, the raw charge of adrenaline still coursing through his veins. "I guess we'd better find a phone, huh?"

As soon as Stan finished parking, they climbed out, locked up, and walked casually away.

* * *

The late morning sun still beat with intensity on the stable yard of the Coulter ranch in Aurora, Missouri. Summer was hanging on late this year, the degree days through the first few weeks of September running well above average. For a change, rainfall had also been plentiful, the ranch's two thousand acres of corn silage yielding the first real bumper crop in ten years. A summer wheat crop, sown across another thousand acres to the west, was also showing a high bushel-per-acre yield.

Francine Coulter didn't much care about silage, her grandfather's fifteen thousand head of cattle, or any season's wheat crop. Her passion was horses, and right here in the middle of her family's fifty-thousand-acre empire, she struggled like a zealot missionary in a hostile land to establish a first-rate stock-breeding facility. Toward that end she possessed unlimited energy reserves, a keen sense of purpose, and perhaps most important, the desire required to make her dream a reality against considerable odds.

This morning, heat or no heat, Francine was out in the yard, working right alongside the hired labor. A photographer and reporter from *People* magazine were scheduled to visit the ranch early that afternoon, and that morning her mother had phoned from Washington to practically beg her cooperation. Her father, who disapproved of her enterprise, was the current front-runner in the very earliest stages of the Democratic primary race. Whether it existed in fact or not, he needed to project an image of folksy family harmony. And that meant having photographers drop by to document his beautiful daughter hard at work; the iconoclast Washington debutante turned maverick horse breeder. As far as Francine was concerned, her father's candidacy could die in the stretch for all she cared, but *People* meant publicity, and she wanted the place to look sharp.

At the terminus of perhaps her dozenth trip, the horsewoman heaved a last load of manure mucked from a quarterhorse stallion's stall onto the heap at the far end of the paddock. Once she let the handles of the wheelbarrow drop, both hands went to the small of her back as she tried to stretch some of the ache out of her six-foot frame. A dense mane of mahogany-red hair was tied away from her face without ceremony. Sweat ran freely between her shoulder blades and down her spine. A filthy T-shirt was plastered to her torso, and if her two Mexican grooms saw anything to get excited about in that, they'd long ago gotten over it. Their twenty-six-year-old boss was a tough taskmaster, but an untiring worker. Taller than both of them and as strong as many men, she'd long ago earned their respect.

The stable yard looked to be in good order as Francine surveyed it with a critical eye. So where the hell was Carter? She'd wanted to get that part of her day's business out of the way early, to avoid having it interfere with the photo session. First thing this morning, when she'd learned from his office that he was just thirty miles away in Shell Knob, she'd called to demand he get his ass up here. Now it was nearly eleven o'clock and he still hadn't showed. She had to start thinking about getting cleaned up. As she turned to trudge off across the yard toward her office beside the tack room, she glanced down at herself. Horse dung caked her knee-high rubber boots. The grime of a morning's toil covered her Wranglers and once-white shirt.

Down off the main ranch road she caught a cloud of dust out of the corner of her eye. A vehicle had turned into the stable-complex approach. Even as she shielded her light-sensitive green eyes from the glare, she couldn't positively identify her visitor, but had to assume it was Carter, as usual, taking his own sweet time. The car was black, low slung, and late model; something fancy. As it approached along the outside rail of the mile-and-a-quarter training track, she figured that if she hurried, she might be able to strip out of the shirt, wash her face, and get into something fresh. Appearances were always important in dealing with Carter. She didn't want to lose the upper hand.

* * *

Francine would not have recognized Carter DeWitt's new Lincoln. It was purchased since his father's death and his last visit. He rode in it toward the stables with the windows run down and the warm breeze fingering his hair. The smells on the air here were those of many of his happiest childhood memories; grouse hunting in the brushlands at the foot of the Great Plain; Thanksgiving pig hunts across this wild, unruly terrain. He loved it down here, and in recent years life as the youngest full partner in his father's firm consumed so much of his time, he'd rarely had the opportunity to break away and come back.

The stable yard looked even more prosperous than it had when he'd come down to negotiate his current business deal with Francine last November. The fencing surrounding the training track and corrals was painted a fresh, pristine white. There were marigolds, petunias, and pansies planted in half barrels outside the paddock gates, as well as along the south side of the hay barn. Francine had a fierce pride in what she did. She worked tirelessly to see her dream bear fruit. All the evidence suggested that it was already starting to happen.

The attorney parked his car next to an open-top Jeep CJ, just adjacent to the tack room. It was strange, this late in the year, to find the air still so oppressively humid. As he climbed out into the midday heat, his Gucci tassel-loafers picked up the fine, powdery dust of the region. Francine's head groom, Jorge Mendez, appeared leading a quarter-horse mare back from exercise as Carter crossed toward the shade of the stable run's broad overhang. He nodded in recognition.

"Meester DeeWeet. *Como esta? Mucho calor, no?*" The diminutive man tugged a bandana from his hip pocket and mopped his brow.

"Hot as hell," DeWitt agreed. "You seen the boss lady?"

"You've got some explaining to do, mister."

Carter's head came around to find Francine, barefoot and in grimy jeans, but wearing a fresh white T-shirt, standing with one hip wedged against the jamb of the open tack-room

51

doorway. For the moment his gambler's cool dissolved and his eyes shifted nervously from side to side.

"Mind if I come in out of this heat?"

She shrugged and stood aside. "It isn't all that much cooler inside. Electricity costs money. And besides, the air conditioner broke the last week of August."

When she called that morning, Francine had refused to discuss what it was that demanded this emergency powwow, but now he could read the anger flashing in her eyes. He was walking into a situation where the wrath factor was an unknown, and that wasn't the sort of footing he'd expected. On the contrary, he'd gotten rather comfortably accustomed to having such a well-connected, beautiful woman need him. The Coulters were rich by any standard, but her grandfather and father held the purse strings tugged tight. The million-dollar trust, bestowed on her by her maternal great-uncle Michael Harrington, had long since been exhausted building this place and developing a line of quarter-horse stock. To make the move into thoroughbred breeding, she desperately needed the money his syndication efforts could raise.

As the attorney moved cautiously into the office, Francine dropped into her desk chair, swung those long legs up to ease her calves over the corner of the desk, and pointed to a choice of seats opposite. The walls of this rough-sawed oak-paneled room were hung with ribbons, plaques, and bits of racing memorabilia. Atop a bank of four-drawer filing cabinets stood a cluster of trophies. Much to her family's chagrin, her line of quarter-horse stock had recently become the toast of private, high-stakes races in West Arkansas and East Texas. Just this past month one of her colts had brought $125,000 after winning a string of races for two-year-olds.

"Aren't you a *sight*," Carter jibed in a nervous attempt at good nature.

"The soil of honest toil, counselor. You have difficulty recognizing it?"

DeWitt focused the best level gaze he could muster.

"We've been friends a long time, Francie. Why don't you cut to it? What's the problem?"

"The problem?" she shot back. "The problem is the phone call I got from one of your *investors* last night. A George Gleason? He said he was going to be in the area next week and wanted to know if he could come by and have a look at our facility. That's the way he put it, Carter. *Our.* I think maybe there's something you haven't told me."

DeWitt had begun to sweat, and it wasn't from the heat. Still, he worked to maintain his composure. "The auction's still three weeks away, Francie. And yes, George is one of several people who have bought into the syndicate. It's going well. You need half a million bucks, and we're almost there. I have a few more tentative commitments. All we need is one to jell and we're over the top. No problem. If it goes the way it looks like it will, you might have a couple hundred thousand extra to play with."

While he spoke, her unwavering gaze bore into him. DeWitt liked to think he knew great physical beauty, and Francine had it in spades. Even when she was angry, her eyes flashed in a face that was all delicate bones and exquisitely juxtaposed planes. A life of hard work around the stable yard and hours in the saddle was keeping that memorable physique of hers in peak condition. Right now there was nothing soft about her.

"I called the bank this morning, Carter. The only money in *our* corporate account is *my* hundred and ten thousand dollars. Where is Mr. Gleason's money, Carter?"

"I haven't deposited it yet." Straight. Matter-of-fact.

"Oh? Your pal George gave me the impression that he made his investment over a month ago."

"That's true. Late July."

"I repeat my previous question, Carter. Where is the money? And how many other people have made investments that aren't in that account?"

DeWitt took a deep breath, stood, and wandered to the lone

office window. There were more petunias in the window box outside.

"There are five investors to date. A hundred thousand apiece. I invested the money to see if I couldn't squeeze us a little more leeway out of it. It's not in the bank because it's in the stock market."

"That's an *escrow* account, Carter! The investment agreement specifies that the money goes into escrow until such time as we've made a commitment of it at auction. What you've done is fraud."

"Technically."

"*Technically?* Fraud is *fraud*, Carter. My father, who happens to have a constituency that thinks pari-mutuel horse betting is a sin, is a candidate for the presidency of the United States . . . or haven't you been paying attention? The media is busy crawling all over his private life and the private lives of his immediate family. His *shit* can't stink right now!"

DeWitt turned from the window to confront her, his shoulders coming up and hands spreading in supplication. "I thought I was acting in our best interest, Francie. I got a tip from a reliable source, and couldn't see how I could pass up an opportunity like this. You want to call it fraud? Fine. I'm the corporate treasurer and I thought I was acting in the best interest of our enterprise."

"Get it back, Carter."

He took a step forward, flashing his best no-sweat smile.

"Of course I'm going to get it back. The auction's still three weeks away, right? And when it comes time to write the check for that horse, the money will *be* there."

She shook her head. "Not three weeks, Carter. Now."

Flustered, he started to sit, stopped, and then went through with it, collapsing hard enough to send a small cloud of dust billowing from the seat cushion of the chair. "The brokerage fee alone would leave me at least twenty-five in the hole if I cashed in today, Francie. I need at least a week to break even."

"That's some hotshot stock," she observed, her tone icy

cool. "This is Monday the sixteenth. Next Monday, the twenty-third, I call the bank. If there isn't at least six hundred and ten thousand dollars in that account, I call the State Attorney General's office. Leeway my ass, Carter. You thought you could skim a few bucks for yourself, and you've been caught with your hand in the cookie jar. You don't get it out, and get it out *quickly*, I'm going to make sure you get your ass thrown in jail."

He looked stricken. "Next *Monday*? Jesus, Francie—"

She wasted no time in cutting him off. "This is just the kind of excuse my dad is looking for to get my grandfather to throw me and my horses off this ranch. My name is on those incorporation papers. If I don't take action against you, I go down *with* you. You're the bright-boy attorney, you tell me what my other options are. If that money isn't safe in the bank by next Monday, I'll wash my hands of you."

Instead of arguing further, he nodded and grabbed the arms of his chair to hoist himself to his feet. "Fair enough. I hate it that it had to come to this, but okay, we'll do it your way. I've always had high hopes for our partnership."

"In a *horse*-breeding enterprise."

He grinned that confident, gambler's grin again, his ride through the roughest waters over. He had a week and he had a plan. What more could an edge player ask?

"You know I've always had other hopes as well."

She scowled in exasperation. "Try cold showers."

Five

By noon retired Taney County sheriff Bosley Scranton still hadn't had so much as a nibble. From the first of April through the end of September he fished this same piece of the White River from dawn until about now, rarely experiencing this disappointment. Some said it was the minuscule freshwater shrimp growing in the abnormal cold at the base of the Lake Taney Como power dam. The trout seemed to love them. No matter the explanation, the fish grew huge in through here. Boz thrived on the fight of these big browns and he also enjoyed the peace to be found here, just a few miles from his own front yard in eastern Taney County.

On what would otherwise have seemed like a fine Monday morning, Scranton was less concerned that his lure hadn't found any fish than with his own inability to find that characteristic peace. His accustomed tranquility was being threatened as he faced an unaccustomed dilemma. For the first time in twenty-eight years, he found himself in deep debt to his Little Rock, Arkansas, bookmaker. This fact would seem less serious if he were not, at the same time, confronted with a cash-flow cutoff. Phillip DeWitt, the bearer of old Senator Franklin Coulter's annual gift of gratitude for past services rendered, wasn't going to be making the usual Turkey Day payoff this year. He'd dropped dead three weeks ago, creating a vacuum that Boz couldn't trust the old senator would fill. People who went through life employing others to do their dirty work for them rarely understood the whole nature of that work. There was also the possibility that DeWitt alone had been making sure the loyal sheriff was taken care of all these years. The annual envelope was always a gift, and never the payoff on a direct squeeze. If Boz had learned anything in his thirty-two years as an elected official, it was that you never squeezed the higher-ups in the party machine. They were the grease that made all the gears mesh soundlessly and the wheels turn smooth. They were also your bread and butter. In the three decades up to his retirement, no Democrat ever mounted a sustained challenge against Boz Scranton and no Republican saw his campaign handbills on a phone pole or tree for better than three days.

Scranton was astonished at just how deep he'd gotten into his bookmaker. Forty-two thousand dollars. Every winter since his retirement he'd traveled south to the house that Coulter money had purchased in Pass Christian, Mississippi, on the Redneck Riviera. This past winter he'd followed the Florida dogs with a bit more enthusiasm than usual, without any sustained luck. Then there were the NCAA basketball finals, where a series of reversals saw the hole he was digging grow deeper. All the while, he'd been confident that once Phil DeWitt delivered, he would get square and once again, everything would come up roses. The bookmaker was being led to believe that he would have his money by December first. Today, just a few short months to Thanksgiving, Boz stood knee deep in the shoal waters of the White River and did a lot of mental scrambling. He didn't see much choice but to confront Franklin Coulter directly. The old man didn't know him, but he was figuring that a subtle, back-door approach might kick over the right rock. He would simply explain who he was, say that he was pinched, and ask for a loan. Without actually mentioning that nasty night in '63, he'd give the old man a chance to catch, as they said down this way, his drift. Forty or fifty thousand had to be little more than a drop in the bucket to a man like Franklin Coulter. To Scranton it was the price of preventing his bookmaker from breaking his legs. Next year, he swore, he wouldn't be such an old fool.

Carter DeWitt loved his creature comforts. Though there were other, more expensive and exotic cars than the Lincoln Continental, he preferred the way this American luxury car pampered him with its quiet buttery-soft ride. That afternoon, after leaving Francine at her stable complex outside Aurora, the car rolled over a bridge spanning the White River, fifty miles to the east. To the north, on the far side, just a mile or so up the road, sat the county seat of Forsyth. But today DeWitt was headed a few miles downstream, following the directions provided by his investigator. He had a Reba McIntyre tape playing soft on the custom sound system. In concert with the cool of the interior climate control and the odor of upholstery leather, he was encased in a cocoon of pure indulgence. This was gorgeous country he'd just driven through, with the exception of that garish freakshow he'd encountered midway, the so-called Branson Strip. Traffic hadn't been too bad, with the tourist season winding down, but Branson's carnival rides, hee-haw show palaces, and souvenir emporiums created an unendurable blight on the Ozark landscape. Out here the White River wound a lazy path through some lush, rolling topography, its waters controlled by the Table Rock and Taney Como dams to the west. Carter remembered that his father had enjoyed fishing along here.

The cottage cluster sat nestled back off the road to his right, about a mile and a half along. Blinking neon proclaimed the availability of LIVE BAIT. Behind that sign sat Sid's Bait and Court, just as Tony Flood had described it. DeWitt pulled the Lincoln up and around the gravel drive, braking in front of unit 6. Like the rest of the cottages, it sat nestled in the shade of massive hickories, the white clapboard and shutters painted fresh, the gardens surrounding groomed pin neat.

The door to unit 6 came open as Carter climbed out into air still heavy with humidity. The leather soles of his loafers crunched gravel underfoot. Flood appeared behind the screen door.

"Any trouble findin' this dump?"

"None at all." DeWitt grabbed the handle of the screen door, hauled it open, and stepped up. As he did so, his investigator handed him a cold Busch beer.

As soon as his employer had entered, Flood quickly closed the door in an attempt to trap the cool air being generated by a feeble old GE air conditioner mounted through the back wall. It wasn't really proving up to the challenge, but labored valiantly.

"Damn near October and still hot as a hooker's poont out there. Pull up a chair, boss man."

DeWitt's eyes took in the room before returning to regard the investigator, The cabin was perhaps twelve by twenty, with a bath off to one side and a tiny kitchenette built along the wall fronting it. As always with Flood's investigative outposts, it gave, with the exception of a single grip sitting at the foot of the bed, the impression that it was unoccupied. And though it was a good size for such an accommodation, Flood, with his fire-plug bulk, seemed too big for it.

Carter crossed to a maple dinette, pulled up a chair, and sat. He and Flood both popped the tabs on their beers simultaneously before Tony climbed onto the double bed. He propped himself with pillows jammed against the headboard, the muscles of his shoulders and biceps dancing with every exertion. The two had last seen each other just yesterday afternoon, when Flood arrived in Shell Knob to report on his weekend inquiry into the finances of Doctors Orton and Solokowski. How he got access to such information when most banks and credit institutions were closed was a mystery to the attorney. When he'd once dared to ask, Flood had assured him that such information was actually easier to come by nights and weekends. The former Army Intelligence master sergeant was known to be something of a computer whiz, a fact belied by his somewhat contrary physical appearance.

"You want Scranton's particulars first, or that accident y'all asked me t'look into?"

In the wake of his meeting with Francine, Carter was glad he'd decided to have Flood check into the death of Constance Dahlrymple. With the pressure he was now under, he felt he might need as much firepower as he could muster. It was important that the official record reflect the same circumstances reported in his father's secreted letter.

"Give me the accident."

Flood reached across the bed to pick up a spiral notebook, leafing through to a specific page. "Constance Dahlrymple. Died the night of twenty-one, January, 1963. Drove her new Triumph offa cliff above Lake Taney Como, just east o' Branson. Dropped it right onta the narrow little flat 'tween the cliff an' shore. Missed the water itself by less'n a hunnerd feet."

"Any speculation on the possibility of foul play?"

"More like horse play. Car crashed a guardrail an' was totaled. Sheriff reported findin' a shattered whiskey bottle on the passenger-side floorboards. 'Nother full bottle was inside a' overnight case inna trunk. Too much booze an' young, frisky-filly wildness. Case closed."

"What about the coroner's report?"

Flood shrugged. "Good question. This ain't the same area as it were back in '63. A pathologist's exam cost money. There ain't no record of one in the county files."

DeWitt absorbed this information, both elbows propped in front of him on the table, the can of Busch held inches from his lips. What Flood was telling him seemed to bear out what his father said. The sheriff had done a pretty thorough job of covering the events surrounding the Dahlrymple girl's death.

"So tell me about the sheriff."

"Old boy served eight terms an' retired back in '86. Still kickin'. Seems he still spends summers here'bouts an' then heads down to the Gulf to weather out the cold months. Lives jest up the road from here, outside Taneyville. Fly-fishes the same spot every mornin' like religion. Eats lunch every day at the Crawford Deli in Forsyth. Collects a pension from the county, has a checking account with next t'nothin' in it at a local bank. I ain't yet gotten into the banks down where he spends his winters. May have somethin' socked away down there, but if he does, it ain't reflected in his TRS credit file. He owns one lousy piece o' plastic, a MasterCard, but don't ever use the damn thing. Seems t'own his house outright, an' the forty acres it sits on. Don't have no safe deposit boxes at any of the local banks, so if he does have somethin' worth your doublin' my fee, he must either have it stashed down on the Gulf or somewheres in that house."

As he concluded his report, Flood hopped off the bed, snatched up Carter's empty beer can, and sidearmed it careening off the wall and into the trash. Two fresh ones came out of the tiny under-counter refrigerator.

"You say he fishes every morning like religion," DeWitt mused as he opened the new can. "That should leave you an opening to sneak into his place and have a look around, right?"

Flood chuckled. "Because you're talkin' breakin' and enterin', can I assume I never heard y'all say that?"

"For what I'm paying you? I'd think that goes without saying."

The unnatural curl to one side of Flood's upper lip seemed almost normal as the rest of his face broke into a broad smile. He raised his can in salute and nodded in Carter's direction before lifting it to his lips.

People's lady reporter and high-energy male photographer had shown up at the Coulter ranch in a rented Pontiac, dressed like they were on safari. If Francine thought that the bush jackets, walking shorts, hiking boots, and heavy khaki socks

61

were already too much, they didn't hold a candle to the accessories. Hats, neckerchiefs, canvas shoulder bags . . . the works.

While Francine and her horses were seen to be a quaint backdrop for their pictorial spread on Senator Richard Coulter's honest-to-God pioneer roots, it was Francine's grandfather Franklin who held their real fascination. Richard Coulter might be the man of the hour, but his father was a living legend. A *seven-term* senator who'd been elected to fill his dead father's seat at the impossibly young age of *thirty-two*, Franklin had gone on to become one of the most powerful and feared men in Washington. Then, at the relatively young age of sixty-six, he'd walked away from it all to return here to Aurora and run cattle. Today, at eighty-three, he was still very much a presence. Unusually tall for a man of his generation at six-foot-three, he had a weather-creased face with much of his granddaughter's bone structure. The plaid cotton Western shirts, rough-cut cowboy boots, and Lee Rider jeans were all part of a folk-hero costume, just like the big, wide-brimmed Stetson hat and oversized silver belt buckle. Franklin Coulter was just as much at home out here on the range as he had been in the Senate chamber for forty-two years. The photographer and reporter from *People* thought it was going to make colorful copy.

They'd asked Francine to saddle her favorite horse and ride him a turn or two around the stable yard. She'd run a comb through her hair, pinned it with a couple of clips, and changed her jeans, but otherwise the statement being made was about the work ethic. Grandfather and granddaughter, working in harmony on the same land that had made their pioneer ancestors giants in the region.

"What's the horse's name?" the reporter asked.

Francine sat four and a half feet above her, the clean white T-shirt gleaming in the blazing hot sun. Behind the reporter the motor drive of the photographer's camera whirred away, the shutter clicking like the shuttle of a loom.

"Buster. He's a quarter-horse stallion."

"He looks fast."

Francine smiled with pride and confidence. "You bet he's fast. Over a short course, he can run like the wind."

"A short course?"

"That's what he's bred for. Sprinting. Unlike thoroughbreds or jumpers. Each is bred for a different type of racing."

The reporter seemed amused. "Should America think this is sort of a peculiar place to find a woman raised in Washington? One with three generations of United States senators on one side and the great Harrington fortune on the other? A woman with blood like yours is as close to royalty as this country gets."

Francine shrugged. "I believe people should go where their hearts take them. I spent winters in Washington and summers out here on the ranch. The ranch won out. I've been to Monte Carlo, and find I prefer fast horses to fast cars."

The reporter soon returned to Franklin, who lounged in the shade of the stable-run overhang. Nearby, his foreman, Hank Tillis, sat inside the open door of the old senator's fully restored 1956 Chevrolet step-side pickup. Also part of Franklin's carefully cultivated folk-hero image, the vintage pickup truck went everywhere he did.

The photographer loitered a few minutes, obviously more taken with the image of a stunning, six-foot redhead on horseback than an old man with his boots up on a hitching rail. Francine threw a leg over, hopped from Buster's back, and started loosening the belly cinch. If they wanted a show, she would give them a show. It helped distract her from the confrontation she'd had with Carter that morning. In retrospect she could think of a dozen ways she'd played it wrong. For starters, she should have demanded to know what this stock he'd invested half a million dollars in was. Secondly, she should have instructed him to give the investors their money back and dissolve the corporation. He'd been persuasive with his plans when he sold her on it late last year, but today he'd proven himself a bit too slick for her more conservative economic tastes. She was dead serious in saying that any scandal involving her business operation right now would be more than enough to see her family evict her. The blood relationship she had to the great Harrington fortune might make for splashy ink in *People*, but her mother was Michael Harrington's niece, not his daughter, and that made Francine his *grand*-niece. The money from her handsome but not huge Harrington Trust was long gone. If she were forced to start over from scratch, somewhere else, her enterprise would be set back at least five years. If she were the reason her father failed to get the Democratic Party's presidential nomination, she would be set back much further than that.

Thirty more minutes of enduring the photographer's drooling and the lady reporter shooting reproachful glares at him between questions aimed mostly at the old senator, Francine watched the two of them pack it in and depart. Before the dust from their car was settled, Franklin was on his feet and waving to Tillis in the truck. Hank slid behind the wheel, kicked it over and started backing it around toward the open doors of her feed shed. Francine turned to confront her grandfather.

"What's going on?"

Franklin's expression was neutral as he refused to meet her eyes and started into the sunshine of the stable yard. "They've run out of oats at the supply in town, and Hank's got all that cutting stock to saddle. We're shipping a thousand head to the Kansas City feed lot before the weather turns bad."

Color rose in the young woman's cheeks. "My oats are special order. There's a vitamin mix in them that costs a fortune."

"I'll write you a check."

She started in after him, moving quickly to fall in step at his side. "It'll take a month for the supply house in Louisville to fill and ship that order. I've got pregnant breeding stock that *needs* that feed!''

Franklin chuckled, the affluent gentleman farmer enjoying this display of pique by one of his dependents. "It's hard to believe a Coulter could have fathered anyone as pretty as you, Francie. Especially when you're worked up. You turned out so all-fired *impassioned*. Why do you suppose that is? Because it's in the genes?'' He'd been having a little fun at her expense, but now his expression sobered. "As long as you insist on carrying on with your tomfoolery on my ranch, you ought to at least be willing to scratch my back the rare times I ask. That's good news about the vitamin mix in those oats. Cutting and running down strays is hard work for a horse.''

The Coulter patriarch turned to leave Francine where she stood and joined Tillis in hoisting fifty-pound sacks of grain into the bed of the pickup. As she watched him, the rage filling Francine had her wishing that his fundamentalist God might strike the old hypocrite dead. As long as she'd known him, he'd always been a bully. Her father, though he espoused a slightly more enlightened-conservative Democrat's philosophy, still embodied a lot of the old man's instincts. Both played at politics like they played at life. To them it was nothing less than a win or lose proposition; that simple. And considering this fact now, Francine saw Carter DeWitt in a new light. He'd been raised with people like them surrounding him on all sides. Men who forever played odds and sought the upper hand. It was no wonder that he now lived his life by those rules too.

The warehouse loft that Robert McElliot and Stan Torbeck called home was situated on the corner of West Nineteenth Street and Sixth Avenue, in the heart of New York's fashion-photography district. It was vast, in a pure square-footage sense, without the trappings and finery of the many similar spaces in the city that had been "decorated." Here no concessions were made to any of the tastes currently infecting fast-lane, mid-Manhattan lifestyles. Instead, the loft they shared was a Spartan affair. Its cavernous interior ran one hundred feet deep and thirty-five feet from wall to wall. The back end, away from the street, was divided into two private rooms with a bath between. Up front, awash in the southern exposure of six huge casement windows, the kitchen stood open to the main body of the place, set off by a long, low peninsula. The remainder of their domain, measuring a full thirty-five by sixty feet, was a wide-open work space, cluttered with equipment, several huge tables, and simple furniture.

In the wake of the debacle on the courthouse steps, the partners had placed a call to the agent-in-charge at the Manhattan Secret Service office and been ordered off the street. Shortly thereafter the phone van had been recovered, along with the videotape from all seven of their monitor cameras. Just after noon the agent-in-charge personally delivered the taped footage to them for examination. The prisoner being transported after arraignment on charges of attempting to plant explosives in a JFK airport baggage handling area was a known Shiite extremist. The most recent CIA and Interpol information had him training in Libya before disappearing sometime in late July. The two passengers in the cab, killed in the attempt to liberate him, were illegal aliens, both carrying documents suggesting they'd traveled to New York from the Detroit area. The driver of the cab was also its owner, a legal resident living in Astoria, Queens. Because the attempt was so well-timed, the FBI had reason to wonder whether other, sympathetic factionalists might have also infiltrated the area earlier that morning in an effort to help plan it. The cameras had been left running throughout the entire incident, and the Secret Service was reluctant to let those tapes out of its hands. It fell to McElliot and Torbeck to scrutinize every foot of all seven reels, isolating every last face of any man who appeared to be of Arab extraction and transferring those isolated faces onto a separate tape.

The process involved hours of grueling, painstaking attention to every detail. They'd been at it since one, and by four had barely scratched the surface. The surveillance on Foley Square had been set up at eight A.M. that morning. The incident took place at ten-thirty. Two and a half hours of tape for each camera, and only two of them to comb through it all, one minute at a time.

"Next guy I see with a mustache, I may just rip it off his face." Torbeck moaned. He kicked his desk chair away from the video console on squeaking wheels and stood to stretch.

Both of them had already seen a lot of faces, paying especially close attention to those that were dark-complected and sporting upper-lip hair.

"Those men are our brothers, Stanley."

McElliot sat at a second machine, a dozen feet away, from time to time electronically transferring an interesting countenance onto his master reel. He too was tired of trying to ferret out imagined Islamic features.

"So're all those great guys over at the Bureau," Torbeck growled. "But I *hate* the fucking Bureau, and here I am doing them a goddam favor, just so they won't accidentally stumble onto the fact that I *exist*."

"Just think of all the favors they'd ask if they *knew* you existed."

The two of them prided themselves on the way they'd managed, with McElliot's father's help, to remove themselves from the Treasury rank-and-file. They attached a certain stigma to being forced to endure the bureaucratic paper shuffling and inept management that came with life as a federal agent. When both had graduated from UCLA with film degrees, then-director Terrence McElliot had lured them into the Secret Service with promises of something other than the mundane. After the required training and the two years spent in the Presidential Protection Detail, they disappeared from all the usual Secret Service data bases and the Government Accounting Office payroll records to be placed in deep cover, working delicate special assignments. During those two years of regular duty they'd learned to scorn the meat-head, ugly-

American mentality of most Secret Service agents, and the supreme arrogance embodied by most FBI men.

Behind them, atop the huge trestle table they used as their desk, the phone purred. The indicator bulb on McElliot's private line lit and he rose to snag it on the second ring.

"Yeah."

"Bobby? It's Jasmine Jefferson."

There was something uncharacteristic in the voice of his grandfather's oldest maid. She was perpetually upbeat, almost to a fault, and this was not her tone.

"What's up, Jazz. You sound . . . strained."

"Your grandfather passed away this mornin'. Your dad tried t' reach you but didn't want t' leave a message. He's on a plane back from his vacation in the Virgin Islands, and asked me to call you."

Michael Harrington had recently suffered a physically crippling stroke. At eighty-three years of age, and with the entire left side of his body paralyzed, the quality of his life had been very much altered. During a visit made to his bedside at Bethesda Naval Hospital, the old man had revealed to his grandson that he really didn't see any point to enduring in the face of this new reality. The grandson remembered those words now, a searing lump forming quickly in his throat. They'd been spoken with clarity, the fierce spark of intelligence still so very much alive in the crippled man's eyes.

"How did he go?"

"I found him in his bed this mornin'."

Michael Harrington had been too proud a man to long bear having his fanny wiped and meals spoon-fed to him in a bed.

"I'll be on a train as soon as I can get a ticket," he told her. "Don't worry about sending Jeff. I'll take a cab."

Stan was back to hunching over the editing console as Bobby hung up. His head came up and around to confront his friend's pain-contorted face and tear-filled eyes.

"The old boy?"

McElliot nodded. "Just this morning. I've got to get down there."

"You want some company?"

A quick shake of the head. "This thing we're working on is important. I'm sorry I've got to leave it in your lap."

"Don't sweat it." Torbeck paused and then looked directly into his friend's eyes. "I'm sorry, Bob. I truly am."

The big, happy-go-lucky Californian knew how much his partner had grown to love his grandfather in recent years. As Ike's U.N. ambassador, Michael was often busy through his grandson's infancy and childhood, but he'd become quite involved with Bobby's life and interests in later years. His wife and their only daughter Beth was dead, and Bobby was Beth's only child. As the old man found himself face to face with his own mortality, his focus had turned to bloodlines and legacies. The boy embodied the entire Harrington family future, and whether he carried the name or not, he carried the blood.

"Don't worry about this shit," Stan said. He nodded toward the console. "I'll really hunker down here, and by the time you get back, it'll probably be in the can. Once it is, I'll be glad you're not around to bug my ass. I'm gonna want to sleep for a week."

Bobby forced a smile, the lump in his throat still burning, the tears in his eyes threatening to brim over and run streaming down his cheeks.

"Unlikely, friend. There are times when I think I know you better than you know yourself."

Torbeck could be counted on to become a fixture at whatever bohemian Manhattan night spot caught his fancy whenever he found himself with a little down time on his hands. All the sleep that Stan would get was going to be in strange women's beds.

Six

The first-class section of the six o'clock Metroliner from Pennsylvania Station was crowded with rush-hour travelers. Before taking his seat, McElliot grabbed a beer from the club car, and then a second as the train pulled into Philadelphia. Outside his window the long, last light of day wasn't doing anything to flatter the bleak cityscape of South Philly's ghetto neighborhoods as the train pulled away from the City of Brotherly Love. The sight of that desperate squalor depressed him nearly as much as the death of his grandfather.

While the beer was more than just slightly tepid, it seemed to be serving its purpose. His cerebral function was numbed a bit around the places where the hurt cut deepest. What he was headed toward was something he'd wished his entire adult life that he might somehow avoid. With his grandfather dead, he was the last stop in the long, ever-narrowing Harrington bloodline. That responsibility was not a mantle he wore well. In recent years Washington society had tried its best to portray Michael Harrington's filmmaker grandson as a sort of swashbuckling diamond in the rough. It was eight years now since a prominent local magazine had named him their most eligible bachelor. The hoopla had died down, but

Bobby knew now that his grandfather was dead, the fires of speculation would be fanned anew. Most troublesome was the fact that his effectiveness as an operative in the field might be affected so long as his face remained fresh in the public eye.

As the train crossed into the northeast corner of Maryland, McElliot downed the last lukewarm mouthful of his beer. He'd been in kindergarten when his mother died. The loss of her was so devastating that he'd withdrawn in emotional confusion. In retrospect he wondered if being forced out of the Harrington nest and into the rural Missouri home of his father's parents wasn't the best thing that could ever have happened to him. He'd overcome the feelings of abandonment and flourished in that environment. While his East Coast opposites were busy sailing and haunting the aisles of Brooks Brothers and J. Press, he'd been learning how to raise beef cattle, drop a streaking jackrabbit at a hundred yards with a single shot, pick a burning short-hop grounder clean off the infield dirt, and sit for ten seconds atop a rampaging rodeo bull. Today he appreciated what those experiences had taught him about hard work, self-discipline, and the endurance of pain. Through his grandfather, he'd inherited a Harrington's understanding of wealth's burden of social responsibility. Through the McElliots, he'd found a prairie pioneer's understanding of survival through persistence.

He must have dozed off, missing Baltimore entirely. When the train slowed, pulling into Washington, he awoke with the sudden flurry of departure activity around him. Bags came down from overhead racks and his fellow passengers crowded the doors in a desire to be among the first off board. It was nine-thirty by the time he stepped into the night air outside Union Station. The rush hour on Capitol Hill was long dead, and with the last trickle of cab traffic carrying fares in to catch departing trains, he didn't have any difficulty hailing one.

The ride out to Whippoorwill, in Potomac, Maryland, ran through several of the District's taxi zones. Bobby paid a pretty penny for it. Unlike the wide-open, barely changing landscape of Nevada, Missouri, the Harrington estate was a lush, white-fenced horse farm in Potomac's oldest and most exclusive reaches. It stunned the young man to realize, as he approached, that all this was his now. A manor house constructed in 1834, in the finest antebellum plantation tradition. One hundred sixty acres of the most highly coveted Washington-area real estate. Fifty-seven rooms filled with the relics of long established fortune: Hepplewhite, Sheraton, and Chippendale furniture, vast orientals gracing inlaid parquet floors, more Georgian silver sitting about than the Smithsonian had on public display, paintings by eighteenth century English landscape artists as well as Renaissance and Impressionist masters. Through his childhood he'd spent perhaps two weeks out of the year in visits here, and it had never seemed like home. Home was a white clapboard farmhouse on the Missouri range.

The cab turned between stone pillars on the River Road, rolling up a tree-lined drive past the gatehouse and a dozen Arabian horses grazing in tranquil contentment. He paid the cabbie, stepped out onto the drive, and stood a moment, facing the massive colonnade which fronted an ornate double-door portico. The air was perfumed with the heady scent of roses from the formal gardens. He took several deep breaths. The parlor floor of the house was ablaze with light, and his grandfather's white Rolls-Royce Silver Spur stood parked just off to one side. That probably meant that his father had arrived home from his trip to the Caribbean.

The front door opened, a tall, thin black man emerging out onto the porch.

"Bobby. Why din't you call, son? It would'na been no problem t'pick y'all up."

As McElliot greeted Jasmine's husband, the oldest of all his grandfather's employees, he waved his concern away.

"How's everyone holding up, Jeff?"

The question was genuine. He knew he wasn't the only

one who felt bad about the old man's passing. Charles Jefferson knew him well enough to answer with easy familiarity.

"Some better'n others, Bobby. Ain't a soul in that house didn't love Mistuh Harrington. Your daddy got in 'bout a' hour back. Talked t'the funeral home t'make sure things was taken care of an' took hisself straight off t'bed. I gather he had trouble gettin' a flight. Looked whupped on his feet."

Jeff's mother had been a Harrington cook. He was born at Whippoorwill. McElliot wasn't sure just how old he was, but knew he had to be getting up around seventy. His grandmother was born here too, twenty years after the end of the Civil War. To him and the dozen others in the family's employ, this was home. Including their salaries, utilities, and property taxes, the general operating budget for Whippoorwill was currently running well in excess of five hundred thousand a year. It was now Bobby's responsibility. There was no way he could close the place up and turn those people out into the street.

"Let's let him sleep." The new master of the house slung his garment bag over his shoulder and followed Jeff into the marble-floored foyer. Overhead, a crystal chandelier threw refracted bits of light onto the walls and ceiling, each tinted in a wash of separate primary color. The surrounding walls were hung with large formal portraits tracing the Harrington line back four centuries. No women. Only the men, decked out in their period finery. Ghosts, all assembled here to stare down at the latest to join them.

"You hungry, Bobby?"

"I am, actually."

Jeff glanced at his watch. "Florence is gone at this hour, but she made an excellent shepherd's pie. That be okay?"

McElliot assured him that it would be, and mounted the sweeping central staircase. Since he was a child, a suite of rooms had been maintained here for him. In size and decor they were every bit as extensive as his grandfather's own private sanctuary. A bedchamber, sitting room with fireplace, dressing room, large bath, and a book-lined study.

73

Over the years, as he collected curiosities in his travels, he'd added them to those left by occupants past.

Instead of going directly to his quarters to unpack and freshen up before dinner, he dropped his bag at the head of the stairs and moved down the hall in the opposite direction. On reaching the door at the end, he entered his grandfather's suite. The bedchamber was the same one the old man had occupied since he was a boy. The decor was what a Victorian might term "manly," with a sturdy mahogany four-poster, highboy dresser, and a writing desk in classic Federal style. The carpet underfoot was a hundred-fifty-year-old Persian from the Holy City of Qum. Mementoes of a richly indulged and robust life hung from the walls and sat arrayed in silver frames on the dresser top. Photographs of Bobby's grandmother and his mother. A photograph of his grandfather and father, both outfitted in morning suits for his parents' wedding. Without really thinking about it, the young man found a chair and sat, all that history of his family surrounding him. For a piece of time he couldn't be bothered to measure, he sat and stared at the bed where his grandfather had died. The bedclothes were made up and the old man's slippers were tucked beneath the side on which, before his stroke, he would daily rise to take on the world. The acute sense of loss, felt in his moment alone with this place, was overpowering. Tears welled up to burn his eyes and run freely down his cheeks.

On Tuesday morning, before sunup, Carter DeWitt climbed behind the wheel of his Lincoln to embark upon his new career as an extortionist. With the weight of the revelations discovered in his father's papers to back him up, he hadn't had much trouble convincing both doctors, Orton and Solokowski, that they should meet to talk. He thought it reasonable to expect them to be hostile, so he'd suggested a big, noisy, and very public coffee shop on Springfield's Jefferson Avenue. It was convenient to the Cox Medical Center, where both had offices, should the negotiations run late. And perhaps more significant, it was situated an equal distance between the courthouse and police headquarters. DeWitt was confident that this proximity would eliminate the worry of being forced to defend himself physically, should one of his targets opt for a violent resolution of their differences.

The Continental coupé handled with surprising agility for an American luxury car. DeWitt had no reservations about pushing it a little as he nosed through the twists and turns of Route 39, on his way toward the intersection with Route 60 below Aurora. He'd finally gotten a completely refreshing night's sleep at the lake house, his internal clock now adjusted to the slow-lane pace of life in these hills. Today he felt fully acclimatized and in sync with his surroundings. Yesterday's run-in with Francine was old news, and today he would once again roll the dice. He was still in the game, and that was all that was important. By the end of the week he would have fully recovered, and today he was driving through God's country. Outside the car windows the hardwood-studded Ozark mountains rolled gently north toward the foot of the Great Plain. The vistas afforded to him at the crest of every hill were nothing short of stunning. Traffic was light and he was making good time. When, after half an hour's drive, he eventually reached Route 60 and started the last twenty-minute leg east toward Springfield, he allowed himself the luxury of increased speed.

As he proceeded, he let the bigger picture play itself over once again in his mind's eye. Francine had no idea how important this business partnership with her was to his overall plan. If he couldn't marry her, literally, then he would marry himself to her dream. Republican platitudes and flag pledging weren't solving the country's deeper problems and people were hungry for change. There was no one who could stand in the way of Richard Coulter, and in a year's time Francine would be the daughter of the new President-elect. In the camera's eye, Carter and Francine would make a handsome-looking couple in winner's circles of racetracks across America. And today the camera's eye and the public eye were one and the same. They drew lines of association in black and white; from DeWitt to Coulter to winner.

Neither man occupying the remote corner booth of the restaurant looked anything like he'd imagined. A hale and hearty, hunting and fishing glow was upon both of the faces that turned to him with open hostility as he approached the table. The silver-haired Solokowski was the larger of the two, with a big-boned, heavy-muscled Eastern European's build, and a round, flat face. His skin, like Orton's, was tanned leather-tough by the Ozark sun and wind. This morning the laugh lines etched around his eyes lay fallow. The eyes themselves were enlivened only by a fierce glint of hatred. Orton, with his more chiseled, handsome face, was not as tall nor as stocky as his associate, but his expression conveyed the same message.

"What's this about?" Orton demanded when DeWitt was barely seated. "How the hell do we know you're who you say you are?"

Carter ignored him, raising a hand and smiling pleasantly at a passing waitress. It was comforting to see how many uniformed cops were numbered amongst the occupants of the other booths. He ordered coffee and a cheese Danish.

"What difference does it make, Doctor?" He'd turned to beam a smile of his best boyish charm in Orton's direction. "You've got a dirty little secret that isn't such a secret anymore. I'm here to propose a way we might get it back into its closet."

Solokowski interrupted, leaning close across the table and speaking in low, tight tones. "You call us up and mention a name. What's that supposed to get you?"

Carter had distilled and transcribed the part of his father's account involving these two. In response to the man's question, he passed a single sheet of paper across the table. "Your names are in there too, Doc, along with a date, description of an event, and the fact that you were paid fifteen hundred dollars for your inept services."

Neither man moved to pick up the paper and scan it. Solokowski abandoned his aggressive posture to ease back in his seat. He wrapped his hands around the mug of coffee sitting on the table in front of him. The waitress brought DeWitt's coffee and Danish. Carter busied himself with dumping nondairy creamer and two packets of sugar into it as Orton spoke.

"Your father came to me with a problem, DeWitt. Tim and I tried to help him solve it. What happened was an *accident*."

Solokowski, still doing a slow burn, broke in. "And I've got to assume he told his *employer* it was an accident."

Carter regarded him coolly. "And what makes you think his employer knew anything about it, Doc?"

Now Solokowski snorted in derision. "If it was your father who'd gotten her pregnant, he wouldn't have come to Erv with his problem. Franklin Coulter was glad to have your father on his payroll because he needed a low-life like him to do his dirty work. If it was his own personal problem, your father wouldn't have bothered with doctors. He would have just shoved her off that cliff, straight away."

Carter sipped his coffee, his eyes going hard as he regarded the man over the rim of his cup. "Those are some pretty high and mighty words, coming from a hack abortionist."

Orton moved to cut through this name-calling. He lifted one of his immaculately manicured hands to point a finger at the young lawyer's chest. "The door swings both ways, young man. I think that Tim is right about one thing, and that is Franklin Coulter's involvement. He had a reputation for chasing skirts. If any of this was to come out, I've got to think he'd be none too happy about it. Not with his boy having just declared for the Democratic nomination."

DeWitt flashed him a nasty little tight-lipped smile. "But it *won't* get out, will it? Not without the two of you being ruined in the process. And I'd be willing to bet every nickel my father left me that he never said a word about who he was working for that night. He was much too smart to do anything as dumb as that. You can assume anything you want. I defy you to prove it." The coffee was nasty stuff. Carter set the cup back down on the table in disgust. When neither doctor made any move to respond, he eased back on the booth bench to regard each of them in turn.

"I probably don't have to remind you that there is no statute of limitations on murder. I've done quite a lot of criminal defense work, and I know the psychology of a typical juror's reaction when confronted with a fat-cat doctor who's butchered a pretty, seventeen-year-old girl."

"It was an *accident*!" Solokowski snarled it through clenched teeth.

"That's what *you* say, Doc. Even in the process of trying to convince a jury of that, you'd be cutting your own throat. If I'm not mistaken, your wife is the Springfield superintendent of schools, isn't she? Come next election, your misdeeds probably wouldn't play so well to the local electorate."

Both men paled visibly; Orton as much as Solokowski. They were trapped. DeWitt picked up his Danish and took a tentative bite.

"What do you want from us?" Orton asked. It was weak and shaken.

"Your agreement to pay me a sum of money. Specifically, two hundred fifty thousand apiece."

The doctors sat rooted in stunned silence while DeWitt continued to munch on his pastry. He was relieved to find it at least better than the coffee.

"You're insane," Solokowski snorted. "That's half a million dollars."

"You'd be insane not to pay it, Doc. And what the hell, I had your resources checked out before I came here. You can well afford it; big real-estate developer like you."

Now Orton spread his hands in a gesture of surrender. "What sort of time frame are you talking about? Neither of us can just write you a check. Not in the kind of dollar amounts you're talking."

DeWitt grinned. "I'm a generous-natured guy, Doc. You've got until Friday evening."

Solokowski went off again. "That's outrageous! I'm not that liquid!"

Carter reached across the table to retrieve his unread document. "Indulge me. Convicted or not in Criminal Court, you'd undoubtedly lose your licenses. And beyond criminal liability, you might face a civil suit brought by the girl's mother for pain and suffering. She's an old lady now with two other kids and a whole slew of grandchildren. The rules of evidence are quite different in Civil Court. That sort of action is all the rage right now. A jury in this righteous Christian climate might make an award that could wipe out both of you and all your heirs. In that light, half a million suddenly looks cheap."

"But Friday's just not possible," Orton argued.

Carter stood. "You don't play by my rules, I take this to the Taney County D.A., Monday morning." He leaned to push the tab for his coffee and Danish across the table to a spot between them. "Get that for me, will you?"

The air smelled somehow sweeter as he stepped outside.

Tony Flood had noticed an interesting aspect of the retired sheriff's daily fishing routine. He'd watched him through the weekend, attempting to determine with some precision just when the old man could be counted on to leave his home every morning and how long he stayed away. Like DeWitt, Flood was pretty sure that if Bosley Scranton had some physical evidence in his possession, and it wasn't in safekeeping somewhere down on the Gulf, then he was hiding it in that big, frame farmhouse outside Taneyville. Now, from the depths of a thick scrub-oak stand about a hundred yards distant from where the sheriff was parked along the bank of the White River, Flood watched him lay out his gear. And there he was, doing it again. Before he climbed into his hip waders, the man emptied his pockets, tied the contents up in a plastic bag, and secreted them in the depths of his cooler's crushed ice.

Once Scranton was geared up and set to fish, Tony trailed him to make sure he'd worked his way well into the shoal waters and was started upstream. He then doubled back to dig out his prize. The knotted plastic bag proved to contain a set of keys, coins, a penknife, and a wallet. The billfold was one of the oversized variety that long-distance truckers and bikers seem to favor. Within it he found a MasterCard, a health-insurance card, fifty-three dollars in small bills, and a number of dog-eared paper scraps. It was on the back of Scranton's driver's license that he spotted a numeric sequence penciled lightly along the top edge of the back side. Eight digits: 07–33–69–21.

There was no time to waste on this sultry morning. Carter had made it clear that he was on a tight schedule, and that if Tony found the evidence he hoped the sheriff was holding, there was another $25,000 in it for his trouble. At the thousand a day Flood charged for his services, that extra money was a free month. He knew that the sheriff could be counted on to kill a few hours over lunch that afternoon at Crawford's in Forsyth, after he packed it in here. It wasn't yet eight o'clock, and Scranton's old farmhouse was just a few miles north of here on Route 160.

Situated up on a little knoll rising nearly a hundred feet above the road, the two-story clapboard box was set back about two hundred yards at the end of a long dirt and gravel drive. Flood parked his Jeep Cherokee a quarter mile off and made his approach on foot. In the course of making a complete circuit of the place, he found an open casement window around back, set at eye level above a tool-strewn workbench. The chickens in the coop behind him raised a ruckus as he got down onto his belly, easing his bulk through the narrow opening. When he touched down inside, he was careful not to disturb anything on the bench.

The tiny high-intensity torch he carried revealed a damp, gloomy room surrounded by stone foundation walls. It was surprisingly neat, as well as being the coolest place he'd been in a week. There was a rack of fly rods hanging on one wall alongside the furnace, and a neatly kept bench dedicated to flytying. The surface he'd just crawled across was tool-strewn for a reason. Scranton had the Briggs and Stratton engine of his lawn mower torn down and carefully laid out on newspaper. Various components stood soaking in canning jars filled with solvent. A further, painstaking search of the room revealed no secret hiding places. Flood eventually made his way upstairs.

It took nearly an hour of careful, economic movement, pausing every now and then to photograph something, before he located the old safe set in the study floor. Cast in concrete, it looked like one of those units he'd often seen up front in grocery markets as a kid. Nothing fancy, but big and as tough-looking as a Sherman tank. With all the windows closed in the house, and no air-conditioning, it was stifling in there. Tony hunkered down to spin the combination dial, reading the numbers he'd found in the wallet.

The noise of the engine was muffled at first. So muffled that Flood's alert ears first filtered it out as road noise. The vehicle was halfway up Scranton's drive before Tony's adrenal cortex squeezed its sensory amplifier into his bloodstream. Suddenly his respiration rate was up, his first impulse being to freeze. Already, what sounded like some sort of truck, quite possibly Scranton's, was swinging into the big gravel court between the house and the garage.

The investigator's eyes darted around the room, searching for any evidence of careless movement. There was a closet in one corner, and he was already heading for it as the vehicle's door slammed and bootsteps thudded up the stoop. To Flood's adrenaline-charged hearing, it sounded like the beating of a bass drum. The closet was jammed with old cardboard transfile cartons, offering no refuge. The only way out opened directly onto the entry hall at the foot of the stairs. The big front door had a leaded-glass panel in it, covered only by a pair of flimsy, sheer curtains. Slowly, squatting down behind the old walnut desk, he bypassed the pistol in his waistband and withdrew the knife from the sheath on his leg.

Instead of hearing the sound of a key in the front latch and the door swing open, the visitor depressed the bell button, twice. Close to a minute lapsed between each ring. A moment after the last, the hinges of the mail slot squealed before footsteps were heard to retreat back down the drive. The truck departed, once again leaving the house enveloped in the quiet of its remote location. Flood got his breathing steadied. The pounding of his heart subsided in his ears. A quick inspection of the entry hall in front of the door revealed a single envelope stuffed with tickets to a pancake breakfast and raffle sponsored by the Forsyth Rotarians.

The first attempt at the safe combination failed as Tony guessed the left-right sequence incorrectly. The second time around the release handle gave and he was able to tug open the heavy door. Guns were the first things he happened across: a Smith & Wesson .357 "Combat Magnum"; a Colt .357 Magnum "Python"; and a five-shot, .44 caliber Charter Arms "Bulldog 44." The old boy was apparently into heavy firepower. Beneath them was a single, banded stack of fifty crisp new hundreds. Not a fortune, but a tidy little sum. There was also a wad of warranty certificates, a life insurance policy, and a large, ledger-lined envelope.

Flood focused on the envelope, removing it to undo the clasp and dump the contents on the floor at his knees. A check of the time revealed that he'd been inside the house for an hour and forty minutes. The sheriff had been out on the river for three hours, and though he'd been seen to stay out longer, he would most likely be reeling it in soon unless they were really hitting. There was always the remote chance that he might stop home before heading into Forsyth for lunch.

As he examined what he had before him, Flood's pulse quickened.

"Oh Carter, you tricky little weasel," he murmured. "Smaller'n a breadbox, my ass."

Backfire

With extreme care the investigator carried the envelope and its contents to lay them out across the dark green surface of the sheriff's desk blotter. One by one he shot them with his Minox camera, using the edge line between the subject document and the blotter background as his reference point for sharp focus. The photographs were going to be more difficult to reproduce than the printed and typewritten sheets, without the aid of focus rings and a stand. Still, Flood had a lot of experience, and relied on it now to do the best he could under the circumstances. Carter had offered to double his fee if he could deliver this stuff, but after seeing it, Tony Flood was already entertaining much bigger ideas.

Seven

The news of his old friend Michael Harrington's death had reached Franklin Coulter when he returned to the big house for dinner the previous night. Franklin made reservations on a Tuesday afternoon flight out of Springfield, informed his still-seething granddaughter over the evening meal, and retired early. Apparently, the former ambassador's death had been one of choice. Unable to bear living in his crippled state, he'd taken an overdose of barbiturates Sunday night and passed on in his sleep. But for reasons private to a man of more than eighty years, the fact that his old friend had chosen this way out was of no comfort to Franklin. He had his health, had always been as strong as a bull, and yet, at eighty-three, stood undeniably near the threshold of his own death. The fact of it scared the hell out of him.

Harrington was Francine's great-uncle, and the man who'd left her that million-dollar trust she'd so shamelessly squandered on those damned horses. Out of duty she would accompany Franklin east, and that fact was no comfort to him either. His granddaughter had never been a comfort to him. In a lifetime where syphilis had been cured and a man had miraculously walked on the surface of the moon, the weaker sex had somehow gotten stronger, and that rankled. The girl was undeniably his equal on too many fronts, and too much like him, to ever be his friend. As they coexisted, so they would also travel together to mourn the loss of a man who had been a friend to them both.

The plane didn't leave until three, and Franklin arose at his accustomed early hour to take care of a few business matters before his departure. It had been some time since he was last in Washington, and while he was there, he thought it might be nice to stay on a few days, visiting with old cronies before they too became bittersweet memories. The day sparkled out on the range, with promise of turning into another scorcher. His foreman and the boys had the preparations for the roundup and Kansas City shipment well in hand, but Franklin spent time poking through the details, just to feel like he was still part of it. By the time he returned home from his trip, his steers would be gone to the feed lot and the money would be in the bank.

When he returned home for lunch, Franklin noticed a strange car parked in the drive, some sort of fancy foreign convertible with the top down. As he entered the house, his Filipino butler, Enrique, informed him that a Dr. Timothy Solokowski was waiting to see him in the library.

"Dr. Solokowski?" Franklin entered through the double doors to stand surveying his guest. "I'm sorry, have we met?"

The big, immaculately tailored man stood, shaking his head.

"No, Senator. I've met your son on several occasions. My wife Muriel is the Springfield superintendent of schools."

Coulter responded with a cautious "Ah," this information making nothing any clearer.

"Something happened to me this morning that I want you to know about," the doctor continued. "I hope I might speak frankly."

The old senator moved to take a chair, his curiosity piqued.

"Please, have a seat, Doctor. I'm flying to Washington in

85

just a few hours, but I should have time to listen to a man who wants to speak frankly.''

As he settled in, Solokowski began relating how he and Erv Orton had been approached by Carter DeWitt in the diner that morning. As he spoke, he watched Senator Coulter frown with deep consternation.

"To tell you the truth, I'm at a loss as to why Phil DeWitt would have left this information with his son. The kid is obviously not interested in protecting your welfare."

"Whoa!" Franklin's voice had sharp command in it. "*My* welfare? I'm sorry, Doctor, but what the hell's this got to do with me?"

Confusion spread quickly across Solokowski's face. There was some obvious irritation at the edges of it. He sat up a little straighter in his chair and leaned forward. "Dr. Orton and I were led to believe that it has a *lot* to do with you, Senator. That Phil was working to alleviate a problem of potential *embarrassment* to you."

"You mean, 'frankly,' that I was responsible for getting the girl pregnant?" As he said it, Franklin came to his feet to tower menacingly over this man who had to be twenty years his junior. He no longer saw any reason to try and control his anger. "Well 'frankly,' Doctor, I don't know what the hell you're talking about. And 'frankly,' I'm beginning to doubt you are who you say you are. What is this? Some clumsy charlatan attempt to shake me down?"

His visitor was suddenly at a loss for words, his indignation beginning to boil over. "Shake you down?" There was incredulity in it. "I'm the one being shaken down! Phil DeWitt's son is demanding two hundred and fifty thousand dollars!" He paused to shake his head in open wonder. "You're good, Senator. Jesus, what did I think I was doing, coming here?"

"I wouldn't have the foggiest, fella, but I suggest you leave."

Solokowski contemplated the face of the old man looming over him, the rage obvious in the way the veins stood out on his temples and neck. He shook his head slowly and pushed himself up from his chair. A couple inches shorter, he was still more than Coulter's match in sheer bulk. For that moment, the two of them stood toe to toe and eye to eye.

"Shake you down," Solokowski muttered in disgust. "That's almost amusing, Senator." And as he thought about it, the notion suddenly struck the doctor as comical. He began chuckling uncontrollably as he turned for the door. "I hope you enjoyed your little charade, Senator. You can rot in hell with me, for all I care."

It was nearly two months since Terrence McElliot had last seen his son. By circumstance, today's reunion was not joyous. Bobby had been busy all morning, meeting with Michael Harrington's senior attorneys in an emergency confab designed to educate him on exactly where he stood. Terrence had agreed to meet with his son for a late lunch in Culpeper, Virginia. It was a location chosen out of longstanding agreement that a particular roadside dive had the best barbecue within an hour's drive of the Capitol Mall.

The dank-smelling roadhouse was typically noisy and smoky with its blue-collar crowd. As the father and son entered, the lunch trade was only just starting to thin. The jukebox still blared tune after loud country tune while a few diehards two-stepped their way around a postage-stamp-sized dance floor. Terry and his son chose a booth in the back, leaving behind all the distracting activity in the center ring of this good-natured circus. There was only one thing on the mind of either man. For Terrence, Michael Harrington was a man who had accepted a hayseed—an admittedly bright, Princeton-educated hayseed—as the husband of his only child and sole heir. In the years which followed, this man of immense wealth had never voiced so much as one word of suspicion as to his son-in-law's motives and intentions. The minute Terry married Beth, he was accepted with open arms into the rarified atmosphere of the Harrington family. Today the ex-director of the Secret Service served on half a dozen

Harrington boards. It was only after his wife's death that Michael had invited him to come live at Whippoorwill, but neither had ever regretted Terry's accepting the offer.

Bobby looked tired. Once the waitress departed with their order, the younger man eased his elbows onto the table and rubbed his face with his hands. One huge breath went deep in his chest and was pushed out between his fingers in a cheek-puffing whoosh.

"It was never going to be easy," Terry told him.

The son nodded. "I just wish I hadn't been so damn busy these past few months. I knew his life had to have turned into a living hell, and where was I? Off playing pat-a-cake with the posse comitatus, and what the hell good did it do? He needed me, Pop, and I wasn't there."

"You couldn't have helped. He practically ordered me to take a week off at the house down in the islands. Said I was starting to get to him, the way I was always around. He accused me of keeping a death watch."

"I didn't get a chance to say good-bye. To try to explain—"

"You didn't have to. He was proud of you, Bobby. Don't kid yourself."

"Why?" his son demanded. "Because my team won the goddam College World Series? Because I've won a couple of awards for making insightful films about America's crumbling industrial infrastructure?"

The older McElliot shook his head, with a worn weariness in his expression that his boy wouldn't find in his own face for another fifteen years. A casual observer would likely contend that the two men resembled each other. Both were tall and ruggedly handsome, with the same black-Irish shock of unruly hair and slate-gray eyes, but Terry McElliot never failed to see his dead wife, Beth, in their boy. Bobby's face had the added presence of his mother in the more angular facial bones and those laugh lines. In Beth, they'd been fainter. In both they created a heart-melting expression with the slightest smile. When Bobby smiled, Terry felt as though he were seeing a ghost.

"He knew, Bobby." The words were spoken softly.

Absolute surprise registered on the young man's face. He was under the impression that his grandfather had thought he'd quit Treasury after those two years of Presidential Protection Detail, in order to pursue his career as a documentary filmmaker. That was the story fed to anyone who'd shown the slightest interest.

"He what?"

"When I eventually got around to telling him that you'd opted to go deep under, he was sore as hell with me. But that was still well before I retired. He kept abreast of your career, and was genuinely impressed."

Terry watched as a hand drifted to Bobby's face, the index finger coming to rest between upper lip and nose. His boy was staring hard at him.

"Why would he be angry that I *stayed*? It's not like he hated the idea of government service. He did his own share of it."

Wisdom twinkled in the father's eyes as he smiled. For a man in his middle sixties, there was still a lot of physical power left in him. He'd rowed single sculls for the United States in the 1952 Helsinki Olympics. His hands were not the soft, manicured tools of the civil servant, but the big, thick-fingered paws of a workman. A regimen of daily exercise kept him lean, minimizing the inevitable thickening suffered by most men his age.

"The things Michael did in his youth and I did in mine were the foolhardy sorts of exploits that all eager young bucks embrace. Your grandfather took many risks during the Second World War that the world will never know about. He traveled to Russia three times, and once each to Prague and Bucharest. I myself did a lot of crazy things working Treasury's funny-money detail when I was too young to know any better. But the older a man gets, the more precious life and health become to him. Sooner or later the weight of experience forces him to confront his old foolishness. And once it does, he wants something different, something safer, for his offspring. When your mom died, you were all he had left.''

As Bobby absorbed what his father said, Terry watched him over the rim of his beer glass. ''Before I retired, he brought a lot of pressure on me to bring you back in.''

''To do what?''

''Train other young guys in your work style. Either that, or to work in analysis. He thought from the time you were a kid that you had that sort of brain.''

One of the boisterous lingerers punched up a Kenny Rogers tune on the jukebox. Terry winced as that sandpaper-and-nasal whine filled the place. Country to him was the music of his own Missouri youth; of the old school, and very few of the stylists who'd come along since. Hank Williams; the Possum; the Merles, Travis and Haggard; Waylon. Willie Nelson could sometimes amuse.

''What did you tell him when he asked you to bring me in?'' Bobby asked.

''That I'd talk to you about it. Not that I thought it'd do any good.'' Terry fixed his son with a soul-searching stare. ''So tell me, ten years down the road. Any regrets?''

Bobby took a sip of his beer and slowly shook his head.

''I think I knew the lay of the land better than most, going in. Better, surely, than Stan did. And I feel better now than ever, knowing that Michael was watching. I like the idea that we did a few things to make him proud.''

Their rail-thin waitress approached the table to ask if they'd like another round. Her pert, unrestrained breasts were stretching a tight T-shirt, and though she wasn't particularly pretty, she had no trouble holding their attention. The effect her nipples were having on that fabric was mesmerizing. They waited until she walked away to write their tab before resuming.

''Any change of heart now?'' Terry asked. ''You're suddenly a very wealthy man.''

Bobby snorted. "I was already making more from my trust than I could spend without looking like a fool. What's different?"

"The added weight of responsibility?"

A shrug. "That's what lawyers and money managers are for. I'm just an eccentric documentary filmmaker, right? Bobby McElliot, the shit-kicking millionaire. Why should he have a change of heart?"

"I had to ask. I'm not just your father, but the guy who got you into this, remember?"

"Don't worry about me and the job, Pop. I think I speak for Stan as well as myself when I say that the minute it turns into just another bureaucratic dog-and-pony act, we're both out of there."

The retired director nodded. "Fair enough." In the background Lee Greenwood was asking God to bless the U.S.A. Lee was another one Terry didn't much care for.

The father and son spent the time it took to get the check and finish their beers, making small talk. Eventually they found themselves standing between Bobby's borrowed pickup and Terry's Jaguar XJ in the roadhouse parking lot.

"Franklin mentioned that Francine is flying out with him this evening for the funeral," Terry told his son. "The news seems to have hit him pretty hard, by the way."

"I guess it would," Bobby mused. "One of your oldest friends, who also happened to be your most eloquent philosophical adversary. I swear, those two *thrived* on all that arguing."

"Without a doubt. Just like I still do. It's long been my contention that Franklin would argue the Devil's side with God if he knew he could get a rise out of Him."

For the first time that afternoon Bobby broke into a wide, uncompromised grin.

"Anyway," Terry continued. "Francine's mother left just a couple days back on some antidrug junket to Latin America with a bunch of Senate wives. I was thinking you could do your bit toward easing family tensions by whisking Francine away to dinner somewhere. Franklin says Richard is pretty keyed-up with the campaign already, and you know how those two always got along.''

Bobby seemed agreeable. ''I haven't seen her in ages. Sure.''

''I thought you could probably use the distraction.''

That grin appeared again. ''Francine's one distraction I can use most any time, Pop.''

Terry hoped the pleasure was obvious in his expression as he shook his head and reached to wrap his son in a tight embrace.

''Thanks, son. While you run interference on that front, I'll call and see if I can't buy Franklin and Richard a drink.''

Timothy Solokowski had already done all the thinking he intended to do concerning the jam he was in. With his wife Muriel away in Kansas City, visiting her sister, and the diagnosis from Sloan-Kettering in New York more than a month old, the path before him was clear enough. He had no way of knowing whether Franklin Coulter's blanket denial was the truth or just an old politician's skilled deception. The fact was that it didn't really matter. Both Franklin Coulter and Carter DeWitt were oblivious to the fact that an extortion demand was only part of the load currently burdening this particular camel's back. Tim Solokowski suffered from terminal cancer of the lower spine, sacrum, and pelvis, the result of an accident during experimentation in Cox Medical Center's nuclear medicine facility. Some years ago the doctor had been exposed to a massive dose of X-radiation. His disease was already too far advanced and inaccessible to allow surgery. The radiologist had less than a year, and more likely, just a few months to live.

And there was something else DeWitt's pampered brat couldn't know about. Ten years ago Tim had divorced his first wife and married a beautiful, ambitious girl, twenty years his junior. In the time since, his good buddy Erv Orton had made no fewer than a dozen overt passes at her. On a number of these occasions the same man who still blamed him for nicking that artery and screwing up the Dahlrymple girl's abortion had waited until Tim was away at conference to make his overtures. Muriel, who was flattered by the attention but firm in her loyalties, never failed to give her husband a detailed report after each incident. The first time, Tim had laughed it off. He knew that Orton was having problems with his own marriage, but then again, Erv had been enduring them from the outset. Betty Orton was that special kind of high-strung provincial rich girl who thought her narrow little world was the entire universe. The daughter of a local charcoal-manufacturing baron, she'd been indulged as the child of some imagined aristocracy since birth. When Erv married her, he'd just as much been marrying her father and the family's social standing. He then discovered, as an eminent local cardiologist, that he could have the social standing without the wife he'd never really loved. Still, the marriage endured, and still Erv persisted in trying to bed other men's wives. Never once had Tim ever brought it up. Today, as he left the Coulter ranch in a fit of anger, Solo-kowski figured that Erv too could rot in hell.

By two o'clock that afternoon he'd piloted his new Saab 900 Turbo convertible east through Springfield to visit a wine store and tobacconist en route to his home on the shores of Fellows Lake. He'd been thinking over the directions of his life for a month now, ever since the diagnosis of his disease. None of it had turned out the way little Timmy Solokowski, in the bright naiveté of a Chicago boyhood, had dreamt it might. Even his Swedish luxury car was a disappointment. All gorgeous facade, and plagued by both a hard ride and turbo lag beneath the hood, it seemed to accurately reflect his own current condition. To the eyes of the world it would appear that he had that world by the tail. But the eyes of the world couldn't see the way the vivacious, ambitious young woman he'd met and married had embraced the fundamentalist nonsense of the Assembly of God Church for reasons of political gain, and then come to actually start believing it.

They couldn't see how much he still loved her and could no longer find ways to bridge the gulf between them. And most important, those eyes couldn't see the dark secret that had been eating away at him for twenty-eight years. The emptiness that secret created was a void so deep that all the matrimonial bliss, all the money, and all the material comfort in creation could never hope to fill it.

The sprawling brick ranch-style house was empty when he pulled into the garage and mounted the short flight of stairs to the kitchen. The pool man had been there that morning, and the housekeeper had left something microwavable out on the counter in his wife's absence. Tim ignored the food, not feeling hungry, and sure that it would get in the way of the wine. He would have preferred something a bit more esoteric for the occasion, but a '78 Margaux was the best selection the place on Glenstone had carried. When he drank it, he wanted to taste not only the nobility of the grape, but also the giddiness an entire bottle of that nectar could be depended upon to produce. After clipping and lighting one of the fresh Honduran cigars he'd picked up, Tim pulled the cork on the wine, decanted it, and set it to breathe.

The gun he took down from the cabinet was his pride and joy; a .12 gauge, double-barrel Purdy sidelock. He'd purchased this rarity at auction in London six years ago for $75,000. That amount was more than twice the cost of his entire medical education. He remembered being amused by that fact at the time. One shell would do the job, but he loaded both barrels for symmetry's sake.

Cigar in one hand, glass of wine in the other, and the Purdy sidelock wedged between his knees, the radiologist lounged on the flagstone terrace behind his house. It overlooked the blue waters of Fellows Lake and the rich-textured green of the tree-lined shore beyond. His view encompassed most of the eight acres that were his rural domain. The bright aqua of the pool gleamed in the afternoon sun. Trees drooped with ripening pears and apples. The rose garden, with his wife's competitively-bred hybrids, still perfumed the late summer air.

There was no satisfaction in contemplating any of this. None of it was his anymore. It belonged to a wife whose star was rising, who was more than attractive enough to find someone else with whom to share it. This evening he was merely saving it from the clutches of a man he barely knew. Strangely enough, he was at peace. He'd dug his hole in hell and stood on the edge of it, peering in, for almost thirty years. The depth of that hole was no longer of any concern. The wine was excellent. The three Honduran cigars he'd smoked were fair enough. There would be no better time.

The doctor lifted the barrel of the gun to his mouth, wrapped his lips resolutely around it, and leaned forward to insert an extended finger through the trigger guard.

The more Tony Flood saw of his employer's recently inherited house on Table Rock Lake, the more he liked it. DeWitt had himself quite an oasis here, with a huge house nestled deep in hardwoods on three sides, an expanse of landscaped lawn rolling down to the beach, and a $37,000 Bass Buggy moored down there in the oak-timber and fieldstone boat house. Right now, as evening approached, the two of them were out on the sweeping stone terrace which overlooked the lawn and water. The sun had recently crept beyond the ridge of the roof behind them, leaving them in a comfortable, relative cool. All was eerily quiet on a Tuesday, this time of year, and Tony liked that too. His Arkansas hillbilly soul felt most at home in this sort of atmosphere, his ears picking up every subtle change of the wind.

"You never really hinted at what we was lookin' at, sheer dollarwise, Carter boy."

Tony leaned against the rock balustrade, tilting the neck of his Busch bottle to point it at the photographs spread on the tiny table at DeWitt's knee.

"If I'm readin' it right, the entries on the outside'a that envelope indicate payments made to our friendly retired sheriff . . . every year, it looks like to me, 'round about the end of November.''

"So it would seem," DeWitt mused, his voice and eyes off somewhere in the distance.

"Ten thou a year until 1970," Flood continued. "Then twenty-five a year until '80, and fifty a year from then till now."

DeWitt's eyes came around, focusing. "But what I *don't* see here is anything *worth* that kind of money." He picked up the four photographs of a bloody bed in some obscure motel room and the copy of a coroner's report indicating that the girl found in that nasty wreck hadn't necessarily died there. She appeared to have died from loss of blood, the result of a botched abortion. "The report points a finger at the cause, and the pictures tend to support it, but I'd been led to believe there was something altogether more damaging."

"Against who?"

DeWitt got a little smile working at the corners of his mouth and slowly shook his head. "I'm not quite ready to play that card. In fact, I may never play it. Not if this is all Scranton had, all these years."

"Your daddy paid him all that money, didn't he?"

Ignoring him, Carter continued to study the documents before him. Flood reported having had to process them in a makeshift darkroom set up in his motel bath, but they were still of fair quality.

"This was *everything* in that safe?"

"I told y'all 'bout them guns, the warranties and that shit. It's everything that was in the envelope. Y'all think this crafty backwoods cop was putting the squeeze on your old man without even havin' the actual goods?"

"It's starting to look that way."

Flood rose from his perch to cross to the cooler. Bending, he set his empty on the flagstone and got himself a fresh one.

"Y'all want another?"

DeWitt shrugged, once again lost in thought. Tony got him

a new beer anyway, twisting the top off and setting it before him.

"Look at it this way, Carter boy. Y'all said you'd double my twenty-five if I got you the goods, and it looks like there weren't none. You jest saved yourself a pile."

DeWitt picked up his beer, pushed back in the lounge, and crossed his legs at the ankles. Dressed in starched khaki shorts, Top-Siders, and a pale green polo shirt, he was every inch the city slicker at his country retreat.

"Made a pile too," he said, smugness in his tone.

Flood grunted. "With *that* shit?"

Self-satisfaction oozed from the way the lawyer let his eyes narrow. "Those two doctors I asked you to research?" He pointed at the coroner's report. "They were the ones responsible for fucking up that scrape-job. I had it on reliable information already, but this stuff you brought me increases my leverage."

"You sly dog. How much y'all gonna hit 'em for?"

"You mean blackmail? That's illegal."

"So's eatin' pussy in most states."

"Half a million dollars. Two fifty apiece."

Flood was up and pacing now. "I *like* it, Carter boy. I always knew you had good instincts. That's a smooth, smooth play."

DeWitt picked up the photos and shuffled them into a neat stack. "That extra twenty-five I was going to pay you? I wouldn't mind having a little backup when I go around to collect this Friday evening. That service and this coroner's report, together, would be worth that sort of money to me, easy."

Tony nodded, reaching out to shake on it. "I like workin' with you, Carter boy. Like I said, you got good instincts."

Without his grandfather's lively, dominant presence at Whippoorwill, McElliot found the place depressing. Francine Coulter's decision to come east for her great-uncle's funeral was timely. A reunion with her provided an opportunity for escape. And if his second cousin was still the same Francine, she might well dispel some of the clouds currently darkening his sky. The last time they'd crossed paths, some five years ago, was the occasion of her graduation from Bryn Mawr. At twenty-one she'd been irreverent, bawdy, and yes, quite beautiful.

They'd agreed over the phone to meet at 1789, the elegant French restaurant in Georgetown. He was already seated at their table, twenty minutes past the appointed time, when she finally made her appearance. Francine hadn't forgotten what her tools were or how to use them; the dress she'd chosen was just short enough to show off the hard-muscled turn of those perfectly proportioned legs; the slinky emerald fabric clinging tenaciously to the curves of her hips and haunches before taking a sharp turn in at the waist. Shoulderless and strapless, the dress left civil engineers in the crowd baffled as to how it sustained support of her considerable breasts. A radiant, deep-tanned face bracketed bright green eyes which refused to roam the room. Her entire carriage was a study in practiced obliviousness. As the maître d' led the way, she spotted her date, broke into a huge smile, and crossed to plant a kiss square on his lips. Bobby was feeling better already, holding her hand as the maître d' held her chair.

"You doubtless already know how fabulous you look," he complimented.

"I'll bet you say that to all the girls."

"At least a dozen, just last week."

They settled in, their waiter pouring from the bottle of champagne already set on ice. Before she arrived, McElliot had been actively wondering how much she might have changed. It was amazing to discover how little the five years had affected her physically.

"I haven't seen you since you moved to New York," she told him, eyes probing his. "You can't tell me you actually *like* it."

"Not really," he admitted. "It took a little getting used

to at first, and I'm never there long enough to let it make me completely crazy.''

"If you don't like it, I'm not sure I understand why you even bother.''

This conversation reminded McElliot of the one he had last Friday night. And that reminded him of Marilyn Hunt. His mind drifted a moment, comparing the tall, stunning beauty sitting before him with the less imposing, and perhaps subtler beauty of the lady prosecutor. Both were very handsome women, worlds apart. One, he'd discovered himself viewing with a disconcerting seriousness, as a sort of equal. Marilyn Hunt was roughly his age, and had achieved about the same level of accomplishment in her career. This woman sitting before him was ten years his junior, and ever since he'd won a National Junior Bull-Riding championship at age seventeen, she'd worshiped the ground he walked on. To complicate matters, she was his distant cousin. There was nothing technically incestuous about their several very secret indulgences in the years since, but in his mind, they'd walked very close to the line.

"Why I bother?'' He couldn't disguise the amusement in his voice. "You remember Stan Torbeck? My pigheaded partner? He thinks we should be located where we're just a cab or subway ride away from an appointment with the people who pay the freight. Trusts, foundations, and the networks. The idea does have some merit, actually.''

"Think you'll change any of that now that your grandfather is dead?''

"Like what?''

Francine, even as a kid, had always been a shoot-from-the-hip sort. Her jumping right to the heart of her curiosity didn't at all surprise him.

"You've always pretended like you weren't a part of this, Bobby.'' She gestured toward the room with a half wave. "One of those people who pays the freight, as you put it. As long as Ambassador Harrington was alive, you could hide in his shadow. Now that shadow is your own.''

McElliot sat back in his chair, both hands spread palms up in an open-book gesture. "I'm not hiding, Francie. I'm a filmmaker. Why would I want to change that? It's what I like to do."

Realizing that she'd come on a bit hard, the young woman reached to cover one of those hands with hers. "I'm sorry. We haven't seen each other in such a long time. My curiosity is getting the better of me. Of course there's no reason for you to change." She squeezed the hand. "There aren't too many guys like you, Bobby. Women either. People like me are forever looking for something they don't have. For years you've given the impression of already having what you want. I envy you."

In his line of work, McElliot wondered what other choice he had but to appear both confident and content. If a man in deep cover suffered existential angst, he either kept it to himself or risked exposure through the chinks in his armor. Francine could never know how much he prided himself on his skill as a liar.

"Look around you, Francie. Every woman in this room is green with envy of you. You're bright. You're beautiful. You're healthy. What else could you possibly want from life?"

"A brood mare with champion thoroughbred lines." She said it ruefully.

He laughed outright. "A brood mare?"

It caused her eyes to narrow in anger. "Go ahead and laugh. Over the last five years I've spent every nickel of my Harrington trust and broken my back trying to build a quality breeding and training facility." She leaned forward across the table. "My family, the Coulter side, is worth at least two hundred million dollars, and from them I can't squeeze a red cent. What I'm doing is *immoral*. In less than three weeks the horse I've got my heart set on is going to go to some other bidder because I can't get a syndicate to back me. It isn't funny. I've got a million dollars and five years of my time invested in a dream my family has done everything in its power to crush, short of throwing me off the ranch.''

In the wake of this impassioned manifesto, McElliot sat regarding his dining partner in a whole new light. The wildly impetuous and, yes, somewhat spoiled girl he'd once known had grown up. This was a different Francine Coulter; one who talked about dreams and claimed to be working hard to see them realized.

"What sort of money are you talking about? For this horse.''

"Between five and six hundred thousand.''

It evoked a low whistle. "I knew they sold for big money, but I guess I didn't know quite how big.''

"This one would be a steal at that price.'' She said it with absolute conviction. "A lot of horses go for ten times that. This mare is a four-year-old whose trainer died. She got shuffled around in an ownership dispute and has never been raced. I happen to know from someone who worked with her as a two-year-old that she turned in some spectacular times on the test track. Foaled from a mare sired by Dancer's Image. She has Lucky Debonair and Cannonade on the stud side.''

"So how about I buy her for you?''

Francine's surprise was absolute. "Say that again?''

"We could work out some sort of partnership. You on the management side and me as a silent partner. You pick the sires and I pay the stud fees. Hell, if I'm going to be one of the bona fide beautiful people, I might as well do something a little wild. For thrills, it beats playing the stock market.''

Beside herself, Francine reached out once again to grab his hand. "Hold on, Bobby. There's one thing I don't get. What's in this for you?''

"Money, I'd hope. Isn't that why people make hunch investments?'' He paused, perhaps a bit surprised too. "Look at it this way, Francie. I've known the other principal in this venture all of her life. She's flown in the face of her family's objections to pursue something she seems to believe in. Passionately, I might add. I'm not much of a card or dice player, but there's still a little of the gambler in me. I'd like to place this bet.''

She withdrew her hand from his and tucked it into her lap, lowering her voice to a hushed, hoarse whisper. "You're not fucking with me, are you, Bobby McElliot?''

"You want me to write you a check, right here and now?''

At that moment Francine's escargots and McElliot's oysters arrived. She waited until the waiter withdrew before taking up where Bobby had left off.

"Partners?'' There was still disbelief there.

McElliot raised his champagne flute and reached to click it with hers. "For all your energy, I can tell when you're not very happy, Francie. Maybe I can help change that. What are friends for?''

Face softening and shoulders relaxing, she bit her lower lip to prevent herself from coming apart. "Yeah,'' she murmured. "What *are* friends for? I've missed you, Bobby. Why is it that we never see each other anymore?''

"I think there was a time when we were worried about what our families might think if they'd known how we were carrying on. Back when you were eighteen, even I felt a little bit like I was robbing the cradle. Then there's the fact that you're the daughter of my mother's cousin. Families get touchy about things like that, even though there's nothing in the Book of Common Prayer that's set against it.''

A finger traced the rim of her glass as a sly, mischievous smile played slowly across her lips. "What would you say to the idea of us heading over to the Inn after dinner and taking a room? Just sitting here across from you has given me an uncontrollable urge to take a stroll down memory lane.''

Eight

When Terrence McElliot phoned Franklin Coulter, suggesting he join him that evening for drinks, the former senator used his invitation as an excuse to also join him for dinner. Franklin's daughter-in-law Julia had broken off participation in an antidrug junket below the border, but wouldn't be arriving home until tomorrow morning to join her candidate-husband and their daughter Francine at the funeral. Meanwhile, the juggernaut of Richard's recently launched bid for the presidency was already steaming ahead at full speed. Franklin's son was scheduled to attend a Democratic celebrity roast, organized by a more moderate, show-biz element of the party than Franklin could appreciate. He had, of course, been invited to attend, and was trying to figure a way to refuse gracefully when Terrence's call came, providing the perfect out.

After a long stretch of isolation in landlocked Aurora, Franklin expressed a hankering for fresh seafood. Terrence suggested Jonah's, one of the old senator's former haunts on Capitol Hill, and picked Franklin up at eight. It still amazed them that, though eighteen years apart in age and much further than that in basic political philosophies, the two of them had become and remained such close friends. Michael Harrington, the man they now mourned, had been the catalyst, his views running along the middle ground between these two. In a town where everyone wanted something from somebody, Franklin had always felt comfortable in an exchange of views with that wealthy, moderate Republican. And because of Terrence's close relationship with Harrington, he had been drawn into their curiously friendly adversarial exchanges. Like the fire triangle of fuel, heat, and air, each had provided his own special element toward a lively combustion of ideas. Tonight, more than the passing of a man was being mourned.

Through dinner the warmth of reminiscence had started as a trickle springing from deep sadness. By the time they'd ordered brandies, the discussion had turned lively once again. Of course, foremost amongst the topics of discussion was the announcement of Franklin's son Richard's bid for the White House. Franklin was at the same time proud of and frustrated by Richard's stands on various key issues.

"You'd think somebody else raised him," Coulter was complaining. "Talking crap like that. The goddam oil is *out* there. We've got a responsibility to ourselves to break the stranglehold all the camel jockeys of the world have on us and our wallets. I understand Richard needs California, but how many of them live at the damn beach? A tiny handful of coastal crybabies is acting like it speaks for all thirty million citizens out there. You and I both know that isn't even close to true."

"I'll bet you'd be pretty quick to dig in your heels with the same logic were I to turn it around," Terry countered. "Discussing something like the abortion issue? The polls say two things, Franklin. After the Valdez disaster up in Alaska, America wants Indonesia, Venezuela, and Mexico to kill off *their* wildlife more than it wants to kill off its own. And seventy-six percent of the voting population believes a safe, legal abortion beats a coat hanger in a back alley. If Richard wants to get himself elected, he knows he's got to say what America wants to hear.''

Franklin, dressed in one of the same Western-yoke jackets, string ties, and gingham checked shirts that had made him one of the more popular characters on the Hill, looked like he was going to launch back into his side of the argument, when he seemed to think twice and stopped.

"Speaking of abortion. The queerest damn thing happened to me as I was winding up my affairs and getting ready to fly out here this morning. Seems this doctor came calling; the husband of a middleweight Springfield politician who Richard endorsed in her last bid. He told me a story made the hairs stand up on the back of my neck. Something about Phil DeWitt and a volunteer from my '62 campaign. She was pregnant, and this doctor says Phil hired him to get rid of it, only he screwed it up somehow and she died."

As the former Director of the Secret Service, this news made McElliot sit up a little straighter. A whole host of dangerous implications came tumbling at him as his law-enforcement conditioning quickly processed the information from a number of angles.

"Why did this . . . doctor . . . tell you this, Franklin?"

Coulter pursed his lips. "That's just what I can't get to add, Terry. DeWitt's boy Carter went to this fella with knowledge of the incident; names, places, the date. Apparently, there's some doctor named Orton, friend of this Solokowski, who was also involved. Carter is trying to blackmail the two of them for a quarter-million bucks apiece."

"And you bought the story?" McElliot was keenly focused and absolutely serious now. "That this man was who he says he is? That this isn't some sort of elaborate con?"

"I out and out accused him of that possibility, and it didn't seem to shake him. I know the climate for candidate scandal in this day and age. Shakedown was the first thing that occurred to me."

"Maybe you should explore that. Call the Bureau and have them check it out."

"There's more, Terry. It isn't the fact that Phil was in my employ at the time that worries me. This man says Phil led him to believe that they were all working at my behest. That I was the one who'd gotten the girl pregnant."

McElliot thought he knew what a major-league hitter felt like, standing in and looking for the fast ball, only to be thrown a hard-breaking curve.

"He's attempting to implicate you *directly*?"

"It's *bullshit*, Terry. But you can see why I can't go to the Bureau with it. Some idiot asks the wrong question in the wrong place, the media gets hold of it, and my boy finds his candidacy in the middle of scandal involving his immediate family. Bullshit or not, there's no telling how fast a thing like that could spread. Scandals are like brush fires."

McElliot still couldn't get the elements of the bigger picture to add, at least not to his satisfaction. "I can't figure why Phil DeWitt would have told his son something like this. Even if it were the truth."

Franklin dismissed any notion of his old manager's loyalty with a backward wave of his hand. "You mean because he owed me so much? Phil was a hustler, Terry. It was in his damn blood. Even back in those days, he always had his fingers in half a dozen different pies. Thought I didn't know about most of the influence peddling he did on the side. Like hell I didn't. He peddled a lot of it by throwing my name around. Things like that tended to get back to me, sooner or later."

Terrence lifted his glass, his eyes peering deep into the amber pool at the bottom of it. "If he claimed he was working for you, I can see how this doctor might have believed him. I always suspected that Phil was a bit of a player, but then again, you've got your own reputation to blame as well. Even Jack Kennedy couldn't beat the legends of your prowess between the sheets . . . at least not until he was dead."

Franklin scowled while hurrying to move off the subject

of his own indiscretions. "So if we both doubt Phil would have actually told something like this to his son, how did Carter find it out?"

"You just got done telling me it was a pack of lies."

Anger flashed in the old man's eyes for an instant. "I just got done telling you that it wasn't me who got any campaign volunteer pregnant. It wasn't me who told Phil DeWitt to hire some greenhorn abortionist. I've got no way of knowing how much, if any, of the rest of this doctor's story is true."

McElliot considered this for no more than a couple of beats and then nodded his acceptance. "Okay, so maybe Phil kept some sort of favor file. Where he documented the leverage he had against certain people. A guy like Phil might have done something like that."

"What sort of leverage is *that*? If the story is true, then he was just as guilty of killing the girl as these doctors were."

Terrence smiled. "Maybe he was a collector."

"What the hell is that supposed to mean?"

"Collectors are like pack rats, Franklin. They don't necessarily collect things because they feel they can use them. They collect them because they like having them around. Pack rats steal buttons and silver spoons, probably because they're shiny; because they fascinate them."

"Are those *my* tax dollars that trained you to think like that?"

Again Terrence smiled. "Don't make too light of the notion, Franklin."

The waiter arrived at that moment with their check. Terrence reached for it, but the old senator snatched it first. As famous as he was for the string ties and the Western cut of his clothing, Franklin Coulter was also famous for being tight. McElliot was surprised.

"At least let me split it with you."

"Nonsense. You rescued me from some ass-paralyzing shindig infested with liberal Democrats; hind-end suckers who make me want to spit. This dinner's a bargain."

Some minutes later, once the valet had brought McElliot's

Jaguar around and they were under way toward the Coulter home in Spring Valley, the old man returned to the subject of their recent discussion.

"I'm a little worried, Terry. Those polls you love so much have my boy at least twenty points ahead of anyone else being mentioned. I worked my whole life to see him get this shot. A scandal right now could blow him off the track, even before he's out of the gate."

"It's only one of a thousand things you should be worried about at this point, Franklin. The convention is still nine months away. A lot can happen during the primaries."

Franklin scowled, waving off this broader sweep of the brush. "Who could you talk to at Treasury for me? You must know someone who could look into this craziness quietly before it rears up to bite Richard on the backside."

Surprised, Terrence glanced over and saw that Coulter's expression was poker-hand serious.

"I want to know if there's any *real* evidence," Franklin continued. "On-the-record stuff. Anything that says how this girl *actually* died."

McElliot took a deep breath. "I think my first instinct was the correct one, Franklin. Take it to the Bureau. I can give you some names."

Coulter shook his head, vehemence in it. "You haven't been listening to me. That's too damn risky. Hell, there's already an army of media pricks crawling over every square inch of my son's life. Somebody gets the notion that I paid to have a campaign volunteer put at risk and accidentally killed, the party would laugh Richard right off the platform."

They rode in silence for several minutes out Massachusetts Avenue. McElliot hated what it was that Franklin was asking him to do, but also understood his position. Franklin was a prideful man; a political dinosaur in the supersonic age.

"Let me talk to Dick Strahan," he said at length. Strahan was his successor at the Secret Service. "I suppose this problem could fall under either of two headings. It could be construed as a threat to a declared, major-party candidate for the presidential nomination. I think it's thin, but that's for Dick to decide.''

''And the other?''

''Conspiracy to commit extortion. On the half-million-dollar level, Internal Revenue might be very interested.''

Bobby McElliot could appear self-confident and a bit aloof to the outside world, but any distance quickly disappeared in bed. Francine had always found him a genuinely tender and a totally selfless lover, just as eager to give pleasure as to receive it.

''I'm sure I'm a fool to tell you this.'' She said it as she stood beside the bed watching him get undressed in the glow of the bathroom light. His body was perfect, lean and broad-shouldered, with the sculpted musculature of Michelangelo's David.

''Then *don't* tell me.''

''I want to. It's just that since I was fifteen I've slept with more men than I'm proud to admit, but there isn't another who's ever come close.''

From where he stood stepping out of his trousers, he chuckled softly. ''And you're *sure* you don't have me mixed up with any of those others?''

She pulled back the blankets and climbed into the bed. ''That was a compliment, you jerk.''

She enjoyed watching the way he draped his slacks over a hanger. He turned from the closet, came over, and took one of her hands in his.

''Have you ever stopped to think about just how lucky we are, Francie? You and me? There are millions of good folk out there who are content to work in sweet oblivion all their lives, drive beat-up Fords, breed brats, and retire to play golf on reclaimed swampland. And that's the American *dream*. Most people in this country never even get *that*.''

As he climbed into bed next to her, his legs slid down along her buttocks and the backs of her thighs. The contact with him was something akin to electric shock. One hand reached to glide slowly across her hip and then up her stomach to cradle one of her breasts. She was proud of her body and the pleasure it could give. She stirred beneath his touch and eased onto her back. They locked eyes.

"I complain a lot about my family," she admitted. "And you just described my vision of hell. Looking at my life in that light, I guess I *am* lucky."

"You've only been chasing this dream of yours for five years, Francie. It might seem like an eternity for you, but you've still got the entire prime of your life ahead. Most people with a dream don't start out with a million bucks and the rent paid. Learn to be patient."

She rolled her eyes. "You gonna fish or cut bait, big boy?"

Her level of excitement vibrated with the delicious tension all along him, her hand tracing down across the muscles of his chest and hard, flat stomach. Back suddenly arching, she rolled over and into his arms.

New Jersey Senator Bill Bradley, the only man being mentioned as a serious threat to Richard Coulter in the Democratic race, was also the only man in Congress with any height on him. Both were Princeton products, but while Bradley played basketball and had gone on to play for the New York Knicks, Coulter rowed heavyweight crew. To Richard's great dismay, both of them had won Ivy League titles in their respective sports, but only Bradley had been named a Rhodes Scholar. Still, Richard was quicker on his feet than Bradley with a calculated rejoinder in pressure situations. His humor came easily, strengthening the image he projected of great physical competence. And perhaps most important of all, he spoke with unusual elegance and persuasion while delivering a prepared speech.

He'd delivered another such speech tonight, the sixth such oration since the declaration of his candidacy in San Francisco, and Phil DeWitt's death. Since his manager's tragic and untimely demise, other political side men had been rushed in to try and fill the void, but none of them would ever make Richard feel the same sort of confidence Phil could. At the political charity fete he'd attended tonight, a roast by half a dozen Hollywood celebrities already declared as active supporters of his candidacy, he'd been a fish out of water without Phil lurking in the wings. In an effort to relax, he'd had a little too much to drink. The flush of it was still in his cheeks as he returned home just minutes before midnight. If Phil were still alive, he would by now have an incisive analysis of how the crowd had reacted to the short speech he'd made after all that good-natured fun-poking. He would have a fix on whether the night had been a great success, unmitigated disaster, or something in between. He would know how the press had reacted and what sort of coverage he might expect in the morning papers. None of the people hired in Phil's stead could give him a good feel for any of these things.

Julia's car wasn't in the garage, indicating that Francine was still out on the town. Franklin had no doubt already turned in, as was his habit, so Richard entered the house quietly. Once indoors, he made for the library to pour himself a nightcap and have a cigar, still a little keyed-up from the night's exertions and not quite ready for bed.

"Would you mind pouring me another while you're at it?"

Richard whirled, his breath catching, to find his father in one of the club chairs near the unlit fireplace, a book open on his lap.

"Damn! You scared the hell out of me. What are you still doing up? It's midnight."

Franklin waved toward the spirits tray with an underhand wiggle of the fingers, indicating that Richard should pour and join him. One fundamentalist Christian tenet that neither chose to obey was the notion of temperance.

"We haven't had a chance to talk," the old senator said. "And tomorrow is going to be a busy day."

Richard splashed straight single-malt scotch into two tumblers, filled two more glasses with water, and selected two cigars from the humidor.

"How'd it go tonight?" Franklin took the offered beverages and then the cigar, lifting this latter to drag it beneath his nose.

Richard had learned long ago to try and paint an accurate picture in his father's presence. Franklin was an acknowledged master at an intricate and often ruthless game.

"I think I was a little tight going in. These Hollywood types have egos that suck up attention like thirsty sponges. They say they're here to help you get elected, but everyone knows that half the reason they're out in the spotlight with you is because it's shining just as brightly on them. Three of the six are has-beens. They don't do movies anymore, they do Vegas. Phil thought them a necessary evil. I haven't heard anything different from the two guys taking his place, so . . ." He lifted his shoulders in a gesture of uncertainty. "I go with the agenda Phil designed until somebody says something else that makes more sense."

Franklin had dug a penknife out of his trouser pocket while his son spoke. Now he clipped the cigar and set it alight. A minute passed while he twirled it slowly between thumb and forefinger, puffing furiously to get an even burn going.

"Cuban," he grunted, slapping his Zippo shut.

Richard nodded. "Soviet Ambassador gave me a box last week. And no, I didn't declare them as a gift."

A slight smile spread across Franklin's face. Archenemy of communism around the globe or not, he recognized that the Russians seemed to be entrenched for the duration, and that Castro's Cuba still grew and rolled the best cigar tobacco in the world.

"Speaking of Phil, I had a curious visit from a fella over from Springfield before I left this morning. A doctor by the name of Solokowski. His wife is the Springfield superintendent of schools."

Richard didn't have to think long to put a mental finger on it. "Sure. Muriel Solokowski. Ran again and won big, just last year." His ability to recall names and facts from within his constituency was acknowledged to be one of the best in either house of Congress. There was a Democrat named Vasconcellos from California who was on a par, maybe better, but not by much. "What's he got to do with Phil?"

Franklin took a sip from his scotch glass and chased it.

"He told me a curious story, about how Phil hired him back in 1963 to perform an abortion on one of the volunteers from my campaign. A girl named Dahlrymple. Apparently, something went wrong and the girl bled to death. Phil managed to fake her death in a car crash and cover it up."

A frown knit Richard's brow. "He says *Phil* did this?"

"That's right."

"Not that I believe it for a minute, but why was he telling *you*? If it's true, Phil is dead and this doctor is still guilty of it, yes?"

"Phil's son Carter came to him about it. He's trying to extort some pretty big money in exchange for keeping his mouth shut. A quarter-million dollars big. Apparently, there was a second doctor involved, and Carter wants the same amount from him as well."

Richard had struck a match and now paused with it halfway toward the end of his cigar. *"Carter?"*

"That's right. Little shit's got a lot bigger pair of balls on him than I ever knew. But what about this story, Richard? You and Phil got a lot closer than he and I ever did. And if my recollection serves me, didn't he have you managing the volunteers during my '62 campaign?"

"Sure did. I wanted to run for the House seat Jerry Wadkins was vacating that next year, and you wanted me to have some experience in the trenches. But hell, there were hundreds of kids coming off college campuses to canvas and stuff envelopes that year. K.C., St. Louis, Columbia, Jeff City, Springfield; all of our offices were overrun with them."

"And you don't recall ever hearing anything from Phil about any girl trouble he might have had? Think hard. I don't know if it's sinking in with you yet, but this can be big trouble for you if it gets out."

"Trouble for me? Because Phil was my campaign manager? This is something he did almost thirty years ago."

"No, you fool! Because he led this Dr. Solokowski to believe he was acting in the interest of his employer. Solokowski came to me this morning thinking I already knew about it. All these years, he's assumed that it was *me* who got that seventeen-year-old pregnant!"

Richard removed the cigar from his mouth and set it next to his drink on the little table beside him. "You?"

His father colored slightly. "Of course *me*. Your mother had been dead for five years. I was something of a ladies' man. If Phil DeWitt had wanted to pass his own problem off as mine, him acting as my go-between, why would this guy doubt it? Everyone always wants to believe the worst about people in positions of power. I'm sure Solokowski thinks that his wife got her support from the party because of *his* past services rendered."

Richard was up out of his chair now and pacing tight circles around the middle of the room. "Phil never breathed a word of this. But he was like that with women. I had no idea he had any intention of marrying Sybil until he asked me to be his best man. How did Carter get hold of this? To my knowledge, Phil never kept anything like a journal."

"Would he have told you if he did? The man played his entire life pretty close to the vest. You admit you knew nothing about the heart condition that killed him. I think it's more than coincidence, the timing of this. Phil DeWitt drops dead, and three weeks later his son surfaces with the goods on two men who killed a seventeen-year-old girl. Solokowski admitted his part in it, so it's not something Carter just made up."

"And if the media gets wind of this, especially that the doctor believed Phil was working on *your* behalf . . ." Richard's voice trailed off. He bent to snatch his drink up and downed a quick gulp.

"That's exactly what I've been trying to say, son. This thing hits the wires and you're a political dead man."

In an attempt to control his composure, Richard took a series of deep breaths, letting the air out slowly, his pulse throbbing in his temples.

"Sit down," his father suggested. "You're not the first person I've discussed this with tonight. I laid the whole thing out on the table for Terry McElliot, and asked him for his help."

"You did *what*?"

Franklin Coulter gave his son a look that had not passed between them in twenty years. It counseled Richard to hold his tongue, leaving no room for argument. Franklin waited silently for Richard to get control of himself. A full minute passed, the old man puffing resolutely on his cigar.

"Terry's first suggestion was that we take the problem to the Bureau. I took pains to explain the danger inherent in that approach, and he was willing to acknowledge it. The list of presidential aspirants who've been politically murdered by scandal is both long and thoroughly bipartisan. He supposes an extortionist plot could be of interest to his old friends at Treasury, for the obvious tax-code-violation reasons. And he admits that it does at least embody *potential* threat against a presidential candidate. If Carter recognizes what this information could do to your chances of gaining the nomination, he may choose to extort compensation for his silence from you."

"Pretty farfetched," Richard contended.

Franklin smiled, shaking his head. "Not *so* far. Carter has already demonstrated the inclination, and his current demand suggests serious greed. Terry seemed to feel that once Michael's funeral is over tomorrow, he might be able to get support from his successor for a clandestine investigation into Dr. Solokowski's allegations. If damning evidence against Carter can be gathered and brought to bear, he might agree to prosecution on a lesser charge, in exchange for letting it die, right there. I don't see as you have any choice but to pursue exactly this course of action."

Richard had recovered his composure and was listening

very closely to what Franklin was saying. The son picked up his cigar to finally light it, his eyes locked all the while with his father's. After shaking the match out, he nodded.

"I suppose I don't have much choice, do I? And I suppose I owe you a debt of gratitude. There aren't many men who can dissect a problem, put a finger on a proper response, and act with such swiftness." His eyes twinkled now. "I guess I've still got a thing or two to learn."

Franklin did not share his son's amusement. "There are only two ways to learn any of life's important lessons—"

Richard stopped him, hand in the air. "I know. The hard way and the harder way."

Nine

Wednesday morning dawned muggy and hazy over the Ozarks. From a high of ninety-six, the mercury had fallen only ten degrees overnight. Retired sheriff Bosley Scranton dragged his seventy-two-year-old bones out of bed with the first faint glow of light in the eastern sky, set coffee to percolating, and stepped outside to pee before feeding the chickens. The mugginess didn't bother him more than anything else did these days. The Ozark summer was older than he was, and just as set in its ways. Once he got down to the river, with his rubberclad feet in the icy water below the power-site spillway, the cool convection breeze coming up off the river would keep him as comfortable as any air conditioner could.

Because it was so quiet and comfortable down on the White River, Boz didn't so much mind that the fishing had been lousy the past couple days. Hell, he generally threw the fish back anyway. Much more important to him was the time his sport afforded him to stand out there with Mother Nature and stew in her juices. There was a deep, contemplative beauty in the art of the perfect fly-cast. And just because Boz might not describe it that way to the boys at Crawford's Deli, it didn't mean that wasn't how he felt about it, down deep. As long as there was fly-fishing, the summers weren't so bad. Winter was a different story, and when *that* old man came blowing down from the Canadian tundra, Boz packed his bags at the first sign of frost. Then, it was his hideaway on the Redneck Riviera and blue water fishing on the Gulf for him.

At quarter of six he loaded his gear into the bed of his new Dodge Dakota pickup, making sure he had plenty of fresh ice in his cooler to take the temperature down on a six-pack of Heileman Special Export beer. If he did get a nice trout and decided to have it for his dinner, he'd want to get it on ice in a hurry and have it last through the quick run he planned to make, sixty miles upstate. Today was the day he intended to speak with old Senator Franklin Coulter about that loan.

The spot he fished every day was considered, at least officially, to lie within the headwaters of Bull Shoals Lake. In fact, it looked pretty much like the White River must have appeared before an army of engineers had started messing with damming up these mountain valleys, creating giant water-project reservoirs. Clusters of hardwood forest ran down to its shores, mostly oak and hickory, but still containing scattered black walnut. Boz pulled his truck onto the river access road just above Kissee Mills, drove down a few hundred yards and bore right again over a dirt cut through the woods to the river's edge. At this time of day only the diehards were out along this stretch. This particular morning none were within sight of where he parked. After the ritual of burying his waterproofed wallet in the depths of his cooler, he carried his little fly box and rod in one hand and waders in the other, making his way to his favorite flat rock.

The boots were getting old. For the dozenth time that month he reflected that it was time to invest in a new pair. They'd taken about as many patches as they were about to and were starting to show discolored fatigue cracks around the ankles. Still, after selecting a fly, tying it to the end of his leader, and removing his shoes, Scranton sat to tug them on and up his legs over his trousers. The long light of the early sun sparkled before him over the waters of the river. This morning he had a hunch that the trout were tired of playing games with him. He felt lucky.

The blow from the rock caught the old man cleanly, toppling him right where he sat. The moment he slumped forward, the crimson gash in the back of his scalp bleeding profusely, Tony Flood stuck him with the syringe and shoved the plunger home. One-hundred-and-fifty milliequivalents of pure potassium chloride raced through Scranton's bloodstream to his heart. The effects were textbook. A man suffering a fatal heart attack wouldn't bleed out much, even if he hit his head in a resulting fall. It was important that the injection kill him in a hurry. And it was evident from the way the unconscious form of him started to seize up that Flood had done his homework.

To give it the look of one of those things that just happens, Tony tossed Scranton's rod out into the river before dragging him down and dumping him in after it. The fly box was left open next to his shoes, just so, and the scoop net was flipped in amongst the rocks of the shoals. The water level of the river was down that morning, but with the torrential squalls they'd had on and off through the past week, the maintenance people at the power site would no doubt be letting a little water out through Taney Como's Ozark Beach Dam. His research told him that this generally occurred in the mid-afternoon, around three. When it happened, there was no telling how far the old man's dead body might float before some other fisherman or boater happened across it.

Flood wasted little time admiring his handiwork. He'd parked his Jeep half a mile away to avoid being associated with the scene, and now started back toward it. Even if someone discovered the corpse relatively soon, he figured to still have an hour's cushion before it was reported. It wasn't likely that the local law would drift around to seal up the house before noon. Tony didn't imagine there was much he could do with that wad of warranties and the life insurance contained in the safe, but he thought it would be a real shame if anyone else got his hands on those several documents and photographs he'd withheld from Carter.

That meeting they'd had yesterday, over at DeWitt's lake house, had been most enlightening. From the minute he'd first cracked that safe and gotten a good look at its contents, Flood was pretty sure where his employer was headed. Carter'd found something in his daddy's papers, telling him about the 1963 incident and the resultant cover-up. And a snake like Carter would want to parlay that information into as much as he could possibly squeeze from it. But Phil DeWitt hadn't given him the trump card, and his boy couldn't get his hands on it unassisted. To Tony's deep appreciation of the perverse, it seemed ironic that Carter had paid him $25,000 for no more than a glimpse at the end of the rainbow. As far as Carter would ever know, there was only a *small* pot of gold.

Since hearing of her uncle Michael's death, Julia Harrington Coulter had been involved in a mad dash to get home from Iquitos, in the Peruvian Amazon, in time for the funeral. A light plane had taken her to Quito, Ecuador, where a scheduled airline hop took her to catch an Avianca flight from Bogota, Colombia, to Washington's Dulles Airport. She'd never been able to sleep on any plane, let alone a small one crossing the craggy Cordilleras of the Andes. She'd finally arrived in the nation's capital just after daybreak. With the funeral scheduled for eleven, just five hours away, she was dead on her feet as she passed through customs to be met by Mark Gladstone, the family chauffeur.

"Morning, ma'am." Gladstone reached to take over the pushing of her baggage cart. "Good trip home?"

"*Horrible* trip home. I'd thought Richard might meet me."

"The senator has a seven o'clock meeting on the Hill this morning, ma'am. I'm to pick him up at eight-thirty. He asked me to tell you that he would meet you at home no later than nine."

This news of Richard's preoccupation only produced anxiety. There was nothing she would like more than to be the next First Lady, but the price she was expected to pay over the next year was going to be very high indeed. If the truth be known, she absolutely loathed the campaign trail, with all its demands for displays of good humor, hours on end of graciousness and maintaining the appearance of strength. It had been Richard's idea that she join those other Senate wives on the antidrug junket, seeing it as an opportunity for her to begin developing First-Lady-type interests in world and domestic problems. After just three days away, she was returning to Washington feeling more worn out than she had after the first whirlwind week following the declaration of her husband's candidacy.

"Francine and her grandfather have arrived?" she asked.

"Yes, ma'am. Last evening." Gladstone, a tall, slightly built man of fifty-two with a hatchet face and snow-white hair, hurried to hold the rear door of the black Lincoln Town Car for her before loading her bags into the trunk. Minutes later they joined the stream of early rush-hour traffic, moving east past Dulles and into the heart of the District.

When Julia arrived home, she found her father-in-law up, already bathed, fully dressed, and having breakfast in the dining room. It was just seven o'clock, but the old senator was an habitual early riser. Her daughter Francine, who had apparently arrived home sometime in the wee hours, was still fast asleep upstairs. After a brief, cordial exchange with Franklin, where she accepted his condolences over her uncle's death, she moved upstairs to draw a bath and try to make herself look presentable.

Richard Coulter returned at eight forty-five to find his wife and father sitting together in the library over coffee and the Wednesday edition of the *Post*. He'd been up early for a meeting with his new campaign manager and Lester Dworkin, his speechwriter. Since Phil DeWitt's death, three more Democrats had declared as candidates and Richard had slipped five points in the polls. He still had a commanding lead, but it was very early on in the process. This entire week would be devoted to strengthening strategies. Gladstone had picked him up and he was en route home when he finally had a chance to scan the front pages of the three Missouri dailies delivered to Washington on the first flight out of St. Louis. Now, after kissing his wife on the cheek and inquiring about her trip and flight home, he dropped Wednesday's edition of the Springfield *News-Leader* onto the table at his father's elbow.

"If I was harboring any doubts last night about Dr. Solokowski's sincerity, I'm not anymore."

Franklin picked up the paper to scan the front page. There the article was, just below the fold.

AREA RADIOLOGIST SHOOTS SELF

FELLOWS LAKE—Late yesterday afternoon, police were summoned to the scene of a grisly shotgun suicide in this exclusive suburban Springfield location. Just after three, a neighbor reported hearing a gunshot coming from the direction of Dr. Timothy and Superintendent of Schools Muriel Solokowski's lakeside home. When Mrs. Georgia Kruder was unable to reach anyone in the house by telephone, she summoned the Greene County sheriff. Officers responding to the call found the body of Dr. Solokowski, a prominent area radiologist, on his home's rear terrace. The Medical Examiner has put the preliminary cause of death as being the result of a single .12 gauge shotgun blast, believed to be self-inflicted. School Superintendent Muriel Solokowski was in Kansas City, visiting her sister at the time of the incident. She told police that her husband had been depressed of late. Foul play is not suspected.

Franklin took a moment to reread the short article, frowning in consternation.

"I have to say that the man didn't seem particularly suicidal when I spoke to him," he ventured. "At a loss, yes, and even scared, but I had no idea he was planning anything like this."

"Like what?" Julia asked. Her eyes traveled back and forth between the faces of her husband and his father. "*Who* committed suicide?"

"A man I spoke to yesterday morning," Franklin replied. He took a deep breath and set the paper aside, glancing to Richard. "I suppose there's no reason Julia shouldn't know about this."

"Know about *what*?" Julia demanded.

For reasons of propriety, Francine and Bobby hadn't spent the entire night at the Georgetown Inn. They'd finally parted company at two, Francine driving back to Spring Valley to get some sleep. She was a sunup riser out of habit, and had forced herself back to sleep for an additional few hours, eventually rising at eight. A long, hot bath went a long way toward raising depleted energy levels. If she did not feel rested as she began to prepare for the funeral, she at least felt revived. As she surveyed her face in the makeup mirror, she was thankful they hadn't indulged in drink to excess. The lack of sleep alone had left her challenge enough.

At close to nine, bathed, dressed, and ready to face the day, she was descending the stairs toward the dining room and breakfast when the voices came to her through the open door of the library. Her mother was speaking, and something in her tone prompted Francine to slow in her tracks. She eased to one side of the stairwell where, by peering down into the entry gallery, she could make out her parents and grandfather through a big framed mirror hanging opposite the library door. Both men were seated while the tall, aristocratic Julia paced before them, her agitation evident.

". . . like Joe Biden or John Tower! Innocent or not, the smear campaign put on by the Republican press would do you such damage that you'd never be able to hold your head up in this town again!"

"I think you're overstating the case a bit, Julia," Franklin cautioned. "Right now, all this ungrateful sonofabitch has done is use his information to blackmail a couple of local doctors. I'll admit that the money is big, and that maybe the threat was enough to get this one fella to kill himself, but the other one isn't likely to open his mouth and admit his own guilt."

"But neither of you had anything to do with this. I don't see why you don't want to go public with it. A preemptive strike, if you will. Anything to throw it back into Carter's face. Put *him* on the defensive."

"Because dirt is dirt, no matter who it winds up sticking to." This time it was Francine's father speaking. "I think asking Terry McElliot to sponsor a Treasury investigation was a stroke of genius. I had my doubts last night, but after a few hours to sleep on it, it looks better and better. If Treasury crawls down the kid's throat with either a tax-evasion or straight-extortion charge, he'll have no choice but to back down."

Francine's heart thundered as she started slowly back up the stairs. The details were sketchy, but it didn't take much imagination to enable her to string them together. Her mother had put the finger on Carter, specifically. Her grandfather mentioned blackmail and big money. One of the people Carter was attempting to blackmail had committed suicide. Somehow, this information had gotten back to her parents, and they saw good reason to feel it as heat. These tiny pebbles of information triggered an avalanche of educated speculation. Carter would never be this reckless if he wasn't in jeopardy . . . in jeopardy of losing the money he'd taken from the syndicate's investors and gambled in the stock market.

A wave of fury flowed over her as she reached the second-floor landing. She knew enough about the ins and outs of the federal power structure to know that retirement had done little to dull the edge of Terrence McElliot's sword. There had to be dozens of men at Treasury who owed him favors.

Once Bobby's dad launched an investigation, its fine focus would eventually reveal her own association with the reckless hustler now seen as a threat to her father's candidacy. Carter had overestimated his abilities this time around. His amateurish blackmail scheme had managed to make it all the way to Washington and to the ears he wanted most to avoid. Francine knew she had to reach Carter quickly and cut him off.

Muriel Solokowski had not slept and was treading numbly through a valley of deep shock when Ervin Orton's BMW appeared in the drive. Late the previous afternoon the police had located the housekeeper and learned where to reach the dead doctor's wife. It was another four hours before she could catch a commuter flight into Springfield and race to Fellows Lake. She'd arrived home to find it crawling with forensics people from the state police. Tim's body had already been carted away, but the terrace was still a mess of blood and blackened bits of flesh. After seeing it once, she hadn't been able to go back out there. In a phone conversation with her secretary late last night, Muriel had asked her to contact the cleaning contractor employed by the school district. Just moments ago their office called to tell her that a crew was on their way out with something called a water blaster.

From the cool, white and brass elegance of her living room, she watched the man her husband secretly loathed climb slowly from behind the wheel of his car. For the first time Muriel wondered if she found her ardent flatterer as odious as she'd once professed. Ervin was at least as well off as Tim, and arguably better looking. He fancied himself something of a cosmopolitan sophisticate beneath a good-ol'-boy veneer; both a man's man and a ladies' man, all rolled into one high-energy, well-tailored package. Muriel seemed to embody everything he desired in a woman; she was seventeen years younger than he and fifteen years younger than his wife. Her look was very much the fresh-scrubbed, *Town and Country* sort. And while Muriel might admit to herself that she'd been secretly flattered by his pursuit, it remained impossible now for her to respect any man who acted as he had and still claimed to be her husband's best friend.

Orton paused for a moment to stare at the front of the house before pushing his door closed and crossing to the front stoop.

"Hello, Muriel." His face was haggard and drawn, his obvious distress suggesting that she wouldn't have any trouble trying to keep him at bay today. "I would have come sooner, but I was up all night with a case going sour. For the love of God, hon. I swear I'm sorry." There wasn't even an ounce of syrup in the way he said it. As she held the door, he slid into and through the entry hall.

Muriel, with her red-rimmed eyes and straight blond hair tied back in a severe, unadorned ponytail, followed him into the front room. She had a stiff scotch in there, contrary to the tenets of her new faith, but had barely touched it. So far, the shock was still providing all the anesthesia she needed. Her tone was hollow as she spoke.

"The police found a letter in his top desk drawer, Erv. From Sloan-Kettering in New York. It confirms a preliminary diagnosis they made while he was out there at that conference last month."

"Diagnosis?" This news took Orton by complete surprise. "What diagnosis?"

She shook her head. "I didn't know either. He had bone cancer. Of the pelvis and lower spine. He's known it all this time, and I had no idea."

"Good God."

As if on automatic, Muriel pressed ahead. "I talked to the funeral home in Springfield. The coroner will release the body to them after the autopsy this morning." She was all flat, detached efficiency now. "They can cremate right away, and I've scheduled the funeral for day after tomorrow. He never actually expressed a desire to be cremated, but . . . he doesn't have a *head* anymore." At that she burst into tears.

Orton's impulse was to rise from his chair and go to her

side. Wrap his arms around her in comfort. Instead, he fidgeted nervously with his wedding ring, awkward with the moment.

"I'm awful damn sorry, Muriel. You think you'll be all right out here . . . by yourself? Betty and I have plenty of room, you know. You could come and stay until you, ah, got your feet back on the ground."

The suggestion, even in her numbed state, struck her as wickedly ludicrous. She never blamed Erv for feeling trapped in his marriage, but had no interest in witnessing its obvious pathos either. The rail-thin, leather-tanned Betty Orton was insufferable, with her sneering obsessions with the "right" Springfield society, tennis and golf. The woman yammered incessantly about hooks and slices. The idea of spending even one night in that house, in the midst of their openly declared marital war, was unthinkable.

"Thanks for the offer, Erv." Composed again, she was suddenly all distance and determined independence. "There's an awful lot still to do. I have a million calls to make, and then there are the lawyers; closing up Tim's practice and getting his affairs in order. Between that and the everyday business of the schools, I'm hoping to stay busy enough to take my mind off the worst of it. I'll be fine."

It was a dismissal. Orton rose to stand self-consciously with his hands shoved deep into the pockets of his suit pants. She was saying good-bye not only for the moment, but also to a chapter in her life. The message was perfectly clear. If he wanted a firm-bodied, vivacious young wife to make him happy through his golden years, he'd better shop elsewhere.

The telephones in the guest suite of the Coulter home were on a private line. Once she'd regained the upstairs, Francine wasted no time shutting herself into these little-used rooms. When no one answered her first call to the DeWitt house in St. Louis, she quickly dialed the lake house in Shell Knob. In desperation she let it ring twelve times before a man picked up, his breath coming in quick gasps.

"Carter?" From the grunt of hello, she wasn't at all sure. "It's Francine."

"What's up? I was tinkering with the Bass Buggy, down in the boat house. Almost didn't hear you."

"One of the doctors you are trying to blackmail committed suicide last night, didn't he?"

A lengthy pause. "I'm not sure I understand what it is you're talking about, Francie. Blackmail?"

"Cut the crap, Carter!" she exploded, her voice a tight hiss. "My father and grandfather are downstairs right now, discussing what it is they want to do about you."

"Your father is in Aurora?"

"Washington. Franklin and I flew out here last night. My great-uncle Michael died."

"Washington?" Confusion strained Carter's tone.

Francine moved to cut through his posturing. "I know. How could anybody have heard about your cute little games way out here? Well, one reason might be that you're nowhere near as slick as you think you are. I'm not stupid, Carter. Something happened to your friend George Gleason's money . . . to the other investors' money."

"Francine, listen to me—"

"No, you listen to *me*! You've got a different problem than getting that money to me now. I don't want it anymore. As soon as I get back to Aurora, I'm dissolving the corporation. Gleason and the rest of them are all yours. I'm a horse breeder, not a felon."

"I can make this right!" he pleaded.

"You might be making license plates instead," she countered. "Franklin's asked Terrence McElliot to intercede at Treasury. They're coming after you, Carter."

"McElliot's a has-been," he retorted. "What's your grandfather expect a guy like that to do? Ask the IRS to audit me?"

"Or maybe ask them to build a fraud and extortion case against you. I'm willing to bet that you didn't invest in that so-called hot stock in the syndicate's name. Profit or loss taken since, I'm also willing to bet that you didn't declare the money from Gleason and the rest as income. Once the IRS puts a freeze on all your assets, you won't be able to pay *anyone* back.''

The chuckle that reached her from down the line was laced with a nervous, false bravado. ''Has it occurred to you that your family might be frightened of what I know for good reason, Francine? That they might actually be involved?''

''Involved in what, Carter? Stealing money and extortion? A man has committed suicide on account of a threat you made. Doesn't that *bother* you? I suggest you take your powers of smooth persuasion back to the courtroom. Right now, you're playing way out of your league.''

Now Carter's voice could be heard to get tight in his throat. ''Just like that? I'm supposed to say thanks for the call, hang up and walk away?''

''I *knew* you'd get it.'' And before he could add another word, she cut the connection.

There was a frightened emptiness gnawing at the pit of Ervin Orton's stomach as he drove his Seven-series BMW back along the gravel access road from the Solokowski house to the county highway. It wasn't a feeling characteristic of his temperament. He hadn't felt it on the night Tim had nicked that artery in Connie Dahlrymple's uterus, and he hadn't felt it all through the years of occasional recollection. Quite to the contrary, he had come to all but forget that it had ever happened, his misdeed buried deep in the past beneath years of hard work and professional success. The girl had sinned, and the wages of sin were plainly spelled out in the Good Book.

But now the old wound was picked open and bleeding raw. For one brief day he'd had someone else to help shoulder the burden, but today he found himself left all alone out here. And because he was alone, Erv felt both helpless and scared. Phil DeWitt's son was in a position to destroy everything he had built through a lifetime of diligence; to bleed him dry.

At the highway the tires of the car hit the blacktop with a squeal as he went quickly up through the gearbox. There had been a coolness in Tim's attitude of late. Erv wondered if perhaps Muriel had advised Solokowski of the attempts made to seduce her. But hell, Timmy wouldn't take anything like that seriously. He had to know that it was never any more than idle amusement. Sport.

Bone cancer, of all the goddammed things.

Some piece of urgent business had come up to call Terrence McElliot away early that morning, preventing him from joining his son in the car to the Washington Cathedral. After rising late to dress and breakfast hurriedly, Bobby left the house to step out into the sunshine of that late summer morning. His grandfather's white Rolls-Royce Silver Spur, deemed inappropriate under the circumstances, was parked in the garage. Instead of it, a Cadillac stretch limousine, kept in mothballs for the most part but dragged out for the occasional use of guests, had been washed and buffed to stand gleaming in the middle of the drive. Jeff was busy with a chamois as Bobby descended, turned out in a reserved charcoal suit, white shirt, and sober navy tie. The two exchanged greetings as McElliot opened the back door for himself and climbed into the spacious rear compartment. As he closed the door, there was a sense of finality to the way it snicked shut. That deep pain of loss, momentarily dispelled by the diversion of his evening out with Francine, returned now to ride in the seat beside him.

They arrived at the cathedral a full half hour early, but already the cavernous Gothic interior was filling with mourners. Bobby loitered on the steps outside, greeting as many of his family's old friends as he could while enjoying the cool, overnight shift in temperature. Indeed, it was a picture-postcard day in the nation's capital, with little white fluff clouds drifting in grand procession across a sparkling blue sky. People he didn't even know were going out of their way to cross and shake his hand, each offering condolences. Many assumed he would recognize their names, and more often than not he drew a cordial but complete blank.

With the scheduled appearance of the hearse still ten minutes away, a black Lincoln Town Car pulled to the curb. McElliot watched as the white-haired driver held the rear door and Julia Coulter emerged. Francine followed close on her heels, and though his old friend and recent lover had dressed in properly mournful black attire, there wasn't a thing in her Washington wardrobe that didn't flatter that physique. The Coulter men emerged from the car last, the family moving up the steps. Julia spotted her cousin Beth's son and moved to grasp his hand, leaning close to kiss his cheek.

"I know this must be terribly hard for your, Robert."

"We all knew it was coming, Julia. Not that it makes the fact any easier. I'm glad you could make it. You had a long trip."

Behind them the Senate Majority Leader and his wife arrived to mount the cathedral steps. In catching them out of the corner of her ever-alert eye, Julia patted the hand she was holding and moved with practiced skill to intercept them.

"Don't be such a stranger," she admonished in parting. "You're the only family I've got left now."

Francine rolled her eyes as her mother moved off to make a fuss over the Democrat and his wife.

"Sit with me?" Bobby asked.

"Sure," she replied. "We family have to stick together."

Ten

The black Buick sedan rolled northwest from the Treasury building at 1500 Pennsylvania Avenue, en route to the Washington Cathedral. From his position in the backseat Terrence McElliot stared out through the smoke-tinted glass while current Secret Service director Dick Strahan sat beside him. Outside their soundproof cocoon the District of Columbia sparkled in brilliant sunshine. Inside, the partition separating the rear compartment from Strahan's driver was run up, sealing them off in complete privacy. Also tall and solidly built, as were most men up from the ranks at Treasury, Dick Strahan had been one of McElliot's deputies and remained a close friend.

"I'm sure you know how tricky this gets," Strahan was saying. "From a strictly legal standpoint, this is more in the Bureau's jurisdiction. Conspiracy to commit tax fraud is a little weak, especially before the fact."

"Granted," McElliot replied. "And if this wasn't a request made by Franklin, personally, I'd be up the avenue at Justice right now. I'm sure you're aware of how important his son's candidacy is to him."

Strahan nodded. "As well as being aware of the fact that,

like his father once was, Richard is the Appropriations Committee's most vociferous advocate of Treasury enforcement."

Terrence turned away from the view to confront Strahan directly. "Franklin believes that if DeWitt isn't hit quickly and hard enough to make his head spin, a scandal-hungry press will get hold of it and turn Richard Coulter into the next Gary Hart."

"And you're inclined to believe the old boy? That he had absolutely nothing to do with this girl's death?"

McElliot sighed, his big hands clasped and drawn up between his long legs. Slowly, his head moved back and forth, real doubt in his eyes. "Dick, I just don't know. Franklin chased anything in a skirt for a while after his wife died. It's entirely possible that he could have gotten any one of them pregnant. And God knows, Phil DeWitt never went to the bathroom without Franklin's okay. On the other hand, this smells all wrong for Franklin. I was what in '62? Thirty-four? By then I'd been watching him in action for twelve years. I think that if he'd gotten himself into that sort of trouble, Franklin would have handled it differently. He could be ruthless, but he was always efficient. I believe that if it had been Franklin's problem, he wouldn't have used a couple of local interns in trying to solve it."

"I suppose I'm inclined to agree with you *there*," Strahan admitted. "A man like Franklin Coulter didn't get where he got by leaving his dirty work to ambitious amateurs. I know you feel you owe him for all he did for you, Terry, early on in your career. So how do you think I should approach this? I owe you a favor or two, myself."

McElliot smiled. "How about Bobby and Stan? From what Bobby tells me, you've got him flown in to cover a manpower shortage, protecting some federal prosecutor. You could cut them loose to fly out and make a quick assessment. If they decide that dragging the Bureau in is the only way to go, then so be it. Maybe they can dig something up quickly that will pin this renegade kid's ears back. If they can do that, it'll take the heat of potential scandal off Richard Coulter's campaign, and I'll have done my favor.''

"And I'll have done mine.''

"I'd maybe even owe *you* one.''

"Speaking of Bob,'' Strahan murmured, changing the subject. "How is Ambassador Harrington's death going to affect his career with the Service?''

McElliot's hands came away from between his legs as his eyes drifted back to the world outside the car. Fingers outstretched, he rubbed the hands slowly, palm to palm. "He was already a wealthy man, Dick. He's a whole lot wealthier now, but I don't think that will change his attitude. What I'm unsure about is the added weight of responsibility. All of a sudden he's got that estate to maintain; a payroll to meet; his interest in a dozen corporations to oversee. Only time can tell what those pressures will do to him.''

With Francine at his side, Bobby watched the hearse arrive. Two flower-laden, cutaway Cadillacs preceded it, and behind it a black government sedan followed to disgorge his father. As Terrence moved slowly up the cathedral steps through harsh sunlight, pausing here and there to greet sympathizers, both Franklin and Richard Coulter broke away from other conversations to greet him. A moment later the ex-director moved on toward his son.

"Hello, Francine,'' the elder McElliot greeted her. "I'm pleased that you were able to come.''

Francine regarded Terrence with something approaching adoration. As a child, this man had fascinated her more than any of her grandfather's other friends. He was handsome, with a sort of elegance and deep courtesy about him. He had always gone out of his way to pay attention, as recently as last Christmas spending the better part of an hour grilling her about her horses. Since she'd learned to speak, she'd always addressed him in the familiar.

"He was always kind to me, Terry. I'm glad I could be here.''

Below them the two Coulter men started up the steps. Franklin reached the younger McElliot first, reaching to shake his hand.

"Bobby. It's good to see you. I'm sorry about the circumstances." For the first time in his relationship with the younger man, the old senator spoke these words as an equal. Such was the effect of seeing the mantle of great economic power passed and received. Franklin understood this underlying event's significance.

"Thanks, Senator. You look well. Ranching seems to agree with you."

Franklin smiled. "The world is changing much too quickly for an old man like me, but the cattle stay pretty much the same. Like them, I seem to be content."

As Franklin started to move away, Richard stepped up. "Bobby." He said it with a nod, shaking hands. "I'm sorry about this. I know how close the two of you had become."

"It was coming and we all knew it, Senator. Congratulations on your candidacy. All the polls I've read give you a nice lead."

Richard waved the notion away. "Polls. They'll be the death of us all. I've got a tough fight ahead of me. I just wanted to say that your grandfather was a greater American than most people will ever know. You've got a lot to be proud of. I am, just to have known him."

They eventually moved into the cool of the cathedral interior, proceeding up the center aisle to take seats together in the front pew on the left. Moments later the President, First Lady, and Secretary of State arrived to take places adjacent to them, surrounded by a small army of Bobby's colleagues from the Secret Service. The main body of the church was nearly filled to capacity by the time the dead ambassador's military pallbearers carried the casket in ceremony to a flower-covered bier at the foot of the altar. As the Episcopalian bishop mounted the steps to the altar and the ceremony began, Bobby's watch told him that they were already half an hour late getting started. After the funeral service was over, there was still the long, slow ride to the Arlington National Cemetery. It would be difficult enough to bear without the awareness of an unsettling attention being paid him. Washington society was close-knit and full of its own importance. He found it frightening in its capacity to both draw conclusions and project expectations.

There was no reason to stay any longer at Sid's Bait and Court, so Tony Flood had tossed his grip into the Jeep and was preparing to clear out when Carter pulled into the gravel drive. It was just noon, and because the young lawyer appeared agitated, Flood wondered if it was possible that the retired sheriff's death had already been reported on the news.

"What's up, Carter boy? Y'all look like you're bein' chased by a swarm of angry bees."

"I didn't know if you'd still be here." DeWitt was making no attempt to hide the relief in his tone. "I need to talk to you, Tony."

Flood nodded toward the door of unit 6. "You're lucky y'all caught me. I was just gettin' ready to move on up to Springfield and find me a motel up there. C'mon inside. I ain't checked out yet."

As Carter entered the familiar cabin, he crossed directly to the dinette and pulled up a chair. "Have you seen a newspaper?" he asked.

Flood knew Scranton's death couldn't have been reported in a paper yet, and was relieved to realize DeWitt had himself worked up about something altogether different.

"Can't say as I have. Why?"

"That radiologist. The one I had you do the digging into. He blew his brains out yesterday."

Flood feigned concern. "That a fact? I guess that's too damn bad for you, huh? What with the way you'd planned t'lean on him and all."

"I *did* lean on him. Yesterday morning. I leaned on him so hard that I had him and his buddy Orton both sweating."

Flood clucked his tongue as he slowly shook his head.

"Tough break. But I guess y'all still got the heart doc wrigglin' on the hook, right?"

Carter ignored the question. "You didn't find anything about him having been diagnosed with bone cancer?"

Now Flood frowned, the man's implication clear. "You asked me t' dig into his financial picture, Carter boy." It was cool and even. "This is the first thing I've heard 'bout any fuckin' cancer."

DeWitt stood abruptly to pace in nervous circles. "I didn't mean it to sound like that. It's just that I find myself in a bit of a jam. . . ."

Tony nodded knowingly. "The dead doc left a note?"

"Maybe worse." Carter frowned, looking for the safest way to phrase what was spooking him. "I got a call from Francine Coulter this morning. Apparently, her father and grandfather know at least something of what I've been up to. How, I've got no idea. The only thing I can figure is that Solokowski came clean before he pulled the trigger."

"T' the Coulters? Why?"

Carter rubbed both hands up and down over his face in frustration. "Oh, what the hell. My father left me some stuff that led me to believe that Sheriff Scranton was holding some piece of evidence damaging to the Coulters. Something that would tie them directly to that accident I had you investigate. Those pictures you found, along with the ledger entries and the coroner's report, only serve to confirm that the event really did take place, and that *somebody* had been paying Scranton off. As far as the Coulters are concerned, all I've got is hearsay."

"An' now *they* know you've got your finger in the pie."

"That's about the size of it. And they know what any scandal involving my father and possible allegations against them would do to Richard Coulter's candidacy. Francine told me that Franklin approached an old friend, Terrence McElliot, about getting me investigated."

"Terrence McElliot?" Flood was drawing a blank on the name. "Who the fuck is he?"

"The retired Director of the Secret Service. He and Franklin are related, some way or another."

"I don't get it. Why not go to the FBI?"

"They obviously want to keep this in the family. Do it quietly. I'm hoping that's to my advantage, but I don't think I've got much time. The Treasury Department can freeze my assets. If they do, some things I've got working would go queer in a hurry." He paused, considering what he was about to say next. "Let's just say that I'm a bit overextended at the moment, and some of the money involved isn't mine."

"You just paid me twenty-five thousand in cash. That yours or someone else's?"

"It's mine for the moment," DeWitt replied. "But if I can't get out of this jam, what the hell difference does it make?"

"The cash you still expect t' get from Orton . . . That gonna be enough t' see you squeak through?"

"Barely." Carter took a moment to draw a picture of his current circumstances, describing how the bottom had fallen out of Sure-Fire. "The two hundred thirty-seven that the stock is worth today, combined with Orton's two fifty, will get me close. I'm going to have to dip into a little cash reserve of my own to make up the difference, if I want to stay out of jail."

Flood seemed confused. "I thought your daddy left you a nice chunk o' change."

"Frozen in probate."

"For how long?"

DeWitt rubbed his face again. "Who the hell knows? *Too* long. What I need you to do now is keep an eye on Orton . . . if not around the clock, then at least most of Friday. Make sure he goes to his bank, and that he doesn't have a couple of T-men with him when he does. I'd like you to be around when I make the collection that evening, just to keep an eye out for trouble. I'm going to make sure he still intends to pay, but I can't ensure he doesn't plan to double-cross me. There's another twenty-five thousand in it for you."

"I thought you said you were strapped for cash."

"Don't worry, I can cover it. Barely. Think of it, Tony. Fifty grand for a week's work. Not bad, huh?"

"No," Flood agreed. "I'd rather be in my shoes than yours, Carter boy."

Fifteen minutes later DeWitt was gone. Flood had told him of his plans to move his base of operations to a Super 8 motel in Springfield, on Kearney near the airport. Now, before checking out, Tony sat with his feet up on the dinette table, trying to organize his thoughts. He didn't like the news about the involvement of this man McElliot. Treasury could use a lot of different angles to come at a problem. Carter said that he wanted him to set up on Orton in an effort to detect the double-cross, but Tony had a few ducks of his own to get in line. One or two of those ducks were going to involve some travel.

As Flood stood to leave the cabin and kick his own plans into gear, he knew time was short. He didn't want to see Treasury agents following Dr. Ervin Orton around on Friday any more than Carter did. He wanted to be back in the area by mid-morning Friday, and it was already Wednesday afternoon. There was an awful lot to do in the next two days.

The McElliots, father and son, rode behind the hearse in the Whippoorwill limousine as the long, slow procession crossed the Memorial Bridge. Trailing them somewhere in the line of cars was the Coulter family, but the dilemma facing them was here in this car, the subject of immediate discussion. Terrence had just concluded explaining the complexities of it.

"We're confronted with a rather irregular situation," the older McElliot mused.

"We?"

"Well, I am. And now Dick Strahan too. Franklin asked me for my help, and I'm sitting here trying to figure a way to ask you for yours."

"I think you just did. And judging from the fact that it was Strahan's car that dropped you at the cathedral curb, I'd guess that you've already aired the idea with him. Care to be at all specific?"

Terrence regarded his son with admiration and a certain amount of relief. Bobby had never been one to pull punches. "Technically? It would be a covert Treasury investigation aimed at determining whether this St. Louis lawyer is conspiring to defraud the government of monies he would owe in taxes. Actually? Franklin wants to know what Carter DeWitt has as evidence about that night in 1963. He obviously had enough on Dr. Solokowski to scare the hell out of him. Franklin swears that he had nothing to do with the events of that night, nor did he have any knowledge of them since."

"And you believe him."

Terrence scowled, obviously still at odds with that issue himself. "I *want* to. But more importantly, you may be able to prove it. At the same time, you could conceivably prevent a legitimate, hard-earned candidacy from being damaged. I think it was obvious that Phil DeWitt always envied Richard Coulter and his position of privilege. Phil did very well by the Coulters, but he always had to hustle, pulling strings behind the scenes while first Franklin and then Richard basked in the spotlight, out front. Festering jealousy can do a lot to twist a man's perception of justice. So can guilt. Phil knew that he was directly responsible for that campaign volunteer's death. Maybe this is the way his mind twisted things to make everything seem right."

"And maybe Franklin *was* involved."

"Granted."

"And meanwhile, I might defuse the DeWitt threat to Richard by getting Dick Strahan the evidence he'll need to come down hard on Carter."

"That's the favor Franklin is asking, yes. But the one I'm asking is that you also try to eliminate any doubts we have. I want to know what really happened that night."

Bobby took a deep breath and pushed it out in a whoosh. "So would I. What do I tell Stan?"

"What do you *want* to tell him?"

"The whole truth. He's my partner. We don't lie to each other. I want to know exactly what's at risk, going in."

"Fair enough."

"Can I assume this is a matter of some urgency?"

"*Franklin* seems to think so."

His father's tone prompted a sharp look. "You're upset about this, aren't you?"

Terrence turned his head away to look off across the pristine rows of white marble headstones as the cortege crept through the gates of Arlington National Cemetery. There was a tightness in his voice as he spoke.

"I think I know how Phil DeWitt felt, Bobby. I wasn't a kid off the streets of St. Louis, I was a kid off the farm. Both Phil and I had little more than our wits to recommend us to the world. I was a Coulter Scholar at Princeton, no less, making me feel all the more indebted to them. When Franklin invited me to Washington, to get me started with all the right breaks in government, how could I refuse? Once I was there, he was the one who took me to the Christmas party where I met your mother. Today, when I think back on those times, I can't really put my finger on when Franklin started to take the fact that I owed him a huge debt for granted. And the funny thing is that I actually like the man, even though we disagree about practically everything. The only thing I don't like is the feeling that is always hanging in the air between us; that I wouldn't be where I am without him."

Eleven

Bobby's departure was delayed for several hours after the burial, as Michael Harrington's will was read at his attorney's offices. It was nearly five before he finished handling everything demanding his immediate attention, and he was lucky to make the six o'clock Metroliner with only minutes to spare. He left Washington with his head buzzing legal jargon and the weight of new responsibilities resting with unaccustomed heaviness on his shoulders. His grandfather's will was simple enough. Everything, down to the last nail head, was left to him. Much of it, over the years, had been transferred to his name to avoid paying a huge, one-time inheritance tax. Other larger chunks were in corporate trusts over which he now had complete control. And control, it seemed, also meant the time-consuming burden of administration.

When his train pulled into Penn Station at nine-fifteen, he flagged a cab on Seventh Avenue, and found no one home when he arrived at the loft. Stan was playing true to form. He'd probably worked eighteen hours at a stretch, finishing the editing of all the footage, and was now out blowing off steam. The completed video cassette was atop the desk with a note weighted beneath:

Hope This Finds You Reasonably Intact After Your Ordeal. Wish I Could Have Been There To Help Prop You Up. This Sucker Is *Clean*! If They Aren't Here, They Weren't There!

The light on the answering machine hooked into Bobby's private line blinked only once. After dropping his bag in his bedroom, he picked up a pen and crossed to retrieve the message. It was from Marilyn. She had set up a time when the Manhattan D.A. would take his deposition. She asked him to give her a call, saying that she would be up most of the night working on some suddenly urgent aspect of her case. He could feel free to call any time before midnight.

It was only a bit past ten. Stan wasn't likely to straggle in before sometime late the next morning. Venturing out on the late-night club circuit in search of him would be an exercise in futility. When Stan got onto one of his postproduction rolls, he functioned much like a shark. Keep moving or die. At best, Bobby could hope to see him by lunchtime.

The lady prosecutor snagged it on the first ring.

"Yeah." All business.

"Bobby McElliot. I'm innocent. I swear."

From down the line a stifled chuckle reached his ear.

"I doubt that very much, Mr. McElliot. No one is."

"Sorry I'm so late getting back to you. I was—"

"I know about your grandfather. When I called to offer my condolences, Stan told me he expected you back tonight."

"I'm surprised you caught him home. We just wrapped a project."

"I was also calling about that deposition. My admirer has filed countercharges of assault with intent. Do you think you could squeeze me in tomorrow morning?" She yawned audibly.

"Even earlier, if I didn't think you'd fall asleep on me."

Marilyn laughed. "Careful, mister. I just won a major case, and I'm feeling decidedly open to temptation."

She related the details of how, just before the case went to jury, the defense had entered a guilty plea in exchange for slightly shorter jail time. In doing so, they were forced to surrender $470 million in seized U.S. assets. She'd been working all evening to complete the paperwork. It had to be ready for the judge first thing in the morning.

"You're not going to go running off to a Club Med someplace before we have a chance to celebrate, are you?" he asked. "I have to go out to the Midwest on family business tomorrow night and may be tied up out there for a while."

"How long might awhile be?" There was disappointment in the way she asked it. "Not that you've got to worry. I'm stuck here until the sentencing, and that's not for three weeks."

"Sounds like you *are* planning a vacation."

"I haven't had one in two years. I think I've got the time coming, don't you?"

"No argument here. So what's the drill tomorrow?"

"Can you meet me at ten, in front of One Hogan Place? It's a block off Centre."

"Not a problem. You sound as tired as I feel. Why don't you try to get some sleep."

"I wish I could. I should have this in pretty good shape in another hour . . . *if* I don't run into any more snags. Wish me luck."

Having said good night, McElliot cradled the phone and wandered toward the kitchen end of the loft to get himself a beer. He carried it back to the cluster of furniture in the middle of the place, pushed the finished tape into the player, and settled into his favorite armchair. It was difficult, at first, to focus on the monitor. His attention was occupied by a new conflict. It was years since he'd had such strong feelings for even one, let alone two women. His relationship with Francine had existed on a casual level from the outset, but now he wondered if his feelings were *still* so casual. Their two fiercely independent souls had each suffered something of an emotional blindsiding the other night. He was fairly sure that

Francine hadn't been ready for the strength of feeling that flowed between them, and neither had he. And now here he was, back in New York, and tasting Marilyn Hunt's free and easy good-night kisses all over again. There was something about the feisty little prosecutor that played mischief with a very vulnerable part of him. With the smell of Francine's perfume still lingering on his clothes, he looked forward with eagerness to tomorrow morning and his meeting with Marilyn Hunt.

By nine-thirty Wednesday night Ervin Orton's nerves were shot. The strain he was under had him thinking about turning in early, when the phone rang. Seated at the desk in his den, he turned away from studying his investment portfolio to answer it.

"Let's talk, Doc."

He didn't like the tone of the DeWitt kid's voice. The effort of figuring a way to squeeze a quarter-million dollars out of his ready-cash investments had left him with a dangerously short fuse.

"Always a pleasure, Mr. DeWitt. What's on your mind?"

"Not on the phone. Your office at Cox. In forty minutes."

Before Erv could focus his fury, Carter cut the connection. For just an instant Orton's thoughts wandered to the loaded Ruger Service-Six revolver he kept in his nightstand drawer. The temptation to use it tonight was strong. But the gun was registered to him. The end of one nightmare would only mean the beginning of another. He had little choice but to go and hear his tormentor out.

Betty was in the living room, watching television and addressing envelopes to the women members of their country club. The envelopes contained invitations to the annual holiday fashion show and luncheon that she'd been selected to chair. She looked up as her husband entered, slipping into his suit jacket.

"Where might you be going at this hour?" It was acid-tinged and laced with suspicion.

"The chest I cracked yesterday morning is developing complications. Looks like pneumonia, but they think I should run up and have a look."

"Isn't there a resident on? Couldn't he take care of it until morning?"

"Probably. And now that he's notified me, if there *is* a crisis, who do you think would get sued for malpractice?"

"What have you been doing in there all night?" A quick shift of subject, and again suspicion.

"Looking at a deal that we might want to get into. Big new anchored mall they're planning to build in Denver. I'm trying to decide if it's for us, *and* if we can afford what they want to get a piece of it."

Her eyebrows went up. "I talked to Daddy this afternoon and he didn't mention you saying anything to him about it."

At Betty's insistence Erv had gotten involved in a number of investment schemes with her charcoal-manufacturing father. Primary among them was a factory-outlet mini-mall on the strip down in Branson that had returned handsomely for a few years and now was going a bit sour. Everyone was building like crazy down there, trying to get a chunk of the tourist trade quick, before they polluted Table Rock Lake and everything dried up, just like it was starting to up at Lake of the Ozarks.

"Probably because I *didn't* mention it. This is something one of the guys in the Kansas City group told me about. Believe it or not, I like to think for myself every once in awhile, just to prove I'm still capable."

Without waiting for Betty's next parry, Orton headed for the door.

At ten-fifteen on a weekday night the doctor's office wing at Cox Medical Center was all but abandoned. Five minutes after Orton arrived he received a call made from a pay phone in the parking lot. He then returned downstairs to join DeWitt in the front seat of his Continental. The lawyer started talking before Erv had the passenger-side door closed.

"If that sonofabitch Solokowski were still alive, I'd say he

146

had some explaining to do to you, Doctor. But he isn't, and he's left you holding the whole bag.''

Panic-stricken, Orton began to protest. "Whole bag? What the hell is that supposed to mean? Nobody knew he had cancer! Not even his wife!''

DeWitt slapped his open palm down on the leather seat alongside his thigh. "What's it *mean*? Well, it sure as fuck doesn't mean that I'm concerned about that sorry bastard's *health*!''

Orton tried to calm himself as he regarded this incensed man, young enough to be his son. "No, I don't suppose you would be. Certain things seem to run in families.''

"Feeling sorry for yourself, *Doctor*? Hell, if I wasn't a fair-minded man, I might be inclined to dump Solokowski's half of the payoff into your lap. As it is, I hope you don't think this changes anything.''

Orton scowled now. "Is *that* the purpose of this meeting? Why would I think you might have changed your mind? Because you're sorry my friend is dead?''

DeWitt continued to ignore the doctor's angry tone. "No, Erv. I got you out here to discuss time and place. It's still two hundred and fifty thousand, and it's still Friday, or I *will* go to the papers on Monday.''

"Friday's too soon,'' Orton argued desperately. "The money is there, but I need more time to figure out how to work it. If I tap any of my pure-cash investments, the interest penalties will be astronomical.''

DeWitt chuckled. "I'm not interested in talking capital gains here, Doc. I'm talking about you saving your ass. What's worth more to you. A few dollars or the last years of your life?''

"*When* on Friday? It can't possibly be early. It's only two days away.''

"What are you doing Friday evening, early?''

Orton retrieved his date book from his jacket and opened it to that week. "My wife is doing some sort of charity cocktail party at the country club. I have to join her there for dinner at seven-thirty.''

"So she'll be out of the house by, say, five?''

"That's right. Earlier than that, I'd imagine.''

"Five-thirty, then, Doc. And you won't have to meet me. I'll drop by.''

Orton's blackmailer terminated their exchange on that note. Erv got out of the Lincoln, stood, and watched him drive off before climbing back behind the wheel of his own car. After a day's careful study, he knew he could call the necessary CD's and bonds by Friday, but doubt still gnawed at him. Where would this young man's greed end? Carter DeWitt could continue to hit him for these huge chunks of cash every few years until the day he died. There had to be some way out. As he drove through the sparsely trafficked streets of Springfield, he desperately tried to discover some weakness in DeWitt's scheme. Eventually, as he piloted his BMW back down the drive and into his garage, he gave up hope. Whatever Carter wanted, it would be better to pay it than lose everything he'd worked for. He would pay the quarter million to him Friday, and keep on meeting his demands until the day he finally got up the nerve to kill him. Carter DeWitt was surely more deserving of death than that poor girl had been.

After parking, Orton depressed the button to close the automatic door before climbing out of the car. As he stood there, watching the mechanism do its lumbering job, he realized that in those twenty-eight years since driving away from Branson that night, neither he nor Tim had ever mentioned the incident again, even to each other.

Twelve

Jimmy Ike Dorsett had looked hard, and still wasn't sure what it was he'd seen. He was working the waters of upper Bull Shoals Lake as he sat in the chair of his flat-bottomed bass boat. That thing floating out there sure *looked* like a man to him. Jimmy Ike's last cast, on the other hand, had been a thing of real poetry, and neither damnation nor high water were going to make him budge until he'd slowly and artfully dragged the lure back alongside. It came at a steady, even speed, governed one crank of his Garcia 321 Plus at a time. That thing couldn't really be a man anyway. Not half a mile from shore and bobbing high in the water like that.

Poetic cast notwithstanding, the smallmouth were refusing to hit on this sizzling hot, cloudless morning. The sun was already high enough to fry his pitiful catch lying there in the bottom of the boat. It was time to head into shore. Way down the lake he could see that the first of the kids were already out, skiing behind a jet boat and most likely wrecking the fishing until dusk. As much as he hated to quit without success, Jimmy Ike racked his rod, climbed down off the pedestal chair, and took the helm. That floater was still piquing his curiosity, and before heading in he thought he'd check it out.

The fisherman was nearly upon the thing before he realized that, for God's sake, it *was* a man! Deader than last week's meat loaf, he was floating facedown, spread-eagle, and most of him below the lake's surface. Pulling alongside, Jimmy Ike grabbed his extendable lure retriever and reached it over to hook the poor bastard's clothing. The body was bloated with the heat of at least one day in the water, his hands gone white as snow. It had to be the gases of decomposition keeping him up like that.

There wasn't much to do but get a line on him and drag him to the dock. One of his waders looked like the least problematic angle to attack from, and the big, work-hardened retiree got a clove hitch around it. After crawling back to the helm, mid-boat, he eased the throttle back a hair and started the slow trip to the beach. The moment the tension went out of the line to the corpse, it started to roll over. Jimmy Ike checked his direction and was trying to keep one eye on his tow. What that one eye saw was enough to cause him to lose his biscuits and gravy. There was no wonder that the bass hadn't been hungry this morning. They'd already eaten their fill of the poor devil's face.

The late-summer heat wave currently gripping the East Coast was promising to intensify as Thursday morning dawned. An habitual early riser, Bobby McElliot spent the wee hours assembling some of the gear he thought he might need in the Midwest. Just after sunup Stan stumbled in with one of his conquests, an Amazon-sized strawberry blonde with glamour-magazine facial bones and a dress that left little to the imagination. She neither smiled nor made any attempt at pleasantry in passing. Torbeck didn't do drugs, so it must have been his body she was after. Bobby shot his partner a mock salute as Stan disappeared behind the leading edge of his closing bedroom door. It would be at least two o'clock before Stanley emerged, said good-bye to this latest lovely, and was capable of coherent conversation.

At nine-thirty Bobby left the loft and hiked the long block west to catch the Number One IRT train at Eighteenth Street and Seventh Avenue. The stench of urine bit his nostrils as he descended the stairs toward the token booth. As much as he never looked forward to the bitter winds of winter, they could at least be relied upon to keep the offal odors of human elimination at bay.

His ride downtown was blessedly uncrowded. Most of the workaday migration had ended an hour earlier, and only a few of the better dressed, later arrivals populated Bobby's car. He was ten minutes early for his rendezvous with Marilyn and dawdled a bit on Foley Square, across from the U.S. Court House, to watch a bent old woman feed the pigeons. The woman dragged a shopping cart with one bad wheel, the basket crammed with filthy odds and ends. It made a young, healthy, and secure man shudder to contemplate what it must be like to grow old in a city that ate the weak for breakfast.

The prosecutor was located lounging against the front fender of a government Chrysler as Bobby approached up the sidewalk. He was surprised to discover her dressed in khaki walking shorts, a red polo shirt, and sandals, some of her hair pulled back with a clip. As he got closer he could read the weariness around her eyes and mouth.

"I'm not sure whether I'm a sight for sore eyes or my sore eyes are a sight," she said, standing on tiptoe to kiss him lightly on the cheek. "I finally got to bed at four-thirty and met the judge in his chambers nearly an hour ago."

Bobby looked her up and down. "Is this the new dress code at the Justice Department? Because if it is, I heartily endorse the trend."

With slight self-consciousness she glanced down at a perfectly acceptable pair of legs. Terrific legs, in fact. Bobby recalled, once again, how he'd perceived her that first time, last Friday afternoon; as statuesque in miniature.

"They weren't going to be getting much more out of me

today,'' she said. ''I figured if I dressed like this, they wouldn't have to wonder whether I was taking the rest of the day off.''

''To sleep, I hope.''

When she smiled, the tiredness in her face seemed to lift a little. ''You look rested. I know you must be tired of hearing it, but I feel for what you've been through. Your grandfather was one of those rare people who was a legend in his own time. I suppose that makes the loss only greater for the people who were close.''

''It's something I'll have to live with. After the stroke, he wanted out, Marilyn. He hated being an invalid.''

''You admired him quite a lot.'' The way she so often put things, it wasn't a question.

''Yeah, I did admire him,'' Bobby replied. ''The whole world was his oyster, and yet he chose a life of public service. I valued his insight, and I suppose that might be the thing I'll miss most. That, and the stability he represented.''

She glanced up toward the door of One Hogan Place. ''Are you ready for this? There's a lot of pressure being brought by somebody in the mayor's office to see the D.A. drop this. The creep with the loose hands countersued me yesterday, for assault with intent to do serious bodily harm. The way he's telling it, an uppity federal prosecutor kicked a fun-loving banker in the balls without reasonable provocation. His attorney says he'll drop his suit if I'll drop mine.''

She turned to mount the stairs, and in her wake, Bobby admired the turn of her ankles. ''It doesn't sound like you're ready to meet his terms.''

''Over my dead body.''

Before she could grab the door handle, Bobby reached around, beating her to it. As they stepped into the relative cool of the interior, he attempted to reassure her.

''If this ever does go to trial, I'll crawl on my hands and knees from the North Pole, if that's what I have to do to get there. There I was, enjoying myself over a beer in a financial-district steakhouse, watching a very attractive woman in the phone alcove, when some jerk comes along to ruin a perfectly pleasant afternoon.''

She tossed her head to strike a seductive pose in front of the elevator bank. "But you also have him to *thank*. If it weren't for him, you'd never have *met* that attractive woman.''

The elevator doors opened. They stepped inside and rode to the sixth floor.

On his way home McElliot stopped off at the supermarket to pick up some bagels, cream cheese, and eggs. While the rest of New York would be thinking about lunch, or perhaps even getting back to work, Stan Torbeck would be craving breakfast. His basic desires were always predictable. When Bobby stepped off the freight elevator and into the main studio space of their loft, it was half-past one. His partner's bedroom door hung open and water could be heard running in the shower. As he put the groceries away and began heating a frying pan, the shower cut off.

"How many for breakfast?'' he called out.

"Just you and me. But there aren't any eggs in the icebox. I already checked.''

"One of us has been up long enough to make eight or nine trips to the store, big guy. What happened to your friend?''

"She didn't have any interest in an enduring relationship. You get a chance to look at that tape?''

"Looks terrific. I called down this morning, and Strahan is sending Reiske up to collect it.''

Stan emerged from the bath with a towel wrapped around his waist. His short-cropped, white-blond hair still glistened with water. "How was the funeral?''

Bobby poured them cups of coffee from the insulated carafe he'd filled earlier. A little milk went into his while Torbeck's remained black.

"How, ever, are funerals? The guest of honor is always dead. I miss this one more than most. As window dressing, our President, his First Lady, and the Secretary of State were there in the front row, and half the U.S. Congress filled the church behind."

"And my best buddy is a bona fide, megabucks rich man now."

Bobby chuckled, slicing open a pair of bagels and laying them out on the toaster-oven tray. He knew that Stan didn't really care much about the Harrington legacy, nor did he fathom the weight of social expectation that went with it. The mystique of the East Coast power network seemed to escape this beach-bred Californian.

"Who was the ice maiden?" he asked.

Torbeck dodged into his room and emerged clad in a pair of loose-fitting, light blue cotton shorts. "Late-innings reliever. Threw hard for a few and flew. Not exactly the stuff fairy tales are spun from, but a guy takes what he can get at three-thirty in the morning. Sun still comes up too early, even this time of year."

A half-dozen eggs, cracked with a splash of milk whisked into them, went into the frying pan. Bobby commenced working them around the sizzling hot surface with a spatula and nodded toward the toaster. "Keep an eye on the bread, will you?"

Torbeck moved alongside. "Where were you up and off to so bright and early?"

"Bright and *what*? It's nearly two in the afternoon. I was meeting Marilyn to give the Manhattan D.A. my deposition."

"Ah, the saga continues. Did she still look good enough to eat?"

"Pure parfait." As Bobby continued to work, scrambling the eggs, his expression slowly changed as he tried to decide how to broach what he was going to say next. "Something's come up, Stan."

"You proposed marriage."

"Real funny. A new assignment, maybe best described as quirky."

Torbeck was pulling the bagels from the heat. The tone in Bobby's voice forced him to turn. "You care to elaborate?"

The eggs were scooped out of the pan and onto a pair of plates. Torbeck stacked the toasted bagels on a third plate, and together they moved to the table.

"After the funeral my father and I rode out to Arlington together. Earlier yesterday morning he had a meeting with Dick Strahan."

As they started to eat, Bobby related the nature of his discussion with his father. When he concluded, Stan sat with a full fork poised midway between his plate and mouth, eyeing him steadily.

"It's old-boy political backscratching, is what it is. You get a good read on how your old man feels about it?"

"Off the record? He's upset that Franklin even asked him to pull the strings. But then again, he owes that old man an awful lot. He could hardly say no."

Stan shrugged. "I don't suppose." He lifted the food to his mouth and commenced chewing thoughtfully. "Ain't been a good scandal yet, so early in the races. Got to be a whole slew of eager-beaver media types just dying to get their hooks into one, huh?"

"There's more," Bobby told him. "Once we're on the scene, Dad's asked me to go it a step further. Franklin claims he's totally ignorant of the event. Claims to remember nothing of the girl. While we're trying to get the goods on this extortionist lawyer, Dad's asked me to do a little checking into the particulars surrounding the girl's death."

"Tempting fate, isn't he?"

Bobby smiled. "Nothing new about that. Terry may owe Franklin Coulter the favor, but he won't play stooge for him. I hope Franklin realizes that."

Torbeck gestured over to a pile of gear stacked near the elevator door. "I noticed you'd thrown a few things together. When do you want to saddle up?"

"We've got to wait for Reiske to get up here and collect

the tape. I made reservations on a six o'clock flight out of LaGuardia, so let's hope he doesn't hang us up.''

Dick Strahan's Treasury courier arrived at three to collect the videotape and Stan's typewritten report outlining his conclusions. As far as they were concerned, it was good riddance to an intelligence-processing nightmare. A total of seventy-three different individuals had been singled out of their surveillance footage for further scrutiny. Of those, sixteen had behaved in directly suspicious manners. It was now up to the Bureau, Customs, and Immigration to ascertain who they were and what their function might have been that morning.

In exchange, Doug Reiske had delivered an envelope from their boss, containing an expenses check for $25,000.

"You planning to deposit that this afternoon?" Torbeck asked. He was seated at one of their two big worktables, the parts of his Beretta Model 92F automatic spread disassembled on the Home section of the Thursday *Times*. Any other equipment they were taking along had already been packed. It was moving on four o'clock.

"I figure the Government Accounting Office is good for it."

McElliot sat across from Stan and was pushing 9mm hollow-point bullets into the eight-shot clip of his Walther P-38.

"That's a lotta dough for a snooping trip to the Ozarks. You ask me, I think the boss intended for us to call the heliport and catch a whirlybird out to Queens. He no doubt knew that it'd beat hell outta sitting around in rush-hour traffic for an hour and a half."

"You know, you might have a point. I got the impression that speed was of the essence here." Clip loaded, Bobby fitted it into the butt of his pistol and slapped it home. The VIP heliport sat just a few blocks uptown and to the west at 34th Street and the Hudson River. For a few hundred bucks they could get themselves and their gear to LaGuardia in fifteen minutes. He reached for the phone and reserved an Aerospatiale Astar for a trip out in forty-five minutes. As soon as Torbeck completed a last-minute check of the electronic-surveillance equipment he was taking along, they were ready to go.

"Biscuits and gravy," Stan murmured, his words dripping disgust. "Grits and eggs, swimming in Wesson oil. And not a hint of a sea breeze for a thousand miles."

"C'mon. The Gulf is closer than that."

"And how many times do I have to tell you that there ain't but three real oceans in this world, Bob? With coastline that sustains some actual *surf*. The Gulf is a goddam cesspool, chock full of drilling scum and sewage. You can't *ride* that shit. All you can do is drown in it."

"So just think how light you'll be traveling, Stanley. You won't have to pack your board and wet suit."

Stan had originally been bitten by the cinematography bug while learning to shoot surf footage as a teenager. He'd built his own waterproof 16mm head-mounted camera, employing it while hurtling down the face of a wave, hunched down on all fours atop a little knee board. Just last year, while on vacation in the South Seas, he'd geared up and climbed overboard off his chartered boat to ride the gigantic open ocean swells generated by an approaching typhoon. Bobby had seen the footage and it was terrifying.

Their subsequent airborne jaunt, made from the bank of the Hudson in mid-Manhattan to Queens and the shores of Flushing Bay, got them to LaGuardia with nearly an hour to kill before their flight out. Three and a half hours later, during the layover between St. Louis and the regional flight to Springfield, the partners grabbed a quick bite in a Lambert Field restaurant. Outside the immense glass windows rising thirty feet along one wall of the Gateway Garden, commercial carriers took off and landed with only the barest sound. Because they'd gained an hour flying west, it was not yet nightfall out here. It seemed like as good a time as any to discuss their immediate strategy.

"The way I see it, we've got to start looking at the basics first," Bobby was saying. "See what they've got in the files of the sheriff's and coroner's offices; local newspaper archives. I want to know how *they* say the girl died."

"Okay," Stan agreed. "And then we want to tickle this Dr. Orton. He's the only live wire we've got on the other side of DeWitt's ledger." The big man was happily sawing away at a Kansas City strip and wolfing it down while Bobby had rather imprudently chosen fettucine with a watery scallop cream sauce.

"We want to avoid making any waves with the local bureaucracy," McElliot warned. "They start showing signs of provincial protectionism, we back straight off. I think it's important that we tread lightly until we know whose toes we have to avoid." He pointed his fork at Stan's plate. "How's your steak?"

Torbeck flashed the okay sign. "Tasty. Like only the American Midwest seems able to grow beef. You struck out, huh?"

"Terrible," Bobby replied.

In pity, Stan cut off a chunk of his beef and set it on his partner's bread plate.

The flight to Springfield was aboard a so-called commuter aircraft; a twin-engine prop plane seating eighteen in tiny seats along each side of a foot-wide center aisle. They encountered turbulence twice en route, an experience a novice to light-plane travel wasn't likely to soon forget. The fact that the cockpit door stood open was reassuring. The passengers could see both the pilot and copilot's backs. Neither wore a parachute.

On the ground in Springfield they picked up the Ford Taurus wagon that Bobby had reserved earlier with Hertz. Branson, where Connie Dahlrymple died, lay fifty miles to the south, accessible only along a road that narrowed to two lanes ten miles outside of Springfield. They purchased Rand

McNally's map of the region from the airport gift shop before starting off, the Hertz version not being terribly rich in detail.

"America's heartland, Bob. Bet it makes your heartstrings hum, right?" Stan had taken the first turn behind the wheel and was piloting them along U.S. 65 at a fairly sedate pace for a man generally in a hurry. He had his window run down and breathed deep of the Ozark air.

"My heartstrings *what*?"

"Hum, Bob. *Hum.* Look at this landscape. It's awesome."

"What happened to that hint of a sea breeze? And the fact that Springfield is one of the prime rhinestone studs in the Bible Belt? And you don't know the half of it. Ignorance is still bliss down in this neck of the woods, Stanley. I'm a boy from the wide-open flatlands. When you get a load of the Branson Strip, we'll talk about humming heartstrings." He shook his head, eyes betraying the hint of amusement. "I'm wondering how we'll do with the crowds. It's still warm, and Labor Day means nothing anymore."

Regardless of how this adopted son of the state might feel about Missouri's southwest region, the country they drove through *was* gorgeous. The sun was down now, the valleys and ravines completely filled with shadow while a pale light still lingered across the peaks and ridges along the horizon. The headlights of a stream of cars, mobile homes, and campers played across the bluffs of yellow rock looming along either side of the road. It was easy to see why the Daltons, James brothers, and a host of other early outlaws had chosen this region for safe haven. The wild Ozarks stretched well down into Arkansas and a hundred miles both east and west. Even today, with the exception of small recreational pockets built near the huge water-project lakes, most of it remained unspoiled. The lake they were headed toward, Table Rock, was one of these monsters, with an excess of eight hundred miles of shoreline. Broad branches of it, and a host of smaller limbs, stretched through thirty miles of dammed-up mountain valley. To the immediate east, on the other side of a little fingerling of a lake with the wistfully Italianate name of Taney Como, another even larger lake stretched deep below the Arkansas border. This was Bull Shoals, with more than a thousand miles of shore.

The down side of the trip south was the traffic. With the warm weather holding and the weekend approaching, late vacationers were flocking into the Ozarks by the thousands. Every fourth vehicle was one of a variety of slow-moving recreational behemoths. The flow moved ever slower as they approached Branson. With a dozen miles left to their destination, they crawled, cars bumper to bumper as far ahead as the eye could see.

"Flatlander or not," Torbeck grumbled, "you know more about this neck of the woods than I do. How many motel rooms they got in this burg?"

"I'd guess a few thousand. Along with scores of R.V. parks and campgrounds."

"No shit. So this place is a real mecca for you flatlanders."

"Let's drop the flatlander handle right now, shall we?"

Stan grinned. "Sorry, Bob. It's late and this traffic is making me ornery."

"Me too. As far as Branson goes, I hear it's changed a lot since I was last here in the early seventies . . . and then, it had already changed quite a bit since the night the Dahlrymple girl died down here in '63. I looked up the population this morning, and the almanac lists Branson at twenty-five hundred. That's probably the 1980 census figure, because my edition is a couple years old. Since then, it's grown like fungus on a wet forest floor."

It was another forty minutes before they finally pulled off Route 65 and into the city of Branson proper. The first thing greeting them, perched above the interchange like some painted, hillbilly whore, was a huge commercial edifice with more gingerbread on it than the house in Hansel and Gretel. A garish, neon and blinking incandescent sign fronted the place, saying all that need be said:

160

T-SHIRTS * HILLBILLY CRAFTS * QEWPIE DOLLS * ARKANSAS
DIAMONDS * GENUINE WALNUT BOWLS * TOURIST INFOR-
MATION

Stan sat craning his neck as they idled at a red light, mar-
veling. "Jesus *Christ.* And I thought the Black Hills around
Rushmore were bad."

"Careful, Stanley. The folk down here aren't too keen on
taking the Lord's name in vain."

Stan scowled. "So what the fuck is an Arkansas Diamond?"

"Big chunk of glass. Natural formation of silicate that the
locals dig out of the ground."

"Do tell. And look at all these cars. Where the hell are
they *going*?"

Bobby nodded toward the west. "That's Route 76. Just a
few blocks down that way the strip begins."

Eleven o'clock rolled around before they finally located a
motel on the far side of town with two rooms available. All
up and down the Branson Strip they'd encountered at least a
dozen country entertainment palaces; several bigger than
most theaters on Broadway. Lights, flashing in the colors of
a nightmare rainbow, had stretched for five miles, and between the barnlike theaters stood shoulder-to-shoulder gift
shops, motels, go-cart tracks, water slides, miniature golf
courses, fast-food restaurants, and "factory outlet" emporiums. A flock of tourists peopled every linear foot of it:
Stan's flatlanders; midwestern families, old folk and teens,
all looking for inexpensive and wholesome commercial
amusement. Cheap thrills.

It came as something of a relief that they'd found no va-
cancies along that strip. Even for a couple of guys accustomed to the Manhattan mainstream, this brand of the
consumer nightmare was more than either could hope to sleep
through. Eventually they found their way east to the opposite
side of the town's central business district. This was more

typical of the smalltown America they'd seen so much of in their work. Here there were banks, storefronts, crosswalks, and a post office. Weary from all the stop-and-go driving, Stan steered them on a course leading away from the craziness and into the more tranquil Ozark countryside. As he followed signs pointing the way to a town called Hollister, he was prepared to sleep on the ground if necessary.

Mr. Winkler's Three Billy Goats Gruff motel was the first they'd encountered all evening that didn't have a full complement of cars in its lot. The surrounding area was tree enshrouded and blessedly quiet. Stan turned the wheel, starting them down the gravel access toward the office.

"Ain't no fucker better walk on *my* bridge," he grumbled. "I'm whipped."

Thirteen

Bobby rousted Stan out of bed before sunup for their customary prebreakfast road work. Theirs was a routine that invariably came apart during the idle times in New York, but once they embarked on a project, fell immediately back into place. It was obvious, considering the temperature of the predawn air, that the mercury would soar once the sun got its hold on the day. They had a lot to do on this Friday, before it became too hot to function; none of the county offices would remain open over the weekend. The six miles they ran, most of the distance burned off at a demanding clip, left them feeling refreshed, their heads clear of travel and sleep.

By six-thirty they were in the car and driving along Route 76, away from Branson and through some beautiful rolling country toward the county seat in Forsyth. Nothing would be open until eight, but they wanted to eat something and get acclimatized before jumping in with both feet. Forsyth proved to be a little triangular-shaped town perched on a hillside above the shores of serpentine Lake Taney Como. They had breakfast in the heart of it, at a place called the Kountry Kettle. Stan limited himself to eggs, sausage, and wheat toast, refusing the biscuits and gravy. He was fortunate

163

to drink his coffee black, while Bobby was forced to order a glass of milk, just to have something palatable to dump into his. There wasn't a dairy product on the table; only margarine and an ersatz creamer sealed in tiny plastic tubs. Their food arrived swimming in pools of grease.

"I hope they don't plan to charge extra for this." Stan was busy trying to sponge up grease with slices of toast and setting them to one side. "What kinda shape are their arteries in around here?"

"Look around you," Bobby suggested. "See anyone who isn't overweight?"

"One old-timer, skinny as a rail, at that gas station we passed on the way in."

"Probably has an overactive thyroid. If you don't like *this* too much, you're going to just love dinner. Out here, it isn't food if it isn't fried."

They hit the sidewalk with a half hour to kill, and spent it wandering through the town as it started to awaken.

"Kill me if I start drawling like that," Stan told Bobby.

Torbeck was prone to unconsciously pick up the speech patterns and cadences of whatever region they visited. Two years ago, during their investigation of a white-supremacist group with antigovernment leanings, headquartered in the Texas/Oklahoma panhandle, he began to sound more good ol' boy than the good ol' boys themselves.

Eventually they worked their way toward a cluster of county buildings situated around a quaint open quadrangle. The County Jail and Sheriff's Department were located in buildings appended to the backside of this setup, away from the Registrar of Deeds, Registrar of Voters, Planning, County Records, and the Building Department. They had just strolled through the fuchsia-planted courtyard, moving toward the sheriff's annex, when a waddling woman of middle years raised the shade on the door to the records room and unlocked it.

"What can I help y'all with?" the matronly woman asked.

Her eyes traveled between them, openly assessing how they dressed and carried themselves.

Bobby handed her a business card. "Robert McElliot, ma'am. From Pleiades International Films. Project Development." The card informed her that Pleiades had offices in Los Angeles, New York, and Paris. "My partner here is the line producer and location scout on the television documentary movie we're here getting organized. Mr. Stanley Torbeck."

"A television movie?" The clerk was impressed. "You mean like a *Movie of the Week*?"

Bobby smiled indulgently, all jovial friendliness. "Sort of, but not exactly, ma'am. This is for *Public* Television. For a series doing in-depth exploration of current issues. This film is going to explore the abortion issue from an historical perspective. We think that 'Death of a Coed' is a very unique and special project."

Stan stepped up. "It's a *true* story, ma'am. One that took place in 1963, right here in this area. The girl had an illegal abortion and died in Branson."

The woman blanched but was not at all dissuaded in her enthusiasm. These men were talking about a movie that millions of people might see. They were talking to *her*, and that made her a part of it.

Stan pressed the advantage. "We thought that as long as we were down here, scouting the locations, we'd drop by and look at your files. I would be interested to see if they shed light on how I set up the final shooting schedule. You know, enrich the texture."

The woman had a pen and pad out in front of her on the counter now. "Nineteen sixty-three is a little before my time here. What was her name?"

"Constance Dahlrymple." Stan spelled it. "The writer puts her death on the night of January twenty-first."

"And what would you like to see? The sheriff's report?"

"And the coroner's. Please."

When the clerk disappeared into the racks of dusty file

cartons, Bobby turned to his partner, grimacing. "Enrich the *texture*?"

Nearly five minutes elapsed before the clerk returned, file in hand and a confused look on her face.

"This is odd."

"How's that, ma'am?" Stan asked.

"The sheriff's file shows a correspondin' coroner's report number, but that report is missin'. There's a gap in the numerical sequence." She laid the file on the counter and pushed it toward them. "We keep purty tight control of them files. I mean, I don't understand where it could'a got to, a file as old as that."

"This is even *more* odd." Bobby spoke the words while peering over Stan's forearm at the sheriff's account of what he'd discovered. "This says that Constance Dahlrymple was killed in an automobile accident. Driving while intoxicated. He reports that she drove her 1962 Triumph TR-3 off a cliff on Route 3, wherever that is. Two whiskey bottles found at the scene, one inside the car and another in the trunk."

Stan turned to him with an impatient scowl. "You worked with the writer on this thing. What did he do, *invent* his so-called facts?"

Bobby shrugged. "He's generally reliable. Has an impressive track record. He claimed to have done his homework."

Stan continued to study the document on the counter before him. "Seems a little fishy. We hear one story, and there isn't a coroner's report to back up the sheriff's findings. Still, we've got a problem, Bob. I don't see how we can represent this story as being true. It's a damn shame, but I don't see how we can go ahead with the project in good conscience. Not when the county she died in has something totally contrary in its records."

Bobby reached over to point to the signature scrawled at the bottom of the report. "Bosley Scranton?" He addressed this question to the clerk. "Am I making that out right?"

The clerk seemed eager to see their production put back

on track. "Yes sir. Sheriff Scranton was our number one 'round here for thirty-two years. Retired back in '85." She stopped abruptly, a funny look crossing her face. "Strange his name comes up. He was found drowned just yesterday mornin' in Bull Shoals. Fishin' an' had hisself a heart attack, they say."

Seated once again in the car, McElliot sat slouched behind the wheel, staring wordlessly into the surrounding town. Stan had one knee up, wedged against the dash on the passenger side, and his head thrown back against the rest. His eyes were closed.

"This DeWitt leans on that dead doctor and his buddy for a quarter-million bucks apiece, and we read an entirely different story of what happened. The official story. And the man who wrote it conveniently floats up dead. That doctor didn't blow his brains out just because he was gonna die of cancer, Bob. He *knew* what he'd done."

"I'd be inclined to agree. It makes you wonder what the sheriff's interest was in a cover-up. That's what we're looking at, right?"

Torbeck grunted. "It's a whitewash, bright as Tom Sawyer's fence." And as he spoke, he unwedged himself and pulled his door release. "Hang on a sec. I want to check something out."

McElliot watched as Torbeck hopped out of the car and crossed the sidewalk toward a pay phone. Amazingly, the booths in Forsyth still had directories hanging in them. Stan checked something and hurried back without making a call.

"The book doesn't have a listing for any Dahlrymples, but it does have a Bosley Scranton, living on a Rural Route 6 in Taneyville. You see that on the map?"

Bobby unfolded the thing to pore over it for a moment before holding it up, his finger on a spot just a few miles to the north. "Right here. Instead of turning this way off that bridge across the river, you go the other direction up 160. What've you got in mind?"

"We're this close. I know we want to get working on DeWitt, but maybe we ought to swing by. Talk to Scranton's old lady, if he had an old lady. If not, we can play it by ear."

McElliot swung the car around and started back through town the way they'd come. "The manager of the motel told me that the Branson paper is only a weekly. He says it might have had something about a death here in 1963, but we'd probably have better luck with the paper in Springfield. The *News-Leader*. I'm hoping to get a few more facts about who this girl was than we found in that report."

"Pretty sketchy, wasn't it? Didn't include *anything* on the car, other than the make and model. No vehicle ID number. No *plate* number. Wouldn't you expect him to record at least that basic registration info?"

"Something stinks," Bobby agreed. "But if the newspaper archives can tell us more about her, maybe we can attack it from that angle. She had to have friends."

As they gained the main road, paralleling the waters of Lake Taney Como, a sign they passed indicated a turnoff to OZARK BEACH DAM and POWER SITE. From that point, their map indicated that they were traveling alongside the headwaters of Bull Shoals Lake. Apparently, the lakes were piggyback, one on top of the other.

Taneyville turned out to be something less than a town. A post office and dueling service stations sat huddled on either side of the road, both stations with general stores attached. Half a dozen other nondescript buildings, most of them ramshackle old wooden structures in need of paint, completed the uninspired picture. Still, the surrounding country was both beautiful and sparsely populated. There wasn't a soul on the road to observe their passing through. They did that twice, driving a couple of miles north and doubling back before locating Scranton's mailbox at the end of a rutted dirt road, south of town. Bobby pulled in and followed the drive a few hundred yards up an incline and around into a flat clearing. A white clapboard two-story house sat in the middle of it, shaded by three giant oaks. In style, it wasn't a lot different than the farmhouse he'd grown up in, about a hundred miles upstate.

Stan climbed out first to circle the house, stopping to inspect the empty chicken coop with its door hanging open. McElliot remained out front, wandering around to look over the immediate layout. It had been a working farm once, with evidence that a barn, corn crib, and other outbuildings had once stood off to the east in a large, overgrown flat. A garage still stood across the drive, in good repair. The house itself was well-maintained. The columns supporting the veranda roof were whole saplings, stripped of their bark and painted a pristine white. Someone's idea of hillbilly elegance.

Torbeck emerged from around the far side. "They've already come by and collected his chickens. The crap is still fresh in the coop. And I doubt we're gonna find any old lady at home."

Bobby had also noticed the bright yellow sheriff's seal affixed to the front door and jamb, over the latch lock. Its large black lettering suggested that anyone desiring access to the premises contact the authorities first.

"What's left of the place is in pretty fair shape." He had wandered over to the door of the garage to inspect the padlock on the big swinging doors. Now he continued around the side of the structure to stand on tiptoe and rub the coat of dirt away from a high window. Stan followed.

"See anything?"

"It isn't easy. Looks like a car in there, under one of those fitted tarps."

"No shit? A sheriff in the land of Buicks and K-Cars who keeps his wheels under a fitted tarp. I think we should take a closer look, Bob."

Torbeck retrieved the tire iron from beneath the rear deck of their station wagon and wedged the flat end beneath the hasp of the garage door's padlock. One powerful jerk, with all of his 220 pounds behind it, saw the wood splinter and the hasp torn aside. Bobby stepped up to swing the double doors wide.

Light flooded in, and they followed to strip back the tarp.

A late-model Mercedes 560 SL convertible was parked beneath. White, with black top and red leather interior.

Stan whistled, long and low. "My, my. Ain't you a beaut."

Curiously, the car had Mississippi plates.

"Isn't it, though?" Bobby murmured. "Think he bought it on his county pension?"

"Nope. That there is seventy-five thou on wheels."

"Makes you curious about what we might find inside the house, doesn't it?"

"Bet your ass it does."

They discovered a transon-type window to the basement which had been pushed shut but not locked. Being the smaller of the two, Bobby slid through and worked his way upstairs to unlatch the kitchen door. A seal had been affixed there as well, and Torbeck broke it to enter. As they proceeded through the interior of the place, both kept ears tuned for the approach of visitors, though neither knew how they could effect an unobserved departure with that narrow dirt drive the only route of escape.

One room at a time, they moved methodically but with practiced swiftness through the kitchen, into the center hall and upstairs. Unlike the car parked in the garage, what they found seemed entirely typical of a residence in a rural location. The furniture was old and well worn. There were three bedrooms; one without a hint of having been recently occupied, one obviously the dead sheriff's, and one that gave them both the willies. A woman's dress, stockings, hat, and gloves were laid out on the quilt of an old iron double bed. There were cosmetics bottles, hair combs, and a brush set out atop a dressing table. A pack of Lucky Strikes and a mother-of-pearl inlaid Zippo lighter sat on an otherwise clean dresser surface. It was as if the sheriff expected this woman to be coming home tomorrow.

"Jesus," Stan murmured.

Bobby nodded. "For some people, they go from every part of their lives but their heads." He turned away from the room, moving back out into the hall. "We're missing something, Stanley. So far, that Mercedes is the only incongruity we've found.''

''There's still the front of the house, downstairs. At least we've narrowed it down.''

Five minutes later they discovered the sheriff's study, just inside the front door. Bobby was the first to advance slowly inside.

''What do we have here?''

Both of them had seen enough places professionally tossed to know the indicators without having to spot an overturned file cabinet. In one corner an armchair was shoved out of place, with indentations visible in the carpet where it had set for years. In the floor behind it the door of a safe, set in concrete, lay open. McElliot played the beam of his penlight down into it, squatting to reach inside.

Stan leaned to peer over his shoulder. ''What you got?''

One by one Bobby removed the contents of the safe and fanned them out on the floor. They were disappointly meager, but he set about examining each in turn.

''Life insurance policy.'' He opened it. ''In the amount of four hundred thousand dollars. It names a Martin Scranton as the beneficiary.''

''You wanna bet it wasn't Marty who rifled this safe?''

''No takers.'' Bobby tore the rubber band from around another wad of documents. The first was the warranty to a 1989 Mercedes 560 SL convertible. Beneath were warranties to an Evinrude outboard engine, a Toro snowblower, a GE dishwasher, and a set of matched American Tourister luggage. It was the last document that caused him to slow and lean close.

''Whoa.''

''What is it?''

''An explanation for why his car has Mississippi plates. The title. It lists the owner as a Morris Purdy, address in Pass Christian. That's one of the little port towns along the Intracoastal Waterway, east of New Orleans.''

''You think our boy was leading a double life?''

''Looks that way, doesn't it?''

"Anything else in there?"

Bobby shook his head, and Stan knelt to examine the safe door.

"This thing wasn't forced, Bob. Whoever got into it already had the combination."

McElliot dumped the contents back into the safe and rose, stretching. "Is this just beginner's luck? We've only been at it a few hours and we've discovered an awful lot of missing pieces. Significant pieces. The coroner's report from the county files. The old sheriff, who turns up conveniently dead."

"Just *yesterday*."

"And now this. I don't know what it is, but there's something missing here too."

In Tony Flood's estimation, Carter DeWitt was unsuited for the game he'd been forced, by circumstance, to play. He was bright enough to survive, but he just didn't have the instincts of a strong-arm heavy. The picture he used to guide his actions was too broad-based, its perspective running away too deep into the future. His trouble was here, now, and still he depended upon his lawyerly ways to see him through it. He spent money to buy expertise because he himself had no experience in certain crucial areas. He expected value for his dollar, because in his world money didn't just talk, it barked commands, it demanded loyalty, it soothed the wounds sustained in the trenches of corporate skirmish.

It was useful that the Coulter bitch had called to warn Carter of the trouble headed his way. Useful because Tony *did* have the tools necessary for not only playing, but winning this game. To him the fact that Terrence McElliot had been approached to help launch some sort of investigation only meant that a wild card had been dealt into the game. Flood knew who held it and how it might be played. The existence of that card might affect his strategy, but Tony wouldn't allow it to instill fear.

Tony was exhausted, having spent the thirty-six hours since Carter's Wednesday revelations on the road, organizing his own end game. He'd slept fitfully on a plane for a few hours, early yesterday morning, and was now relying on his emergency stash of methamphetamine to keep him alert as he made the trip north to Springfield from Little Rock. The Orton collection was scheduled for early that evening, and the threat of Orton's playing this out with the feds behind him was very real. McElliot hadn't had but two days to get some sort of strategy in place, but Tony had long since learned not to underestimate the power of bureaucracy. It could move when the incentive suited it. No, Flood wanted this collection to go smoothly, so that Carter and his measly couple hundred thousand would be out of his hair. Then would come the sweet part, making all this other tail-chasing worthwhile.

With what he had from the dead sheriff's safe, Tony was going to be putting the squeeze on someone for a hell of a lot more money than a few hundred thousand. And if Carter could be spooked by the mere mention of feds and a has-been like Terrence McElliot, then he didn't deserve this shot at the big brass ring. The world was populated with chicken-enshits like him. That's why the horses on the inner ranks of the carousel had seat belts.

The Springfield *News-Leader* was a bustling regional daily with pleasant enough offices and staff, all located very near the world headquarters of the Assembly of God Church and the Lester Cox Medical Center on the fringe of the old downtown. The back-edition archives were all on film. Once McElliot and Torbeck produced press credentials, a slightly overweight and overcoiffed young woman named Lisa took them under her wing.

The chairs were comfortable, the coffee they'd been offered a little weak, and after two hours of staring at the reader screen, both were beginning to suffer eye fatigue. They started with the morning of Tuesday, January 22, 1963, and worked their way through the rest of that week. The Dahlrymple death had not made the Tuesday edition, but was front page, above-the-fold news on Wednesday. That first article, and the three that followed through Saturday, provided them with a wealth of information. Matriculated as a freshman at Southwest Missouri State, right there in Springfield, she had just started her second semester at the time of her death. A year earlier she'd been elected Homecoming Queen at Branson High School, graduated as Senior Class valedictorian, and been awarded a small scholarship by the First Baptist Church. She was survived by her mother Ruth, of Forsyth, and two sisters.

According to Dr. Solokowski, the girl had worked as a volunteer for Franklin Coulter's 1962 senatorial campaign. It was a reach, but maybe they could run across an article or photograph of Constance Dahlrymple somewhere on the campaign trail. If a photo caption or news article mentioned her, then it might also name one or more coworkers.

Easier said than found. There was plenty in that year's papers about the Senate race, but mostly about the challenge being mounted against the incumbent, and not the incumbent himself. Franklin Coulter, already a two-termer, was being considered something of a shoo-in when a dark horse by the name of Harold Appleton came charging to the fore of the Republican ranks from off a mid-state hog farm. He was outspoken, charmingly rustic, and just enough of an old-time populist to catch at least part of the electorate's fancy. Franklin Coulter had been forced to actually campaign for a change. Phillip DeWitt was put in charge of that campaign in early August, when it became apparent that too much had been taken for granted. DeWitt, seeking to take advantage of the Kennedy/Peace Corps fervor gripping the nation's idealistic youth, had gone onto college campuses across the state, looking for legions of student volunteers. One article, late in the campaign, spoke of how Richard Coulter, the senator's charismatic twenty-eight-year-old son, had been put in charge of organizing these volunteers. Apparently, the ploy worked. They recruited nearly two thousand canvassers. Torbeck turned the spool crank to bring up the front page of the

Backfire

Wednesday, November seventh edition, and they saw their first photographic evidence that Constance Dahlrymple had been one of the volunteers on that winning team.

"Whoa! Hold it right there!" McElliot was hunched forward in his chair, staring hard at a photograph dominating most of the top half of the front page, just below the headline:

COULTER CLEANS UP!

Pictured in the foreground was a beaming Franklin Coulter, standing on a rostrum at what looked like his campaign headquarters. There were streamers and bunting in the familiar stars and stripes motif. And behind him, directly to his left, stood his son Richard and the man Bobby recognized from a childhood visit to Aurora as Phillip DeWitt. Strange, he'd forgotten having ever met the man, but now the face came back; a city slicker who'd stayed behind when the rest of the gang saddled up to ride out across the range after breakfast.

And there was the jubilant, ecstatic face of a beautiful girl who stood between and just half a step behind them. There was no mistaking her identity.

"Well, lookee that," Torbeck muttered. "You see any *other* campaign volunteers in that picture?"

"Right up there on the winner's platform," Bobby agreed. "I think Franklin told Dad there were hoards of volunteers. Too many to remember any one specifically."

"Maybe, but forgetting this one would be like forgetting the young Audrey Hepburn."

They had seen the high-school picture used with stories about the tragic accident. It depicted a dark-haired girl of rare, delicate beauty. Torbeck leaned closer now to study that face more intently, along with those of the three men. "Nope, that ain't a face you'd miss in a crowd. Not if you've got red blood in your veins. And judging from the way these three are standing"—he pointed to DeWitt, Richard Coulter, and the Dahlrymple girl—"good old Phil may have been the guy fucking her, but all three of them definitely knew each other."

"I want a copy of that," McElliot said. He checked his watch and stretched. "Then I think we'd better get set up on Dr. Orton."

Tony Flood arrived to park his Jeep Cherokee in one of the spaces outside the Cox Medical Center's office wing just minutes before Dr. Erv Orton emerged, carrying a briefcase. The meth Tony had ingested six hours earlier was beginning to wear thin, and he had the little square of chemical paper unfolded on his lap as he prepared to recharge his batteries. With the tip of his commando knife dug gently into the pile of powder, he watched Orton climb into his black BMW, buckle up, and turn it over. The drug burned like holy hell, going up into Flood's nostrils. Eyes watering, he hurriedly refolded his stash, dropped it into the breast pocket of his shirt, and got his own vehicle under way.

Orton left the lot to drive a few blocks south and then west to a branch office of the Landmark Bank. Two o'clock; only an hour before the close of business for the weekend. The doctor was cutting it close. When he left his car, he carried the briefcase with him, and emerged from the bank twenty minutes later, empty-handed.

Flood sat up a little straighter in his seat and hunched forward over the wheel to watch Orton as he hurried across the sidewalk to unlock the driver's door of the BMW. Everything had gone without a hitch to this juncture. There was no evidence of the doctor being either accompanied or followed. So what was he doing without the damn briefcase? Where was the money?

And then, with an abruptness that looked as phony to Flood as a whore's orgasm, Orton straightened as if he'd forgotten something, turned, and hurried back into the bank. When he reappeared less than a minute later, he had the briefcase in hand. Tony was at a loss to figure out what the hell was going on, but whatever he'd just observed seemed to indicate he should proceed cautiously.

Fourteen

McElliot and Torbeck spent a few minutes in the car, studying the map, before departing the *News-Leader* offices in search of Dr. Orton's home in Wildwood Estates. On the surface, Springfield didn't look a lot different to them than cities like Omaha, Nebraska, or Oxnard, California. Like so many places, it started with an older, concentrated core and sprawled outward. Much of the downtown was decayed and in the process of being revitalized. The railroad, once the city's lifeline, cut the downtown off from an area of less desirable residential areas to the north, while miles of newer, wider thoroughfares ran south past strip malls, fast-food eateries, and corporate clusters. Most everything they passed, going south, was clean. In all, it was totally uninspired, but seemed to indicate a healthy economic climate.

"You digested enough of that breakfast grease to think about lunch?" Torbeck asked. "It's two o'clock, and for some reason my stomach ain't growling yet."

"It's still in shock. Let's skip it and hang this wire. I like our chances of doing it unobserved while it's still the middle of the workday."

One of the items of equipment they carried was an external

phone-line tap with a low frequency transmitter. Their plan was to do Orton's house first and then return downtown after business hours to do his office. They had the doctor's address culled from the local directory, and followed the map to a remote, semirural location well south of the city where an up-market developer had created an exclusive enclave over-looking Lake Springfield. Torbeck, the gadget expert, was relieved to see that the two-acre-lot parcels were going to afford him plenty of shrub cover. Every residence on Orton's Melbourne Road was spaced at intervals of at least two hundred feet.

"That would be it there." McElliot pointed to a brick and shingle house nestled down below the road, set back about fifty feet, on the lake side. The surrounding grounds were planted with a variety of ornamental bushes; several decid-uous, but most of the evergreen variety. The house itself was overhung with a pair of huge oaks.

"The good doctor hasn't done so bad for himself," Stan observed. As he spoke, his eyes were tracing the phone line away from the roadside pole and down to a spot at one end of the house enshrouded in a clump of sculpted cedar.

"And if I'm not mistaken"—Bobby pointed to a Cadillac Allante parked half in and half out of the garage—"someone is home."

The car's convertible top was down and the trunk lid up. A set of golf clubs leaned against the rear bumper.

"Wife or girlfriend," Stan announced.

"You prescient?"

"The pink pom-poms. No self-respecting man would carry anything like that on his woods. So. You ready to stroll up there and distract her with your charm while I do the dirty work?" He pointed. "That house over there on the left looks pretty sleepy, the drapes drawn like that. Let's go back around so you can drop me off up there. I'll work my way back."

"Good plan," Bobby growled. "And I'll pretend to be the Avon lady."

Minutes later Torbeck was dropped off to skulk away into

178

the undergrowth while McElliot swung the wagon around and pulled up in front of the Orton residence. He took a moment to remove a different card from his wallet than the one presented to the Forsyth records clerk, grabbed a notebook, and climbed out to walk down a winding path to the front door. Stan, meanwhile, found the going even easier than expected. He'd dodged his way along a shallow depression between this and the next house, found cover behind a natural rock outcropping, and was kneeling next to Orton's phone junction box before his partner emerged from their parked car. The line-monitoring device he had was state of the art; a tiny unit, not much bigger than a standard Zippo cigarette lighter, that was automatically activated each time the line was engaged. Its low frequency transmitter was capable of broadcasting to a minicassette receiving unit up to 150 yards away. Installation required no more than a screwdriver to remove the junction-box cover. Within seconds of reaching his current position, Stan was clipping the unit to the red and green terminal bolts.

No sooner had he lifted the receiving unit and switched it to the test mode than the device kicked on, tape starting to roll past the recording heads. Surprised, Stan jammed an earplug into the monitor jack and fitted the ivory plastic piece into his ear.

"Helen and I played Shady Rest today instead of the country club, and you know that dogleg to the right on the sixteenth over there? Third time I've played that course this month, and I did it *again*, Beulah! I put my tee shot right into that nasty old bunker in the crook. I swear, my game has gone to H in a handbasket. Hang on, will you? I think I hear the door."

Torbeck unplugged the earpiece, replaced the junction cover, and began retracing his steps.

"Yes?"

Mrs. Orton certainly fit the doctor's wife image that McElliot had in his mind. Terminal tan. Straight, silver-gray hair cut short in the active woman's bob. Thin, muscular legs in British walking shorts, flat-chested torso in a country-club-crested polo shirt, possessed of a handsome if not slightly pinched face. At the moment she was barefoot. Bobby guessed her age to be around sixty.

"Tom Treadwell. Equinox Features Syndicate. Missus . . . ah?" He handed her his card.

"Orton," she replied, examining the thing closely.

"I'm the production manager for a feature film we're shooting here in the Springfield area, and I'm out here in advance of the crew, scouting locations."

Betty Orton's look roved over this handsome, healthy specimen, settling finally in direct contact with his eyes.

"And what is it that I can help you with, Mr. Treadwell?"

The woman's manner was openly flirtatious. Bobby took advantage, adjusting his posture toward an appearance of casual ease. With it, he flashed a conspiratorial smile.

"The featured character in this film is a girl in her late teens who comes from a very nice home in a good neighborhood. I've been scouting Springfield from one end to the other, and until I drove down Melbourne Road, I hadn't found a thing that satisfied me. Your house is, I think you'd be proud to admit, the nicest of any on this side of the street, facing the lake. It is *exactly* what I've been visualizing."

He had her. Betty Orton was mesmerized.

"Please don't go away, Mr. Treadmill. I was right in the middle of a phone call. Come in, please. I'll go hang up."

Bobby stepped just a few feet inside the door, leaving it open. It *was* a nice place, with glass all along the north side of a sunken living room, affording a pleasant view of the lake below. While the lady of the house was away, completing her call, a black, Seven-series BMW pulled into the drive outside. He turned to watch as a spare, distinguished-looking gent climbed out and approached, carrying a briefcase. Up above, on the street, he saw the passenger door of the Taurus open. An instant later Stan's head appeared. The man in the suit had to be Dr. Orton.

* * *

Ervin Orton's briefcase was packed loosely with banded, five-thousand-dollar stacks of hundred-dollar bills. All the way home he'd been as nervous as the manager of his bank had been, filling out the disclosure papers required by the IRS and handing such a sum over to him. Erv had tried to effect the same casual bravado as he'd used on his Merrill Lynch broker, speaking of a once-in-a-lifetime investment opportunity and the necessity of having the cash right at hand. In an effort to put any overly eager bank employees off the scent of such a sum, he'd requested access to his safe deposit box and feigned stashing the cash. It hadn't been easy for him to leave his briefcase on the manager's desk, walk out of the bank, and return as though he'd forgotten it.

He could only hope the ruse had worked. As he drove south through Springfield toward his home, Erv felt absolutely exposed. The driver of every car he passed knew he had that small fortune there on the seat beside him. Twice he would have sworn that a white Jeep Cherokee was following him, only to lose it in his rearview and have it reappear, three miles later. He knew, with what little rational clarity he had left, that the world was full of white Jeeps; that nobody who glanced over at him on the road was doing any more than admiring his seventy-thousand-dollar car.

All that raging paranoia left Erv in an easily excitable state. When he parked in the drive and hurried to the house, the man he discovered standing inside his front door gave him quite a scare.

"Who the hell are you?" he demanded. There was not only heat in his voice, but as the adrenaline level rose in his bloodstream, beads of cold sweat broke out across his forehead and soaked the armpits of his shirt.

"He's from the movies, Erv!"

Orton glanced up to see Betty hurrying toward him from the kitchen. "A location scout . . . and he loves our home!"

The doctor scowled at this casually dressed man with the notebook clutched in one hand. "You're a *what*?"

"His name is Tom Treadwell. From the Equinox Features Syndicate." Betty pushed the card toward her husband. To take it, he had to shift the briefcase from one hand to the other. "They want to use our house in a movie."

Betty was as high-strung as a thoroughbred racehorse. Since childhood she'd been indulged by her entrepreneur father, and had come into her marriage with expectations of those indulgences continuing. For thirty-two years Erv had struggled to meet her expectations, while growing to hate her obsession with being seen in all the right places, with all the right people. He hadn't had the guts to tell her that he was being blackmailed to the tune of a quarter-million dollars and that they might have to tighten their belts a bit. This movie business was all he needed right now.

"Listen," he told the young man. "My wife is a bit of an enthusiast, but we are really very private people." As he spoke he handed the card back. "I'm afraid you're going to have to find someone else's house for your movie."

He'd passed through the entry hall and stood now, expecting the young man to thank them for their time and excuse himself. Instead, their visitor closed the front door.

"My name isn't Tom Treadwell and Equinox Features doesn't exist, Doctor."

The man knew Orton's profession, and that was nearly as disconcerting as the new, icy edge in his speech. His accent wasn't from around here, but did have some sort of regional familiarity.

"My name isn't important," the young man continued. "Let it suffice to say that I represent a certain prominent man's many interests. I'm retained, if you will, to resolve, ah, *problems* that come up from time to time."

Orton was stricken. He backed slowly toward the wrought-iron railing that separated the entry from the living room, stumbling and nearly falling as he came up against it. Betty turned on him.

"What is this about, Ervin?"

"It's a private matter, Betty." Orton turned to his visitor.

"I'm sorry, but I will *not* discuss this any further in front of my wife."

The man's gray eyes had turned cold. "I think she should hear this too, Doctor." Everything about him suggested competence, from his imposing stature to the way the veins crisscrossed his muscular forearms.

"I . . . I wish you wouldn't insist on that," Orton begged. The man lifted his eyebrows and slowly shook his head.

"I'm here to see *all* the cards laid on the table, Doctor."

Betty was beside herself. "What *cards*, Ervin? This is an outrage, this man coming into our home like this."

"Shut it!" It was delivered quietly, but the young man put enough cold steel in it to freeze Betty's tongue. "My employer thinks that he might have a problem, and I intend to see it cleared up before I go anywhere. You and I are going to reach an understanding, Doctor."

Orton found himself gripping the rail behind him with such force that his hands ached. Beside him, Betty moved to create as much distance as she could between herself and their visitor.

"My employer is concerned about a conversation he had with your friend, Dr. Solokowski, last Monday morning. In that conversation your friend tried to implicate my employer in a nasty piece of business you engaged in with a Mr. Phillip DeWitt. He would like your assurance that you don't share your friend's opinion of him."

Betty Orton, even in her terrified state, couldn't contain her curiosity. "Who is he talking about, Ervin?! Why don't I know anything about this?"

Orton scowled, trying to force himself to confront the young man's hard stare. He ignored his wife.

"Any business I did with Phillip DeWitt was just between him and me. You can assure Franklin Coulter that I have no intention of implicating him in *anything*."

The young man smiled a vicious, narrow-eyed smirk. "I never mentioned Franklin Coulter, Doctor."

"Franklin *Coulter*?" Betty blurted it. "What nasty piece

of business have you ever been involved in with Franklin Coulter?''

Again Orton ignored her. "Then tell your *employer* that there is no problem. That I understand his position and respect it. That I know I'd be a fool not to.''

The young man simply nodded, turned, and opened the front door. In the next moment he was gone. The ensuing, dead silence that hung in the entry hall reeked of fear.

"Ervin. I demand to know what in the name—''

Orton took an abrupt step forward, raising his hand as his face went purple with rage.

"Shut *up*, Betty! Don't you say another *word*!''

Where Melbourne Road had a ninety-degree turn in it at its west end, it became Chapala Drive. Tony Flood had slowed to park just short of that bend as his subject proceeded along to turn down into his driveway. From his slightly elevated vantage, Tony had a clear view of the house when the big, rugged-looking blond man appeared skulking along a rock ledge to the left of it. The guy ran up a little depression in the terrain and dove behind the cover of a parked Ford Taurus wagon. With an alarm klaxon shrieking in his mind, Flood watched the way the man lifted his head to observe Erv Orton's progress through the car windows until he entered his home. Then the man opened the passenger door to climb in and sit with his head down.

Flood grabbed his field glasses from the glove box to get a better look at this interloper. From his angle he was able to peer down into the car with good visibility. His first assumption, that Mrs. Orton had been caught stepping out with the golf pro from the club, was called into question when the man made no attempt to escape. Instead he tossed a canvas tote into the backseat and set about extending the antenna of a tiny gray box held in his right hand. The field glasses immediately swung back down across the landscape to follow the rock ledge in its path toward a clump of cedars at the west end of the house. Directly above, the phone line ran in from the road to a terminus up under the eaves.

The guy had hung a wire, and that meant he probably wasn't the golf pro. Tony's mind raced as he reached into the backseat for his own investigator's bag of tricks. The blue plastic telephone lineman's handset he removed from it was generally used to check a group of lines in a large terminal board before hanging a wire of his own on a specifically targeted number. Right now it was his only hope of being able to determine what this other character's interest might be. Carefully, he let himself out of the Jeep to steal across Melbourne Road.

Dr. Orton and his wife were left to fight it out as McElliot hurried back up the path to the street. He'd been surprised by the doctor's midday appearance, and had made a split-second decision to wing it. They'd intended to monitor telephone conversations over the weekend, hoping to get something incriminating on the cardiologist. Instead he'd seen an immediate opening and gone for broke.

So how had he done? Had he hit the nail on the head or mangled it? Generally, his tight-spot instincts and reactions were pretty good, but right now, as he opened the driver's door and climbed behind the wheel, he was having his doubts.

"Sorry, Bob," Stan apologized. "There was no way to warn you. That sucker came outta nowhere."

McElliot started the car without a word, drove it to a spot across and a hundred yards up the street, and pulled up to park. He then leaned his head back and closed his eyes.

"I guess we can count ourselves lucky that he didn't see you climbing out of his bushes."

"So how'd it go?"

With his eyes still closed, Bobby shrugged. "Only time will tell. I was standing there, suddenly confronted with a golden opportunity to either speed or screw things up, so I goosed him." He went on to recount how he'd taken a flyer at putting the fear of God into Orton, in front of his wife.

"So what the fuck?" Stan told him. "Now's as good a time as any, ain't it?"

"You're starting to drawl, Stanley."

The single-frequency, minicassette receiver had been hooked into a two-inch auxiliary speaker and sat propped on the open glove-box door at Torbeck's knees. A tiny red light nestled atop it suddenly started to glow, indicating phone activity. Stan adjusted the gain knob.

Flood was midway along the rock ledge when the door to the house opened and the second man emerged to ascend the path and climb behind the wheel of the Ford. This one wasn't as large as his friend, but was still good-sized, moving with assurance. Tony watched as the car started away from the curb, moving diagonally across the street to park again about a hundred yards farther along. They were waiting for something, and there was no time to waste.

"Hello?" The voice came on nearly the instant Tony clipped on to the junction terminals and thumbed the handset into action. It was tinny but very clear.

"DeWitt? Orton."

A slight pause, and then: "This had better be an emergency, Doc, and not some lame excuse for why you haven't got the money together."

"Franklin Coulter just sent one of his thugs around to shake me down," Orton retorted. "Right in front of my wife. I'd call that an emergency, wouldn't you, DeWitt?"

"He did *what*?"

Flood listened intently as Orton proceeded to relate the essence of his encounter with the uninvited guest.

"Son of a *bitch*!" Carter hissed. "That was some friend you had there, Doc. Seems he's *still* causing you problems."

"He's causing *me* problems? This is all your fault, young fella! Damn it; I thought this payoff was supposed to buy me some peace of mind."

DeWitt could be heard to chuckle. "Add it up, *Doctor*. I only have a financial interest in your secret. Coulter obvi-

ously has *other* interests . . . like not seeing it in the papers
Monday morning. Franklin Coulter sent that man because
he's scared. Your friend Solokowski was scared enough to
blow his brains out. Everyone is scared, except me. You'll
pay me this evening and be glad you're still on my good side.
I appreciate this call.''

There was an audible click as the line went dead.

"Bingo," Torbeck murmured.

"Every once in a while . . ." McElliot said, the relief
obvious in his voice. "Must be all that clean living."

Stan quickly rewound the tape and listened to make sure
they'd gotten the conversation clearly. When it concluded, he
switched the player off and started scanning the roadside. To
enable them to monitor other calls, he needed a place to hide
the receiver. "Some interesting notions surface," he mused.
"Like maybe Franklin Coulter *does* have something to hide."

"You get that feeling too?"

Torbeck nodded. "Solokowski seemed to think so. DeWitt
sounded like his own suspicions were being confirmed. And
Orton wouldn't have taken your bait if it wasn't on his mind
as well."

"DeWitt said the payoff is scheduled for this evening, and
judging from the way Orton was carrying that briefcase, the
money is already in the house." Bobby glanced at the time.
"Quarter of three. What do you figure 'this evening' means?"

"What's on your mind?"

"Constance Dahlrymple. I'd like to take a run by the registrar's office at Southwest Missouri State before they close
for the weekend. See what we can dig up there that'll give
us something to chew on until Monday."

Torbeck thought it over while picking up the map to find
the university and figure the quickest route.

"Looks like a fifteen-minute drive, this time of day. Once
rush hour starts, you can probably double that. It's smack in
the middle of town."

"So figure forty-five minutes, round trip. If we left now,

we'd have an hour there, and a chance to set up something else for tomorrow if it starts to get interesting. We could be back here by quarter of five.''

Torbeck pointed to the road ahead. "So what are we waiting for?''

Within seconds of breaking Erv Orton's connection, Carter DeWitt was punching in the Coulter family's Washington number. It was a desperation move, surely, but even though Francine had threatened to cut him off and see him in jail, he hoped that she was still a good enough friend to tell him what the hell was happening. All that bravado he'd slung at Erv Orton over the phone had no substance to it. As he spoke the words, he'd stood watching his last desperate play slip away.

The Coulter housekeeper answered to inform him that Francine was away at the health club and not expected to return before dinner. Carter left no message. When the doctor called, he'd been sunbathing. Now he pulled chinos over his Speedo briefs, jammed his feet into loafers, and threw on a madras sport shirt. That quarter-million dollars was his birthright. Even if Francine couldn't confirm his suspicions, he knew they had to be correct. It would be just like Franklin to mount a rearguard action. Trusting Terrence McElliot to launch an effective Treasury investigation would be too much like putting all his eggs into one basket. Carter knew that he no longer had a lock on gracefully bailing himself out of his current dilemma. He was going to have to scramble. If Flood was doing his job, he would hopefully have some line on who these Coulter interlopers were. Tony would know whether it was safe to push the timetable up a few hours, move in and collect the cash. Once he had his hands on the money, Carter figured he'd have a clear enough head to think about the next step. On his way out the door he grabbed a fresh pack of Camel filters. He'd quit smoking the day his father dropped dead, but kept a carton of butts handy, to test his will. Right now he didn't give a damn about any will but the will to survive. Behind the wheel of his sweltering-hot Lincoln, he shook one out and lit it before starting the sixty-mile, hour-and-a-quarter trip to Wildwood Estates. Nearly suffocating with the heat, he ran the climate control up to maximum cool.

The wire hung on Orton's phone was so up-to-date that Tony hadn't yet seen that particular model, and he made it a point to keep abreast of developments in the field. His gut feeling told him that the interlopers were feds, and that led him to wonder precisely how long they'd been here in the field. The way they moved, their size, and the way they'd made their approach told him that they were definitely cream of the current federal-enforcement crop. It was interesting that Treasury had chosen to go at Orton this way, literally through his front door. They hadn't sought to enlist his aid, but were attempting to frighten him into something . . . like making that call. Orton had been effectively shaken right down to the shoestrings and fooled into playing into their hands.

When the cardiologist answered the door, he was expecting to see the man who'd just left. From where he stood, Flood could see Orton's wife standing a few yards behind in the entry hall, looking more angry than apprehensive. Both of their faces registered confusion as they were confronted by this second, also unfamiliar, visitor. Tony saw no sense in waiting for either of them to invite him in.

Orton never saw the blow that broke his nose. It knocked him stumbling backward and to the floor, his wife watching him fall in open-mouthed horror. Blood flew in bright crimson splashes across the toes of her shoes, and as she turned to flee, Erv's attacker was on her next. One moment she'd turned and was moving away toward the living room, and the next, a hand caught a fistful of her hair, jerking her head back hard. Out of reflex, Betty tried to turn her gaze, attempting to read the man's intention in his eyes. It was then that she saw the glitter of bright steel and felt the cold, sharp prick at her throat.

Flood waited until the writhing doctor had recovered. Eventually he ceased his moaning to focus on the sinister commando knife being held at his wife's throat.

"Wh-What do you want?" His hand reached up tentatively to touch his nose. He was close to sixty years old and probably hadn't suffered a blow of such ferocious impact since childhood. The pain of his own touch saw him wince and work to swallow a yelp.

"I want the briefcase, Doctor."

"M-*My* briefcase?" The man wasn't much of an actor, but at least he was game. "I-I left it at m-my office."

In a flash of action that stunned the cardiologist to the core of his being, Flood spun Betty, threw her hard against the nearest wall, and whipped that knife laterally across her abdomen. Almost instantly a bright crimson line appeared along the dead-straight rent in her shirt, just below her breasts. Betty Orton screamed, clutching at herself in a desperate effort to staunch the flow of blood. Erv watched in horror, struggling to his knees.

"The briefcase, Doctor. The same one my partner just watched you carry in here."

"Ah-Ah-Ah-On th-the t-top shelf. In th-the c-closet." He lifted a hand to point toward the door at his wife's hip. "Y-You d-didn't have t-to do th-that. Sh-She d-didn't k-know."

"Well, now she does, shit-bird." In his impatience, Flood kicked the wounded woman aside to open the door and pull the case down from an overhead shelf. Setting it on the floor, he knelt to thumb the latches. It was packed loosely with banded packets of hundred-dollar bills. Several were selected at random, notes pulled from them for closer examination. When he ran them through a series of rudimentary checks, they proved authentic.

Flood surveyed the doctor's pleading face as he closed the case, hoisting it by the handle as he turned to leave.

"You might tell your friend DeWitt how much Franklin Coulter 'preciates the donation."

Fifteen

Southwest Missouri State University was a good-sized institution sprawling over a large section of central Springfield, with an enrollment of nearly seventeen thousand. Founded just after the turn of the century, its central core, including the administration building, had a substantial, brick-constructed dignity about it. The rest of the place was an architectural hodgepodge, each new addition reflecting something of its era's dreams.

The recently launched academic year was in full swing as the partners parked in a fire zone and hurried across an open, tree-dotted quad. They paused to ask directions of a kid in an acid-washed denim jacket and were pointed toward a big building, dead ahead. The student was relatively sure that the registrar's office was somewhere on the second floor.

"Definitely not a geography major," Torbeck commented, his eyes sweeping the terrain before him, assessing the local talent. "Been awhile since I've been on a college campus. Kinda makes me feel depraved to realize I used to screw girls this young."

"You still do."

191

"Be nice, Bob. So what line of shit do we feed to this crowd? Another film project?"

McElliot shook his head. "Time is too short. I suggest we go the legit route. Nothing like having a couple T-men come calling to stir up a lazy Friday afternoon."

They discovered the registrar's office on the first floor instead of the second, but soon learned that administrative records were kept in an archive upstairs. The keeper of that particular domain was an attractive, prematurely gray woman of around forty, with huge blue eyes and an easy smile. The little gold Treasury-agent badges seemed to impress her as McElliot explained that while their time was short, the information they sought was conveniently specific.

"I'm sorry we can't explain further," he apologized. "But we're investigating certain circumstances surrounding the death of a girl who enrolled as a freshman here in 1962 and was killed in a car crash in late January of '63."

The archivist, who had introduced herself as Holly Reed, moved immediately to a computer terminal and stood with her fingers poised above the keyboard.

"Most everything has been moved from hard copy to computer data base since then. We keep photographs and other pertinent documents on microfilm. Her transcript file will give us the corresponding cross-reference numbers to her film file."

Bobby spelled the Dahlrymple girl's full name, and moments later the abbreviated transcript came up on the monitor screen.

"Yes. She only completed one semester. Major declared as Political Science. Here, take a look."

The archivist swung the monitor on its swivel base, affording the partners a clear view. From it they learned that Constance Dahlrymple had been born in Walnut Shade, Missouri, on March 9, 1946; graduated Branson High School with a cumulative GPA of 3.96; enrolled at SWMSU with a major in Political Science and had taken four courses that first semester.

After digesting these and very few other meager facts, Torbeck turned to Holly Reed. "There was mention of a church scholarship made in the newspaper articles about her death. Where would her financial information be kept?"

"That's all on film," she replied. "Hang on a minute."

A sequence of reference numbers was copied onto a scrap of paper which she then took into a back room. The efficiency of her system was impressive. She emerged only a few minutes later with a microfilm cassette in hand.

"This would contain everything else we've kept on her. I have to warn you that there may not be much. It's expensive to duplicate every scrap of file paper on film. If the staff didn't consider it important, it was thrown out."

Once the file on their subject was located on the film-reader screen, all three of them began to read as Holly Reed slowly cranked the information across their field of view. The first document it contained was the dead girl's original application for financial aid. Much of the information recorded there only served to confirm what they already managed to glean from articles at the *News-Leader*. Constance Dahlrymple was the dependent of a single parent, residing in Forsyth. She'd been given scholarship moneys in the amount of five hundred dollars from the Branson First Baptist Church. Her mother's assets and income were well within the range qualifying her for maximum assistance.

In the follow-up document they read the offer of aid made to her by the university. In a combination of state and federal money, along with a low-interest student loan, she was being fully funded. Then Torbeck spotted something.

"Hold on. She paid the loan *back*?" He pointed to an attached record of full repayment.

Holly scanned it. "Not just the loan. The entire aid package." She pointed to a section in the middle of the form. "And this indicates that her tuition and dormitory fees were paid in full for the remainder of that academic year."

The next document was a copy of her dorm-lease agreement with the university, amended on the first of January,

1963, to reflect that Constance Dahlrymple was no longer being subsidized by the financial-aid office.

"Look at this," McElliot murmured, pointing. "A fee paid on a dorm parking permit for a 1962 Triumph TR-3, license number TJA-673." He turned to Stan. "Why didn't that occur to me? This poor kid from the hills was driving a brand-new sports car the night she died. Where'd she get it? And where did she get the money to pay all those school costs?"

Torbeck shrugged, turning to Holly Reed. "Can we have copies of these?"

Back out on the street, moving south through early rush-hour traffic on Campbell Avenue, Torbeck and McElliot tried to put their information in perspective. They'd spent only forty minutes inside the registrar's archives and had plenty of time to make it back to Dr. Orton's neighborhood before five. Still behind the wheel, McElliot was speaking.

"It wasn't obtained legally, but that tape will probably be enough for Strahan to coax a prosecutor aboard. Hell, confronted with it, DeWitt might even be frightened enough to make a deal."

"He's a lawyer, Bob. He'd want to see the authorizing warrant."

"True," McElliot allowed. "You'd need to couple the tape with Orton's threatened testimony in order to really scare him. Orton had the money in that briefcase. I saw the look on his face when he discovered me standing inside his front door."

Stan grinned. "Damn. I'll bet he nearly shit his pants."

"For all I know, he *did*. A simple investigation of his recent financial transactions will show that he's liquidated certain assets and converted them to cash. Confronted with that evidence *and* the tape, he'll make any deal the prosecutor asks him to make."

"Especially if it doesn't involve him going to jail." Torbeck paused, thinking back over their analysis. "So when you add it up, we've already done what the boss man asked us to do. He wouldn't want to arrest DeWitt without a prosecutor in place to start making deals.''

McElliot knew that his partner was right. "Even if we took him down holding the bag, the only thing we could possibly charge him with is unlawful possession of currency.''

"And we'd have a tough time showing reasonable cause for search and seizure without bringing Franklin Coulter into it. We can't use the tape, and Coulter's the guy the dead doctor talked to. I suggest we dump it back into Strahan's lap.''

They'd reached the intersection with Weaver Road, where Bobby went left, still headed toward the Orton home in Wildwood Estates.

"So I guess we've got a decision to make. Do we sit around outside the good doctor's house all night, in hopes of getting pictures of what DeWitt could claim is a social call, or do we fly back to D.C. and let the front office run with it from here?''

Torbeck had reached out to fiddle with the knobs and buttons of the car radio, searching the dial. He settled on a country station playing a George Jones tune. In the lyric, the possum was asking who'd chop his baby's kindling when he was gone.

"Me? I'd like to spend another day digging into this dead sheriff's story. Him turning up dead right now is a huge coincidence. Maybe too huge. I'm wondering if an autopsy's been performed. It could change the whole way Strahan wants to approach DeWitt if we turn up something that points toward the old lawman being the victim of foul play.''

"Then there's this new data we've got on Constance Dahlrymple,'' Bobby added. "I'm curious to know what Missouri Motor Vehicles has on that Triumph. It's an expensive little car for a poor girl from the sticks to be driving. We know *somebody* got her pregnant, and now it's starting to look like she was being kept.''

George Jones wound it up and the radio station launched into its quarter-hourly news update.

"To repeat the story coming to us from Washington, D.C., this afternoon: former Secret Service director Terrence McElliot was found murdered in Rock Creek Park today when a golfer left the fairway to search for his ball in heavy undergrowth along the creek bank. McElliot, the son-in-law of recently deceased former United Nations Ambassador Michael Harrington, had been shot once in the head and is presumed to have been dead for several days. FBI and Washington Metropolitan police have no report of McElliot being reported missing, and no motive . . ."

The car swerved crazily, nearly skidding off the road. Torbeck reached over to fight Bobby for control of the wheel. The rest of the announcer's description was lost on them as their hearts thundered in their ears and both broke into cold sweats.

Stan's voice seemed to come at Bobby from down a long tunnel, shouting but barely discernible. "Pull it *over*, Bob! Just stop the fucking car!"

The next thing McElliot knew, they were off the shoulder and Stan was running around to the driver's door to jerk it open and unclip his sear belt.

"C'mon, buddy. We're gonna get you out of there for some air. You just about killed us both."

From the depths of numbing shock, Bobby forced himself to form words. "Tell me I didn't hear what I think I heard."

Stan's face and voice softened. "We both heard him the same, Bob. I'm awful goddam sorry."

It had all the earmarks of a filling-station sting. Carter had been low on gas and pulled into a Texaco station just beyond Billings. It was two in the afternoon and he hadn't eaten since breakfast. The nervous churning he'd experienced since Erv Orton's call was making his stomach sour, so after asking the pimply, shiftless attendant to fill it, he'd crossed to the station office for a diet Dr Pepper and a Snickers bar. He emerged just as the kid was slamming the hood, saying his water and oil were just fine. And why shouldn't they be? The car didn't have six thousand miles on it. Minutes later, halfway up Route 60, between Billings and Republic, three miles from *any*where, not one, but two of his engine belts snapped.

Once, while drinking in a bar in upstate Louisiana, he'd overheard a patron telling stories of working the service-station circuit in Wyoming, Colorado, and Utah. To hear him, there were places all over America where the men working the pumps paid the owner for the opportunity to ply their trade. The deal they struck was a simple one; for every tire or accessory they sold, they got a straight percentage of the above-wholesale net profit. Preying on city slickers, geriatrics, and road-weary pilgrims a long way from home, they employed linoleum knives concealed in grease rags to cut belts and slash tires; shorted batteries dead with screwdrivers; told tall tales of death on the highway . . . of fictional family men who had failed to heed a particular manufacturer's defective-tire recall. The gullible were fair game, or anyone who was fool enough to leave his car unattended to call his private investigator and grab a candy bar.

Tony hadn't been in his room at the Kearney Street Super 8, but with the developments Orton had reported, that fact meant that he was probably out doing his job. More immediately, Carter would be damned if he was going *back* to that same Texaco. Instead he walked the three miles ahead into Republic and engaged the owner of a Phillips 66 station to tow the car. It was five-thirty before he got back on the road, and nearly six by the time he entered Erv Orton's Wildwood Estates neighborhood. With every minute he'd been stalled, his paranoia grew. His inability to locate Flood's Cherokee on any of the area roads did nothing to bolster his confidence. By the time he reached Melbourne Road, he was convinced that Franklin Coulter's thugs were laying for him. Still no Tony. Reasoning it out, he concluded that the investigator was no longer watching the Orton house, but sticking with the new threat. It made sense that they were probably lying in ambush somewhere nearby, waiting until he was out alone on some remote stretch of pavement before making their move. He hoped that Tony was armed. Fool that he was, Carter hadn't brought along the Colt Python .357 that his father kept locked in the gun cabinet.

While cold sweat soaked the armpits and side panels of his madras shirt, Carter made some decisions. To elude anyone who might be keeping an eye out for his arrival, he parked his Lincoln nearly half a mile away from Orton's house and climbed out to scramble down through the brush and rock-strewn terrain to the railroad tracks running east-west along the shore of Lake Springfield. Once gaining them, he started west and approached the doctor's home on foot, out of sight of Melbourne Road. Everything appeared tranquil as Carter eased cautiously from tree to tree, ascending the steep slope of Orton's property, past a large in-ground pool and onto the back patio. The sliding glass door leading off what appeared to be the living room stood open to catch a breeze on this sultry late-September day. Rather than surprise the occupants with this less-than-orthodox approach, DeWitt knocked.

A moment later he knocked again. Louder this time.

"Dr. Orton?"

When there was no reply, Carter eased back the screen to enter, pulling it shut behind.

"Dr. Orton?" DeWitt's pulse quickened as he moved farther into the room. "Anybody home?" The ticking of an antique pendulum clock on the fireplace mantel was the only sound to reach his ears.

Curious now, Carter advanced toward the dining room and then to peer out into the front drive through louvered shutters. A Cadillac Allante, with a set of golf clubs leaning up against its open trunk, sat half out of the garage, top down. Orton's BMW was nowhere to be seen. By now it was more than half an hour past the appointed time of their rendezvous. And what was the wife's car doing parked with the trunk open like that? Erv had said she had some sort of country-club reception to attend; that she would be gone and he was scheduled to join her at seven-thirty for dinner.

Something was wrong, and Carter was suddenly angry. Orton had obviously panicked after receiving that threatening visit, and elected to take flight. It was even possible that he'd told his wife of the jam he was in and they had left together. All caution was now thrown to the wind as the infuriated attorney stormed across the living room and mounted the short flight of steps to the entry gallery.

And then he saw the blood. Lots of it. Splattered across one wall. Pooled in some places and smeared in others over the terra-cotta entry-hall floor. Carter grabbed for his mouth as his stomach lurched. Barely digested Dr Pepper and Snickers squirted out between tightly clenched fingers to dribble down his chin and shirtfront. Coulter thugs forgotten, he tore the front door open and sprinted up the winding path to the street.

The appearance of those two feds, masquerading as Coulter heavies, was looking like a stroke of the purest kind of luck to Tony Flood. Instead of being forced to stand by and watch until Carter collected his winnings and left the game, Tony had drawn to an inside straight and simply blown him out of the game instead. Carter would have no choice but to withdraw. Tony could afford to hold the youngster's hand and pat him consolingly on the back. He would offer him a few words of advice, suggesting that Carter lay low for a couple of days until things cooled down. Maybe, in a day or so, he'd allow that he had a little mad money tucked away and that if the kid was in a real bind, he might see his way clear to take that downtown St. Louis condo off his hands for the right price. Luxury high-rise places like that had to be worth a couple hundred thousand easy. He would see if he could take it off DeWitt for a hundred and a quarter. This wasn't just a lucrative job anymore; it was turning out to be fun. Tony didn't expect to get that second $25,000 DeWitt had promised, but he had the first, and now Orton's two fifty, and the *real* power play hadn't even been run yet.

It was eight-thirty, Friday evening, and Flood had just plugged the feed lead back into his room phone when the phone started to ring. That would be Carter now. While toweling his torso dry from an invigorating cold shower, Tony moved to answer it. Five hours of uninterrupted shut-eye had left him refreshed, the post-methamphetamine numbness now vanquished, his mind naturally alert.

"For the love of *God*, Tony! I've been trying to reach you since two this *afternoon*! Where the hell have you *been*?!"

"Hold on!" There was cool, professional command in the way Tony barked it. "Where are you?"

There was a pause, probably while DeWitt leaned out of his phone booth to scan for a street sign or other landmark. Flood could hear traffic noise in the background.

"The Northtown Mall parking lot. Near the corner of Kearney and Glenstone."

"You're right close by. Get back in your car an' drive straight west on Kearney toward the airport. It's the Super 8 on the right, not the Regal. Y'all know the room number."

Before Carter could say anything else, Flood broke the connection. With the casual ease of a man confident of his direction, he tossed the bathtowel over the top of the bathroom door, wet a comb to drag it twice backward along the sides of his close-cropped hair, and dressed. Ten minutes elapsed before he saw DeWitt's black Lincoln pull into the motel lot and alongside his Cherokee, downstairs. The attorney mounted the exterior stairs to the second level and found Tony standing at his open door, clad in sneakers, jeans, and a tight, sleeveless T-shirt. Flood held a beer in each hand, one unopened, passing the latter across as he nodded in greeting.

"Orton didn't come up with no dough, right?"

DeWitt crossed to the room's big recliner without a word, collapsed into it and popped the tab on his beer. Eyes closed, he drained the whole thing in a series of huge gulps and tossed the can toward the trash basket. As Carter sat, Flood noticed the smeared chocolate stain on the front of his shirt.

"I think he's dead. What happened? Why weren't you there?"

"I *was* there, up till a few hours ago." Tony related how he'd followed Orton from his office to the bank and then home; how he'd watched the two men pay the doctor a visit, leaving with the same briefcase Orton had carried from the bank. "I followed 'em all the way out to a county road south o' Aurora, an' remembered that's where the Coulters have their spread." Tony wanted to keep it credible.

DeWitt covered his face, nodding slowly and speaking through his hands. "Orton called me early this afternoon, after getting a visit from some guy representing the Coulters. I tried to calm him down, and then I made a beeline to collect the money. I tried to reach you from a pay phone, and then I broke a fan belt out in the middle of nowhere. I didn't get to his house until after six."

"Why d'ya think he's *dead*?"

"There was no one home, Tony. The entry hall is covered with blood. His car was missing, and that's what I don't get. You followed those guys away from there, and they didn't have Orton with them?"

Carter's eyes had emerged from behind his hands, and Flood peered directly into them, slowing, shaking his head. "Nope. I was all set t' head back an' see what happened once you arrived, jest like we'd talked about, but then *this* came up." He walked to the long, low dresser set along the wall at the foot of the bed and picked an envelope off the top of the television. With a flick of the wrist he shot it through the air to land in Carter's lap. "I'm listenin' t' the radio an' on the news is some 'nouncement 'bout Sheriff Scranton washin' up dead yesterday down on Bull Shoals. Heart attack or some shit. I had t' get my ass down there t' make sure nobody else ran across this." Tony pointed at the envelope.

Carter had already opened it and now scanned the contents. On the outside was the same list of ledgered entries that Flood had photographed for him. Inside, it contained the originals of the photos he'd been given, and a yellowed coroner's report.

"I didn't think you'd want that shit fallin' inta anyone else's hands, and there weren't much I could do 'bout the Orton thing."

DeWitt was still staring at the sheaf of old photos and documents in his hands. "A heart attack?"

"That's what the news said. Floated up deader'n a doornail out in the middle o' the lake."

DeWitt was shaking his head. "This is too much of a coincidence, Tony. Scranton floats up dead. Coulter sends people to not only shake Orton down, but maybe even murder him. Christ, I've been driving around in circles for two hours since leaving his place, one eye glued to the rearview mirror and trying to make sense out of it all. Jesus, what if I'm next?"

"Want 'nother coincidence?" Flood asked. "I don't s'pose y'all listened t' *any* news if you didn't know 'bout Scranton. They found Terrence McElliot in the bushes o' some Washington park. Bullet in the brain pan. Everybody who knows anythin' 'bout this nasty business is windin' up dead."

The news about McElliot stunned DeWitt all over again. "But Franklin Coulter is the one who approached McElliot with the problem in the first place. Any connection there would make no sense."

"Maybe he knew somethin' we don't. How the fuck do I know? What I *do* know is that your ass is in danger right now."

"Danger?" DeWitt asked, derision in it. "Even if Franklin Coulter doesn't see me dead, his granddaughter is going to see me in jail, Tony." He threw the envelope and its contents to the floor in despair.

Flood pulled out the desk chair to sit, hunched forward over the back of it. "Y'all wanna know what I think you should do?"

DeWitt lifted and dropped his hands, the despair still heavy in his eyes. "Right now, I'm willing to listen to anything."

"Okay; I think y'all oughtta hand ol' Tony the ball an' let him run with it. Lay low an' let me see if I can work summa these coincidences t' our advantage. You still got a powerful weapon in that shit there." He jerked a thumb at the papers strewn across the carpet. "What Coulter is tryin' t' do is workin'. He wants t' scare the shit outta you. Get you t' back *off*. But he don't know you got one ace up your sleeve who don't scare off so easy. That ace is me."

"You? What could possibly be in it for you at this point, Tony?"

Flood waved his misgivings away with an impatient swat at the air. "You're not thinkin' clear right now, Carter boy. Y'all jest moved inta your daddy's house in Creve Coeur. Coulter don't know nothin' 'bout that, right? So you'd be safe there, at least for a little while. Meanwhile, y'all still got the goods t' cause a media scandal . . . make some fuckin' dickhead reporter the next Pulitzer Prize winner. I'd think Franklin would pay a pretty penny t' prevent that from happenin'."

DeWitt had calmed considerably as Flood spoke. His gaze had less panic in it now as he contemplated his investigator. "Like I asked just a minute ago, Tony. What's in all this for you, *ace*?" Suspicion had crept into his tone.

Tony gave him an easy grin. "I was jest gettin' t' that part. I'm lookin' at a straight fifty-fifty split."

"A fifty-fifty *split*? Of *what*?"

"The dough we coerce from ol' Frank Coulter."

"How much?" DeWitt's confidence was coming back fast.

"I was thinkin' an even million. Half o' that would get you outta your jam, an' the other half'd do me fine."

DeWitt shook his head to the negative. "Two. A Coulter will only respect you if you hurt him, and I've come too far to settle for less."

"Fine. Two then. A cool million apiece. But I think it

might be a good idea t' let it cool off a few days. You head back t' St. Louis an' I'll go back t' lock up the lake house."

"I want to be there, Tony."

Puzzled, Flood frowned. "Wanna be *where*?"

"With you. In Aurora, when you lean on Franklin. I've known him all my life, and negotiating is what I do for a living. This is going to be done right."

"Oh-kaaay." Flood drew it out, caution tempering it. This was delicate territory, and he didn't need Carter to be fostering suspicion right now. He needed to get him on ice; to clear the way. "I guess I ain't got no problem with y'all bein' the mouthpiece. You're the one with the silver tongue."

"So I'll see you in St. Louis tonight? You think Creve Coeur is safe for now, but I'm nowhere near as confident."

"No sweat, Carter boy. As soon as I lock up in Shell Knob an' check out a few details on how Scranton bought it, I won't waste no time drivin' up. I'll head back here an' hop onna plane. It could be late, but I'll definitely be there."

Carter nodded his agreement. "You want me to pick you up?"

"Naw. You look like you could use the shut-eye. If y'all got a spare key, I'll take a cab from the airport."

Sixteen

Without bothering to return to Branson and pack, Torbeck and McElliot drove directly to the Springfield airport and booked a charter pilot to fly them to Washington. While waiting for him to fuel and file a flight plan, they called their motel, extending the rental of their rooms indefinitely. The flight, in a twin-engine Beechcraft King-Aire, took four hours, landing them at Washington National at nine-thirty. From the airport they placed a call and learned that Dick Strahan had just left the office to return to his home in Silver Spring. They called Dick's wife to say they were en route, and flagged a cab.

The Secret Service director was quite obviously shaken, his generally confident demeanor gone, his face haggard.

"I tried to contact you, Bob. Your motel said that you were out. I left messages on both your New York machines."

Torbeck and McElliot accepted stiff whiskeys and now sat at either end of the leather sofa in the director's study. Strahan occupied a wing chair, opposite.

"We heard it on the radio news," Torbeck told him. "But what I don't understand is that we were in the Springfield

205

News-Leader offices from ten until noon and didn't hear a thing about it.''

"The Bureau had a blanket thrown over it. The golfer found him just after eight this morning. It was another hour before the FBI was called in. Metro knew from the cut of his clothes that he wasn't riffraff, but he had no identification on him. The first agents on the scene didn't recognize him. Until Chad Collins, the D.C. Field Office agent-in-charge, showed, everyone was assuming it was diplomatic. His suit was tailored in London. That's all they had to go on.''

"What are the early leads?" Bobby's question had a toneless quality to it.

Strahan frowned. "The Bureau and Treasury have mobilized a special joint task force. We've got a total of fifty agents scouring every square inch of this. Chad Collins is heading it up, and I got my last update from him before I left the building at nine. So far, we know that he was killed at very close range by a .32 S and W roundnose bullet, and definitely not at the site where he was found. The Bureau's preliminary computer check hasn't turned up anything yet. The forensic pathology lab is now putting his time of death as sometime either late Wednesday night or very early Thursday morning. The airports, trains, and buses have turned up a host of leads that are being run down now. The most promising is from National Airport, Wednesday night. An arrival on a flight from Tulsa had his wallet stolen in the men's room. One of his credit cards was used just minutes later to rent a Pontiac Gran Prix from the Avis counter. That car was discovered abandoned in the airport's metered parking lot on Thursday. There were three tickets under the wipers, the first one written at four A.M. Thursday. Whoever rented it didn't need it for long. We have an Identa-Kit description from the clerk who handled the Avis transaction, and it seems to match the description of a man who paid cash for a ticket to Dallas, first flight out on Delta, Thursday morning.''

Stan and Bobby were both surprised with how much progress had been made, developing this angle, in just a day.

Admittedly, the investigation could be chasing a worthless lead toward a dead end, but it was good indication that they were doing all the right things. The manpower mobilization and interagency cooperation were both impressive.

Stan came forward in his seat, his expression thoughtful.

"What about people fitting the description who flew into D.C. either on that same Tulsa flight or around the same time as the wallet was stolen?"

Strahan shook his head. "So far, we've struck out there. It's involved a lot of tracking people down who have moved on to other destinations. Collins has dispatched a special team to work with their Tulsa Field Office. The Avis clerk distinctly remembers the guy being big enough to be impressive. Not unusually tall, but powerfully built; on the young side of middle age, and speaking with either a southern drawl or a Texarkana twang." He paused a moment, thinking back over the terrain he'd just covered, and shook his head. "You realize that this whole thing is odd as hell. Terry hadn't worked enforcement for thirty years. There isn't a single person still alive who he personally put inside, so the personal-grudge angle is weak. He's been retired for three years. None of the staff at the house in Potomac knew where he was going that night when he left at around ten. His car was discovered on the third floor of one of those multilevel parking facilities on M Street in Georgetown. None of the restaurants in the area had him on their reservations lists as a late diner. A sweep made earlier tonight couldn't turn up a single bartender or cocktail waitress who remembered seeing him."

"Somebody set him up." There was no doubt in Bobby's voice.

"I think so too," Stan agreed. "If you're on the right track with the guy from Tulsa, and it's a long shot, he was just the shooter. I'd be paying close attention to the files on people from that region who do contract work."

"We're right there with you," Dick told him. "The Bureau has people working overtime in their computer center tonight.''

McElliot rose, his hands going deep into his pockets and his shoulders hunched in frustration. ''We can't work this, right?'' It wasn't really a question.

Strahan shook his head, his eyes saying that he knew exactly what his dead friend's son was going through. ''Not without destroying your cover. Maybe later, when all the facts have been shaken from every conceivable tree and you don't need Bureau support to proceed, but not right now. At this point it's an informational game. All I can tell you is that every available resource we have is being exploited. I'm impressed with the organizational abilities of this man Collins, and I'll keep you fully updated at all times.'' He paused, eyes traveling from one to the other, waiting for at least a nod of agreement. When he got them, he moved on. ''I realize there might be better times to ask this, but you're here and you've just returned from a rather sensitive official investigation. Any developments to report?''

On cue, Torbeck produced the minicassette tape made of the Orton–DeWitt telephone conversation from his shirt pocket and handed it across.

''We made this just this morning, after Bob put some pressure on the other doctor. The cardiologist. He panicked and got straight on the horn to DeWitt. Obviously, it wasn't a legal tap, but it should establish grounds for launching a bigger investigation.''

''Orton as much as admits his guilt, and DeWitt is plainly blackmailing him,'' McElliot added. ''We also uncovered evidence that would suggest the Taney County sheriff was involved in a cover-up. The sheriff's report and all the newspaper accounts say Constance Dahlrymple was killed in a car accident. DWI. The coroner's report is missing from county records. And just coincidentally, the old sheriff washed up dead on a local lake yesterday. We took an unauthorized peek inside his house and found a floor safe pilfered. The party interested in the contents of his safe *wasn't* interested in a four-hundred-thousand-dollar life insurance policy or the seventy-thousand-dollar Mercedes roadster we found parked in his garage.''

Dick Strahan let all this sink in, lifting his drink to his lips and sipping slowly. "It looks like it might be time to find ourselves a sympathetic U.S. attorney. You two covered one hell of a lot of ground in just one day.''

McElliot returned to pacing the length of the room. "We were led to believe it was urgent, sir.''

The director nodded. "But I wouldn't blame you, in light of your personal circumstances, if you wanted to pass on pursuing it further.''

Bobby seemed not to hear him. "I think I know a prosecutor who might be hungry for a new case right now. I won't say she owes me a favor, but I do think she'd be inclined to cut us the leeway we'd need.''

"Marilyn?" Stan asked.

Bobby nodded. "She just won the case she was prosecuting, and I'm willing to bet that for something involving the potential coercion of a United States senator, she'd be willing to travel out of New York.''

"Marilyn *Hunt*?" Strahan asked. "This week's golden girl?''

"That's right," McElliot replied. "She's proven she's good, and if she could bring this to some satisfactory resolution, and Richard Coulter just happened to get himself elected President, she'd be a shoo-in for a spot on the federal bench.''

"You'd be risking your covers even by approaching her.''

Bobby glanced at Stan before speaking. "This is the last thing my father asked me to do for him, sir. You just finished explaining why his son can't risk getting involved in the investigation of his murder. I've met Marilyn Hunt and believe I can trust her enough to justify taking this risk. We've already uncovered a few things that are going to demand the help of a committed, hard-working prosecutor, working as our information-gathering apparatus. Where, for instance, did the dead sheriff get the kind of dough it takes to buy a car like that? And how did he really die? Stan and I think his death is a bit *too* convenient.''

"You think DeWitt could be tied to it.''

"The possibility has occurred to us.''

"And, to be perfectly candid,'' Torbeck added, "it's also occurred to us that Franklin Coulter may not be out of the woods yet.'' He went on to describe what they'd discovered at the *News-Leader* and in the SWMSU archives, producing the newspaper photo and registrar's documents to back them up. "First thing, once we convince Marilyn or some other prosecutor to take this on, we'll want her to contact the Missouri DMV for a title search on that car. As soon as we leave here, Bob and I intend to pay the Coulters a visit and ask both of them about that picture. There hasn't been a red-blooded man born who could forget a face like that.''

The call from Jack Essex, the Justice Department's Chief of the Criminal Division, summoning Marilyn Hunt to Washington, couldn't have come at a better time. In the wake of her big victory, she was already feeling at odds with the limbo she would have to endure until sentencing in two weeks. On the one hand, she was exhausted and glad for the down time. On the other, she was antsy. The pressure and the grind had an addictive quality that a woman of her temperament had trouble kicking. The summons from Essex meant that she was about to be rewarded for all her hard work with an offer of more. The prospect made Marilyn's spirit soar.

Marilyn's opposite numbers, working the civil, the tax, or the antitrust sides of the Justice Department street, considered everyone of her breed to be grandstanding showboaters. And Marilyn was convinced that those gray-suited automatons had something other than blood running in their veins. The wars they waged were against emotionless, faceless monoliths, and there could be no passion in fighting such wars. But Criminal Division's war was different. When a criminal prosecutor stood before the bar, she had to feel an absolute loathing for not only her opponent, but the evil that person embodied.

She'd stayed late at the office, tying up the loose ends that would allow her to leave for Washington Sunday night without anything left in abeyance. It was ten-thirty by the time she arrived home to pop a Lean Cuisine frozen entrée into the oven and draw a hot bath. When the phone rang, she was just stepping into the tub.

"Yeah."

"Marilyn? Bobby McElliot. I'm sorry about the hour."

"Bobby. God, I'm so sorry about your father. Where are you?"

"Washington. Do you have a minute?"

"Of course. You didn't fly out to the Midwest yesterday, I hope."

"I'm afraid so. I just got back about an hour ago. Nobody could reach me, and I didn't hear the news until late afternoon. I'm calling to ask if you have plans for the weekend . . . and if you can break them."

It caught her completely off guard, and she had to scramble to regain her balance. The big mirror on the door to the bathroom revealed that the bruise on her left hip and thigh had gone a hideous yellow, and for an instant the memory of the indignity she'd suffered came flooding back.

"Say that again?"

"It's not quite the way I made it sound," he apologized. "Something pressing has come up that I think you might be interested in. Professionally. Stan and I would like to discuss it with you, and I'm stuck down here, for obvious reasons."

"Professionally? I'm an Assistant United States Attorney, Bobby. In light of that, would you care to be a bit more specific?"

"Not much more. At least not over the phone. As specific as I can be is that it involves extortion, tax evasion, and perhaps murder. There could be more. You're the expert."

"More?!" She blurted it, not very professionally.

"I don't want to say anything else on an open line. Could you possibly break free and come down here tomorrow?"

"I'll be on the nine o'clock Metroliner. I believe that would get me in at twelve-thirty."

"I'll pick you up at the station. We can talk over lunch."

Marilyn paused, not at all sure what was going on here. The most recent source of romantic excitement in her life was trying to push romance and her work together. In her experience, they never mixed well. A sudden wave of sadness washed over her. Bobby McElliot, her warm-witted documentarian, had just spoken in terms of open lines and capital crime. Something was very much out of whack.

"This is all very mysterious, Bobby. Please bear in mind that I'm sworn to uphold the law. And that no matter how much I like you, the minute I detect any attempt to compromise my position, I'll reach for the handcuffs. I'm dead serious about that."

"I don't doubt it. Union Station; twelve-thirty. And thanks, Marilyn. I'm sorry if I've upset you."

"Never mind," she replied. "I'll trust you. I think I owe you that much."

The oven timer commenced to buzz as she hung up the phone. She grabbed a robe, figuring she could always draw another bath. It wasn't until she reached the kitchen that she realized she'd lost her appetite.

With the exception of the Harrington funeral, the visit east had been better than most for Francine Coulter. Her father was too busy with the campaign to spend much time on her back. Her mother was behaving in a more accepting manner than usual. The reunion with Bobby McElliot was delicious, though all too brief. Still, Francine had been away from her horses for the better part of a week, and it was time to be getting back. Friday morning, in a phone conversation with her head groom, Jorge Mendez, she'd learned that her grandfather had apparently prevailed upon her specialist feed supplier in Louisville to express ship the replacement of her high-nutrition oats. It would seem, for the first time since she'd undertaken her enterprise, that the olive branch was being offered. In the light of this new peace, Bobby's offer to act as her financial backer lifted her spirits each time she thought about it. Then, midway through this last day of her stay, came the news of Terry McElliot's murder.

Late that afternoon Francine called to change her flight reservations to Monday, after the funeral. The prospect of seeing Bobby again under these horrible circumstances plunged her into depression. It was a different depression than she'd ever suffered before; one far beyond the realm of self-pity. For the first time in her young life she was being forced to confront certain inescapable absolutes. The despair she felt at the death of her distinguished childhood hero seemed as wide and deep as an ocean, no shore in sight. It forced her to wonder whether she had the emotional strength to offer comfort to Bobby without falling apart.

That evening, after supper, she packed her gym bag and drove to the health club on Connecticut Avenue. There, she spent the usual hour on the machine circuit, another half hour in the pool, and finished with a few games of aggressive squash. Instead of taking the accustomed steam, she packed it in after a quick rinse in the shower. Tonight she was in no mood for the chatter that filled the air in the steam room.

Once she returned home, she drew a bath in the upstairs Jacuzzi tub and immersed herself. The previous night a group of her old friends from the Cathedral School had dragged her out to make the Georgetown rounds. She'd ended up eating food too rich and having too much to drink, and rose that morning feeling sluggish. The mirror in the bath had revealed bags beneath her eyes. In the womblike warmth of the tub, she felt the weight of an overall mental and physical sinking spell.

Headlights swept the drive outside, brightly illuminating the second-floor bathroom for an instant as she climbed from the tub. A car door closed with a whump and seconds later she heard the doorbell ring. She reached for a towel and rubbed the water from her hair while surveying herself in the full-length mirror mounted opposite. All in all, everything was pretty much where she'd last left it. There were a number of workout fanatics in her group of old chums who'd begun to suffer the inevitable posterior drop, but hers still rode up high like a sixteen-year-old's. She attributed this phenomenon to all the training time in the saddle. Riding was terrific exercise for the legs, buttocks, arms, and abdominals. And even though there was no exercise that could prevent gravity's effect on a woman's breasts, hers had not been visibly affected. Exercise could only help preserve an ideal tone. Genetics did the rest.

It was after eleven before she drifted downstairs in cotton shorts and an old T-shirt to make herself some tea in the kitchen. Germaine, the housekeeper and cook, was at work alongside her mother at the prep island, assembling hors d'oeuvres for a charity function the following night. In that same interest, Francine had been enlisted to join her mother and other ladies of the committee on an expedition to the Baltimore flower mart the next morning at an ungodly hour.

"Looks good, whatever it is you're up to," she commented.

"Crabmeat croustades and a caviar brioche," Julia Coulter replied.

Francine filled a kettle, set it to boil, and pulled up a stool. These two had been working side by side like this ever since she could remember. The Coulter kitchen had always been a great experimental laboratory, where nearly anything that piqued an interest would be tried at least once. Germaine, a bean-pole black woman of indeterminate age, had been in the household since Francine's infancy.

"Who did I hear at the door?" she asked.

Her mother glanced up, all levity disappearing from her expression. "Robert . . . and Stan Torbeck. They're in the study with your grandfather."

* * *

Tony Flood was feeling pretty pleased with himself. Already this week he was nearly $300,000 richer, tax free, and that was looking like just the beginning. A little careful planning and some precautionary measures, taken in time, had helped, but fate also marched in lockstep with his desires. When it came to big ideas, guys like Carter DeWitt were always proficient at puffing out their chests like frigate birds, but they generally ran scared when the tide turned. Carter had needed little encouragement to send him scampering, the specter of murdering bogeymen chasing him all the way up I-44. He was probably just passing through Rolla right now, his hands aching from the grip exerted on the wheel.

DeWitt's lake house was all locked up snug, and Tony now drove north toward Aurora on Route 39, his own grip loose and easy. At ten past eleven old Franklin Coulter wouldn't be expecting any visitors, and that was going to increase the investigator's element of surprise. He just hoped the old man didn't have a heart attack when he got an eyeful of what Tony had from the dead sheriff's safe. If Carter thought two million was a fair price to ask for his circumstantial evidence, then five seemed reasonable to Tony for the hard evidence that could blow the Coulter clan back to the days when they ran hardwood lumbering camps. For five million Tony would even throw in Carter's head on a platter, just before he left for Rio and one nonstop parade of young pussy and fancy tropical drinks.

Aurora sat at the foot of the great North American plain that stretched from the Ozarks to the Arctic. It had the earmarks of a place once destined to be another sparkling gem in a necklace of American prosperity that would stretch from sea to shining sea. The railroads were meant to forge the links of that necklace; in this case, the St. Louis and San Francisco. There was a huge grain elevator down by the tracks. The downtown was laid out on a grand scale, with its avenues broad and its storefronts brick. Everything about its construction, most of it having taken place at the turn of the century, promised a prosperous future. Today the St. Louis and San Francisco still passed through, but was no longer what it used to be. Trucking had taken a fatally huge bite out of its business. While the main streets still struggled to maintain some semblance of dignity by embracing the quaint and nostalgic, a thick, dusty veneer of decay was more than cute could scrub away.

In the dead of that late Friday night, Tony Flood drove into town not seeing any of this. Its history meant nothing to him. He was a man of the present and of the future. When he stopped at a service station to fill his tank, he asked the attendant where he could find the Coulter spread. And just as Tony knew he would be, the man was more than happy to point the way. He knew this because he liked to think he knew people. He knew that the folk of Aurora would consider it a cut above other rural Missouri towns simply because the home of three generations of United States senators was located nearby. And like the city of Independence, upstate, it might soon be the home of a President.

Flood found the Coulter ranch on a county side road, situated five and a half miles southeast of town. He took it slowly, proceeding between two huge stone pillars and along a paved road. He remembered Carter telling him that the Coulters had once owned nearly 200,000 acres in through here, and after various sell-offs, still controlled about fifty thousand. Carter had also reported that the ranch supported a huge herd of Hereford beef cattle because cattle were Franklin's passion.

At the two-mile point on the ranch road, Flood still hadn't seen a sign of life. For all he knew, there might be as many as a hundred hands living on a ranch of this size, but where they were remained a mystery. Then, away off to the north, atop a moonlit knoll, he spotted the main house, the sight of it evoking a chuckle. Franklin Coulter's grandfather, the legend who built the family's first fortune by lumbering hardwood for the St. Louis sash mills, had fancied himself a Jeffersonian. The house he'd built was a nearly exact replica of Jefferson's Monticello. The immediate grounds were said to duplicate the original's Virginia hill-country setting, all the way down to the domed cistern, semiunderground storage, wine cellar, and winery on the premises. It sure looked like the real McCoy in that moonlight, and Flood found the spectacle amusing.

On the last approach to the house, still perhaps a half mile off, he finally encountered some other signs of habitation, where a fork in the road sported a sign pointing the way to STABLES and BUNK HOLLOW. Minutes later he parked on the road to approach the main house on foot up a long, brick-paved central path. When he rang the front door bell, it was eventually answered by a geriatric Filipino in a nightshirt.

"Yes?"

"Tell Franklin Coulter I'm here t' see him."

"I find it difficult to believe he might be expecting you, sir."

Tony grinned his best nasty grin. "Surprise visit, Charlie. Why don't you be a good little gook an' go mention the name Connie Dahlrymple to your boss."

"And if he is not able to come to the phone?"

Flood's hand shot out to grab a fistful of the houseman's shirt, pulling him so close that the two of them nearly touched noses. "Touch a phone and I'll shove it up your ass, Charlie. Just get him."

The Filipino maintained a remarkable cool in the face of Flood's hot-breathed threats. "That would be difficult, sir. Senator Franklin is in Washington."

Seventeen

The tension in the study of the Coulter family's Washington home was so charged with electricity that Stan Torbeck thought he'd detected the taste of ozone on the air. Stan had decided that this was more his partner's turf and was letting him walk point. That may have been a tactical mistake. Bob was in a no-bullshit mood. The information they'd uncovered that afternoon had raised some thorny questions, to which he wanted real answers instead of a politician's patronizing reassurances.

"What are you suggesting, Bobby?" There was heat in Franklin Coulter's demand. "That I *lied* to your father? That *I* got that girl pregnant and hired Phil to take care of it?"

The reproductions of the November 1962 newspaper photograph and the university's financial-aid records lay on the surface of the glass-topped cocktail table between them. The appearance of Terrence McElliot's cinematographer son had shocked the old man initially, and he still wasn't ready to accept the fact that Bobby and his partner were the agents Dick Strahan had sent to investigate Carter DeWitt.

"I'm *suggesting*, sir, that you look at the picture. It's not the only one we saw of her. I'm *saying* that she doesn't look forgettable. Maybe once the senator sees it, the face will ring a bell the name didn't.''

Richard, it seemed, was back out on the campaign trail, having left for his home state Thursday morning to participate in the dedication of an electronics manufacturing plant in Joplin.

Franklin ignored the point McElliot was trying to make.

''I still don't understand what you're trying to get at, Bobby. Your father approached Dick Strahan in an effort to get Carter DeWitt safely on ice before he destroys my son's primary run. I assume that is what you were sent to Missouri to do.'' He paused to pick up the documents on the table and shuffle quickly through them. ''So what is this? Phil DeWitt meets a pretty skirt during the '62 campaign. He gets her into trouble, hires a couple of bumbling hacks to get her out, and they screw it up. To cover his tracks, he shoves her off a cliff. He was a friend of this family's, God rest his soul, but if you want the truth—and Richard will back me up on this— he was a consummate schemer. This sounds elaborate enough to be something he might do.''

Now Torbeck spoke up. ''And he left the whole story for Carter to find after he died? Just so the kid would be sure to know what a swell guy his father was?''

Anger touched the corners of Franklin's eyes and mouth for just a twitch before he pushed it back. Stan studied him, fascinated with his control.

''You didn't know Phil. He sought out and played advantages. He was up-by-the-bootstraps, off the inner-city streets of St. Louis. His wits were his only stock-in-trade. At the risk of sounding elitist, I will say that I believe he developed more than a few bad habits on his way to the top. And no, I don't think he'd bat an eye at leaving negative information about himself, as long as he saw it as a tool Carter could employ toward profit and social advancement. That was his legacy to his son. A house in Creve Coeur. A partnership in a prestigious law practice. A little coin in his pockets to give him ballast. A few dirty secrets to play as wild cards, somewhere down the road. Unfortunately, Carter doesn't have his father's innate political savvy. I'm afraid things like that just aren't genetic.'' As he spoke, Franklin rose to pour himself a brandy from a decanter across the room. ''Quite honestly, I was a bit taken aback to learn that you two fellas are still with the Service. Washington isn't very good at keeping secrets. I suppose you're evidence that it can keep a precious few. It is obvious that you are very good at what you do; to gather all this information in so short a time. I can't speak for my son, but I can say in all honestly that even looking at that photograph, I have absolutely no recollection of that girl's face. I know what you are asking, Bobby . . . about the money for her tuition and such a fancy little car. And I don't know where it all came from. Phil was invaluble to me, even in those early days, but what I paid him was by no means enough to allow for those extravagances.''

''I approached the other doctor, Orton, this afternoon, pretending to be in your employ, sir. I spoke in vague terms about an understanding you thought you had with him, without actually mentioning your name.'' Bobby had eased back in his seat, enabling him to regard Franklin on a straight trajectory, without having to crane his neck. ''*He* mentioned it. Apparently, Phillip DeWitt had him convinced that it was Coulter business he and Solokowski were about that night. I'm wondering if Phil told his son the same thing.''

Franklin lifted his snifter to his lips, appearing to think on it a moment before sighing and shaking his head. ''Maybe, once this prosecutor you've got lined up nails his fanny to the wall, Carter will enlighten us.''

''One point of clarification, sir,'' Torbeck interjected. ''We don't exactly have the prosecutor 'lined up' yet. We intend to talk to her tomorrow. See if she's interested. If she isn't, we're back to square one.''

''She?''

''That's right, sir. Probably the hottest property in the Criminal Division stable right now. We'd be lucky to get her.''

The old man softened quickly, a smile stretching his lips. ''I'm sure you two are better judges than I am of who is hot right now." He turned to face McElliot directly. "I'm sorry if I got a bit anxious there, Bobby. I'm pretty preoccupied with the threat to Richard's campaign. He's dancing on a hotter greased griddle right now than you can imagine. All of a sudden his entire life is under a microscope, and he's got to keep his mind clear enough to think months ahead. It's a lot of pressure on the family as well."

Franklin extended one of his big, tough-looking hands in a gesture of conciliation.

"I'm awful sorry about your dad, Bobby. I think you know that if there is anything any of us can do, all you have to do is ask."

When Bobby and Stan emerged from their conference with her grandfather, Francine waited for her mother to finish offering her condolences before suggesting she give them a ride out to Potomac. Bobby accepted gratefully. Francine had never seen him look more tired and more his thirty-six years. Any trace of boyishness was gone from his face, replaced by a deep, unfathomable sadness.

The three of them rode out into the increasingly rural Maryland suburbs with the windows of Julia Coulter's Chrysler New Yorker run down, the warm night air washing over them. With Bobby seated next to Francine, and Torbeck sprawled exhausted across the backseat, Francine found herself at a loss for words. She felt badly for her friend, but how could she say it in a way that meant more than her mother's practiced utterances?

"I loved him too, Bobby."

She spoke so softly that he wasn't certain that he'd heard her.

"I know you did, Francie. There was always something special between you two."

She nodded, eyes straight ahead, on the road. "He never treated me like I was inferior because I was female. Even when I was little, he would take time out for me. Ask me questions and actually seem like he was listening to the answers."

"He *was* listening." Bobby's eyes had begun to tear up and he made no move to control his grief. "I can't remember

221

him ever asking a question when he didn't want to hear its answer.''

"I'd like to stay tonight, Bobby. If you think it might help.''

His smile broke through the glitter of tears. "I thought you'd be gone back to Aurora by now; that you had a going concern to run.''

"I was booked to leave in the morning. I changed my flight to Monday night.''

"Thanks, Francie, but I'm afraid I won't be much fun.''

From the backseat Torbeck stirred in his sleep with a violent snort and settled right back into a steady, rhythmic breathing of exhausted oblivion. The noise, movement, and the notion of having fun on a night like tonight caused Francine to smile.

"Fun? Getting that big lunk into the house is all the *fun* I want to have tonight. Just think of me as something warm and familiar, next to you in the bed. For fun, I'm driving my mother to the Baltimore flower mart tomorrow at the crack of dawn.''

A sense of foreboding clung to Marilyn Hunt. The train ride to Washington wasn't helping to dispel it, with McElliot's words still echoing in her memory with the same clarity as though they'd just been spoken. *Murder. Extortion. Tax Evasion. Open Phone Line.* She'd reminded him of her sworn duties; that no one, no matter who he was or what great loss he'd just suffered, got preferential treatment in the eyes of the law. McElliot, like any citizen, was going to state his case and take his chances.

Since the completion of the restoration construction three years ago, Union Station was once again an awe-inspiring monument to those days when the steam engine and rail travel were king. If New York's demolition of the old Pennsylvania Station was one of the great crimes committed against American architecture, this was surely one of that architecture's greatest triumphs. Since the plywood barriers had come down, Marilyn rarely flew south to Washington anymore. She loved the wide-open comfort of the train, and she loved arriving here. At noon,

on a Saturday, the place was already the scene of high-volume
foot traffic. Travelers rushed to and fro across the expanse of
the great, glass-roofed central concourse.

McElliot awaited her arrival at the gate, reaching to take
both her bags as he greeted her. The drawn, strained edges
of his smile said more about his feelings than his attempted
levity.

"Did I indicate that we enforce a dress code down here?"
The remark was made in reference to her suit skirt, heels,
and silk blouse, with the jacket thrown over her arm. In
contrast, he wore jeans and a shirt with the cuffs turned back.

Her return look was cool, professional. "You asked me
down here to discuss a criminal matter, Bobby. This is my
prosecutor persona. I don't know if you're going to like this
side of me."

He led the way, carrying her bags out through the main
doors. When they reached the sidewalk, he set them down
to turn and face her.

"I got your message last night, Marilyn. Loud and clear.
Before we go any further with this, I want you to know that
I'm just as reluctant to pursue it as you are. I regret involving
you like this because I was very much content to leave us on
the level we'd started to establish last weekend."

"But you can't."

He shook his head. "I was content with a lot of the aspects
of my life. Then death and duty reared their ugly heads."

Against a backdrop of the white marble buildings on Capitol Hill, the gleaming Rolls-Royce Silver Spur stood apart
from every other car parked along the Massachusetts Avenue
crescent. As they approached, Jeff released the trunk and
emerged from behind the wheel to open the back door.

"Marilyn, this is Charles Jefferson. When we're finished
with lunch and our meeting, he'll take you . . ." McElliot
paused. "I'm sorry, I never asked where you were staying
. . . or if we could put you up."

"Thanks. I've got a reservation at the Marriott."

He nodded. "Okay. I apologize for not being able to take

you personally, but I've got an appointment with the funeral director at three-thirty.''

"I understand." If just meeting her most recent romantic interest under these circumstances was making Marilyn uncomfortable, the $200,000 car didn't do anything to put her at ease. She felt conspicuous.

And neither did Whippoorwill do much to relax her tension. Her breath caught involuntarily at first sight of the place; the huge wrought-iron gates and the fieldstone gate house; sleek Arabian horses grazing in luxuriant green pastures; miles of gleaming white fencing. They followed a long, tree-lined drive through it, arriving before a three-story plantation house with two-story colonnade. And as hard as she worked to repress the effect it all had on her, she knew she was betraying some of it.

"Not exactly neutral ground, is it." She tried to make it wry, but was unable to suppress a smile.

"I think you'll like the lunch," he replied.

Inside, they paused before mounting a sweeping staircase to the second floor as a matronly black woman informed her host that Mr. Strahan hadn't yet arrived but that Mr. Torbeck was already seated in the upstairs dining room.

"Did I hear that correctly?" Marilyn asked as she was being led toward the second-floor landing. "Strahan, as in Richard?"

"He'll be joining us."

They moved along a wide, oriental-carpeted hall toward a smaller, more intimate dining room than Whippoorwill's huge, formal refectory downstairs. This was where the Harrington family customarily took meals when not entertaining in large numbers. The room they entered was furnished with a huge mahogany table, chairs, breakfront, and sideboard, all in late eighteenth-century Hepplewhite style, and all authentic. The table was set for four, at one end, and Stan Torbeck already occupied one of the places, drinking a bottled beer from a glass.

224

Torbeck rose, clad in the same sort of casual attire as his friend. "Hi, Marilyn. Good trip?"

Her eyes traveled around the room in open appreciation of all they saw. "So far," she said cautiously.

Marilyn dreamed of someday owning perhaps one lowboy table created by any of a handful of history's great furniture makers. Right now the pieces in that room were singing to her. Never had she dreamed of actually dining in a place where such things were used as everyday furniture. But that was how they were intended, and this was a rare treat indeed. Seeing Stan's beer bottle sitting on that glorious wood was not.

"That's two hundred and twenty years of nearly extinct history you're trying to desecrate," she told him. "Put something under that bottle, for God's sake."

McElliot chuckled as Torbeck hurriedly moved the bottle onto his place mat.

"What's this about Richard Strahan joining us?" Marilyn demanded. "You didn't mention anything about him on the phone last night."

McElliot held a chair for her and she sat.

"We'd rather not start any of this without him," he told her. "Beer or wine? It's a nice Chardonnay."

"Wine, please." And as she said it, the door to the room opened and the Director of the Secret Service was shown in.

"Dick Strahan, meet Marilyn Hunt," McElliot introduced them.

She rose from her chair to shake the director's hand. Strahan took hers with an easy smile, gave it a courteous shake, and started around the table to join Torbeck on that side. He accepted a glass of wine as he sat and then wasted no time in addressing the subject they were gathered to discuss.

"Mr. McElliot and Mr. Torbeck are deep-cover agents of the United States Secret Service, Miss Hunt. Their records have been expunged from all Treasury files and the Government Accounting Office has no record of them being paid as employees in any branch of government. This is no doubt something of a surprise."

The prosecutor's eyes traveled from one face to the next, finally coming to rest on Bobby McElliot's. "Yes, it's something of a surprise," she admitted. "So tell me, Bobby. That afternoon we just happened to be having lunch in the same steakhouse . . ."

"Not exactly a coincidence."

Strahan moved to ease some of the building tension. "Your superiors at Justice thought you might be in some danger from the people you were prosecuting. Because it was a Treasury case, and the Bureau's New York office was short-handed, they asked us to help out with the manpower."

She nodded, her unflinching gaze still holding McElliot's eyes. "How much the fool should I be feeling right now?"

"Not at all. I can't apologize for lying to you about what I do, Marilyn. It's my job to lie to people."

She turned away from him to confront Strahan. "What's this about, sir?"

Strahan forced a smile. "It's about a rather sticky case that has fallen into our laps, and about the fact that McElliot and Torbeck here happen to think that a combination of your credentials and their evaluation of your integrity might make you the right person to approach with it. It is of a very sensitive nature, and I hope they're right."

She gave a noncommittal nod. "Last night Bobby mentioned extortion, and possibly murder."

"That's correct. I was there when he spoke to you. We didn't think it advisable to go into any detail. Now, before we do, I'll need your assurance that, take the case or not, what we discuss here today goes no further than this room."

Marilyn considered the proposition. "If I don't take it on, you've got that assurance, sir. If I *do*, then it has to go one more step; to my division chief, Jack Essex."

Strahan waved this detail away. "Of course. That is understood." He then launched into a detailed account of how he had been approached by Terrence McElliot with Franklin Coulter's concerns and unusual request. At the conclusion, he set a minicassette player on the table in front of his plate and let Marilyn listen to the recording Torbeck and McElliot had made the previous afternoon.

When the conversation between Ervin Orton and Carter DeWitt concluded, Marilyn took a few minutes to process what she'd heard and to organize her thoughts. As she did this, a first course of linguine and white clam sauce was served. All of them waited until the house staff had departed the room.

"Can I assume that none of us believe Franklin Coulter's side of this story outright?" Marilyn asked.

Strahan turned to his right, nodding. "Bob?"

"There are some problems with the story that the Coulters are sticking by," he told her. And as he spoke he pushed the same packet of SWMSU and Springfield *News-Leader* archives material toward her that they had shown Franklin the previous night. "Richard is off on the campaign trail, but the old man claims he still doesn't remember her."

Marilyn opened the envelope and dumped the contents out at her elbow. The first item she picked up was the 1962 campaign victory-celebration photo. McElliot paused as she examined it.

"You'll also find evidence that a fair amount of money, by sixties standards, was thrown around to make her happy in the weeks before her death; that her tuition was paid in full; that she suddenly started driving a brand-new sports car. Also disturbing is the fact that the coroner's report is missing from the records room in Taney County, where she died, and that the sheriff's report is so sketchy that the license number of the car she supposedly crashed in wasn't included. And finally, the day we showed up to start digging into those files, the retired sheriff who ran the department in 1963 washed up dead on a nearby lake."

Marilyn glanced up, catching his eyes. "Your Midwest trip on 'family business'?"

"Like I said, it's my job to lie to people."

Torbeck broke in here. "If our extortionist had anything to do with that death, we want to nail him for it. And if it was Franklin Coulter, rushing to cover his tracks, we want him just as badly. But what I don't understand, if it was Coulter, is why he would have taken it to Terry in the first place.''

As the parameters of the case unfolded, Marilyn had unconsciously begun to roll up her sleeves. Now she turned to the Secret Service director.

''I can see what you meant by sensitive, sir. The extortion beef could definitely be construed as your jurisdiction, if Bobby's contention that Dr. Orton already had the money in hand is correct. We could probably establish that fact through his banking and brokerage records. Falsifying or removing government documents, albeit *local* government, can be seen as a federal offense inasmuch as those documents have bearing on a federal case. But as far as the perceived potential for damage to a declared presidential candidate goes? I'm afraid any such stance is rife with conjecture. And at this point, until something suspicious turns up, the death of the retired sheriff is purely a local matter.''

''That would tend to mirror my own thinking,'' Strahan agreed. ''We can make a request of the coroner down there, as an interested party, asking for a toxicology workup. If something turns up, we could press them to pursue a more in-depth investigation. But I am more interested in the extortion case against the lawyer. Bob and Stan seem to feel that they already have plenty of evidence for you to use in putting pressure on the cardiologist. He would have an awful lot to lose if he refused to make a deal. With that deal in place, the evidence indicates that he could deliver Carter DeWitt to you.''

''And let's not bullshit each other,'' Torbeck added. ''No matter how 'rife' the threat is with 'conjecture,' the events of January twenty-first, 1963, are a serious scandal threat to the presidential hopes of Richard Coulter. Faced with seven to fifteen in a federal lockup, Carter DeWitt won't be pressing any advantages. The Coulters will be painted by the media as paragons of political virtue who risked their own reputations to see justice served. The prosecutor who helped them would no doubt bask in some of the glory of the moment herself.''

Marilyn had been toying with her linguine, eating little during this exchange. Now the door to the kitchen stairs opened and the entrée of broiled boneless breast of chicken arrived. With regret she allowed her appetizer to be whisked away. What little she'd eaten was wonderful.

When the door to the back stairs closed, leaving them alone once again, Dick Strahan paused with his knife and fork poised above his plate to ask the question she'd known would be coming next.

"So, Miss Hunt. You've just completed a successful prosecution up in New York. You've heard the facts and understand that this is going to demand immediate action. Are you free, and are you interested?"

As Francine stooped to examine a Proteus bloom in the flower mart, pulling her hair from her face, she realized she'd left her grandmother's diamond-stud earrings on Bobby's nightstand. They were heirlooms, a gift before her social debut, and a reminder of a happy, carefree time of her life. For the rest of the morning she fretted over the possibility of a Whippoorwill maid finding and perhaps stealing them. Her good sense told her that this was unlikely. Still, they were small and could be inadvertently dusted onto the carpet and sucked up into a vacuum cleaner. As soon as she was free of assisting her mother and the other ladies in selecting the flora for tonight's function, she begged off lunch and raced back to the District. It was close to one o'clock before she reached Potomac.

The Arabian horses in the pasture had her yearning again to get back to her own stock, but otherwise Francine felt strangely at peace as she drove up the Whippoorwill drive. She had good instincts for her business, unlimited energy for the hard work it would take to make it a success, and now she had the financial backing. With Carter's syndication proposal, there had always been the inkling that aside from the money he stood to make as a partner, some other part of his ambition was also peeking through. He would sooner or later want something else from her; something his association with her family name could buy him. But with Bobby, she knew what she saw was what she was getting. He already had every advantage that Carter dreamed about, and was content to spend his life making films about the American condition. He understood horses and the passion they could inspire.

On reaching the house, she parked in the drive and hurried up the steps to the front door.

Marilyn Hunt had lifted her own knife and fork as Strahan finally pinned her down. Instead of imitating his own pose, she set them down and took a sip of her wine while formulating her reply.

"I'd be crazy to say no. I'm being asked to take a case by the Director of the Secret Service, instead of some agent-in-charge at the field-office level. This case has heavyweight political implications, and politics are the name of the game when the federal bench is your ultimate goal. So I'll take it sir, but with the following provision: If it looks to me, beyond a reasonable doubt, that Franklin Coulter can be implicated in this directly, I'll do my best to tear his heart out, and Richard Coulter's candidacy be damned."

While Dick Strahan listened, he'd lifted a bite to his mouth. Now he chewed, his gaze betraying a slight glimmer of amusement. "Fair enough." He set his utensils side by side at the top of his plate, wiped his mouth with his napkin, and stood. "Then I think I'll leave you three to work out the details of how you'll proceed. I know that Bob and Stan have certain information they'd like access to and more specifics they can share. If your division chief has any problems with this, ask him to contact me directly. These gentlemen have my home number."

Eighteen

Francine was fairly sure that the man who passed her as she entered the house had once worked as some sort of deputy to Bobby's father at the Secret Service. Not quite as tall as Terrence, he was perhaps ten years younger, balding and burly, even in a beautiful English-cut suit. Jasmine, one of the older Whippoorwill maids, informed her as she stepped into the huge entrance gallery that Bobby was having lunch in the upstairs dining room. He was with Stan and a Miss Hunt, and had asked very specifically that they not be disturbed. Francine assured her that she was only there to pick up a pair of earrings, and hurried up to Bobby's suite. The bed had been made, the room straightened, and there they were, just where she'd left them on the nightstand. She paused a moment in the bathroom to put them on and comb a few flyaway strands back into the morning's hastily tied ponytail.

As she started back down the hall toward the head of the second-floor landing, the door of the dining room came open, a very pretty, business-attired blonde emerging into her path.

"It's that door there," Bobby's voice was telling her. "The one straight across."

At the same moment Jasmine appeared, climbing the

stairs, a feather duster in her hand. "You find them, Francine?"

The blonde turned in surprise as Bobby's head emerged from behind the door. Francine slowed to avoid colliding with the stranger.

"Yes, Jasmine. Thank you. They were right where I left them." She looked past the blonde to Bobby. "Something I forgot. I meant to sneak in and then right out again. I'm sorry if I've interrupted anything."

"Not a problem," he replied. "Francine Coulter, Marilyn Hunt."

Francine's expression brightened in recognition as she extended her hand. "I read that article on your case in the *Post* Thursday. Congratulations."

The blonde took her hand, shaking with surprising firmness.

"Coulter. As in Senator Richard?"

Francine gave it a mock frown, nodding. "My dad. Again, I'm sorry for interrupting. It's nice meeting you." She tilted her head, affording her a view into the dining room." 'Bye, Stan. Later, Bobby. I'm out of here."

"She's beautiful."

Marilyn and McElliot had just exited the front door and were crossing the colonnaded porch toward the front drive.

"Yes, she is," he agreed.

"Aren't you worried about a conflict of interest? Your relationship with Franklin Coulter's granddaughter affecting your objectivity?"

"Aren't we jumping to conclusions here?"

"*You* tell *me*, Bobby."

"Until she came east for my grandfather's funeral, I hadn't seen her in five years, Marilyn. Monday, after my dad's funeral, she's going back home. No, I'm not worried about any conflict of interest. I've known Francine since she was born."

McElliot was relieved when Marilyn let it drop. They emerged into the bright sunlight of early afternoon, moving toward Jeff and the awaiting car. Marilyn paused in the middle of the drive and let her eyes roam over the setting surrounding her.

"I've visited a few museums like this, but never one that was still a residence. It's . . . magnificent." Her face tilted upward as she considered her host. "It's a whole other world, isn't it? And though a part of you wants nothing to do with it, the other part was born to it. Where I stand, in admitted awe, you tread with accustomed ease. Your friend Francine walks through this world the same way you do. It's where you're both from. You're lucky to have a friend like Stan, Bobby. He's not from this, and he's still able to see himself as your equal."

McElliot smiled. "Only because he is. He comes from the California beach; a comparatively classless society."

Now she smiled too. "I envy him. I also know that you didn't want to bring this case to me, Bobby. Franklin Coulter was your father's friend and his granddaughter is yours. It's a family thing; I can see that. But there's something else that drove you to get involved, and that I *don't* understand."

"Sure you do. It's the same thing that prevents you from entering private practice and making a fortune *defending* scumbags from the other side. For me, it's something I inherited from my grandfather; the Harrington tradition of public service. I was raised to believe that instead of pissing life idly away, you try to give something back. Yours is a different tradition, but you were raised to believe the same thing."

Grabbing hold of an arm for support, she got on tiptoe to peck his cheek. "I'll be in touch as soon as I learn anything."

Marilyn turned to climb into the backseat of the Rolls. Bobby stood and watched as it moved around the drive to disappear amongst the trees.

Instead of going directly home to his place in Creve Coeur, Carter had driven into downtown St. Louis and spent what was left of the night on the sofa in his office. Because it was a Saturday, there had been no noise in any of the outer offices to awaken him. He slept straight through to eleven. His clothes were rumpled, there was still that foul-smelling chocolate stain on his shirt, and his face looked like hell as he splashed water on it in the partners' washroom. Though his stomach growled ferociously, reminding him that he hadn't taken real food since the previous morning, he decided to head home for a shave, shower, and change before breakfast.

To his great relief, Tony had arrived sometime earlier. There were no Coulter henchmen hiding in the shrubbery, and in fact, the private investigator had picked up some eggs and bacon at a nearby convenience store. While Carter was upstairs, shaved and showered but not yet dressed, he placed a call to the Coulter residence in the District of Columbia's Spring Valley. The housekeeper informed him that Francine had gone to Baltimore with her mother but was expected home sometime that afternoon.

When he tried the call again, an hour later, she still hadn't returned.

"Who you callin', Carter boy? Sounded like long distance."

"Francine, in Washington. I want to know what the hell is going on. Since she's right there inside the house, she may have heard something."

"I thought you told me she's runnin' horses on the family spread."

DeWitt glanced over with an impatient scowl. "She and her grandfather flew out east last week for Ambassador Harrington's funeral. He was family on her mother's side somewhere. Now, I figure they're all stuck out there until at least early next week."

"Oh? Why's that?"

"Terrence McElliot was murdered, remember. McElliot was one of Franklin's oldest Washington friends."

In a gesture that seemed a bit curious, Flood rolled his eyes and then pointed back toward the phone. "If you don't want anyone to find y'all here, I suggest you lay offa that. If you gotta make a call, make it short. An' if it rings, for Christ's sake, don't answer. Jest let me; I can give 'em some bullshit story 'bout refinishin' the floors or some shit.''

It wasn't until two o'clock that Carter finally got through to Francine. When she heard his voice, she immediately asked if she could call him back on a different line.

"What was that all about?" he demanded.

"You're kidding, of course. Your name is *mud* around here, Carter. Why are you calling?"

"Because I think your fucking elders are trying to kill me."

"Oh really? I thought maybe you wanted to tell me that your friend Mr. Gleason's money is back in the escrow account; that I can call the bank, Monday morning, and find every nickel where it should be."

"Come *on*, Francie. I may need a couple more days than that. And for God's sake, I need to know what your grandfather is up to. There's crazy shit happening out here and—"

Before he could finish the sentence, he heard the line go dead. Slowly, the receiver came away from his ear. Gaping open-mouthed, he stared at it in disbelief. From a nearby chair Flood gave him a quizzical look.

"What is it?"

"She hung up on me. The uppity little *bitch* just hung up."

Jack Essex, the Justice Department's Chief of the Criminal Division, paced the floor of his Chevy Chase living room. Marilyn Hunt had never seen all parts of her chief prosecutor's body at rest at the same time and wondered how he managed to sleep. At fifty-four years of age, a time when most bureaucrats went wide from knee to neck, the perpetual motion of Jack Essex had burned away every last ounce of fat on his slight, narrow-shouldered frame.

"Dick Strahan's been around long enough to know that

this isn't how the game is *played*, Marilyn. He should have called *me*. Seen who I had available."

"Don't tell me I can't have this one, Jack. I want it. I just finished winning a battle that you yourself told me was a no-win situation, going in. I won it because I worked my ass off. Today I learn that the Chairman of the Senate Appropriations Committee, who happens to be the Democratic front-runner for the presidency, needs his back scratched. I won't let you take this opportunity away from me."

"Try not to forget who you're talking to, young lady."

Marilyn had been in the Justice Department harness for ten years, and at thirty-four wasn't feeling even remotely young.

"Two Secret Service agents approached me with the director of their goddam agency, Jack. The *director*. It is a longstanding policy of this division for senior assistants to choose their own cases from the current case load. All Richard Strahan has to do is call or file a memo and *this* becomes part of that load. I took the Asian-cartel case as a favor to you because the two bozos you originally assigned had royally fucked it up. I'm not the only one who came out smelling like a rose. By the time this new case goes to trial, *if* it ever goes to trial, you'll probably be sitting on the bench."

She'd spoken forcefully, and for the first time since meeting him a decade ago, Jack Essex had stopped moving.

"I should relieve you of this right here and now, Marilyn. Give it to someone with a less impassioned perspective. I hope you realize that you're walking a high wire here. If Franklin Coulter had anything to do with that girl's death, this whole thing will blow up in your face. You'll find yourself in the center ring of a show that'll make the trial you just finished look like a fucking *flea* circus."

She flashed him her best nonplussed smile. "Well, there's always private practice, right boss?"

Just as she'd known he would, Essex took a deep breath, rubbed a hand furiously across a head of thinning hair, and capitulated.

"I want to be kept abreast, day to day, on this. It isn't just your ass we're hanging out there in the breeze. Mine's out there too."

She heaved herself out of her chair and held out her hand. There was a look of absolute determination frozen on her face as he took that hand and shook it.

"For starters, I'm going to request the St. Louis attorney's telephone records from his local operating company and long distance carrier. Already this afternoon I called the Taney County coroner and asked him to get tissue samples of the dead sheriff to the Springfield Bureau office for express mail out here, with a request for complete toxicology analysis. Strahan will have Internal Revenue investigators dig into the cardiologist's recent transaction record. Monday morning, first thing, I'll get hold of Missouri Motor Vehicles and have them run a title search on the dead girl's car."

Nineteen

Monday morning the same crowd McElliot had seen on Wednesday of last week now packed Holy Trinity Church in Georgetown. And though the President hadn't seen his way clear to grace them with his presence, current and former members of his protection detail had turned out in great numbers. Two former chief executives once served by the fallen man sat among them. Bobby had the dizzying, disorienting experience of déjà vu as he walked up the center aisle, past all those familiar faces, to take his place with Stan and the Coulters. It was a different church, but he felt that same nasty clutching in his bowels.

Unlike his grandfather, who had served with the OSS at the naval rank of Commander, Bobby's dad was not a veteran. He elected in his will to be buried alongside his wife in the Harrington plot at Whippoorwill. After the funeral mass only a few of his very close friends gathered at the Potomac estate for the interment. Though the Autumnal Equinox had occurred in the early hours of that same morning, the late-summer heat had not broken. Most of those gathered at graveside were thankful that the little iron-fenced cemetery stood in shade.

Bobby didn't really notice the heat. Yesterday he hadn't gone to view his father's body, having already seen too much of the damage bullets could wreak. The sealed box was little more than a symbol of his loss, of his connection to those others buried there. As he watched it lowered into the ground, he'd never in his life felt more alone.

The mourners were beginning to depart when a taxi appeared in the drive to pick its way carefully through the crowd of cars parked in its path. Torbeck nudged his partner.

"Our lady prosecutor."

Marilyn Hunt had emerged from the cab. They watched her progress as she started toward them up the walk. The black, worsted wool dress she wore had to be hell in heat like that, but she seemed oblivious to it. As she approached she pulled a tie from her hair and shook her head. Bobby left Stan's side to greet her, his jacket open and hands shoved deep in his pockets.

"I'm sorry to barge in like this. It was the only place I could be sure to catch you."

"It's not a problem," he assured her. "Let me say good-bye to some people and get them on their way. If you don't feel like hanging around here, Stan can take you over to the house."

He started to turn away and stopped. "I'm sorry. Are you in a hurry?"

A hand settled lightly on his sleeve. "Please, Bobby. There's no rush. I'm fine."

He moved to attend to his father's friends. Last condolences were received and thanks expressed as the crowd of cars began to thin in the drive. When the Coulters were the only mourners remaining, Bobby walked toward their car with them, Stan and Marilyn trailing a dozen yards behind. As soon as they were a discreet distance from the cemetery, the funeral director's people emerged from the shade of a distant tree to complete their task.

Francine was scheduled out on a flight at four that afternoon. She and Bobby had already said their good-byes early that morning. Now it was her mother's turn, and she watched as Julia took Bobby's hand in hers.

"I want you to keep in closer touch, Robert."

He forced a smile, leaning forward to kiss his mother's cousin on the cheek. "You're all the family I've got, Julia."

She lifted her chin toward Torbeck and Marilyn, thirty feet distant. "Stan's girlfriend? She's adorable."

Bobby smiled again at the thought. "A business associate." He turned to slip an arm around Francine's shoulders, pulling her close. "So long, friend. I'll be in touch."

In another minute the Coulters were moving off down the drive as McElliot hurried to join Torbeck and Marilyn.

"I was just updating her on the Bureau's search for your dad's killer," Stan told him.

Late Saturday, Strahan had gotten them a copy of the FBI Identa-Kit sketch of the man who was still emerging as their prime suspect. Unfortunately, interview teams in both Dallas and Tulsa had thus far been unable to pick up the trail. No other leads had emerged from an exhaustive examination of the events in Terrence McElliot's life for the week or so before the shooting. There were some elements of the joint FBI–Secret Service task force who were openly wondering if the retired director hadn't fallen prey to a particularly ruthless local element. They were suggesting that it wouldn't be the only time in recent years that a well-dressed man, driving a Jaguar, had been first robbed and then shot, just for good measure.

"So what have you got for us?" Bobby asked her.

"Bad news on that front." Marilyn nodded toward the tail of the Coulter's disappearing sedan. She had a cardboard accordian file clutched in her hands, and lifted it now. "Can we go somewhere and sit?"

Ten minutes later they were gathered in the parlor of McElliot's private second-floor suite. Stan had opened a couple of beers for himself and his partner, while Marilyn drank a diet Coke. She opened the folding file and withdrew items which included a thick wad of computer-generated printout.

"Before I get started with these, let me bring you up to date. Your boss called me last night to say that the Internal Revenue investigators have managed to confirm that Ervin Orton did liquidate two hundred and fifty thousand dollars worth of CD's and bonds. Merrill Lynch is sending duplicate confirmations. The manager of Orton's Landmark Bank branch confirms that he delivered cash on the Merrill Lynch certified check. He claims that Orton said he wanted to keep that much ready cash on hand in his safe deposit box. All the proper IRS forms were completed, and there is record of the doctor having gotten access to his box Friday afternoon. The bank manager is off the hook."

"Just like that?" Stan asked.

"Sure. The only proof we have that Orton had the money in his possession is Bobby's gut feeling . . . until we can get access to the bank box." She paused, glancing at her notes. "I spoke with the Director of Missouri Motor Vehicles and he has promised to have a title search run on the Dahlrymple girl's TR-3, pronto. No word as of yet. The tissue samples from the Taney County coroner didn't arrive at the Bureau's pathology lab until late last night. We won't have the results of the tests until tomorrow at the earliest. But I did find out a few interesting things about our Sheriff Scranton. You were right. He was literally leading a double life."

Several documents came off the top of her tidy little stack.

"Mississippi FAXed me this information this morning. The plate number you gave me off the Mercedes is registered to a Morris Purdy, address in Pass Christian, down on the Gulf. One Martin Scranton is listed as the president, and Purdy is listed as the treasurer, of a day-trip fishing and excursion outfit in Pass Christian which owns three boats. I talked to the local law in Pass Christian this morning too. They say Purdy is a fixture down there come winter, but that he disappears every summer. The IRS has no record of this Morris Purdy. They *do* have a record of Taneyville's Bosley

241

Scranton. According to them, he's never filed more than twenty-six thousand dollars in income for any given year.''

While she paused to let this avalanche of information sink in, Torbeck and McElliot regarded her in open astonishment.

"Jesus," Stan marveled. "When did you sleep?"

She winked. "As soon as Jack Essex gave me the green light on this, I pulled in a couple of eager beavers from down low on the totem pole. I can't say I've slept a *lot*, but lack of sleep has become a routine condition lately."

"Speaking of Essex," Bobby asked. "What sort of reception did this get with him?"

"Cool at first." She thought about what she'd said and chuckled. "He was so mad he had steam coming out of his ears. I didn't tell you this, but he'd already called when you did; to get me down here this morning and talk to me about the immediate future. You guys beat him to the punch by two days."

Torbeck, eager to press on, pointed to the computer print-out. "So what's with this?"

"Phone records. Yesterday I asked Contel, Southwestern Bell, and AT&T to FAX me Carter DeWitt's telephone activity for the past month. I was hoping to get proof of calls made to Doctors Orton and Solokowski. And I did . . ."

Stan was reading the look on her face. "But that ain't all."

Marilyn nodded. "He no longer maintains any listings in his own name, but there are two active phones listed to his recently deceased father; one in the St. Louis suburb of Creve Coeur and the other in Shell Knob, in Barry County, Missouri. Both saw activity over the past two weeks, Creve Coeur from Sunday the eighth through Tuesday the tenth, and then again, this past Saturday. Shell Knob is the only number that saw activity from Wednesday the eleventh through Friday the twentieth."

She paused to take a sip of her soda and run her finger down her notes. "Early last week calls were made to the offices of both doctors at the Cox Medical Center, in Springfield. He also called a motel in Forsyth, Missouri, any number of times that same week. Wednesday evening he called Dr. Orton at his home. On Saturday, from the number in Creve Coeur, three calls were placed to Senator Richard Coulter's residence in Washington, D.C.''

The last fact hung there in the air between them, as heavy as a pregnant cow.''

"Then I stuck my neck out,'' she continued. "I requested the past month's long-distance records for the senator's home and office numbers.''

Both partners glanced at each other, impressed. It was the sort of move that could generate a lot of heat if Coulter chose to take offense. In Washington, he had tremendous clout.

"No calls were made to any of DeWitt's numbers from Capitol Hill. His Washington house, in Spring Valley, has three separate numbers, all unlisted. A call was made from one of these numbers to DeWitt's Shell Knob phone on the morning of Wednesday, September eighteenth, at nine thirty-six. On Saturday, the twenty-first, a call was made to the Creve Coeur number just minutes after DeWitt's last Washington call.''

"The plot thickens quickly, doesn't it?'' Stan muttered.

"That isn't the end of it,'' Marilyn told him. And then she turned to Bobby, firing the next question point-blank. "What do you know about your friend Francine's association, relationship, or whatever you want to call it, with Carter De-Witt?''

Bobby scowled, obviously puzzled. "She knows him, I suppose. Phil DeWitt worked for one or the other Coulter senators for years. I'm not sure what you're getting at.''

She produced a last document with a flourish. "This.'' And handed it across.

It was the first page of an income tax return for a Sub-chapter S corporation calling itself C&D Holdings Inc. The president was listed as Francine Anne Coulter; the treasurer, Carter Phillip DeWitt.

* * *

The events of that past week had been a tremendous interruption to the early momentum generated by Richard Coulter's presidential campaign. Certainly, both the Harrington and the McElliot funerals were good public exposure opportunities, the media not failing to catch him trodding the same turf as the current and two former chief executives. Associations were sure to be made as to his connections by marriage to deceased patriots of such caliber. But all the while, Richard felt as though he should be reaching out, bouncing jovially on the balls of his feet among the grass roots. It was difficult to exude confidence at a funeral, and confidence was what he wanted to project right now. Like an undefeated heavyweight champ, he wanted to be out there where the challenges were, walking the walk and talking the talk. Washington was a fishbowl, where a senior senator was forced to swim slowly and regally through waters of filtered, crystalline clarity. But Richard was on the campaign trail, where slow, regal swimming was for bait fish. He was a shark, having totally immersed himself in the shark mentality: attack, engorge yourself on opposition weakness, keep moving or die.

This afternoon, as Richard eagerly anticipated getting back into strategy sessions with his manager and advisors, anticipated the *People* cover story which was said to focus on his folksy roots, anticipated getting back into some two-fisted pounding on the heavy issues, he found himself back in the library of his stately Spring Valley residence. Standing with his back to the book-lined shelves, with his father seated beside him in one of Julia's chintz upholstered wing chairs, he faced Bobby McElliot, Stan Torbeck, and Marilyn Hunt. There was a look of astonishment on his face.

"You?!" It was aimed primarily at McElliot.

Richard's eyes met his father's. Franklin was watching his reaction to the news of young McElliot's involvement in the DeWitt investigation with something that looked like amusement.

"You raced off to that plant dedication so early Thursday that I didn't get a chance to bring you up to speed, son."

The candidate's head was still spinning. No sooner had the family returned home from the burial and Julia left to accompany Francine to the airport, than McElliot and Torbeck had arrived on the front stoop, the pretty little blond woman in tow. He, himself, had only just flown in that morning from an all-too-brief campaign trip to the heartland.

Franklin turned to the visiting trio. "The senator had obligations in Joplin and Kansas City. With the women around all morning, we haven't had a chance to talk."

The blonde had been introduced as Marilyn Hunt, and that name rang a bell in even Richard's information-overloaded memory.

"Mr. McElliot and Mr. Torbeck are covert agents of the United States Treasury, Senator," she explained.

Richard was at a loss for words. "Damn, Bobby. I had no . . . *idea*."

"You weren't supposed to, sir. But let's move beyond that. Marilyn's been working to develop some of the directions produced by our first foray into the Springfield/Branson area."

Richard was again stunned. "Hold on a minute. You've already been out there?"

"Yes sir. We left Thursday."

"Thursday? I don't understand how you could move so quickly."

Franklin turned once again to glance up at him. "Terry was already talking it over with Dick Strahan by the time you and I spoke to Julia, Wednesday morning."

"Senator," Marilyn interrupted. "I've turned up a link between Carter DeWitt and your daughter Francine. I'd like to know what *you* know about a corporation the two of them have formed."

Richard bristled at the way this aggressive young woman cut into the exchange he'd been having with his father. That

245

irritation quickly disappeared as he absorbed the impact of this latest bombshell.

"A what?!"

Marilyn handed over the copy of the tax return.

"C and D Holdings, Senator. Formed to do business in the breeding and trade of thoroughbred racing stock. That information is not all there on the return. We determined it just half an hour ago through a call to the state offices in Jefferson City."

Richard was more than disturbed by this news. He was outraged. "I—I can't believe this!" He turned to his father out of reflex, and read absolute ignorance in the old man's expression. He turned back to Marilyn Hunt. "What *else* do you know? This is only the first page of the return. How much money is involved?"

"This is the first year they filed, sir . . . for the final two months of 1990. The corporation was formed in the last week of November; they reported no income and paid only the nominal franchise tax."

"So it's possible that this is something that never got off the ground, right?"

"There's more, Senator," Bobby said. "The return listed a bank account number in St. Louis. Marilyn called that bank this morning and learned that one hundred ten thousand dollars is currently on deposit. Last Tuesday night, when I had dinner with her, Francine told me about a horse she hopes to buy at auction next month. It's expected to go in the neighborhood of half a million dollars. She didn't mention names, but talked about her efforts to raise money through syndication and how they'd failed. I assume that's what we're looking at here. It could also explain why Carter chose this moment to extort half a million dollars from the two doctors."

Richard turned pale. "What is it that you're implying?"

Marilyn took control again. "Last Wednesday morning, a call was made from this house to a number listed in Phillip DeWitt's name, in Shell Knob, Missouri. Just Saturday, three calls were made from a number listed to the same name in

Creve Coeur, Missouri, to this house. Minutes after the last of those three calls was made, someone in this house called that same phone in Creve Coeur. Can we assume that it was neither of you two gentlemen who made those calls?''

Ignoring the question as rhetorical, Richard started to move about in his agitation, that broad Coulter chin buried against his breast. As he tried to think, Franklin spoke.

"We told Francine nothing about any of this, Bobby.'' The old man's upraised index finger moved back and forth in the air between himself and his son.

"Was she in Aurora when you got the visit from Solo-kowski?'' Torbeck asked.

Franklin frowned, thinking back, and then shook his head.

"We'd gotten the news about Michael's death, and there was a lot she had to do if she wanted to make that plane out of Springfield at three. I'm certain she was still down at her stables.''

"How about here?'' Stan pressed. "Were there any discussions here in the house?''

"Not that she was privy to,'' Franklin asserted. "Definitely not.''

From where he stood at the far corner of the room, Richard's chin came up, his jaw set in a scowl of determination. "I intend to get to the bottom of this.'' He was addressing his father directly. "I have meetings tomorrow, but I'm canceling them and going out there. Francine is going to tell me what the hell is going on if I have to shake it out of her. I'm running for the presidency of the United States. Carter is doing his best to see me ruined, and my own *daughter* is climbing into bed with him!''

Marilyn took a step forward to confront him. "Perhaps you should wait to see what our investigation produces,'' she cautioned. "A federal judge is issuing eavesdropping warrants on both DeWitt and Dr. Orton. With what we've already managed to establish, we may be able to convince Orton to make a deal as early as midweek. With his testimony, the threat to your campaign could be nailed cold.

Anything you say to your daughter might reach the wrong ears. I understand that you are already at odds with her in this area . . . her business interests.''

Now Richard whirled on Bobby. "*You* told her that! God *damn* it! I won't have you airing my family's dirty laundry in public!''

"I consider her point to be relevant," McElliot returned coolly. "As is the information, to Miss Hunt's understanding of the case.''

"This isn't public, Senator," Marilyn assured him. "We are conducting an extortion investigation. In my experience, the one stone left unturned is often the one that ultimately trips you." She paused. "Now. I can't prevent you from confronting your daughter. I can only recommend against it at this juncture.''

Richard was in no mood to be dissuaded, and had just opened his mouth to speak when Franklin interceded.

"I'm sure the senator can understand the necessity of Bobby's revealing this information, Miss Hunt. Meanwhile, there could be some profit in examining Francine's position. Who knows? She may reveal something material to your case. It sounds like you three are going to have your hands full for the next few days, and let's be mindful of the fact that I have certain leverage against my granddaughter. She has a lot of money invested in a rent-free facility built on my ranch. I don't think we'll have any trouble keeping her in line.''

A return to Whippoorwill and a final strategy session produced a plan of action. It was decided that Bobby and Stan would begin surveillance on Carter DeWitt while Marilyn continued on to Springfield. Once there, she would hook up with the FBI's supervisory resident agent and begin figuring the best route toward approaching Dr. Orton. Because the telephone records Marilyn obtained indicated that DeWitt had returned to St. Louis either Friday night or early Saturday, Stan worked to conclusively pin down the attorney's whereabouts.

He placed a call to DeWitt's St. Louis law firm, asking to speak with Mr. DeWitt regarding a personal matter. The receptionist informed him that Mr. DeWitt was on vacation until the end of the month. Torbeck then allowed that his personal matter was a pair of box seats to the last Cardinals home game of the season. He had to be out of town and couldn't use them.

"But it sounds like my good buddy can't use 'em either. Do me a favor and let him know I called."

"Well, he *did* return from the Ozarks over the weekend, Mister . . . ?"

"He's here in *town*?"

"Yes sir. I expect him to check in for messages sometime this afternoon. If you'd like to leave your number . . ."

"No sweat. If he's here in St. Louis, I'll just call him at home."

He broke the connection and returned to huddle with Bobby and Marilyn.

"DeWitt's still in St. Louis."

"Good," Marilyn replied. "If he isn't trying to take the money out of the country, it means he'll probably try to launder it locally."

"You think he'll approach a factor?" Bobby asked. "Pay a percentage? That gets expensive."

"But it's safe," Marilyn argued. "After that panicked phone call you recorded between him and Orton, you have to figure that he knows there's heat on. Once the money is clean, he can lock it in a bank box somewhere and spend it one small chunk at a time."

Stan had folded his huge frame into one of McElliot's club chairs and now sat staring out a window and into the gardens beyond. "It sure seems like a giant waste of effort, for a chunk of dough that size, doesn't it?"

"Right now, it probably seems like a royal pain in the ass to him too," Marilyn replied. "Don't lose track of what he originally set out to do. He tried to shake down *two* doctors, for a total of half a million. Bobby tells us *that's* what he needed for his partnership with Francine, to buy this horse. From what I've been able to learn from his and his father's banks, he doesn't have all that much ready cash, and the liquid end of Phillip DeWitt's estate is still tied up in probate."

Torbeck continued to stare off into the distance. "So what do we do, exactly? Hang a wire on his phone and then stick to him until he makes the wrong move?"

"For the moment, yes. That's all you *can* do, until I get the paperwork organized in Springfield. When we approach Orton, the evidence we have against him is going to have to be so airtight that his attorney will only be able to give him one bit of sound advice. Leading a horse to water is never quite good enough. It's my job to make damn sure he's thirsty when he gets there."

That reporter from the *Post-Dispatch* had already given Doreen Philby a crisp new hundred-dollar bill up front, just to prove he was good for another if she made the call. All she had to do, the minute old Senator Coulter stepped off a plane, was drop a quarter and call the number he'd scribbled inside the matchbook, collect. For three days she'd been hoping to God that Coulter might land on her shift. That way, she wouldn't have to split the two hundred with Jerry Speakes. Jerry worked days, and had been just as eager to see it work out the other way around.

Five minutes ago, as Doreen drove the baggage cart up to the belly of TWA Flight 21, she'd hit the big casino. Not just one Senator Coulter had descended the rolling stairs to the tarmac of Springfield Regional Airport, but two. At that very moment, as she was lifting the receiver of the pay phone in the crew lunchroom, Southwest Missouri's two most distinguished citizens were loitering in the luggage area, waiting to collect their bags.

Carter had four scotches under his belt and had just announced that he was turning in, when the phone rang. Tony had expressly forbidden him to answer the phone, but it was ringing right at his elbow as he passed. He snagged the receiver out of reflex.

"I have a collect call from Doreen? Will you accept the charges?"

"Who?"

"Doreen." It came at him from somewhere down the line past the operator. The way she said it, there was no doubt that he was supposed to know her. Behind him, he could hear Flood rising from his chair in the living room to approach.

"Uh, sure." The line clicked and the distant caller's voice gained clarity.

"Mr. Horvath? Both Senator Coulters just arrived. Do you still have my address?"

"Beg pardon?"

"For where to send the money."

Slowly, DeWitt turned to face his investigator, his hand groping blindly to replace the receiver in the cradle.

"What's going on, Tony? Who is Mr. Horvath? And who is Doreen?"

Flood silently damned DeWitt to hell for touching that phone, and struggled to mask his anger as he explained.

"Doreen is a night-shift baggage handler at the Springfield airport. I got Horvath from a byline in the St. Louis paper. I told her I was him an' give her a C-note t' call me when Franklin showed. It seems t' me that the quicker we lay it out to him, the sooner he calls off his dogs."

"And mentioning that Doreen might call just slipped your mind, right?"

Flood's eyes flashed anger. "No, Carter. Wrong. Maybe y'all forget the state you were in when you come crawlin' back here. Since Saturday you've personally put away two fuckin' fifths of that shit whiskey you drink. Y'all left damage control up t' *me*."

Carter had been feeling the effects of an evening spent in his cups, but now that haze vanished.

251

"The agreement was two million, Tony. A fifty-fifty split. You weren't planning to leave me here in the lurch and grab it all for yourself, were you?"

Flood's anger grew. "Use your fuckin' head, Carter. Who has the goods on Franklin, an' where *are* they?"

DeWitt smiled, nodding. "I do. That set of originals, here, and the copies hidden away in a nice, safe place down in Shell Knob."

"An' I'm too fuckin' hillbilly dumb t' add all that up, right, Carter boy? That afore Coulter could pay me off an' send me on my way, you'd be in there, right behind me, makin' your own play with the duplicates." As he snarled it, Flood headed for the foot of the stairs. "I'm settin' the alarm for five-thirty. Tomorrow, you an' me are gonna collect that other set, do this deal, an' after it's done, I don't give a fuck if I *never* see your sorry ass again."

Twenty

By the time they'd touched down at Lambert Field, seen Marilyn to the gate of her Springfield connecting flight, and rented the little Ford Probe GT, it was nearly ten-thirty, Central Time. All their gear, with the exception of gadgetry they'd taken with them Friday morning, was still down at the Three Goats Gruff in Branson, so the little two-seat coupé afforded them plenty of room. They'd requested this unit because it was painted silver-gray, a color they hoped would help them work unobserved. The turbocharged power plant would afford them speed, and the fully reclining bucket seats would allow them to switch off sleeping through the hours of boredom that invariably accompanied surveillance. Sunday, while purchasing Stan a dark suit, they'd picked him up several changes of casual clothes at a big-and-tall shop. On the way out to Creve Coeur they stopped at an all night Consumers to buy a large-capacity thermos, and then at a Dunkin' Donuts to fill it. While he was at it, Stan grabbed a bag of their glazed and old-fashioned for ballast.

Creve Coeur proved to be a swank, sedate suburban enclave, west of the city and away from the Mississippi River. It graced a gently rolling terrain which seemed to lend itself to a lot of rural landscaping and the construction of golf courses. Most of the residences in the neighborhood were the sort built by the nouveau riche before the crash of '29. With the aid of a detailed street map, McElliot had no trouble directing his partner to the huge red-brick Victorian that Carter DeWitt was reportedly calling home. The doors of a separate three-car garage were down. There were no vehicles parked in the drive. Nonetheless, lights burned in half a dozen different windows, on both the first and second floors.

No matter where he traveled, Torbeck's gadgets always included a pair of compact, roof-prism binoculars. He picked a parking spot with good sight lines, about thirty yards from the house, and had clear viewing once he'd fiddled the glasses into focus. While Stan worked at it, Bobby played with the radio, trying to find a decent country station.

"Flip for the first shift?" Stan asked.

"No, I'll take it. You see if you can catch some shut-eye. It's hard to believe that it was just this morning that I buried my father."

"Long day," Torbeck agreed.

"Yep. I'm still pretty wound up."

No one was more surprised to learn her father had arrived at the Aurora ranch than Francine. The last she'd heard before leaving Washington was that her grandfather intended to stay on at least another day and that her father had meetings with his campaign advisors scheduled through the rest of the week. She'd thought that she would spend tomorrow getting back into the routine of running the stables, but instead Enrique the houseman had just awakened her to report that both men were here in the house. They were requesting that she join them in the library, immediately.

Flustered and a bit alarmed, she climbed hurriedly into a pair of jeans, pulled on a sweatshirt, and left her room barefoot. When she passed a mirror in the hall, she realized she hadn't bothered to even run a brush through her hair. It looked like hell.

As she entered the big, octagonally-shaped central room, Francine discovered Franklin seated in one of the leather up-holstered armchairs at the refectory table. Her father stood across the room near one of the huge, double-hung windows. While Franklin watched her arrival over steepled fingers, Richard had his back to her. The window he appeared to be staring out through was open a foot, top and bottom, creating a light con-vection breeze to stir the air. Without turning, her father growled.

"Sit down."

"I think I'll stand. Thanks."

Her defiance brought him around, his jaw clenched tight and the veins of his temples protruding. "That wasn't a re-quest, young lady!"

Francine struggled to maintain her cool. She and her fa-ther had been battling over one thing or another for years. She knew there was no profit in fighting fire with fire here.

"And if I refuse?" She asked it with an infuriating calm in her voice. "What will you do, Dad? *Knock* me down?"

Richard had turned to advance a step in her direction when Franklin raised a hand to stop him.

"Last November you formed a Sub-chapter S corporation with Carter DeWitt. We'd like to know why you never men-tioned it, and what C and D Holdings is all about, Francine."

Her mouth opened and closed quickly. "How do you know about that?"

Franklin shook his head. "We *do* know. That is all that's material here."

Without realizing she'd done it, Francine sank into a wing chair positioned behind her. "It was an idea Carter had . . . to solicit investors to purchase syndicated shares in breeding stock. Thoroughbred. It's done all the time." She didn't know the details of *how*, but something icy in the pit of her stomach told here *where* this was going.

"Your corporation's 1990 tax return indicated that from the date of your incorporation last November, to the thirty-first of December, it had no income," Franklin pressed. "What about through the first nine months of this year?"

Francine took a deep breath, closed her eyes, and let it out slowly. "Right now, we have a hundred ten thousand on the books. Money I invested after selling a quarter-horse two-year-old."

She'd opened her eyes again and was confronting her grandfather straight on.

"Just your own money?" her father demanded.

Continuing to ignore him, Francine spoke again, addressing her grandfather. "There should be more." She went on to explain how one of the investors, a George Gleason, had called wanting to come down and inspect the facility, how she'd confronted Carter over the balance in the corporate escrow account.

"When he told me he'd invested half a million dollars of other people's money in some over-the-counter stock issue, I hit the roof. I told him that if the money wasn't on deposit in our account by this morning, I was going to call the State Attorney General."

"And was it?" Franklin asked the question just as evenly as his granddaughter was speaking.

She shook her head. "I don't know. The day turned into hamburger. I intend to call St. Louis first thing in the morning, but I doubt there'll be any good news. Carter called me in Washington on Saturday, sounding panicked. He babbled something about you and Dad being out to kill him. I told him I only cared about his returning the money he stole and hung up on him."

Beside her Richard was pacing like a caged tiger. "For the love of *sin*!" he snarled. "Why the hell didn't you *say* something about this?"

Francine turned to regard him for the first time since entering the room. "To you? Because I was sure you'd use it against me to get me and my horses thrown off the ranch. I didn't think Carter was fool enough to risk jail, and I was hoping the problem would resolve itself."

Franklin quickly returned to the questioning at hand before this escalated into full-scale war. "What do you know about your business partner's efforts to extort half a million dollars from two Springfield doctors, Francine?''

"Only what I overheard you, Mom, and Dad say in the library last Wednesday morning. I heard what you said about that doctor . . . how after Carter approached him, he killed himself. I called Carter and told him that we were returning the money to his investors and that our deal was off. He was out of control, and I had no intention of doing business with anyone so irresponsible. I told him I've worked too damn hard to get where I am, to have some con artist destroy me.''

Her father stepped over to lean threateningly into her face.

"And you expect us to believe that if he came up with the money, you wouldn't have welcomed him, and it, with open arms?''

She twisted to slip from the chair and move quickly to the far side of the room. Her tone was still measured, but it took everything she had to keep it so.

"Yes, I *do* expect you to believe me. It's the truth. I didn't want to find myself in this position any more than you wanted to find me here.'' She paused, turning to face him full on. "You can still recognize the truth when you hear it, can't you, Dad? Of course, after all these years of watching yourself on television monitors, maybe you've lost touch. This is me, your daughter, not somebody you hired to tell you what you want to hear.''

"You realize that this sort of thing can put your father's candidacy in serious jeopardy?'' Franklin asked. "That your association with Carter, when examined in this new light, might make ripe pickings for the scandal mongers?''

Francine shrugged in frustration. "Carter and his father were always as close as family. I've always thought of him as being a sort of obnoxious, but bright older brother. Are you saying that I'm at fault for listening to his proposal in the first place? You know as well as I do that there was no way I could anticipate this sort of turn. The man's a full partner of a prestigious St. Louis law firm, for Christ's sake.''

When Francine turned abruptly to pull open one of the

double doors and hurry from the room, Richard's jaw dropped. It was obvious to Franklin that his son did not feel the matter was at all settled. The senator stood staring down at the wing chair from which his daughter had so skillfully leaped to dodge the brunt of his wrath. In frustration he lashed out in fury, his fist hitting the chair back with an impact that sent the chair crashing into the wall.

With a sigh, Franklin heaved his weary bones to his feet.

"Sometimes you disappoint me, Richard." He left the room, his head shaking.

Springfield Supervisory Resident Agent Joe Riley was not in one of his better moods. For starters, this U.S. attorney he was scheduled to meet could have picked a more decent hour. And then there was the fact that the Springfield Regional Airport didn't offer much in the way of amusement for a loitering, red-blooded male at *any* time of day. He'd already read the October issue of *Field & Stream*, most of the weekly news magazines, and the Monday editions of the *Kansas City Star* and *St. Louis Post-Dispatch*. As a rule, he wasn't much for pulp fiction, and nothing had caught his fancy in the gift-shop rack. He'd been reduced to girl watching, and at eleven-forty on a Monday night the pickings were slim.

Riley was forty-six years old, with twenty-one years of service with the Bureau. A native of Natick, Massachusetts, he'd seen duty in half a dozen different field offices and resident agencies before being assigned as the top federal cop here, four years ago. To him, an Irish Catholic who'd attended Holy Cross, Springfield had at first seemed like a foreign posting. His wife Eunice was better adapted to the tempo of life here, teaching biology in one of the local high schools. Joe, a naturally hyper guy, just wasn't cut out to be a good ol' boy. The pace was too slow, the pervasive fundamentalist climate spooky.

This prosecutor and whatever she was after remained a great confusion. He'd been getting requests about this Orton all weekend, but none of it was adding up. Then, one of the deputies at Justice called, asking him to extend her every courtesy. Just ten years ago lady prosecutors at the federal level were as scarce as hen's teeth, but the world had changed. He'd gone home with the few free hours he had, grabbed a quick bite, drunk a couple of beers, and watched the news. That cardiologist and his wife were still clammed up about who had nearly killed them, and even the scandal-starved local media were losing interest. Now here Riley was, bored and without a pretty girl in sight.

When the St. Louis flight finally arrived, fifteen minutes late, a dozen passengers disembarked out on the tarmac. Riley stood and watched them through the plate glass as they approached the terminal. He already knew what this prosecutor was going to look like. A real battle-ax, from the way she sounded over the phone; one of those young, Georgetown Law go-getters who put on an extra thirty pounds just so she could throw it around. There were four women out there, two in their late twenties and one who fit the mold. Another was in her mid-thirties, a bit on the short side, but a knockout. The last was around his wife's age, with one of those midwestern matronly builds he saw a lot of out here.

When they entered through the outside door, Joe moved toward the heavyset woman in her late twenties and was just opening his mouth to greet her when a hand touched his sleeve.

"Agent Riley? I'm Marilyn Hunt."

Riley was astonished to see that it was the small blonde addressing him. A boring evening suddenly saw a little life injected into it.

"That's right." He took her extended hand to shake it. "Call me Joe."

"Nice meeting you, Joe. I'm sorry about the hour."

"Not a problem. Washington told me that you're juggling something hot."

"I guess we'll find out how hot." He could see a real weariness in the way she moved, in a tightness around her

259

mouth and in her eyes. "Why don't we find my bag and I'll bring you up to date in the car."

Minutes later, as they got settled into his government-issue Pontiac, Riley described the immediate arrangements.

"I booked you into the Howard Johnson just a few miles from here on Kearney Street. It's convenient, and most of the people we take there think it's nice, but if you don't—"

"Like it?" She moved quickly to dismiss his concern. "I'm sure it's fine. Right now, I'm so tired I think I could sleep on a bench at the bus depot."

"After all the request traffic for bank records and the like, I have to believe that this is about Dr. Orton. Am I right?"

"Partially," she admitted.

"Well, I don't know if you've been in touch with the Springfield P.D., but neither Orton nor his wife is saying a word. They're stonewalling."

Riley nearly arrested as the prosecutor jerked completely around in her seat to face him. "The local *police department*?! Jesus *Christ*! My directive was hands *off*! And how the hell would they even know?"

The resident agent scowled. "How would they *know*? The woman showed up at the emergency room of Cox Med Center South with her *guts* hanging out."

The Hunt woman's runaway anger was stopped dead on the tracks. "Say that again?"

He shrugged. "Orton is claiming that some madman knocked on his door Friday afternoon, assaulted him and his wife, and left without taking a thing. He suffered a broken nose. His wife was badly cut across the abdomen. Are you telling me that you don't know any of this?"

It would be difficult to say which of them was the more confused. With her perceptions reeling, trying to make sense of what she'd just heard, Marilyn slowly shook her head.

"No. Nothing. I flew out here to investigate an extortion plot. We know that Orton had the money together and was set to pay off, Friday night." Her voice started to trail off. "It looks like something went haywire."

Twenty-One

McElliot and Torbeck had been catnapping in shifts since midnight. In hopes of getting a little circulation to stir the soupy night air, they had the windows run down, and had been plagued by mosquitos. Aside from the few lights switched on and off between eleven and midnight, there hadn't been any observable activity in the red-brick house. As dawn broke, Stan shook Bobby awake and then climbed out to pee in the depths of nearby shrubbery. When he returned, McElliot was already pouring coffee into two Styrofoam cups. They broke out the doughnuts.

"It'll be just our luck that the shyster spends all day at the office," Stan muttered. "Maybe play a little handball this afternoon while we sit in this sardine can, working up a case of piles."

Bobby didn't bother to respond as he handed him his coffee. It was his experience that Stan's aggravated orneriness, the edges of his patience rubbed raw, actually helped keep him focused. At seven-thirty their vigilance finally paid dividends. One of the three garage doors rolled open and a late-model Lincoln Continental eased slowly back into the drive. No sooner had the car come to a stop than a man with a powerful build emerged from the house, carrying luggage. McElliot came forward to peer intently at him, while Torbeck observed in a more relaxed posture behind his field glasses.

"Looks more like a bricklayer than a lawyer," Stan mused.

He handed the binoculars to Bobby. As McElliot focused to scan the man, a second subject emerged from behind the wheel of the car as the trunk lid opened automatically. This one was more the prototype of the young, affluent attorney. He was dressed in a turquoise sport shirt, the sleeves turned up to mid-bicep, designer denims, and brown loafers. At perhaps six feet, he was taller but didn't carry the brute bulk his friend had. This other had a linebacker's neck and shoulders, a flat stomach and slim hips, all outlined by a gray, skintight T-shirt, navy athletic shorts, and sneakers. Where he bounced slightly with each step, the taller man carried himself with deskbound stiffness.

The one they assumed to be DeWitt hurried to the front door of the house to check that it was locked before returning to climb back behind the wheel. Once the trunk was packed, his associate joined him. The Lincoln eased out onto the tranquil residential street while Stan kicked over the throaty little power plant of the Probe. He gave them plenty of room before following.

"What's he up to?" Stan wondered. "That other guy looks like some sort of muscle, doesn't he?"

McElliot nodded. "If I was having any trouble seeing this yuppie lawyer as an extortionist, I think I see the capability now. Anyone can entertain big ideas, but that other guy looks like the hands-on part of the program."

The Lincoln moved east several long blocks on Olive Boulevard to the intersection with Lindbergh. There, it turned south. This was a main artery, running through the suburban outskirts of the city. It was easy, with the early rush-hour traffic, to maintain a distance of a dozen car lengths without being forced into any acrobatics. There had been no break in the heat since they left the area on Friday. Already, at quarter to eight, the mercury was sliding up past eighty degrees. They had the windows run down and the wind in their faces as the car ahead followed Lindbergh Boulevard all the way out to the intersection with I-44. At that junction it climbed up onto the Interstate and headed west. Stan allowed half a dozen cars to slip between them and the Lincoln before settling down to a comfortable cruising speed.

Two hours into the journey, as it began to look more and more like the destination was Springfield, the Lincoln signaled off the Interstate at Rolla. Torbeck followed cautiously as it pulled in to park alongside a McDonald's. The surrounding area was one of those fast-food oases where a number of rival establishments sit clustered together in hope of luring the brand-loyal customer. A Wendy's directly across the street allowed Stan and Bobby to park and observe without rubbing shoulders with DeWitt and his heavyset friend.

"Can I assume that we're intrigued enough by the muscle man to make him an object of further inquiry?" Torbeck asked. He'd just set the brake and was reaching for the thermos.

"I'd say we're *very* intrigued," McElliot replied.

"What if they spilt up?"

"I've been wondering the same thing. We know that DeWitt has a place in Shell Knob, and that's about an hour southwest of Springfield, down on Table Rock Lake. You think we can assume that's where he'd end up?"

Stan shook his head. "I've got no idea. Maybe? Probably? It doesn't make any sense that he'd even be returning down here. Not so soon after taking Orton off. But then again, maybe he's just as cocky as he sounded during that call we recorded. The muscle can't hurt in reinforcing it."

"And the muscle could also be a weak link. Who would you rather try to catch with his hand in the cookie jar? The brains or the brawn?"

"So if they split up," Stan concluded, "we let DeWitt

go. Concentrate on this other clown for the moment; try to get some sort of ID on him.''

While the Lincoln loitered on in the lot across the street, McElliot climbed out to take a turn at the wheel while Torbeck hurried inside the Wendy's to refill the thermos. Five minutes later, when DeWitt's back-up lights came on, Bobby got them rolling. Stan had picked up a copy of the Rolla paper from a curbside rack and settled back now to thumb through. Ahead, the Continental moved onto the access ramp and picked up speed, again heading west.

Twenty minutes of uneventful travel had passed when Torbeck suddenly came upright in his seat.

''Holy shit!''

''What's that?''

Stan had the paper folded over backward and lifted it now to point. ''A little follow-up article here on the back page. It says that Springfield police haven't made any further progress in their investigation of a bizarre—their word—violent assault against prominent cardiologist Dr. Ervin Orton and his wife Betty. They were attacked in their Springfield home, Friday afternoon. Circumstances are still clouded in mystery . . . neither victim able to shed any light on attacker's motive. Orton's been released from Cox Medical Center while his wife remains there, in stable condition.'' Stan let the paper fall to his lap. ''Hot damn, Bob. Friday afternoon. That would make it sometime after you shook Orton's tree and he made that panicked call to DeWitt.''

''It doesn't make sense,'' Bobby muttered. ''Orton had the cash. We've established that.''

''You yourself said there seemed to be tension between the doc and his old lady. Maybe when DeWitt showed up, she threw some sorta fit.''

Bobby shook his head. ''You saw DeWitt. Nobody who turns up the sleeves of his turquoise shirts and wears Bass Weejuns puts sixty-year-old ladies in the hospital.''

''A guy capable of murdering that old sheriff might.''

McElliot punched at the wheel with the heel of his hand,

his eyes glued on the tail of the Lincoln ahead. "Once we get to Springfield, I'm going to hop out at the first convenient spot. You stay with these guys. By now Marilyn knows all about this. She's going to want to confront Orton with it, and I want to be there when she does."

Two and a half hours west of the fast-food plaza in Rolla, DeWitt's Continental left I-44 at the turnoff for the Spring-field airport. Puzzled, the partners pursued their quarry as the Lincoln rolled past the terminal building and pulled into the long-term lot to park behind a white Jeep Cherokee. From the passenger side the lawyer's muscle emerged to col-lect his grip from the trunk. As he crossed to unlock the Jeep, the driver's window of the Lincoln came down. He and DeWitt exchanged a few parting words.

McElliot unbuckled and reached for the door release. "The Jeep is all yours, Stanley. I'll hang around here long enough to make sure DeWitt isn't flying off somewhere. Then I'll rent another car and track Marilyn down."

Torbeck's size prevented him from crawling over the coupé's drive-train hump. He had to climb out and go around to get behind the wheel. "How do I get in touch?"

"As soon as I find her, or something happens here, I'll leave a message with the manager of the Goats Gruff, down in Branson. You do the same, once you get a chance, and we'll check in every hour or so."

"I s'pose it's better than Dixie cups and string." Stan sounded dubious. "Good luck with Orton."

"Luck? I know a few things the Springfield cops don't. He's going to be putty in my hands." Bobby nodded toward the Cherokee. It was starting back out of its space, down the way. "I've got a gut feeling that our mystery man is the key to quite a few doors, Stanley. Don't lose the bastard."

Torbeck followed the Cherokee east on Kearney from the airport, beyond the intersection with the Interstate and on into the northern reaches of the city. A little more than a mile past the freeway, it pulled off into the parking lot of a Super 8 motel. The subject didn't bother to visit the motel office, but parked and carried his duffel straight to a second-floor room facing the street.

As he watched, Stan's lips curled into an involuntary smile. "Home sweet home," he murmured.

Proceeding at a casual pace, he turned left with a break in traffic to park in the lot of a furniture showroom across the street. His subject was just closing the door to his room as Stan pushed the console lever to the park position. Seconds later the curtain over the room's one big window parted and ran back.

No more than fifteen minutes passed before Torbeck saw the curtains pulled closed again. Seconds afterward the door opened and the subject emerged, changed into slacks, a short-sleeve dress shirt, and brown leather shoes. He carried a navy-blue blazer over his shoulder and had a tie clutched in his other hand.

It looked like the guy had some sort of meeting to attend. And while Stan wanted desperately to break into that room on the second floor, he had to hope the opportunity to do that would arise later. Right now his quarry was dressed for business and on the move. Resigning himself to follow, he reached for the ignition key as the taillights of the Cherokee came on across the boulevard. He followed it back along Kearney toward the airport, but instead of going on across the Interstate, they went south on something called the West By-Pass. In short order they'd hooked up with Route 60 and were heading into the country to the southwest of the city, moving at good speed.

Marilyn was surprised to learn that McElliot was in Springfield. After one night spent trying to catch up on an entire weekend's sleep, she'd called Joe Riley at eight, met him for breakfast in the motel coffee shop, and rode with him to the Bureau's resident-agency office. She wanted to get to work examining the documents subpoenaed from Orton's brokerage house and bank as soon as possible and had elected to forgo renting a car until later in the day. It was just noon and she was thinking about lunch when Rick O'Casey, one of Riley's three resident agents, poked his head in and asked her to pick up the phone.

"I assume that you know by now about Dr. Orton and his wife?" McElliot offered this comment in lieu of greeting.

"I do," she confirmed. "But how would you?"

"A little back-page article Stan spotted in the Rolla newspaper."

Marilyn was about to ask how his part of the investigation was going when something didn't add. "Rolla? I thought you were supposed to be in St. Louis."

"So was DeWitt. He got up at the crack of dawn this morning and moved out. Stan and I just finished following him all the way to Springfield and then the airport."

"The airport? Is he flying somewhere?"

"Not right now. He had some other character with him, a real typecast heavy. The guy had a Jeep parked here in the long-term lot. Must have flown up to St. Louis. When DeWitt didn't book a flight, we let him go, figuring we could find him later. Stan's on this new player, and I bailed to join you when you grill Orton."

She was flustered. This was all happening too fast. "I'm not sure I'm quite ready to proceed against him, Bobby. I just got started here, and I want to be absolutely sure our guns are loaded."

"I'm the guy who gave him the first nudge," he reminded her. "The story we read didn't say what the attacker did to him and his wife, but I'm willing to bet he did one thing that Orton definitely didn't tell the cops about."

"What's that?" she asked.

"Ripped him off."

Marilyn was scrambling to keep up. "Why would you assume that?"

"Because I listened to the conversation between Orton and DeWitt. Carter knew the doctor was ready to pay off. Today, he returns to the area in the company of a man who looks like a heavy hitter. I'm betting that somebody beat DeWitt to the prize. I'm also betting that DeWitt has his own list of suspects; somebody from the brokerage house or bank . . . or better yet, someone from Franklin Coulter. I planted that possibility myself when I shook him down Friday.''

Marilyn thought she could see where he was headed. ''What you're saying is that no matter who robbed Dr. Orton, he's the only one who knows what his attacker looks like.''

''Correct. I think he could be in real jeopardy.''

The prosecutor saw no choice but to capitulate. ''Okay, we'll talk to him. Can you meet me out in front?''

McElliot asked for and was given rough directions to the resident agent's office. ''Give me fifteen minutes,'' he told her.

After being closed up over the weekend, the house in Shell Knob was hot as a pizza oven. Carter spent the first ten minutes after his return racing around, throwing open every available door and window. He then filled his cooler with beer and pulled up a lounge chair on the terrace. There had been no Coulter thugs to leap out of the bushes and turn him into fish food. No attempts had been made to get to him or warn him off. Franklin Coulter was no doubt convinced that his action against Orton was a clear enough message. And that was fine with Carter. The more surprised the arrogant old buzzard was when he and Tony came calling, the more likely he was to see just how neatly and completely his fox was boxed. Carter was still surprised to have learned that neither the doctor nor his wife had been killed, but was not surprised at all that neither had talked to police. Orton might be out the quarter million, but he was going to be out that anyway. To talk would mean being ruined, and even his wife had to understand that fact.

It was hot, even in the shade, but not unbearable. Out on the deep blue surface of the lake below, a speedboat raced past, towing a water-skiing middle-aged woman. Her course cut a graceful swath of white water against the blue. Here and there the surface was still dotted with those big, boxy "party boats," even this late in the season. Aboard them, the gin-drinking geriatrics had the rest of their lives to relax away. The good life, mid-America style. In fact, every aspect of life out on that lake looked worry-free. Bought with honest bucks, made through honest toil. Carter knew it was too late, at least in his case, to give the concept much thought. By now Francine knew that he hadn't replaced the money in the corporate escrow account. She'd sworn that she would call the Attorney General, and it was only a matter of time now before the law came calling.

He downed a first beer quickly, dropped the can to the flagstone, and threw his head back to stare at the sky. God, he was tired. One more play and he could walk away. One more. For a little piece of it, he could get one of the younger attorneys at the firm to handle his father's creditors; to see the estate through probate. One of the syndicated realty chains could handle the liquidation of all his Missouri property; the house here in Shell Knob, the house in Creve Coeur, and his condo apartment. By the time all the smoke settled, he'd probably pull between two and a half and three million out of everything his father had left him. That, and his share of the Coulter shakedown, invested conservatively, would net him in the neighborhood of $350,000 a year, pre-tax. It would be enough to enable him, at thirty-three, to join his own little club of leisure-time gin drinkers; join them far away, in some comfortable foreign backwater where a guy with cash could still get laid once in a while and get plenty of ice for his drinks on days like today.

"Y'all got one o' them cool ones for me, Carter boy?"

Tony Flood, now changed into his idea of business attire, emerged through one of the open glass sliders off the living room.

DeWitt had come nearly a foot out of his chair, his heart thumping in his chest like a trip-hammer.

"God *damn*, Tony!"

"Relax, boy. Y'all didn't hear the Jeep?" Flood wandered over to the cooler and pulled two cans out of the ice. The first he tossed to Carter and the second he carried to his customary perch on the stone balustrade. "What y'all so deep in thought about?"

With little or no traffic on the roads, even in the middle of the day, DeWitt's mystery man made good time over the sixty miles between Springfield and Shell Knob. As soon as he saw the city limits signs, Torbeck had known where he was headed, and the black Continental he spotted—nosed up against the garage door of the house the Jeep approached—confirmed his suspicions. The subject had changed his clothes for a reason. Something was getting ready to go down.

DeWitt's fancy fieldstone lake house was situated down along a narrow road providing access to the water from the main road running through town above it. On the way in, Stan had spotted a service station kitty-corner across Route 39, in plain view of the turnoff. There had to be a phone there that he could use while keeping an eye on traffic.

Shell Knob wasn't so much a town as it was an overblown supply depot; a vacation staging area. There were several of the basic town requisites—the post office, two wood-frame churches, and a strip mall—but there the resemblance ended. On the other side of this cluster, merchandise marts, supermarkets, and boating outfitters stretched for half a mile. There were a handful of motels and filling stations, but very few actual residences. These, Torbeck guessed, were situated as was DeWitt's; along the irregular shoreline of nearby Table Rock Lake.

Torbeck had dropped McElliot off at the airport an hour and a half ago. Hoping he might still catch Bob and Marilyn there, he dialed the number of the Springfield FBI office first. The agent answering the phone reported that Marilyn hadn't left any forwarding number when she departed half an hour ago. Stan knew he had a decision to make. His quarry was just down the road, leaving the motel room empty, at least for the time being. There was no way of knowing where DeWitt and his muscle might head next, or when they would leave, but this was also the only *sure* shot he was going to get at finding the motel room unoccupied. He dialed the number of the Three Goats Gruff and left a message for Bob. In it he said that the fish were biting in Shell Knob. He read the name of the service station to the motel manager and asked him to tell McElliot to meet him there in two hours.

The past four days had been even more of a nightmare for Dr. Ervin Orton than the four preceding them. The only pleasant surprise was his wife. Betty may have been in shock when that monster opened the briefcase on the entry-hall floor, but she'd seen what was inside it. She'd seen where it had come from; out of their own entry closet. And she'd seen enough in his eyes to know to keep her mouth shut. On Sunday morning he'd had no choice but to come clean with her. Betty, above all else, was a pragmatist. She probably didn't love him, but she did love her life. The tidy little fortune he'd amassed in support of that life was considerable. She enjoyed an elevated standing in the community and the respect of her social peers. In the final analysis, once he'd confessed all, she did not feel that telling the truth about the attack she'd suffered was worth the scandal and shame that would surely result.

Monday, a detective from the Springfield Police had stopped by early to check a few facts. Erv's nose still hurt like the very devil, but at least the throbbing that kept him awake nights had stopped. The same cleaning contractor Muriel Solokowski used to reclaim her patio had refurbished his entry hall, removing all traces of that horrible incident. And, happily, Carter DeWitt had not made any attempt to contact him.

By Tuesday noon life had returned to a level of relative normalcy. Betty was scheduled to come home the next morning. A visiting nurse had been hired so that Erv could return to his practice. He had just removed two frozen bean-and-cheese burritos from the microwave and carried them on a plate into the dining room when the door bell rang.

"Yes?" Orton said it as he swung the door panel inward. His glance took in a very pretty, diminutive blond woman dressed in business clothing. Then he saw the tall, menacing man who had visited him and his wife Friday afternoon. The color drained from his face as he tried, frantically, to get the door closed again. The man stopped it with his foot.

The woman spoke. "Dr. Orton? I'm Assistant United States Attorney Marilyn Hunt. This is Special Treasury Agent Robert McElliot. May we come in?"

Orton saw the black leather wallet held outstretched in the tall man's hand. Both an official-looking photo ID and a tiny gold badge were visible. His confusion overwhelmed him. His eyes left the badge to confront the face.

"I—I don't understand."

"May we come in, Doctor?" the woman persisted.

With a feeling of utter defeat settling in his gut, Orton stood to one side.

Twenty-Two

As Carter led Flood into the game room, with its hunter-green walls, mounted buck and boar heads, fishing trophies, and heavy leather club furniture, the investigator smiled inwardly with smug self-satisfaction. DeWitt had no way of knowing that the original documents Tony'd given him from Scranton's safe were only half the take. He was unaware that Tony had another complete set of duplicates tucked away for safekeeping in Springfield. Today Carter believed that he would emerge phoenixlike from the fire of failure, original scheme incinerated, but with a fix on an acceptable avenue of escape.

As DeWitt walked to the far wall and swung back the painting of two mallard ducks in flight, Tony eased himself up onto the end rail of that beautiful old English snooker table to watch. He couldn't help notice the way Carter interposed his body in front of the wall safe as he worked the combination and swung the door. The youngster was deliberately obstructing Tony's view of the safe interior as he reached inside to withdraw the envelope containing the letter his father left him, along with the duplicates of the evidence stolen from Sheriff Scranton.

"Can I assume that these are the *only* copies of this stuff?"

As Carter asked it, he quickly closed the safe door again. Too quickly. Goods in hand, he turned to confront his investigator.

"For the kind of money we're going to ask, Franklin Coulter is going to want to be sure he's getting every . . ." His voice trailed off.

Flood was sitting there on the edge of the snooker table, legs dangling. DeWitt's attention was focused less on his casual demeanor and more on the gun in his right hand.

"Been a little change o' plan, Carter boy. I been thinkin' a lot lately 'bout how I ain't gettin' no younger; 'bout the fact that poundin' the pavement an' poundin' my pud don't hold a candle t' lyin' in some pretty senorita's arms."

"Wh-Wh-What are you saying, Tony?" Carter was too shocked to feel the idiot he looked, standing there and holding out the two envelopes at arm's length, his hand shaking. "I thought we were partners." He stopped, eyes downcast as he shook his head in disbelief. "Jesus Christ, Tony. I paid you good money for this and agreed to cut you in for *half*."

Flood took the envelopes and opened them to peer inside.

"What I'm sayin' is that I've decided t' go solo on this trip. Y'all play a cutthroat game, y'gotta be prepared t' get your throat cut. Don't worry none 'bout the senator, Carter boy. I'll be sure t' give him your regards. An' once I get where I'm goin', I'll send y'all a postcard."

"The evidence is all there, Doctor."

The folder lay open on the coffee table before him, but Ervin Orton hadn't bothered to do more than glance at the contents. A cold sweat was gluing his shirt to his neck and making the palms of his hands slick. Without pausing, the woman sitting across from him continued to count down the items of evidence.

"Transcript of your phone conversation with Carter DeWitt. Record of your CD and bond liquidations. A photocopy of your broker's certified check. The cash receipt, signed by you and the manager of your bank. A copy of the search warrants granting us eavesdropping authorization and the IRS access to your safe deposit box. A report of the items found there.''

"Am I under arrest?" Try as he might, Orton could not control the hollowness in his voice.

The lady prosecutor gave it a dramatic shrug. "Maybe . . . maybe not, Doctor. There is someone else who we want a lot more than we want you. The government would be within its rights to arrest you right now, but I didn't come here to do that. I came here to make a deal."

A glimmer of hope crept into Orton's eyes. "What sort of a deal?"

"What sort of a deal do you *think*, Doctor?"

Orton squeezed his eyes shut hard, trying to clear his mind and string together a series of coherent thoughts. "You want me to admit that DeWitt was blackmailing me . . . to be willing to testify to that fact. But what I need to know is whether I'll be prosecuted for the *reason* DeWitt was blackmailing me.''

"I'm looking to make a deal on extortion-conspiracy and currency-statute violations, Doctor. If you play ball with me, I assure you the local authorities will be made aware of your cooperation. Depending upon how enthusiastic you make me feel, a U.S. attorney can be pretty persuasive on the local level.''

Orton sat staring at his hands and at the file on the table in front of them. "Okay," he muttered, nodding. "This has already gone way too far. I'll tell you whatever you want to know.''

Agent McElliot now leaned forward in his seat on the sofa.

"Describe the man who came here Friday afternoon. The one who broke your nose, cut your wife, and robbed you.''

Torbeck nosed directly into a slot in the Super 8 motel parking lot. There was no way to be certain that Carter's pal hadn't forgotten something and wouldn't soon return, but Stan figured he had time, and aimed to make the most of it. Before climbing out of the car, he checked to make sure he hadn't misplaced the little leather case he carried in the back pocket opposite his wallet.

There wasn't a Treasury training course in clandestine surveillance gimmickry that Torbeck hadn't passed at the top of his class. Locks of all sorts, from the electronically controlled to the simplest mechanical devices, were a specialty. He was gifted with the ability to shut everything else out and maintain an absolute focus until any barrier, no matter how problematic, yielded to his superior will and skill. The lock to room 16 offered little challenge.

Lead time or not, he made sure he had one in the chamber of his Beretta, and kept it handy. He had no warrant and was committing an illegal act. This made him mindful of the fact that anyone who shot him could claim reasonable cause. The room he entered was typical for this particular motel chain. From his experience of renting adjoining rooms with Mc-Elliot, while on the road, he knew that units 15 and 17 would reflect the same layout in reverse; same furniture and decor, the bathrooms taking advantage of the mutually plumbed drainage and water risers. There was a king-size bed, a table that doubled as a desk, two Windsor chairs, a recliner, and a television mounted atop a long, low dresser. The room didn't look particularly lived in. There were half a dozen empty Busch cans in the wastebasket and a cardboard ice bucket with water in the bottom. One towel had been used and was thrown over the top of the bathroom door. Half of the complimentary matches were gone, and there were eight Lucky Strike butts in the ashtray.

As he took inventory, Torbeck was careful not to move any item even slightly out of place. The clothing the man carried in the one nylon duffel and a hard-sided suitcase was the typical gear of the blue-collar stiff on vacation. Socks, underwear, jeans, shorts, and casual shirts. The occupant hadn't bothered to unpack anything into the dresser drawers, and there were only two items, both shirts, hung in the closet. After completing a circuit of the entire room, he got down on his belly to peer beneath the bed. The large, molded aluminum case he found there got his pulse rate up.

"Hello," he greeted it softly. "And who might you be?" Very carefully, he dragged it out into the dim light of the room.

Before attempting to open the thing, he played his penlight over every square inch of it. He found the hair around on the right side, midway along the seam between the lid and body of the case. The owner had wet it and stuck it far enough back that anyone not as careful as Stan would certainly have overlooked it. Torbeck removed a card from his wallet, creased it, and placed the hair in the fold where it wouldn't get lost. He then went to work on the two juxtaposed latch locks. They were trickier than they looked and took nearly ten minutes a side. Once freed, they gave with precise little clicks. He then eased the lid up a bare quarter of an inch and played the light all the way around the lip. When he was confident that there were no booby traps, he pushed it back and up. A low whistle escaped his lips.

"Well lookee here."

Two hundred fifty thousand in crisp new hundreds caught his eye first, but nestled next to them lay an Ingraham MAC-10 machine pistol and two fully loaded, 32-round magazines. Stuffed into a pocket in the lid, Torbeck also found a manila envelope. When he dumped it out onto the carpet, he found a passport issued to an Anthony Edward Flood, a passbook to a numbered account on Grand Cayman Island, and a sheaf of eight-by-ten, black and white photographs.

Torbeck checked the time. He had been inside the room for twenty-six minutes. He then lifted the photographs and closely examined each one of them. The first seemed to be a copy of ledgered entries, done in an amateurish fashion on the back of a large envelope. Three more were photographs of a bed, its sheets stained with copious amounts of what looked to be blood. Another was a picture of a wrecked car, license plate prominent and clearly readable. There were also pictures of Constance Dahlrymple's driver's license and a coroner's report, indicating that the dead girl had not died in an automobile crash, but from loss of blood, suffered in the wake of a botched abortion.

As he replaced everything exactly as he'd found it, shut the case and glued the hair back in place, Torbeck once again checked the time. He was scheduled to meet Bob back at De-Witt's lake house in forty-seven minutes. It was at least an hour and a quarter, getting down there. He was going to be late.

In hopes of avoiding her father before he flew back to Washington, Francine worked well into the usual noon lunch hour, returning to the big house after one o'clock. She was surprised to find her grandfather still at his meal in the dining room.

"Is Dad gone?" She made no attempt to hide the hopefulness in her tone.

Franklin lifted his head from the copy of the *Wall Street Journal* at his elbow to shake his head. "Today was completely shot. He saddled one of the cow horses a few hours ago and said something about trying to unwind." He paused to regard his granddaughter with tired eyes. "Your revelation last night didn't help any, but I think the pressure was already getting to him."

This was a lot more information than the old man might generally offer. To further confuse her, there was no attempt made to mask the despondency in his tone. He nodded at the pendulum wall clock.

"Sit down, Francie. I didn't think you were coming up for lunch. Let's you and me talk."

There was none of the accustomed command in his voice. Instead, it was clearly an invitation. As Francine pulled up the chair directly across the table from him, the cook entered to ask if she'd like soup. Split pea. Francine told her she'd eat split wood. She was ravenous.

"Holding companies. Syndications. Buying thoroughbred stock at auction. You're really very serious about all this, aren't you?"

It didn't have the heat of challenge in it, but out of reflex the young woman moved to defend her position. "The idea of incorporating and letting Carter raise the money sounded like a good idea at the time. Some breeders make a life out of raising quarter horses, but for me it was never any more than a way to get my foot in the door. I spent every penny of my Harrington trust, getting where I am right now. I can't take the next step without backing.''

''And syndication is one of the very common routes, I take it.''

She nodded. ''Unless you're the Aga Khan.'' Pausing, a smile played across her lips as her gaze momentarily lost its focus. ''Or Bobby McElliot.''

Franklin was surprised to hear Bobby's name mentioned in this context. ''What does Bobby have to do with this?''

As the cook arrived with her soup, Francine drew herself up in her chair, squaring her shoulders. ''Last Tuesday, before I heard anything about this madness Carter is involved in, Bobby offered to back me. I know my dad doesn't believe it, but even if Carter had been successful in extorting that money, I no longer even had a *reason* to take it.''

''And you told Carter that?''

''I didn't tell him why, but yes, I did say our deal was off.''

The houseman, Enrique, entered by the main double doors from the entry hall.

''The man I mentioned, sir. The one who visited here the other evening. He's here and is demanding to see you.''

Franklin frowned, irritated by this interruption. ''Demanding?''

''Yes sir. He seems quite insistent.''

''More than *quite*, Charlie!'' As the voice boomed in the hall outside, Enrique was rudely jostled aside and a burly, tough-looking man in a jacket and tie stepped into the room.

''What is the meaning of this?'' Franklin rasped. ''You can't come barging into a man's home like this. Who the hell do you think you are?''

Without missing a beat, Tony Flood strode toward the table to pull up a chair and sit at the far end. ''Anthony Flood, Senator. My friends an' even my enemies generally wind up callin' me Tony.'' He paused to turn toward the redhead sitting across from the old man. "An' you must be Francine. Carter *did* say you was a looker.''

"Carter *DeWitt*?'' Franklin demanded. "You're a friend of his?''

Flood chuckled at this notion. "Not exactly. I used t' work for him. Now, I'm workin' free-lance. I gotta feelin' it's gonna pay better.'' As he said it, he tossed the bulky manila envelope he'd been carrying onto the table. It slid along to stop between Franklin and Francine.

When both Coulters hesitated to reach for it, Flood lifted his chin in a gesture of encouragement. "Go ahead. Take a peek inside'a there.''

Franklin grabbed the envelope impatiently and tore open the flap without bothering with the clasp. From it, he withdrew a sheaf of curling photographs, yellowed documents and a number of smaller items, paper-clipped together. Scowling, he began to examine them.

"What is it?'' Francine murmured.

Franklin shook his head and looked down the table to this man who wanted to be called Tony. "A driver's license. Some pictures of a car wreck. More pictures of what looks like a bed soaked in blood?''

"I'll save y'all the time of readin' the coroner's report. It states that the girl on that driver's license died of a fucked-up abortion. The sheriff an' the papers all reported that she died in that there car accident. Them pictures of the bed are where she *really* died . . . after your boy Richard got her pregnant an' had his buddy Phil DeWitt hire a couple'a hack doctors t' fix it for him.'' Flood pointed to another item, clipped to the driver's license. "That last document there? That's a title report on the car she wrecked. It says the Triumph TR-3 was registered to her name, but purchased from the Kansas City dealer by a Richard Coulter.''

His face gone deathly pale, Franklin thrust the envelope items away into the middle of the table. "Where did you get this?'' There was little heat in his tone now.

Flood was on his feet and moving along the table to reach over and gather his treasure back into a nice, neat pile. "From the sheriff who DeWitt got to help him out of the jam he was in. He obviously ran the plate with the DMV an' put it all t'gether." Flipping the envelope faceup, he pointed to the ledger-lined setup and annual dollar-amount entries. "It looks like he had enough t' keep somebody real grateful. He got a nice tidy sum come every Thanksgivin' since. That was a nice touch, old man. Thanksgivin'."

Franklin's eyes went narrow and his jaw tight. Across the table from him Francine sat in shock. What she'd just heard left her immobilized.

"What do you want from me?" Franklin croaked.

Flood grinned, reached into the inside breast pocket of his jacket, and handed a piece of paper to Francine. "Give that to your granddaddy, will you, sugar? It's the number o' my Grand Cayman Island bank account." He turned to Franklin. "I'll sell you everything there, but it ain't gonna come cheap. If y'all want that boy o' yours t' be the next President of this wonderful land o' opportunity, you'll pay."

"How much?" Franklin growled.

"Five million sounds like a nice round number, don't it?"

Francine's glazed-over eyes had not left her grandfather's face. In some remote part of her consciousness she worried that the old man was going to burst an artery. His face had gone from livid to red with speechless rage. Flood pressed ahead undaunted.

"This is Tuesday. Next Monday at noon I'm gonna telephone the manager o' that Grand Cayman bank. If he don't have some real good news for me, I'm gonna package up copies o' that there envelope an' send 'em, along with a letter of clarification, to the *Kansas City Star*, the *St. Louis Post-Dispatch*, *The Washington Post*, an' *The New York Times*."

Twenty-Three

At the filling station described in Stan's message, McElliot pulled in, checking the time. They were fifteen minutes past the appointed hour and his partner was nowhere to be seen.

"What do you think?" he asked Marilyn.

"I think that if Carter DeWitt is home, we should move on him. We can't discount the possibility that your motel manager got the message wrong. It could be that Stan is already there, or it could be that he got hung up somewhere."

Bobby climbed out of the car and hurried across to the glassed-in operator's kiosk. The attendant inside had some heavy metal cranked up to ear-splitting levels on a portable player, and to get his attention, McElliot had to rap hard on the glass. He requested with a hand gesture that the kid turn it down.

"You know of a DeWitt around here? On Rural Route 3?"

It got him a look like he had a hole in the middle of his forehead. "Everything's Rural Route 3 'round here, dude. Who was that, d'ya say?"

"DeWitt."

The kid thought a moment, running a hand back and forth across the impeccably maintained surface of his flat-top crew cut. "Nope. Don't ring no bells. But hang on a sec." That said, he lifted the receiver of his phone and punched in a number from memory. Whatever he tried to convey didn't take long.

"That was my sister," he reported. "Works part-time for the P.O. durin' the summer crunch. Says there's a DeWitt on County 39–9. Jest a quarter mile down that way, onna right. Say's it's the biggest place down there. Stone house onna lake side."

McElliot thanked him and started back for the car as the air was filled once again with strains of Twisted Sister. Once they located the county road they had no trouble finding the DeWitt place. The shiny new Lincoln that Torbeck and McElliot had followed that morning from St. Louis was parked in front of the garage. Its left rear end was jacked up off the drive, the tire, presumably flat, leaning up against the bumper. The trunk lid of the car was up, all the curtains of the house drawn back and the windows cranked open to catch the breeze off the lake.

Because they wanted to avoid spooking the lawyer, as well as check around for signs of Stan, McElliot continued another hundred yards down the road, turned around, and parked on the shoulder, still a good distance away.

"I guess we can handle this alone," Bobby told Marilyn. "Looks like Carter's right in the middle of fixing a flat." And as he said it, he pulled his Walther automatic from his waistband holster to check the action. "You ready?"

"He's an attorney," Marilyn reminded him. "So he's likely to see reason once I delineate the points of the case I can build against him. In the face of it, I have to believe he'll be willing to cooperate. Let's give him every chance, all right?"

After listening to Ervin Orton's story, Marilyn was now convinced that DeWitt had been double-crossed by the man Bobby and Stan observed in his company. The heavyset sidekick certainly fit Orton's description, but McElliot was still skeptical.

"You seem convinced he was double-crossed, and I'm not. Carter's goon fits the description Orton gave us, but there's just as good a chance that the whole rip-off was some sort of ruse."

They'd been arguing this point all the way along their seventy-minute drive from Fellows Lake to Shell Knob.

"Either way, Bobby, I'm fairly certain that it will come clear pretty soon. Let's go talk to the man."

McElliot nodded, balancing his weapon gingerly in his right hand. "This is just to ensure that you get to say your piece, unhindered. Once you arrest him, are you going to want cuffs?"

"I don't think they'll be necessary, but you use your own judgment. We want him feeling cooperative the next time we sit down to talk with him."

"Okay. Let's do it."

The front door of the sprawling ranch house was slightly ajar. When McElliot rapped at the panel with the back of his fist, it swung wide to reveal an entry wall hung with prints of waterfowl and other game birds. Off to his left a large, vault-ceilinged living room, awash with afternoon light, appeared to be empty.

"Mr. DeWitt?" Marilyn called out.

When they received no answer, Bobby turned to her. "Door hanging wide open in the middle of the day. No one home. Does this look like reasonable cause to enter, counselor?"

"I think so."

Together they stepped inside onto a waxed flagstone floor and passed through a timber arch into the living room proper. Out through three huge sliding glass doors to the east, a flagstone terrace stretched thirty feet to a rock balustrade, the surface of the lake gleaming in the distance below. One of the glass doors stood open, a cooling breeze flowing through the room from off the water. Marilyn called out DeWitt's name again as McElliot moved forward into the room and across it to a doorway at the far end.

Backfire

"I'd advise you to stay right where you are," he suggested, tossing it back over his shoulder.

"What?" Marilyn demanded. She ignored his warning, hurrying forward. The sight of the dead man, lying just feet away, with half his skull blown off and brain matter falling away into a huge pool of blood, saw her pull up abruptly, reverse field, and run for the terrace.

"I warned you," McElliot muttered. Behind him he could hear the sound of Marilyn's spasmodic wretching off the terrace balustrade outside. He avoided looking down at the gore close by and stepped around the puddle of fresh blood to move toward something catching his attention at the far end of the room; a wall safe, in the classic hiding place behind a hinged painting, the door hanging open. There was a small grip zipped open and set on the far end of the pool table, an envelope bulging with money set atop it.

With one finger hooked beneath the full Windsor knot, Flood worked the tie loose, yanked it away from around his neck, and threw it out the window. From the vantage of his sideview mirror he could see it caught in the turbulence behind his speeding vehicle, twisting and fluttering like a paper streamer in a Chinese New Year parade. Down in Rio, he'd be damned if he would ever wear a tie again. Hell, down in Rio he'd be damned if he wore much of *anything* again.

There was still one last piece of business that needed addressing before he returned to Springfield and then St. Louis to prepare his departure. It had started to nag at him again on the road to Aurora. The more he thought about the way Carter tried to hide the interior of that safe, and the way he'd closed its door, the more convinced he was that something of value remained within it. Maybe it was only the attorney's ever-increasing paranoia he'd witnessed, but it was just as possible that Carter *had* held something back, and Tony didn't like loose ends.

DeWitt's car remained exactly where Tony had left it, both rear tires slashed, in the drive. The trunk lid was up and the

Christopher Newman

spare was now on the right wheel, while the wheel opposite was jacked in the air, the flat removed and left that way. Carter was no doubt waiting for a wrecker from one of the local service stations to arrive and help bail him out of this jam. Flood felt a moment of real sympathy for the kid. Proud of his cunning, his skill as a strategist, and his gambler's moxie, Carter was probably still trying to figure out how he'd so royally screwed up such a sure thing.

It seemed a little odd that the front door stood open like that, but DeWitt was most likely still trying to get under way, his efforts only temporarily thwarted. Tony entered the house without knocking or ringing the bell, moving down the hall to the kitchen dead ahead and grabbing himself a cold Busch from the refrigerator. He was back out in the hall and headed for the living room when he heard the sound of movement behind him, coming from the direction of the bedrooms. Pulling up, he eased his Smith & Wesson snubnose from beneath his belt.

"You ain't outta here quite yet, Carter boy. We still got one more little piece o' business t' discuss."

The good-looking blonde who poked her head out the master-bedroom door quickly lost the quizzical expression she wore. Yet, in spite of the gun, she stood her ground.

"The only piece of business we have to discuss is the fact that you're under arrest."

Her cool bravado had an unsettling effect on him. He stood there with the muzzle of his .38 trained on her, his mouth smiling in disbelief.

"Y'all wanna say that *again*?"

And as he asked this most reasonable of questions, a blunt object smashed into the base of his skull.

McElliot tempered the blow he delivered, not wanting to kill the guy. That was a mistake. As he closed to spin the man around and hit him again, he could see that he'd only stunned him. The guy staggered forward a half step, looking like he might go down, and then caught his balance. Too

286

late, Bobby realized that he was too close and wide open on his left side. His opponent's gun hand came back with surprising quickness, hard and tight. The fist with the revolver in it caught him just below the sternum with such force that it knocked him staggering backward, the wind expelled in a whoosh from his lungs. His adversary planted his feet now, got his knees flexed, and launched himself. While Bobby was fighting to blink the stars from his vision and get some air, Marilyn's prisoner was all over him like a swarm of bees.

The reflexes of the survival instinct kicked in, damage control telling him that he wasn't really hurt, while simultaneously he tucked an elbow in tight to his side and drove it directly upward to land crashing into his opponent's jaw. He had a lot of leverage behind it, and caught the man square at a point which should have seen his jaw hinges explode. The two eyes, just inches away from Bobby's own face, glazed for no more than a two-count before the guy shook his head like an enraged bull in the ring, screamed, and began landing sledgehammer blows with his fists. The best McElliot could do was cover a few of the half-dozen vital areas suffering the brunt of it. One shot to the right kidney sent a bolt of pain all the way up his back to his neck. Another caught him dead in the middle of his upper right arm. The whole thing went numb, clear to his wrist.

Somewhere in the back of his mind fear crept in to roost. He'd had the drop on this guy and lost the advantage. He'd made a serious mistake, and now that mistake was going to cost him his life.

As close as it was, the *shick-clack* of an automatic pistol's action sounded like the crash of dueling sabers.

"Twitch and I'll blow your fucking gray matter all over that wall." It was hissed; a mean and sinister voice that was music to McElliot's ears. The torrent of stinging blows suddenly ceased. Eyes wide, Bobby slowly turned his head to see Stan Torbeck crouched down, one knee planted in the middle of the assailant's back, his Beretta jammed up against the base of his skull.

* * *

McElliot was left to nurse his wounds while Stan got the man now identified as Anthony Flood into a chair and Marilyn got her cuffs on him. It was a wing chair, the most difficult thing Torbeck could find for a man to sit in with his hands secured behind his back. For the moment, all four of them were gathered in the living room, Torbeck and his weapon working in support of Marilyn as the interrogator. Bobby sat to one side with a dishtowel full of ice held to his throbbing head.

"Killed him?" There was open incredulity in Flood's voice. "Not me, lady. Y'all might be able t' pin rippin' off that candy-ass cardiologist on me, but there ain't no way I did Carter." He paused to shake his head in disbelief. "Damn, lady. Use your head. What the *fuck* would I be doin' comin' back here if I'd just killed DeWitt?"

"Maybe you'd forgotten something . . . like eighty-five thousand dollars in cash?" Marilyn suggested.

Flood snorted. "Right. He's dead an' I come strollin' back in here, grab m'self a cold beer an' call out to him there in the hall? What was I doin', lady? Beggin' you feds t' hang my ass? Man like me don't *forget* eighty-five grand."

As Flood spoke, Torbeck had crossed to hand McElliot his pistol. Now he turned to Marilyn. "If I were you, I'd get on the horn with the resident agent in Springfield and have him get a warrant to search room sixteen of the Super 8 motel on Kearney Street. Right now, I think I'll step outside and poke around inside this character's car."

Marilyn's interest was piqued. "What's up, Stan?"

"I've got a strong feeling that they'll find an item or two in that room that will shed some light on what our friend here's been up to."

"That's an illegal search!" Flood snarled. "You've been inside my room!"

"Who has?" Stan asked. "Not me, Mr. Flood."

Once Stan left, McElliot kept the Beretta trained on the prisoner while Marilyn called Agent Riley. Some of the throbbing had gone out of Bobby's scratches and bruises, but he knew he was going to feel like hell when he tried to get out of bed tomorrow. It was some minutes before Torbeck returned from outdoors, carrying two large manila envelopes. Out of Flood's hearing, Stan bent close, showing the ledger-ruled side of one envelope to his partner.

"I saw a photographed copy of this same ledger setup just a couple hours ago," Stan murmured. "Found it in a case under this guy's bed. Case had a couple guns and a lot of cash in it, but get a load of what's inside here."

Stan untied the string clasp, lifted the flap, and spilled the contents out onto the mottled steer-hide cushion between them. One at a time Bobby picked up and scrutinized the yellowed documents stolen from Sheriff Boz Scranton's floor safe. As he did so he began to get a sick feeling in the pit of his stomach. After reading the title report, delineating the provenance of Constance Dahlrymple's wrecked TR-3, his eyes came slowly up to be confronted by Stan's own knowing look.

"He talked about coming out here to confront Francine, Bob. Flood's got a point about that eighty-five grand. Who would ignore something like that but a guy conditioned to be indifferent to it?"

Bobby just shook his head in continued disbelief. "It's crazy."

"No, Bob. *He's* crazy. You would be too, if you'd been in a position like his and sitting on a secret like this for thirty years."

Across the room Marilyn hung up the phone and turned to watch these two, deep in murmured conference.

"What did you find?" she asked Stan.

"Deep shit," was Torbeck's reply.

"Take a look," McElliot offered. He held the sheaf of documents out to her.

Twenty-Four

At several remote locations across the seventy-eight square miles of open range land, stands of timber, and rugged ridges that comprised the Coulter ranch, seven remote bunking stations had been constructed to provide ranch hands temporary shelter. Each station consisted of two ten-wide mobile homes, one with a fully stocked kitchen and the other outfitted with eight bunk beds. There was a corral built nearby for horses, a small feed shed which also housed a diesel-powered generator, and a weather-tight outbuilding, inside of which was parked a military surplus jeep.

As Richard Coulter thumped and jounced across a stretch of open terrain, en route back to way-station 6, he was more concerned with catching his six o'clock flight out of Springfield than with eluding detection. Early that morning he'd taken pains to determine where the foreman had his crews working. He'd checked the service records in the ranch office to make sure the jeep at station 6 was in good repair. And lastly, he'd plotted a route off the ranch that would bypass all work parties. He'd left the main house just after breakfast, the knowledge of Carter DeWitt's business involvement with his daughter still burning in his gut like spoiled meat. The fact was little more than insult added to injury, but it helped strengthen his resolve as he corralled the horse and backed the jeep out of the station 6 shed for the trip south to Table Rock Lake. On a Tuesday at the beginning of the off-season, traffic down Route 39 toward Shell Knob had been light, the journey taking less than half an hour. Richard arrived in the area at eleven-thirty, continuing on through Shell Knob and beyond to the town of Viola, just a few miles distant. Within twenty minutes of parking and beginning a surreptitious survey of the lakefront on foot, he spotted a nifty little runabout tied to a private dock. The house fronting the dock was isolated and empty. The boat proved to have an OMC Cobra power plant which turned out to be as easy to hot-wire as an old Farmall tractor. By noon Richard was under way across the water toward the DeWitt spread's private beach and dock. It wasn't much of a trip, and once he'd gotten up a good head of steam, he cut the engine a hundred yards out and drifted in on the prevailing breeze.

When the senator returned to station 6 at two-fifteen that afternoon, he found Ginger, the big cutting-horse mare he'd ridden out that morning, expressing her displeasure at being left for three hours without food or water. Earlier Richard had been so preoccupied with his mission that he'd barely remembered to remove her saddle. Now she whinnied and kicked viciously at the boards of her confinement. Unfortunately, it was still an hour's hard ride back to the stables, and Richard was on a schedule. There was no time to waste pumping water by hand into the corral trough if he wanted to make his scheduled flight back to Washington and the campaign trail.

As he stooped to lift the saddle and throw it onto the irritated horse's back, the barrel of his .32 caliber Smith & Wesson revolver gouged him in the small of the back. He had no holster for it and stuffed it into the waistband of his trousers after climbing out of the jeep. Carter had been standing with his back to him, preoccupied with stuffing an envelope full of cash into a nylon sport bag, failing to even hear his killer's approach through an open door from off the terrace. It had taken only one bullet to finally put to rest the torture of twenty-nine long years, and five more roundnose, S&W long loads still remained in the cylinder.

Torbeck's Ford Probe was abandoned for the larger Taurus wagon. A call to Dick Strahan in Washington had revealed what the investigation team already suspected. Senator Richard Coulter had canceled all of his Tuesday meetings to accompany his father home to Missouri Monday night. With Anthony Flood in her custody as the prime suspect in Friday's assault and robbery at the Orton home, Marilyn phoned Supervisory Agent Joe Riley to report that she was on her way to the Coulter ranch. Riley was asked to report DeWitt's murder to the Barry County sheriff and to request they seal off the scene until an FBI forensics unit could be flown in to process it.

Stan had them moving through the twists and turns of Route 39 at tire-squealing speeds as they made the thirty-minute trip north. Marilyn rode shotgun, her nails digging into the dash, while an aching McElliot occupied the backseat with the prisoner.

"Richard was married in 1962," Bobby recalled. "I was five years old when my mom died, and it wasn't more than two years later that Julia and Richard tied the knot. I remember it clearly because I didn't understand why everyone was making such a big deal of it at the time. Richard's father and grandfather were both U.S. senators, but his marriage into my family gave him old money respectability. There was a big hullabaloo when Julia lost her first baby about a year later. I was in Washington for the usual month I spent there every summer. I can still remember, like it was yesterday, how hard she took it."

"That was when?" Stan asked. "Before Richard made that first run for Congress?"

"Must have been right around there. Maybe before, but

close. The politics all run together. To a little kid, it seemed like someone was always running for something.''

As they turned right off the highway and onto the county road leading to the ranch, McElliot spotted a low-flying, fast-moving helicopter skimming the treetops off to the east. ''Your Bureau friend?'' he asked Marilyn, pointing.

The prosecutor frowned, letting go of the dash long enough to risk a peek at her watch. ''That's some pretty quick response.''

''Just mention you intend to arrest a United States senator for murder,'' Torbeck muttered. ''Works most every time.''

Two miles in, along the ranch road, Bobby spotted a man on horseback about a half mile distant, across the rolling range to his right. And at that instant the rider seemed to spot the approaching helicopter. The horse reared back on its hind legs, twisting in protest as it was reined in hard, turned quickly, and was urged away at a dead run. The man in the saddle appeared to be unusually tall, and the move had panic written all over it.

Bobby pointed at the sign to Francine's stable complex. ''Pull it in there, Stanley! I think that's the senator out there.''

Torbeck reacted even before he'd absorbed what his partner was up to. The Taurus ran a quarter mile along the gravel access road, skidding to a halt in the middle of the stable yard. Ignoring the stiffness of his injuries, Bobby was out of the car and running before it came to a complete halt. Francine's groom, Jorge Mendez, was taken completely off guard as the former Junior Rodeo Champ came toward him at a dead sprint, yanked the nylon-web halter from his hand, and leaped aboard the gelding Jorge was leading back from the exercise paddock.

The fifty-six-year-old senator was exhausted, no longer used to the rigors of more than a pleasure ride. The horse was also wearying of having to sustain the bulk of Richard's six-foot, five-inch frame. The demands he was making on the animal were beginning to tell. Bits of foamed saliva flew away from its mouth to streak both neck and flanks. Richard didn't know who the occupants of that helicopter were, but he didn't like the way it was moving. The paranoia that had gnawed daily at the lining of his stomach for almost thirty years had spread like wildfire over this past week. It now raged, an all-consuming inferno.

There was rugged high ground just a mile off; boulder-strewn and brush-choked. The way the helicopter flew on along the ranch road to the west, he knew he hadn't yet been spotted. The high ground was the only available cover, and Richard urged the mare toward it, the thudding of its heart reaching him through its rib cage. It was a thudding nearly as panicked as his own.

No saddle, no bridle and bit, Bobby McElliot clamped the gelding's flanks with his knees, climbed as far forward over its neck as he could get, and rode with one hand wrapped in the halter lead and the other in mane hair. Together they streaked around the outside fence of Francine's new oval flat track, crossed the main ranch road, and hurdled four feet of barbed-wire range fence. If the horse hadn't been moving at high speed, the landing alone would have probably thrown Bobby. But then, if it hadn't been moving at such speed, it never would have cleared the fence in the first place. This was a quarter horse, not a steeplechase mount. The horseman he'd spotted toward the southeast was no longer anywhere to be seen. Still, he set course in that direction, cheating it a bit due east to try and take advantage of the higher ground.

The pilot of the helicopter had obviously noticed the station wagon's departure from the main road toward the stables, and had swung around to hover fifty feet above the yard. No sooner had he arrived than Torbeck was out of the car and waving frantically, signaling for the pilot to land. The dust rose in a choking whirlwind and horses screamed in their stalls as the pilot set it down dead in the middle of the stable yard. Marilyn was out of the car and running behind Torbeck as he approached the copilot's side door of the chopper. Joe Riley, pulling his headset off to hear her shouting above the rotor racket, leaned out.

Marilyn pointed to Resident Agent O'Casey, sitting in one of the two backseats, and then toward the car.

"I need him to watch my prisoner!" she hollered. "And then I need you to get us into the air as fast as you can!"

Still leaning out, Riley jerked a quick thumb at Torbeck.

"Who's he?!"

"Treasury!"

Without further argument, Riley twisted in his seat, signaling and shouting something to O'Casey. The resident agent dropped his headset and popped the passenger compartment door.

The far-off, muffled roar of the helicopter hovering, landing, and then taking off again intensified the raw panic already short-circuiting Richard Coulter's rational processes. This was a nightmare. He was scheduled to address a breakfast meeting of labor officials at the Washington Hyatt Regency tomorrow morning. He was going to miss his plane. And up through the haze of confused concerns rose the absolute conviction that once the helicopter got back into the air, he had to get rid of his horse and get to ground.

The rugged ridge that he hoped might offer refuge ran directly above his right shoulder, and Richard now gave up paralleling it, looking for a spot where he could urge the horse to begin the climb. As he reined the mare in, prepared to dismount and go it on foot, the horse stumbled, surged forward, and went down. Like a fool, Richard reached with his right hand to break the fall. His wrist gave with the impact, a searing pain shooting up his arm as he was thrown, tumbling head over heels. In the next instant the horse was back on her feet, eyes wild with her own panic. As Richard lay facedown in the dirt and sunbaked weeds, she bolted.

Ten feet away from where he lay, his eyes caught the glint

of blue gun metal. Rolling onto his back, he sat, trying to assess the damage done by the fall. His wrist hung limp, a fierce pain numbing his arm up past his elbow. He couldn't move any of the fingers in his right hand, but his trembling legs still seemed to function as he moved to his knees. One foot planted at a time, he got himself upright, the heavy thrum of the helicopter now clearly audible as it rose high in the air to the west. Breath coming in gasps, a cold sweat of shock now replacing the hot sweat of exertion, he stumbled forward to retrieve his weapon. The first rock outcropping offering refuge was still fifty feet away. Washington, Julia, his beautiful home, the halls of power, tomorrow morning's breakfast meeting, and his missed flight all surfaced to swim along on the rushing torrent of jumbled cogitation as he started for those rocks, left hand cradling his pistol and his useless right.

McElliot was moving along the crest of a rise that afforded him good views of the rolling terrain running away to the north and a valley rimmed by a rugged ridge to the south. At the foot of that southern ridge he spotted a riderless horse, head down and grazing, its saddle askew on its back. Only ten minutes ago Bobby had seen that horse with its rider. If he was on foot, the senator could not have gone far from where he'd dismounted. Raised on this land, Richard Coulter was surely familiar with the terrain. And back in Washington he probably played a little squash or handball to stay trim, but he was no longer any spring chicken. The question now was where he'd gotten off that horse and started up into the rock cover above.

The gelding was urged down off the rise and across the floor of the hollow to where the grazing horse stood. As he moved, McElliot could hear the helicopter complete a first sweep to the north and begin to come back toward him. An air search of terrain like this, with its rock formations and thick stands of hardwood growth, would demand a lot of low-level ferreting out if it were going to be of any assistance.

Backfire

The mare he approached was soaked with sweat and breathing hard, shiny patches of foamed saliva streaking its muzzle, face, and neck. The belly cinch of the saddle didn't appear to be loose, and yet the thing had been wrenched over fifty degrees. It occurred to Bobby that Richard may not have dismounted voluntarily. While the weeds to the west appeared undisturbed, there were definite signs that the horse had approached its present position from the east. With the gelding now moving at an easy walk, its own breath labored, McElliot leaned down to scrutinize the broken range grasses below as he followed the spent mare's trail along the foot of the ridge.

"There!"
Marilyn was leaning forward, the top of her head pressed against the Plexiglas window on her side of the craft. Index finger extended, she was pointing to a spot off to their left, at ten o'clock.
"You see him?" The pilot glanced back to get the direction and eased the stick over, dropping the bird into a swooping left-hand dive.
Stan was leaned almost up against her and peering over her shoulder now. What they both could see was a man on a horse, moving slowly along the foot of a geologic jumble of rock and brush and away from a riderless horse.
"Coulter's on foot," Torbeck told her. He leaned away to tap the pilot on the shoulder and point downward. "Let's work the top of that ridge. As low as you can go, and be prepared to get the hell out fast. The man is armed."

When Bobby encountered the area of trampled grass, he had no doubt that Coulter had been thrown. Dirt was torn up where the mare's hoofs scrambled to get purchase, and a large patch was flattened nearby where she'd fallen. More grass was bent and flattened along a path leading up into the rocks.
The gelding darted off once Bobby slipped from its back

and slapped it hard on the haunches. Overhead, the helicopter was making enough racket to scare the beast far afield. As Bobby started along the senator's trail up the ridge, he watched the whirlybird's progress as it dropped to treetop level and made a first pass, directly above. When the first bullet ricocheted off the rock formation he was ducking to pass beneath, Bobby leaped aside and rolled frantically for cover. The rush of adrenaline came on quickly. The protesting of his bruised ribs and aching right arm were quieted almost as quickly as they were voiced. A second shot rang out, and now the chopper rose crazily away from the ridge top, its engine straining to deliver full power.

If his ears weren't deceiving him, McElliot was pretty sure that the last shot had been fired from a spot above and west of his own position. While he took care to make as little noise as possible, he eased back away from his cover and worked down along a ledge running farther east. Behind him, out in the middle of the little valley, the chopper could be heard setting down. He hoped it would provide enough distraction to allow him to start uphill.

Twice Richard had blacked out from the pain. His hands and feet gone cold, he was shivering on a day when the mercury had crept into the high eighties. He knew the helicopter was sweeping the area in search of him, and he was concentrating on eluding detection from the air when the man on horseback appeared at the foot of the ridge. He couldn't force his exhausted body into further retreat up the hillside, so he lay in wait until his pursuer was less than fifty feet away. With the thunder of the helicopter engine creating a deafening din overhead, he steadied his unaccustomed left hand across the top of a rock and squeezed off that first shot. If only he could have used his right hand, he thought he would have gotten the man. As it was, he got close enough to send him scurrying.

The helicopter afforded a much easier target, its entire profile exposed to a second shot which hit somewhere amidships. It was time for Richard to force himself higher up into the heavy growth of oak, just above. He needed desperately to clear his mind, to think over his options. Now, as the helicopter landed down in the valley, the damned noise of its engines cut to create a refreshing silence, he forced himself to swallow his pain and move. He was a Coulter. Coulters were survivors. They were leaders of men. God-fearing Christians. Anointed.

So why was he crying? Why couldn't he control the trembling of his limbs and the tears that rolled freely down his cheeks? Where was the helping hand of his God?

"Drop the gun, Richard, or I'll shoot you dead where you stand."

The voice came from on high, overhead. A familiar voice, yet strange. Strange and cold, it had power, but not the power to save him. And as he struggled to focus his perception, he lifted his gun to stare at it.

"Give it up, Richard. Put the gun *down*."

His eyes raised, Coulter watched as a man emerged from behind a tree and through shadow to stand confronting him in the afternoon sunlight. Not his God, but a man with a gun leveled at the center of his chest.

"Bobby?" The tears still ran freely and his voice quavered as he asked it.

"That's right, Senator. You're under arrest. Make any sudden move and I'll shoot you."

Richard was still focusing as one thing came suddenly clear.

"Because I killed your father." The warmth of new understanding flowed over him, displacing the chill of all those many years of fear as he fitted the barrel of the revolver into his mouth. He was free now, no longer concerned with why Bobby's eyes went wide and his face seemed to pale. Richard watched as Bobby opened his mouth to scream. The words were something Richard never heard.

Twenty-Five

Six hours of high-intensity investigative frenzy followed in the wake of the prominent senator and presidential candidate's suicide. Federal officers were flown in immediately from Kansas City, St. Louis, Tulsa, and Little Rock. Within a few hours of that first wave's arrival, Bureau and Secret Service heavyweights began trickling onto the scene from Washington. The Coulter ranch had been sealed off from a hoard of clamoring media hounds, and now, as the frenzy subsided, the rolling Ozark landscape lay in relative peace beneath a waning but still fat moon. At eight o'clock Julia Coulter had arrived via chartered jet and helicopter. Ultimately, she was sedated by the family physician and put to bed in the same room she'd shared with her husband of thirty-one years. Bobby McElliot did not want to dwell on where her dreams might take her through this night.

Just as the solution of his father's murder was taking its toll on Bobby, the ramifications of it were taking their toll on the surviving Coulter family. The reunion with her mother was difficult for Francine. The two had never been emotionally close, and as Bobby witnessed their attempts to come to grips with this tragedy, the awkwardness was painfully apparent. Francine proved better prepared for dealing with the shattered Franklin. Once they got Julia to bed, the old man seemed grateful for the opportunity to get out of the house with Francine and Bobby. Together the three of them had walked out through the night air to a promontory, several hundred yards behind the house to the north.

"I don't believe I've ever felt a bigger fool," Franklin muttered. In the moonlight his eyes glistened with the tears of grief held barely in check. One of those big hands was looped into the crook of his granddaughter's arm. Before them the world dropped away in a pattern of low, silvered ridges and patches of deep shadow. The low glow of Springfield could be made out on the horizon to the east. "Richard was always a strange mixture of where he came from and where he wanted to go, but I never once imagined he was so out of control."

"None of us did," Francine returned softly. "You weren't any more a fool than the rest of us."

Franklin shook his head. "Somewhere along the way, I lost track of who my own boy *was*. That shakes me, probably because I'm such a prideful sonofabitch." He paused to turn to Bobby. "I have to confront the fact that I can never make this up to you. That hurts almost as much as having my only son dead."

Bobby was staring off in the direction of that glow to the east. He knew that Stan, who'd departed several hours earlier to retrieve the car in Shell Knob and their gear from the motel in Branson, would likely be checking into Marilyn's motel near the Springfield airport about now. He knew that both Stan and Marilyn were exhausted, but if they were still as keyed up as he felt, it would be some hours before any of them would be able to sleep.

"Give Francine your blessing," he told the old man. "If you want to make anything up to anyone, make your peace with her. Her dream might be different than the one you envisioned for Richard, but it's a good one, and she cares deeply about it."

Francine's right hand crossed her body to cover her grand-father's in the crook of her arm. "I think maybe he already has," she said softly.

Hands deep in his pockets, and shoulders hunched forward, McElliot took a step back. "It's been a long day. I think I'll head back to the motel."

With the foot of the Great Plains as her backdrop, Francine had never looked stronger or more capable to him. A light breeze had sprung up out of the southwest to tousle the strands of hair she reached to pull from her face. It was still a beautiful face, but with a strength of character he'd never really seen before.

"I suppose we've all got the pieces of our lives to pick up," she said. "I'd say right offhand that none of us envies the other his task."

Bobby shook his head. "Nope. I don't imagine."

When Torbeck finally checked into the Springfield Howard Johnson just minutes before midnight, there was a message from Marilyn, asking him to meet her in the lounge. He took a few minutes to splash water on his face and change his shirt before descending the stairs to the lobby and wandering toward the lounge. Even at that late hour the place was still alive with the overflow from some sort of business convention. At least seventy or eighty revelers crowded the lounge, where a four-piece combo, fronted by a sequin-gowned songbird, was mixing homogenized popular tunes into the smoke-filled air. Stan spotted Marilyn sitting alone at a corner table and crossed to collapse into the chair opposite.

"Hope you haven't been waiting long," he apologized.

She dismissed his concern with a shake of the head. "These jokers have kept me amused. They've been stepping up at a rate of one every ten minutes. Seems to be a real shortage of women in the boat-accessory business. Bobby still hasn't checked in?"

"Nope. No messages either." Torbeck thought he detected a hint of disappointment in the way she twirled her drink straw and flipped it into her empty glass. He twisted in his seat to flag the waitress.

"We got that toxicology report on Scranton," she reported as his attention returned. "When you told me you'd found that vial of potassium chloride in Flood's room, I called the Bureau's pathology lab and mentioned it to their staff chief."

"And?"

"At best, the potassium values they found in the tissue are inconclusive. The way he explained it, once decomposition begins, the electrolyte levels in the blood are constantly changing. Fortunately for us, Scranton floated in the cool waters of the lake for a couple of days, the temperature of the water slowing decomposition down. The coroner got the body on ice fairly quickly, and packaged the tissue samples he sent to Washington in dry ice."

Stan was scrambling mentally to follow. "What do you mean by inconclusive? It sounds like conditions were favorable. A big dose of potassium chloride induces heart attack. That would dovetail with the diagnosed cause of death."

"I wish it were that simple," she replied. "Yes, the potassium levels were slightly high, but not measurably high enough to cause death."

"Because the body was allowed to sit a few days."

"Right. With the decomposition rate factored in, the levels were *theoretically* much higher at the time of death, but theory alone isn't going to be enough to convict our friend Flood of Scranton's murder."

Torbeck tried to look at it philosophically. "I guess a vial of the compound isn't exactly a smoking gun, huh?"

"Maybe not," she allowed. "But I sent the state police forensics people down to Scranton's house in Taneyville. If they can get me even one match—hair, clothing fibers, anything—I think we'll try throwing the book at Mr. Flood. I'll admit it's a bit of a long shot."

When the waitress finally made it to their table, Stan ordered Marilyn another vodka and tonic, along with a Beck's beer for himself. After all the Busch he'd consumed while on this case, he was ready to escape the region entirely. With the waitress disappearing back into the crowd, he returned to the discussion at hand.

"I don't think I've ever seen Bob look so shaken. You think the senator really did kill his dad?"

The prosecutor shrugged. "Bobby told me that the senator referred to it like it was something he must have already figured out himself . . . like *that* was the reason Bobby had hunted him down. When I spoke to Agent Collins in Washington this evening, he told me that their primary suspect turned out to be a bag man for the oil lobby. He flew into D.C. the night Mr. McElliot was killed to make some sort of laundered-cash payment to a couple of congressmen. The stolen credit cards and abandoned rental car were part of an attempt to avoid being traced."

Torbeck grunted. "Little did they know. So when did they promise the ballistics report on the senator's gun?"

"Maybe as early as tomorrow."

"You staying out here or headed back east?"

Marilyn dipped a finger, pointing at the floor. "Here, at least until Jack Essex can send me a warm body down from Chicago. Then *that* lucky soul will get to sort out the case against Anthony Flood, and I'm out of here. I think I'll take a week off, lock myself into my apartment, and catch up on my sleep." Her eyes left his to flicker back through the crowd on the other side of a tiny dance floor. Stan turned to follow her glance and spotted McElliot.

As Bobby grabbed a chair and sat, he turned immediately to Marilyn. "I appreciate the way you got all those people out of there once Julia arrived. I owe you one."

Marilyn frowned at the suggestion. "It was fairly obvious that she knew nothing more than we thought she did. How is she holding up?"

"Not so well, I'm afraid. Julia's always been a little high-strung, and this was more than she could take. The family doctor gave her a shot of something and put her to bed. I promised I'd drop back out there tomorrow, just to see how she's doing before we take off.''

The waitress arrived with drinks, and Bobby, thinking Stan's German beer looked good, ordered one as well. As they waited for it to arrive, Torbeck brought McElliot up to date on the brief conversation he'd had with Dick Strahan. As far as their boss was concerned, they were only involved inasmuch as Marilyn might need depositions from them. Other than that, they were to steer clear. This was expected. As covert agents, they couldn't very well stick around and talk with the press.

When Bobby's beer arrived, Torbeck drained his own bottle with a quick gulp and pushed himself to his feet.

''I think I'm gonna turn in. Breakfast around nine?''

Marilyn thought ten sounded better. Once Stan disappeared, she sat confronting Bobby, her fingers unconsciously toying with her swizzle straw, tying it in knots.

''How are *you* holding up?'' she asked.

Those gray eyes got a faraway look in them for an instant and then refocused. ''Better than I was a few hours ago, I guess. On one level, none of it makes sense. On another, the last piece has fallen into place. I keep telling myself that Richard had to be crazy to do what he did, and when I think more about it, I have to conclude that's exactly what he was. I can't imagine the pressure of living with a secret like that; the having to come up with the ten, twenty, and then fifty thousand a year to keep it down here in these hills. It must have eaten into everything else he thought and did. My father was just another obstacle in a fear-crazed and obsessed man's path.''

''You realize that the media are going to crawl all over this one.''

He nodded, resignation in his expression. ''In that regard, I feel more sorry for the Coulters. Tomorrow they're going to find themselves staring into the teeth of a shit storm like none of us can imagine. Julia's going to have the toughest time weathering it. Francine and Franklin are made of sterner stuff. It might even make them stronger.''

Marilyn's own expression went far away now. "On that count, I guess I'm surprised to see you back here tonight.''

"You mean Francine.'' Not a question. Bobby was reading all the unspoken thoughts behind Marilyn's words. "You've got it all wrong, Marilyn. Francine is part of what little family I have left, and maybe more importantly, she's a friend.'' He stopped just a moment to think about what he'd just said. Seemingly satisfied, he nodded. "That friendship has changed over the years, slipping into realms neither of us expected or, to this day, understands. But that's still what it is . . . a friendship. Francine knows that. It's how we both want it.''

Instead of responding to his statement, Marilyn sat quietly regarding him. After a moment of uncomfortable silence, Bobby continued.

"I hated involving you in this, but you were the right—'' He paused to take a deep breath. ''—man for the job. Today, you know a lot more about me than I was willing—or able— to share with you a week and a half ago. I certainly wouldn't blame you if you felt like you'd already learned enough . . . and you don't want to learn any more.''

"You mean more things like the fact that you're a federal cop? I think I can handle them, Bobby. Or that you've just inherited an immense fortune and all the responsibilities that go with it? I admit your family heritage is somewhat intimidating, but there's still that other side of who you are. The side that finds feisty women and wide-open spaces attractive. I don't believe that the events of the past week have changed who you really are.''

McElliot noticed that in her agitation she'd finished her drink before he'd gotten halfway through his beer. He pointed to her glass.

"You want another one of those, or are you ready to call it a night?''

Backfire

She shook her head, chin up and eyes unwavering as they held his. "Neither. I want to dance."

Before he could respond, she was on her feet and grabbing a hand to tug him toward the dance floor. The singer had just began vamping her way through "Blue Bayou," her lounge lizard's rendition about a million miles from Roy Orbison and not a lot closer to Linda Ronstadt. None of the occupants of the dance floor seemed to care, including the couple who now slipped in to join them. The tune was low and syrupy, calling for the intimacy of dancing cheek to cheek. The height difference between the two of them made cheek to cheek or even head to neck impossible, but as Bobby slipped his arms around Marilyn and she came gently to rest against his body, he was once again surprised at just how right it felt.

About the Author

CHRISTOPHER NEWMAN lives in New York City. He is also the author of MIDTOWN SOUTH, SIXTH PRECINCT, MAÑANA MAN and KNOCK-OFF.

Is there no rest for Detective Joe Dante?
Not in Christopher Newman's exciting police novels!

MIDTOWN SOUTH

Dante was ready for light duty, away from the drug beat. But when your precinct borders on Times Square, easy police work is hard to come by. And when uncanny lookalike prostitutes are being murdered, the case is as hard as they come.

SIXTH PRECINCT

Newly assigned to the Sixth Precinct, Dante is working on the bizarre murder case of art collector Oscar Wembley, who was hacked to death with a kitchen knife. Another, more grotesque murder adds an unusual twist to the case, and a new challenge to Detective Dante, who thought he had seen it all.

KNOCK-OFF

A hot designer in the competitive world of high fashion is found bludgeoned to death. The stolen designs for the new fall line point to a piracy ring. The case brings Detective Joe Dante to Fashion Avenue for the toughest case of his career.

Also by Christopher Newman...

MAÑANA MAN

When Henry Bueno's old CIA friend gets knocked off by a mob hitman, Bueno goes in search of the killer. The search leads him right into an elaborate scheme involving stolen guidance missile systems, political assassination and six divisions of the U.S. Marines. But the plan does not include Bueno, whose personal vendetta draws him into the devious intrigue, from South America to Silicon Valley to the Nicaraguan coast.

	SBN	Price
MIDTOWN SOUTH	13064-9	$3.50
SIXTH PRECINCT	13174-2	$3.95
KNOCK-OFF	13294-3	$4.50
MAÑANA MAN	13173-4	$3.95

Newman's books are available in your local bookstore, or use your major credit card and call toll-free 1-800-733-3000. To expedite your order please mention Interest Code "MRM 17." Please allow at least 4 weeks for delivery.

Prices and numbers subject to change without notice. Valid in U.S. only.